THE CARUSO COLLECTION

A NOVEL BY

TOM ULICNY

This book is a work of fiction. Fictional names, characters, places and incidents are entirely the products of the author's imagination. Any resemblance to actual persons, living or dead, or to actual e events or locales is entirely coincidental.

Printed in the United States of America

ISBN-10: 1523300027
ISBN-13: 978-1523300020

For Colleen, Sarah and Kate

ACKNOWLEDGMENTS

The idea for this story originated on a tour bus rolling through Prince Edward Island with my wife Joyce beside me. We tossed the concept around for a while and, while still on the bus, I started chapter 1. Thanks to Joyce for her own twists to the story and for her tolerance of me discussing plot points rather than the beautiful scenery (though I enjoyed both). And as always, thanks to family, friends and associates for your suggestions, encouragement and helpful criticisms throughout the writing process.

The Caruso Collection

CHAPTER 1

The murder of Peter Caruso occurred in Room 48B, in a Brownsville apartment building on Brooklyn's east side. The direct cause of death: three bullets to the chest. A third-stringer working the night-desk at the *Times* obtained the preliminary police report and wrote a short article about the incident which ended up being squeezed into the morning edition near the bottom of page six.

Even the third-stringer knew that few New Yorkers would see it there and fewer still would care who Peter Caruso was and why he was killed. Like high rent and bad pizza, murder was just another one of those unfortunate facts of big-city life. Most people learned to live with such things and tried not to give them much thought.

But the article on page six managed to catch the eye of Nate Parks, a morning rider on the inbound B-train. He read through it dry-mouthed, unable to believe that the victim was the same Peter Caruso he'd known as a boy. On reading the description of the decedent as a *once promising artist*, he no longer had any doubts. This was Peter all right.

After the initial shock, it was the finality of it all that bothered Nate most. Peter Caruso was dead and would never paint again. And he'd been murdered—why would anyone want to kill Peter? They hadn't been close since high school, yet Nate's hands shook as he folded the newspaper and tucked it into the front flap of his messenger bag. He took in a deep breath and let it out slow, like he'd just been sucker-punched. It was the hint of stale beer in the cold, dry air that reconnected him with the swaying of the B-Train and the occasional elbow and shoulder bumps from the morning commuters packed around him. The rails click-clacked by. He re-gripped the handhold overhead and spread his feet slightly farther apart then checked his watch—only forty minutes until his breakfast appointment at the Waldorf. After the news about Peter his meeting seemed trivial, except it wasn't and Nate wasn't about to call it off. He had worked way too hard to bring it about and what grief he had for Peter would just have to wait.

He ran a finger inside his collar, and straightened the lapel of the suit that he wore beneath his gray winter coat then let his gaze wander. He shared the subway car with the usual Brooklyn collection of business types: college students, tourists, a few colorful hipsters and a few derelict junkies. The pony-tailed girl standing in front of him, a grad student maybe, wore a North Face parka, jeans and a baseball cap. Somehow she managed to hold in one hand both a McDonald's coffee and a phone. Through the forest of commuters, Nate caught her reflection in the window – sort of pretty, mid, maybe late-twenties. He thought he saw her glance at his reflection and he shifted his attention to the subway map above the windows. Five stops to go.

Another few minutes crawled by. Thoughts of Peter circled Nate's mind, threatening to bring back boyhood memories or worse, to start him wondering what it would be like to get shot three times in the chest. He swallowed hard. His right foot had just begun a nervous tap when the train lurched and something hit the floor with a splash raising a few shouts and curses. The North Face girl jumped back, bumping into him.

"Crap, crap, crap," she shouted. "My fault, I'm sooo sorry."

Nate looked down. Puddles of coffee flowed across the floor. Then he noticed his pants. Wet streaks accented both legs up to the knees. Something like an anguished moan escaped his lips as he felt the warm liquid soaking into his socks.

"I'm really sorry, that looks like a good suit," said the girl.

Nate's jaw clenched then he cleared his throat and tried to sound cavalier. "It was the train's fault, not yours. They should fix these damned tracks."

"I was careless. I feel terrible."

"Don't. It's all right - really."

"I'm not an authority or anything, but when you get home you should get some soapy water on it – or is it club soda?"

Nate had no idea which it was and didn't care for at that moment his eyes caught hers. They were a deep brown, looking up at him from beneath the brim of her cap. He froze.

"My name's Cat – short for Catherine. You're Nathan Parks

the artist, aren't you? I've been to one of your exhibits in the village, seen you on the train before too."

Nate had never been good with small talk and now, with Peter's death on his mind, it felt especially unnatural but he attempted a smile and slowly the words came out. "Yes, that's me and that exhibit was my only exhibit." Then he wondered if she liked his work but he didn't want to ask the question directly. "So, you like art?"

"I like most art, not all. Some of it can get pretty strange, like the artist is trying to make you feel unworthy or dumb if you don't understand it. I don't like that kind."

In a blare of static, the conductor announced the next station.

"This is me," said Cat unshouldering her purse. "Too bad I couldn't have held onto my coffee just a few minutes longer—right?" The train slowed to a stop and for a moment she seemed to hesitate. "Well, good-bye then. Sorry again about your pants." She piled out along with ten other commuters as more came aboard. "It's club soda I think," she shouted back.

Nate waved to her through the closing doors thinking only then that he should have at least gotten her last name. By this time his friend Eduardo would have had all her information entered into his phone and would have had a date set up for Friday night. But that was Eduardo, the girl-magnet from the apartment above his who seemed to have someone new on his arm every month. Nate thought about Cat's hair brushing up against his chin when she'd backed into him. It had a fresh, clean smell. And she had brown eyes – he was a sucker for brown eyes. He wondered again if she liked his paintings. Well, at least she'd remembered his exhibit and his name. He wondered how many people still remembered Peter.

He'd been a big deal baseball jock at William Bennett High near Scranton. Nate had never figured him for artistic skills of any kind back then, but like Nate, Peter had gone on to study at Columbia's School of Visual Arts. Unlike Nate though, he had graduated with highest honors, and soon after that, made a big splash with an exhibit on campus. He had shown only five paintings but even the toughest critics had given him glowing reviews. Nate had been nearly sick with envy and couldn't bring himself to congratulate Peter as he knew he should have. How could the ace of the sand-lots he once knew be capable of such masterful work?

After his exhibit everyone predicted rock-star status for Peter but a few months passed, then a year with nothing new from him. One year stretched to five and as Nate worked hard to make his own name as an artist, the name Peter Caruso faded. Now, only the most ardent members of the New York art community might still remember him.

Nate shook his head and tried to compose himself. Right now he needed to be calm, smooth and self-confident. He needed to be the artist that his breakfast companions, the elderly mogul Teddy Sinclair and his wife Meredith, would be willing to sponsor. That meant no more dark thoughts about Peter and no thoughts about three bullets to the chest.

He got off at Rockefeller Center, dodged through the turnstiles and trotted up the wet concrete steps to street level. Outside he barely noticed the snow and slush.

At the Waldorf a uniformed doorman waved him through the private entrance off 50th street and into the lobby where he left his coat at the coat-check. According to the clock over the entrance to the Astoria dining room, he was five minutes early. He ducked into the men's room and tried to do something about his pants. The foamy soap didn't seem to help and he couldn't quite raise his leg up to the level of the hand-dryer. If anything, his scrubbing had made the coffee streaks even more prominent.

Nate gave up on the pants and splashed cold water on his face then dried off and looked at himself in the mirror. His hair was neat, his gray jacket and dark blue tie were straight and his bright, salmon-colored shirt hugged his chest without a wrinkle or a blemish...*or a bullet hole.* He wiped his eyes clear with both hands. He made a couple of practice smiles that didn't feel quite right but were close enough, then stepped out of the men's room. He was as ready as he'd ever be to take on the Sinclairs.

Nate surveyed the dining area. At a table near the window he saw Teddy's well-receded, frosty white hairline. He was standing up, waving Nate over. The blonde opposite Teddy turned. She had to be Meredith. He'd known she was younger than Teddy but until this moment, he hadn't realized how much younger. As he crossed the room to their table, he saw her glance at his stained trousers - so much for first impressions.

Teddy greeted him warmly then introduced his wife.

Meredith's sparkling blue eyes and radiant white skin completed the Scandinavian look that went with her hair and her sky-blue pant suit. Her hand was petite and cold in Nate's.

"Pleased to meet you, Mr. Parks." She said this with a smile. Nice teeth – she was almost too perfect, thought Nate. He didn't know Teddy well but he did know that he always went for the best. He supposed you had to respect the guy for that.

"Likewise, Ms. Sinclair," said Nate.

She told him to call her Meredith and he told her to call him Nate. They ordered and then, over a round of mimosas, Teddy raised his glass and looked at his wife. Knowing what was coming, Nate braced himself.

"Nathan Lido Parks is one of the best new artists in the city," said Teddy with a ceremonial flourish. "For this, your twenty-eighth birthday, I've commissioned him to paint your portrait. He promises that it will be something truly special. Happy birthday my dear."

"My portrait?" Meredith flashed another smile at Teddy then at Nate.

Nate was unable to read her expression. Was she really pleased? Maybe not. "Happy birthday, Meredith," he said. Then he improvised: "I hope to make the ordeal as painless as possible." Most wealthy couples chose the artists they sponsored by having them do a personal painting or two. If they were happy with their work, more commissions would follow. This initial job came with a thousand dollar retainer. It was money that Nate had already earmarked to cover some past-due bills. A relationship with the Sinclairs could mark the end of his struggles and the start of the successful career he'd always hoped for. A lot was riding on this. He kept his smile steady.

Nate felt Meredith's stare. She seemed to be checking him out, her eyes drifting down from his wavy black hair to his hazel eyes before settling on his over-sized nose which Nate had always been self-conscious of. She asked some questions: How had he gotten into art? Had he ever painted anyone famous? And she asked about the painting process. How long would it take? Would she have to sit still for a long period of time? What should she wear? She fired these off as they ate and seemed to be gathering enthusiasm for the project. So was Nate. He wanted to ask her a few questions of his own: Where did she grow up? What interests did she have? Why would she ever marry an old goat like Teddy? But he didn't.

Nate found himself enjoying the food and the company of the Sinclairs. He pegged them for your normal, everyday, near-billionaire couple trying to get by as best they could. He knew that Teddy had made most of his money from commercial real estate but fortunately, that mundane topic never came up. A round of cappuccinos finished off the meal after which Nate sensed it was time for a graceful exit. He consulted his watch as if he had another pressing appointment, then thanked Teddy and stood to go.

"When do we begin? The painting, I mean," asked Meredith.

"I've set aside my next few Tuesday mornings. Teddy said that would be best for you?"

Meredith seemed about to disagree but then said: "Yes, of course. Tuesdays are good."

"I have a room all set up at the house," said Teddy standing, sliding his chair back. "It should work out just fine."

"Until Tuesday then," she extended her hand to Nate.

It felt warmer this time and, as he caught her gaze, Nate felt a sexual charge course through him. He held her hand and her eyes a little longer than he should have. When he released both he saw that Meredith's smile had vanished. Nate cleared his throat. "I'll be there at nine o'clock, if that's all right. We need to catch the morning light."

"Nine is fine."

Teddy's smile was gone too. As he shook Nate's hand he drew him closer and spoke low. "If you even think about touching my wife I'll see that you never sell another painting in New York or anywhere else. Are we clear?" His grip tightened.

Nate's mouth went dry. "Yes, right – perfectly clear." Teddy was a man of influence and power. Nate knew this was no idle threat.

Teddy released him then gave him a pat on the shoulder. "Very well then, we'll see you on Tuesday."

"I'm looking forward to it." With relief, Nate turned and headed for the door. Things could have gone better, but they could have gone worse too. The portrait would be a five week project and his only concern was that his image of the perfect Ms. Meredith Sinclair might end up being devoid of character, looking almost too perfect.

He needn't have worried.

The rest of Nate's day was overshadowed by thoughts of Peter. He went through the motions of teaching his two art classes at Manhattan College, ignoring the late-arriving students that he usually berated in a semi-good-hearted way. And he dismissed a question from one of his favorite students about conceptualist art and its deep psychological and emotional message by simply saying it was beyond the scope of this particular class. A steadfast realist, Nate would normally have taken the opportunity to explain his thinking that the emotional content of a painting should appear naturally in the artist's choice of pigments and in the flow and the texture of his brushstrokes which were always applied in concert with, and not at the expense of, what was actually being painted. He was usually passionate about such things, but not today.

He took his time leaving the campus and it was dark by the time he walked from his subway stop and gained sight of his building in Prospect Heights. There was a dim light in the third-floor window. On the roof, the snow lay deep and heavy. Spears of ice hung from the gables. Beneath this burden the building seemed to lean over the street, its black shape matching Nate's mood as he trudged closer. The snow had tapered off but the wind still howled. His ears were frozen, feeling as if they'd break like fortune cookies if bent the wrong way. He climbed the stairs and entered his second floor apartment where he rubbed his hands over them to bring back the circulation then changed into sweatshirt and cut-offs, tossing his suit into a pile for the cleaners. He knew he should scrub out the stains but didn't want to take the time. Then he remembered the girl on the train.

Thinking about it objectively, Nate considered himself medium-lucky with women but a dismal failure with love. For the medium-lucky part, maybe it was something that came with being an artist. Women seemed attracted to him as if his artistic skill might somehow manifest itself in other ways. He knew he wasn't a good conversationalist but most women didn't see that as a problem. They thought of him as a good listener, apparently deciding that his economical manner of speech, well punctuated by periods of thoughtful silence, were part of his artistic aura. Nathan Lido Parks: brilliant painter, deep thinker and man of mystery. As for the dismal-failure-in-love part, there wasn't much to say. None of his relationships had ever really taken hold. Nate was thirty-two years old and had never been in love—not even close.

The plumbing clanked and rumbled from the floor above where Eduardo was probably entertaining his girl of the month. Nate nosed a carton of left-over moo shoo pork and heated it up. He plopped down on his plaid sofa to watch the local news, expecting to see something about Peter's murder. Five shootings were covered. The weather followed, there'd be more snow in the morning. Then, after a commercial, there was Peter.

The first image showed him in happier times just after his

Columbia exhibit with as much of a smile as he was ever capable of—his mouth taut but his eyes showing a rare exuberance. Next, a jerky hand-held video showed a shrouded gurney being wheeled out of a run-down apartment building in Brownsville. What was Peter doing in a place like that? Is that where he lived? The female announcer used the same phrase as the *Times* article: *Three bullets to the chest*. Nate wiped a drop of soy sauce from his chin and leaned closer to the TV, but the segment wrapped up quickly saying the police had little in the way of evidence and no leads to suggest that the murder had been anything other than an unfortunate act of random violence.

Nate glanced at the dead-bolt on his door then put down the empty carton and flipped the TV off. He leaned back and closed his eyes, letting his mind wander, remembering a time when he was a boy and Peter had joined his family on a trip to the art institute in Scranton. Peter had seemed unimpressed but Nate had known even then, that his friend had a strange way of showing his feelings. On returning home, they'd retreated to Nate's room where Nate pulled out some of his art supplies, placing them in front of Peter. "Go on, try it if you think it's so easy."

"I didn't say it was easy," Peter had said. He stared blankly at the canvas-board for a full minute then wet a thick number ten brush with dull black. Purposefully, he started in the upper right corner and used the brush like a mop, filling the entire space with thick wavy parallel stripes.

"It's a zebra – right?" Nate guessed with a laugh.

Peter shook his head then added a single diagonal streak of bright red and set the canvas on edge so that the red paint dripped down. "It's a dead zebra."

Nate was about to laugh again at the joke but Peter's face was a mask of seriousness. There was always something about Peter that was a little weird. It made Nate wonder now about the random violence theory. He opened his eyes. Could Peter have been into drugs?

Eduardo, who never permitted anyone to call him Ed, stopped by the next day and Nate told him about the murder.

"Who would want to kill an impoverished artist?" asked Eduardo from the couch.

"Maybe he wasn't impoverished."

"I thought you said he lived in Brownsville; everyone there is impoverished. And another thing, five years is a long time to go without hearing from someone who was supposed to be a good friend."

"We were close when we were boys, not so much after that," said Nate from his computer. In truth, he did feel guilty for not at least trying to stay in touch, but Peter could have called or written him too, and hadn't.

"So you're over there trying to figure out what he was up to all that time?" asked Eduardo.

Nate grabbed a few almonds from the bowl next to him and tossed them in his mouth, talking as he chewed. "There's plenty on the internet about his Columbia exhibit but not much else. Here, look at this." Nate pulled up one of Peter's paintings.

"Wow," said Eduardo after coming over.

"He called it, *Woman in Winter*," explained Nate, leaning back to give him a better view. "It's from the Columbia exhibit."

On the screen, the tall, graceful image of a woman rose from a snowy foreground. Her features were young but the long strands of hair trailing down her back were a stark white suggesting a much older woman or maybe some kind of inner wisdom. Only the texture of the hair differentiated it from her white clothing and the white snow around her. Her face, pale and sad, looked out from the canvas imploringly. Her body stood in mid-step heading into the background of the painting that held only the vague suggestion of tall pines in the distance.

"She wants us to follow her," said Nate.

"She wants to make love," said Eduardo with certainty. He went to the fridge and grabbed two beers, handing one to Nate. He took some almonds. "A man who could paint like that, wouldn't suddenly give it up would he? Where is this painting now?"

"I don't know," said Nate in answer to both questions. It made him wonder what had happened to the paintings from Peter's exhibit. And could there be others?

They watched a Ranger's game then Eduardo left and Nate went back to his computer. From it he learned that there had been a mandatory autopsy after which the body had been released to his father for burial back in their hometown of Maysville, PA. No date was given for the funeral.

On Sunday morning, Nate called his parents who still lived near Maysville. His mother told him that, yes, they'd heard the awful news about Peter. She said that the funeral had been scheduled for Tuesday and they planned to attend. Nate knew he should be there too. He thought for a moment then told her he'd drive out late Monday and they could go to the funeral together the next day.

"Oh, that'll be so nice, all going to church together," his

mother replied. "Too bad it's for a funeral."

Nate then gave Teddy a call. Meredith answered with a friendly voice and he changed his appointment with her to Monday morning.

The Sinclair estate lay crouched on a rolling, sugar-pined hilltop thirty-miles north of the city. The snow had stopped two days earlier so the trip in Nate's older model Ford Focus was easy and he arrived on time at the front gate. He punched in the security code Teddy had given him and followed the curving drive onto the grounds. Short stone walls topped by thick caps of snow guarded both sides.

Nate had never taken much interest in painting landscapes but here he saw how his pigments might flow, with startling whites, brilliant blues, and earthy browns and greens. Expansive sheets of snow sparkled in the bright sun, dotted by fallen pinecones and sculpted by the swirling wind. Pines and maples towered over the scene, their limbs heavy with snow and ice. At the house he got out of his car. The fresh cold air hit his face. Birds chirped, squirrels bounded and melting snow drip-dripped from a hundred drooping branches. The evergreen scent was everywhere. With a gloved hand on the roof of his car, he took it all in.

"You're coming inside I hope?" It was Meredith. In jeans and sweatshirt she stood inside the half-opened door at the fieldstone entrance to the sprawling house.

"Just admiring the view." Nate pulled his drawing kit from the back seat and, before squeezing past Meredith at the entryway, stomped the slush off his shoes. "Thanks for changing your schedule for me."

"Were you close? Your artist friend who died - were the two of you close?"

"We grew up together but went our separate ways. I hadn't seen him in years."

Nate followed her down a carpeted hallway. He had been in the house once before when Teddy first talked with him about the painting and he knew they were headed to a small guest room that faced the east. It was a good setting for the painting.

"We're through here." She took a right turn. "Two artists, living in the same city - it hardly seems like separate ways to me." She opened a door. "Here we are. All set up. I made coffee. Will you have some?"

"Sure." He normally drank chai but felt awkward turning down the courtesy. "We grew up together but lost touch after college."

"That's too bad, childhood friendships are usually the ones most worth keeping." She poured the coffee. "It's quiet as a church in here, isn't it? There had been a bed over there in the corner but Teddy had it taken out. I suppose he doesn't trust you." She handed him his cup then sat down on a couch and took a sip. "Should he trust you, Nathan?"

Nate felt half the oxygen leave the room. She'd spoken his name as if she were an elementary school teacher who'd caught him about to do something bad. "Of course he should trust me. You should trust me too." He stirred some cream into his cup and took a swallow, glad to have something to be occupied with just then. "I'll put my things over here. You'll be seated over there." He pointed to a chair near the window. "I want to capture you accented by the morning light streaming in."

"Capture me, huh?" She took her place and assumed a bland pose looking back at him without a smile. The sunlight, softened by the gossamer shears hanging in the window, backlit her hair. It shimmered like a halo around her face. "Like this?"

This woman had no bad side. Nate and Teddy had discussed possible poses. He had intended to have her look out from the painting through the oval mirror that hung over the dresser to one side of where she now sat, but Nate saw now there was no need for such cleverness. Meredith's beauty, caught in a simple pose would carry the work. He even liked the contrast of the jeans and sweatshirt with the richly appointed furnishings behind her. "Yes, just like that. But I'll have to get here earlier to catch the right light." Already the angle of the sun was diminishing the effect he wanted. He sat down on a stool.

"How will you start? I don't see an easel or a canvass."

"Every painting begins with a sketch." Nate pulled out his sketchpad and a thick HB pencil. "Look directly at me."

"Oh, we're starting right now? You want me in these?" She pinched the fabric of her sweatshirt.

"Yes, I do. Is that all right with you?"

"The question is: Is it all right with Teddy?"

"After I show him this sketch, yes, I'm sure he'll go along with it. Besides, I like to have my subjects comfortable."

"Teddy's not here today you know. I forgot to tell him you changed the day. We're alone in the house."

Nate shifted on the stool. "I'll show him the sketch later this week then."

"I want to see it first."

"Sorry, Teddy insisted that you see nothing until the painting's finished."

Then Meredith spoke slowly, looking directly at him with her piercing blue eyes. "Teddy would never know, Nathan."

Nate felt the blood rush to his face. He remembered Teddy's threat and took another sip of coffee. "All right, hold still now." As he sketched, thoughts raced through his head about what the two of them could be doing right now. Her husband was out of the house. The door was locked. Who would know? But then he saw it and stopped his pencil in mid-stroke. There, discretely mounted on the cornice above the mirror, was a small box no larger than a cigarette lighter. From its center a glassy dot poked out like a fish-eye.

"Yes, it's a camera," said Meredith. "Teddy had it installed a few days ago."

"Were you going to tell me?"

She tucked a strand of hair back behind her left ear. "Maybe, maybe not. I was waiting for you to try something that I wouldn't want Teddy to see."

Nate lowered his sketchbook.

"I'm a conniving bitch. Is that what you're thinking?"

He was silent for a moment then, like a shield, he brought his sketchbook back into position. "I'm here to paint you, not to judge you."

"Oh, good line," said Meredith, "I'll bet you use it a lot."

Nate resumed the sketch, his strokes bolder now, his shading darker. He began to wonder what was really going on behind that beautiful face in front of him.

CHAPTER 2

Nate left the Sinclair estate in the early afternoon and headed for Maysville. What was normally a two hour drive stretched beyond four due to the icy roads through the Poconos. He had both hands glued to the wheel the whole time as he negotiated the curves and steep inclines and was exhausted by the time he pulled up to his parent's house. The sun had set half an hour earlier. His stomach was growling and he hoped his mother had dinner going. He grabbed his duffle bag from the back seat and headed up the snow-dusted walkway. The glow from the front window lit the wooden porch and the snow made it sparkle. The frozen wood creaked beneath him in an old familiar way and as he approached the front door he savored the homey smell of his Mother's born-again beef stew. The door wasn't locked. He stepped into the warmth and called out: "Hello."

Sal, an aging golden retriever, woofed and came bounding up to give him a couple of sloppy licks. "Hey, you old dog," said Nate putting down his bag. He took off his coat and draped it over the couch.

"Hey, yourself," said his mom coming out from the kitchen, with dad trailing behind. "It's about time you paid us a visit." She gave him a hug and kiss, then assumed her usual voice of command. "Supper's ready. Go wash your hands...and hang up that coat." After a vigorous handshake from his father, Nate followed his orders.

It had been almost a year. His mother was right, it *was* about time he came back. Over stew and homemade bread, they got caught up. All was well here on the farm which wasn't really a farm any more. The house sat on just a single acre. The fields had long since been sold to a co-op outfit that worked them with all the latest equipment, planting corn and soybeans much more profitably than his father ever could. Dad had quit farming years ago and, like most of his neighbors, had taken up work in the steel mills. “A hell of a thing,” Dad always said, “where you don’t see the sun or get a whiff of fresh clean air for days on end.” He’d been retired from the mill for four years but its rough, char-brown residue still remained on his face as if burned into his skin.

Nate had been an only child and his mother had worked odd jobs here and there as he grew up. She was retired now too, spending her time sharing and perfecting old family recipes like the one her own grandmother had always concocted, born again from the week’s leftovers in the fridge.

“Funeral’s at ten,” said his mother.

Nate was cleaning up the last of the gravy in his bowl with his third slice of bread. “Have you talked to Mr. Caruso? How’s he taking it?”

Dad dabbed his mustache with his napkin. “We haven’t seen Frank in quite a while, but he sounded okay over the phone.” He leaned back in his chair, the wood groaning under him. “I expect he’s still in shock just as we would be if something happened to you. I’ve always said that New York City is a dangerous place to live.” His expression went on to tell Nate that the same thing could have easily happened to him.

“There’s crime everywhere dad,” said Nate. “Maybe I’ll move back here someday.” It was his stock answer when the subject inevitably came up but more and more he had found himself thinking about it: a talented but reclusive artist tucked away in the Pennsylvania country-side. It had a certain Thoreau-esque appeal. That night Nate slept in his brass-framed bed upstairs with Sal sprawled out on a throw rug by the door. Nate had named him after Salvador Dali when he was just a pup. The room was cold. The wind rattled the frosty windows and the house made the noises it always had. Nate kept warm, curled under four layers of blankets as memories of his childhood came rushing in and with them, thoughts of Peter.

On long summer afternoons when they weren’t playing video games, they used to fish together at a tree-lined creek not far from Peter’s house up the road. The current was strong and the water cold and they’d always jump in to cool off before heading home. On one of those days, Nate slipped on a rock, falling hard on his shoulder and sliding into deeper water. He remembered floating there, stunned for a moment. The pain had been numbed by the cold water but he found himself unable to move his arm, unable to fight the rushing water as it carried him downstream – slowly at first but then with increasing speed. He yelled out for help, his eyes darting along the shore for any sign of Peter, but he was nowhere in sight. Where the hell was he? The water surged and Nate could no longer touch bottom. He tumbled over, trying to catch his breath, sucking in water. The current had him now, launching him another twenty feet downstream where he struck a tree limb and was finally able to hold on. With his good arm, he pulled himself toward the bank then got to his feet and staggered into the shallows, huffing and puffing, completely out of breath. He bent over, spitting water. When he straightened, he looked up and there was Peter, sitting calmly on a rock by the side of the stream eating a Snickers bar. "That was a dumb thing to do," he said.

Nate was furious. "You could have helped. I think I broke my shoulder."

Still sitting, Peter squinted at Nate. "Yup, it does seem like it's at a funny angle. Probably busted your collar bone. Here." He handed Nate the last of his Snickers as if it might have some pain-killing properties.

Sal stirred in the darkness and Nate rolled over in the bed. Peter had been right. He'd broken his collar bone that day and even now it ached in the cold weather. He pulled the covers around him more tightly.

Maysville, Pennsylvania had been carved into a hillside so that there wasn't much level ground to it. According to the sign on State Route 92, its population was five-hundred and twenty-two and the unpaid city fathers, there were two of them at any given time, seemed to have no interest in growing the town beyond the twenty or so businesses that lined Main Street. Set back two blocks from Main Street, the tall wooden steeple of Saint Mark's church overlooked the town.

The morning dawned bright and clear and cold. Nate drove to the church, his father beside him, mom in the back seat.

"Not many folks here," observed his father when they pulled into the parking lot and got out. There were six cars, seven now with Nate's.

"Peter's father wanted a small ceremony and small it is," observed Mom.

Inside the church, Nate's eyes adjusted slowly to the muted reds, blues and yellows from the stained glass. Flowers and incense scented the air and all was quiet. At the head of the center aisle in front of a white-marble alter, a stone container about the size of a boot-box sat on a wooden stand. The ashes inside were all that was left of Peter. There were a few flower arrangements on either side. Someone coughed.

Maybe fifteen people dotted the first five pews although Nate noticed a lone woman in a dark coat sitting in back. Nate's Dad led the way slowly up the aisle. Nate recognized Peter's father in the front row. On seeing them, Mr. Caruso stood. They all shook hands. "Sorry for your tragic loss," said Mom.

Mr. Caruso, mid-sixties, with a sparse horseshoe of gray hair, nodded. "Thanks for coming," he said, the words spoken softly, almost below a whisper.

The service was short and dignified and the aged Reverend Howe, who had been posted at St. Mark's forever, spoke simply about the boy that Peter had once been here in Maysville and about the beauty of the art he created when he left for the city and became a man. And then there was anger in his voice: "His life has been stolen from us all, taken by a violent pestilence that seems to have infected every corner of our world today. It's a deadly plague of hate and uncaring for the welfare of our fellow man." He spread his arms. "It's a plague whose only cure lies in the faith and the hope residing within these walls. Let us all believe that Peter carried that faith and hope with him until the end."

Afterward, a stately procession on foot led to the family burial plot in the church cemetery where the reverend said a few prayers and a few more kind words. Nate remembered other funerals and sermons from times passed. Though he looked a little more weathered now, the Reverend Howe was still good with kind words.

Nate and his parents offered their condolences again to Peter's father who, as far as Nate knew, was Peter's only living relative. The elder Caruso wore no hat. His eyes were glassy, his face red from the cold.

"Your son was a good friend to me growing up," said Nate, shaking his hand. "He was the most gifted artist I've ever known."

"Thanks Natey. I know that Peter thought a lot of you too."

It was good to hear Mr. Caruso call him Natey as he had when he and Peter were kids. Nate nodded, not sure what else there was to say. He stepped to one side to let others express their sympathy. Some were neighbors, others were just familiar towns people who, as they themselves grew old, had taken on the habit of attending funerals and saying goodbye to folks whether they knew them well or not. Nate didn't see any of Peter's classmates and he didn't see the woman from the back of the church. He noticed there were only six cars in the lot now, not seven.

Nate never knew Peter's mother and had always assumed she'd died a long time ago. He wondered about that. It must have been tough for Frank Caruso to raise Peter by himself, and now, without Peter, there was apparently no one left to share his life with. He felt sad for the old man.

Dad evidently felt the same. "Come with us, Frank," he said as they were leaving. "We can get some lunch."

Mr. Caruso seemed touched by this but declined. "Thanks, but I think I'll stay around here a while longer."

Dad nodded with understanding but on the way back to the car, Mom noted: "The Carusos never were the sociable type."

Nate stayed the rest of that day and was getting ready to leave the next morning when his mother asked if he had a girlfriend. Just to placate her, he showed her his sketch of Meredith.

"She's good looking enough," said his mother, giving voice to her critical eye. "What do you know about her?"

"We just met. It's probably nothing."

"I would never pass a woman off like this as 'probably nothing,'" said his father, holding the sketch while ignoring mom's good-natured glare. He handed it back to Nate. "Nice drawing though, son. I'm always amazed by your talent."

In shaded charcoal, he had captured Meredith as if in mid-speech, causing the viewer to wonder what she was saying – what is she thinking? The portrait of Meredith Sinclair would be simple yet provocative.

Nate kissed his parents good-bye and Sal gave him a slurp.

The route to the main road took Nate past the Caruso house. It was the same size and style as his parent's house; probably built about the same time. A tall lifeless elm stood in the front yard. At the end of a frayed rope a tire hung from one of its limbs. It swung slowly in the wind. As he approached, Nate turned off the radio and lowered the passenger-side window. The snow-caked gravel crunched as he slowed, then stopped. He leaned over for a better look.

Everywhere on the house, faded white paint peeled in layers exposing the gray wood beneath. The porch was buckled. The place looked abandoned except for the black Chevy parked beside it. Nate had seen the car at the church so he knew Mr. Caruso must still live here. Then he remembered Peter's dingy Brownsville apartment building from the news video. He had never thought of the Carusos as being poor but that fact was obvious now. Peter would never have been able to afford Columbia without his full-ride scholarship.

Nate's eyes moved up the wooden structure of the old house. Peter's room lay behind the cracked upstairs window. There were no curtains and the room was dark. He and Peter used to play up there when they were kids, smoke and argue there in their early teens, and break into outright fistfights there in their late teens. Peter had a ferocious temper and sometimes he'd bully and tease Nate into a fight just to show him who was tougher, yet somehow Nate had always thought of him as a friend. Nate stared at the dark, cracked window then finally straightened and closed the passenger side window. No more Peter. He thumbed the steering wheel then eased up on the brake. As he watched the old house recede in his rear-view mirror, he felt as if he were closing an old family photo album. When it finally disappeared behind the next rise, he sped up and headed for the interstate.

Two days later, Nate sat across from Teddy and Meredith in the great room of the Sinclair house. A warm fire crackled in the hearth.

Teddy had been silent for a time, holding Nate's sketch while keeping it from Meredith's view. He'd just been staring at it with no reaction at all. Nate felt his foot begin to tap. He uncrossed his legs and took a sip from his half-finished glass of merlot. He hated merlot.

Then Teddy looked up. "I love it," he said to Nate with a broad smile. "You will too, my dear. I know just where we'll hang it."

"I don't understand why I can't see it," said Meredith.

"I want to see your face when it's unveiled, that's why. It's a surprise. Besides, it's customary that the subject sees it only when it's finished. Isn't that right?" He gave the sketch back to Nate.

"That's how it's usually done," said Nate. "There'll be four more sittings here, then I'll do the finishing touches back at my studio. It should be complete by the end of next month."

"Excellent," said Teddy without the least hint of the suspicion he'd displayed at the Waldorf.

Over the next two weeks Nate learned more about the woman he was painting.

She grew up Meredith Sipriano in a gritty Italian neighborhood in the Bronx - father a high school math teacher, mother a part-time store clerk. Meredith had won a scholarship to Pace College where she majored in psychology. After graduating, she was hired by Sinclair Associates as a marketing analyst where she quickly drew the attention of the recently divorced Teddy. "I needed the money," she'd explained to Nate. "He got me some promotions that maybe I would have earned on my own – maybe not. We dated a few time, made love a few times, then we got married. I was poor, he was rich. He had the hots for me I had the hots for his money – simple as that."

Nate swirled his brush, picking up a dab of cyan then spicing it with an earthy brown. He added an almond tint and touched it to the image of Meredith just below the lower lip, accentuating its shape in subtle strokes always conscious of the maxim: There are no lines in nature – only shadow. "Do you love him?" He asked this almost absently, lost as he was in the creative process. But now that the question had been asked he found himself hanging on her answer.

"He's a good man, Nathan. I don't want to hurt him."

Well, that was a resounding no. Maybe it was the act of painting the gentle curve of her lips that caused him to press the point further. "Just like the song then - Late at night the big old house gets lonely..."

She smiled sadly. "Yes, there is a price for every refuge isn't there? What's your refuge, Nathan? Is it your art?"

His brush stopped moving. He'd never thought of things that way. Was he married to his art? Had it become his refuge because he'd never truly loved a woman? Nate straightened. "Turn slightly. That's it – right there," he said, realizing that he had just answered her question.

That thought bugged him for the rest of the week and he decided that maybe it was time to be pro-active about things.

Nate's favorite place for a good omelet was *The Egg Cracker* and he met Eduardo there at least once a month. It was Saturday morning and the place was packed when he grabbed a booth and ordered a cup of chai. Eduardo was coming from across town after spending Friday night God knows where. He was late, as usual. As Nate sipped he opened up his tablet. It would be his third time going through the local women-seeking-men personals, flagging the ones that looked promising. He hadn't actually contacted anyone yet, that was something he was working up to. He selected two of the newer ads which gave him a total of six, then checked the time.

Nate had first met Eduardo a few years ago when he'd come down from his upstairs apartment asking if Nate would do some graphics for his acting portfolio. From this, Eduardo gave him partial credit for his big break on Broadway: landing the Latin gigolo role in *Legally Blonde*. He had held the part for nearly two years now.

Eduardo apologized when he finally arrived. "I only meant to be a little late. Then I missed the train." He whisked off his scarf and coat and tossed them on the cushioned bench then slid in beside them.

"Why did you want to be a little late?"

"I'm late for everything Nate, haven't you noticed that about me?"

Nate picked up the menu and they ordered.

By the time they'd been served, Nate had told him about Meredith. Then he mentioned his women-seeking-men search.
Eduardo spoke as much with his hands as with his mouth and he expertly timed his full-fork gestures with his chewing. "So you want to meet a woman. It's not that complicated. Half the world's population is women. How can this be a problem? Have an affair with this Meredith girl. Maybe she's the right one for you. Is she good looking?"

"She's married and yes, she's good looking. But I don't want another affair," Nate felt his voice trailing off as the image of naked Meredith floated through his mind. "Still, if I was to have one more affair with anyone, it would be with her." Then he shook his head, dismissing that thought entirely. "I need to settle down into a real relationship – something long term."

"So, introduce me to Meredith. I'll have the affair and you can get on with your quest for the right woman. Just give me her phone number – that's all I need. If you don't, that means you want to have Meredith *and* you want to have your Ms. Right – you want both."

"You make me sound like a polygamist."

"No, you're normal – like me."

"I'm tired of living alone and I'm tired of having affairs that never become anything more."

"But you still want Meredith for yourself."

"I told you, she's married."

Eduardo added a second cream to his refreshed coffee and stirred thoughtfully as if only now appreciating the seriousness of Nate's situation. "What have you come up with on the ads?" he pointed his dripping spoon at Nate's tablet.

Nate read the ones he'd selected and Eduardo hmmm'd and shrugged at each of them. "So, call them. Maybe you'll get lucky and meet *THE* one."

"You're supposed to email them. Women are afraid of being hit on by a pervert. They want to check you out."

"And they can do this through email?"

"Email, then phone, then meet – that's the way it's done."

"You've done this before?"

"I've sat through *Sleepless in Seattle*."

Eduardo's eyes rolled up to the ceiling. He was totally disinterested now. He finished his food and stayed for one more cup before remembering: "Oh, I have something for you." He rummaged through his coat and pulled out a white envelope and handed it to Nate. "It's just been printed. This is an advanced copy I got from a friend of mine. I knew right away you'd be interested – knowing him like you did."

The envelope was unmarked and the textured paper was expensive, feeling almost like fine linen. Nate was immediately curious – knowing *who* the way I did? He pulled out the card inside. It was an invitation:

THE LIVINGSTON GALLERY ANNOUNCES
AN ART EXHIBIT
THE COMPLETE WORKS OF
PETER LAZAR CARUSO

Below this it gave a Park Avenue address and a date three weeks out.

Complete works - so there must be some new paintings created by Peter since the Columbia exhibit. Nate realized that this could be one of the most important showings of the year – maybe the decade.

"It's just for wealthy art aficionados," said Eduardo, "and some of the press – very exclusive. You will go, of course?"

For a moment, Nate forgot about the women in the ads and his mind whirled. He remembered the jealousy and self-doubt he'd experienced at Peter's Columbia exhibit but he'd long since accepted the fact that Peter was just a better artist. Even with Peter dead, Nate might still harbor some jealousy, but it was time to get over that. "I'll need a tux," he said.

Eduardo smiled and spread his hands. "I know some people in wardrobe."

The following Tuesday, Nate had his final sitting with Meredith. He entered the house and was escorted by Teddy to the east room where Meredith waited, the morning sun streaming in behind her. They exchanged good-mornings as she took up her pose, then Teddy left them alone.

"Close the door, Nathan,"

From behind his easel, he locked eyes with her. "Meredith, we can't..." But her look was insistent. He got up and closed the door then walked back to his stool and picked up his brush and pallet. He began lightening a black that would become the gray fabric of her sweatshirt. Almost without realizing he was speaking his internal thoughts aloud, he said: "I'll miss our mornings together."

"Oh? And why is that, Nathan? Is it because you like me? Or is it because you want me?"

"Stop with your teasing, Meredith."

"Only if you stop with your innocent little *I'll miss our mornings together* comments. Do you ever say what you really mean, Nathan? Or do you always let your paints do the talking for you? It's much safer that way, isn't it?"

Nate's mouth turned dry. He had no idea what to say.

Meredith got up and took a step toward him, her eyes more menacing now than seductive, her face reddening but only for an instant as her calm demeanor once more took over. "I just wanted to make you realize that, while I may be locked into a marriage of convenience, I've long ago accepted that fact. I've come to view it more as a challenge than a restriction." She turned for the door and put her hand on the knob. "I'm not the one with the problem here, Nathan - it's you." After opening the door, she walked back to her chair and resumed her pose as if nothing had happened.

Neither of them spoke much for the rest of the morning and it was a strain for Nate to get through it. As he worked, Teddy made his presence known every now and then by rummaging about in the kitchen or poking his head through the door of the east room asking how things were getting on.

Nate completed the painting of Meredith Sinclair in his studio near the end of February and the formal unveiling was held in Teddy's great room a few nights later. Teddy proclaimed it a black-tie event and invited a few close friends.

At eight o'clock, a bell chimed and crystal flutes of Champagne were passed out. People gathered in an arc around the veiled painting and Teddy stepped forward with Meredith beside him.

"Ladies and gentlemen, thank you all for coming. This is indeed a happy occasion for Meredith and I, and a moment of achievement, I believe, for the renowned Nathan Lido Parks. I say 'I believe' since I have yet to see the painting myself." He gave Nate a nod then looked directly at Meredith. "This work was commissioned by me to celebrate the birthday of my beautiful wife and to thank her for doing me the honor of staying with me for these past five years. Our anniversary is coming up in just a few weeks." This elicited some polite applause. "Well, I won't delay things any longer. Ladies and gentlemen, I give you my wife, Mrs. Meredith Sinclair." He stepped up to the easel and eased the white shroud off the canvas.

The room hushed and the people furthest away craned for a better look.

The image of Meredith Sinclair was seated in casual elegance, silhouetted in front of her bedroom window. The colors, shadows, living skin tones, and vivid sunlight created the first impression but what lingered, just as Nate had intended, was that face; beautiful certainly, but there was much more than that. Here was vulnerability and sensuality and here was mystery – What is this woman thinking? What is she about to say?

Someone shouted "Bravo" as everyone put down their glasses and broke into enthusiastic applause.

Nate kept his eyes on Meredith whose face was turned from his as she saw the painting for the first time. She wiped a hand across her cheek and gave Teddy a kiss. Then she turned to Nate. Her lips wavered as if straining against her emotions. A tear escaped from the corner of her eye and she didn't bother drying it. She walked over and gave him a kiss on his cheek. "Thank you, Nathan. It's beautiful."

"It was a privilege, Meredith." It felt to him like she was saying goodbye, as if she had made the choice to end their unfulfilled affair. But then, as she turned back to Teddy, she let her bare arm brush against his sleeve sending another message entirely.

Nate's studio was a low-rent, second floor room located a few blocks from his apartment. He spent most of the following week there grading student papers and catching up on some older projects, but his heart wasn't in it. He couldn't stop thinking about Meredith. He had to see her again but had no idea how he could do that without arousing Teddy's suspicion. He didn't have Meredith's cell number so he couldn't just call her but, even if he did, what then? Would he invite her here to his studio? The place was a mess and his apartment wasn't much better. Would she be shocked to see where he worked? Would she think he was a low-life? He stared at his overstuffed brown couch and the stains on the walls near his sink and microwave that served as a kitchen.

Who was he kidding? Meredith had just been toying with him. She didn't really want him. He was the classic starving artist working in a dump with bills piling up that would never get paid. There'd been no follow up commission from Teddy as he'd hoped and the pittance he received from his teaching barely lasted to the middle of the month.

Nate sank down onto his couch and put his head back, staring at the cracks in the ceiling plaster. A cold shiver ran though him and he closed his eyes. Would he always be poor? Would he always be alone?

Nate sat there for a long while contemplating his bleak future then forced his eyes open. These dark, enveloping moods seemed to come more frequently these days and, with or without Meredith he knew he had to put a stop to them. He made a fist that he pounded once into the couch then went to the sink and splashed some cold water on his face, drying off with a towel still damp from breakfast dishes. At least for now, he was done feeling sorry for himself. It was time to get back to work.

He noticed a painting in the corner of his studio that he'd abandoned six months ago. It was to be a study of a man in a bakery shop - a simple idea that, when he'd put it on canvas, had taken on too much of a Norman Rockwell flavor. He didn't know how to fix it – how to make it his own. He cleaned it up and placed it on his easel. Arms folded, he stared at the image then finally picked up his brush and pallet and added a few brush-strokes that Norman never would have approved of. He stepped back. Yes, that was better—more expressive. Encouraged, he put everything else out of his mind, turned on some Gershwin and plowed ahead, making progress in muting the realism yet boosting the sensory content; the texture of the rising dough, the tantalizing colors of the pastry shelf. He almost didn't hear the knock on the door. He never had visitors here.

He turned down the music and opened the door. He took a step back and his heart thundered. There she stood in a bright green winter coat and hat, her purse under an arm. "Meredith."

She hurried in, her face flushed. She put down her purse.

Nate closed the door and their eyes met. "Can I get..." No, she wasn't here for something to drink. He dropped his pallet and brush and turned the dead-bolt. He rushed to her and pulled her close, wrapping her in his arms. She trembled, but there was no resistance - only passion. They kissed and his hands explored her body beneath her coat, touching her in ways he had dreamed of for weeks. Her coat fell to the floor. He backed her down onto the couch. Her lips parted and she reached for him hungrily, pulling him down, her breath hot on his cheek. She arched her back against his and their bodies pulsed in a frantic, natural rhythm. He fumbled with her clothes, then with his own. There were no words between them and when it was over they lay on the floor, spent.

Nate couldn't remember rolling from the couch to the floor but somehow they had and he was thankful that the one throw-rug he owned had been well positioned and just large enough to accommodate them both. He reached for her coat and covered them both.

She took a deep breath. "Like the song, Nathan. Here I am on the cheatin' side of town."

"It's just a song."

"No, it's more than that. It's been my life."

"It doesn't have to be."

"Do you want me to leave Teddy? I will, you know. I can do that."

"Leave him for all this?" He waved a hand at the peeling wallpaper.

She rolled to her side and elbowed her head up, her breast angling down tantalizing him again.

"I wouldn't leave empty-handed," she said.

"Teddy would ruin me." He cupped her breast in his hand.

"And I would ruin Teddy."

"He deserves better."

"And so do I." She said this with peculiar curl to her lower lip that he'd seen before. Slowly, he pulled his hand away.

"Besides," she continued, "you could...we could, start over someplace else."

Nate's heart jumped. He immediately thought of Maysville—a reclusive but famous artist living happily in the hills of Pennsylvania with his knock-out wife.

"Maybe Europe," she said. "We could live in Paris. What a gas that would be, don't you think?"

He didn't answer. He pulled her close and kissed her, gently this time. "How did you find my studio?"

"I went to your brownstone. One of your neighbors saw me and told me you might be here."

"I wish you'd called. I could have picked up the place – pretty dingy, smells like paint."

"It's not the Waldorf but I came to see you, not your studio. I think of you every time I see your painting and I miss our Tuesdays together. The past week has been torture."

"I've been a hopeless mess, thinking that I'd never see you again." Nate cupped her breast again and felt her body respond. They made love again then lay there for a while without a word. Finally, she stood and began putting on her clothes. He did the same.

She straightened her blouse then stepped into his arms. "Is your art more important to you than me?"

She was standing in front of his easel and his unfinished baker stared back at Nate over her shoulder as if just as concerned. "Meredith, you're the most important woman in my life, but you can't ask me to give up my life's work."

Before she could say anything, he pulled her close. They kissed, long and passionately and Nate found himself lost in this beautiful woman. He was racing down the rails, hands over his head and he knew there would be no stopping this roller coaster ride. At that moment he might have agreed to anything Meredith asked of him, even Paris. But evidently, she was done with questions.

"So, I'm the woman of the week—of the month if I'm lucky and you're my man of the here and now. That's okay, Nathan. I stopped believing in forever a long time ago and no, I would never ask you to give up your art. It's your refuge, remember? Just like Teddy is mine – just so we understand each other." She reached for her coat and put it on, then picked up her purse. She gave him another kiss – just a peck this time.

After she left, Nate stood with his back against the door wondering what had just happened, but overall, feeling much better about things.

CHAPTER 3

Two weeks later, Nate stood on the sidewalk along Park Avenue in his overcoat and his borrowed tux waiting to get into the Caruso exhibit. It was eight at night and there were about fifteen people in front of him. His breath rose in clouds as he shifted his weight back and forth to keep warm, slowly approaching the gallery entrance. The Livingston Group was famous for sponsoring high-profile artistic events and tonight, besides Peter, they were also honoring Peter's father. This was according to yesterday's press release. Nate imagined Mr. Caruso somewhere inside the gallery, nibbling on cheese cubes and feeling very out of place. The same press release had said that there would be a total of thirty-nine paintings on display, thirty-four of which had never been shown before. The remaining five were from the Columbia exhibit. All the paintings had been found in the same Brownsville apartment where Peter had been killed. As Peter's only living relative, Mr. Caruso now owned the paintings. Selling them would suddenly make him a very wealthy man.

A black Lincoln pulled up to the gallery.

"Some VIP," said the guy behind Nate.

The doorman stepped up to the vehicle and opened the door. He extended his hand to offer assistance but the woman inside, wearing an unbuttoned, brown checked coat, got out on her own. She stood there for a moment as cameras flashed. Nate could see she was young with short blonde hair and below the hem of her coat he saw that she wore slacks and—were those tennis shoes? The doorman escorted her inside; she had apparently come alone.

The guy behind Nate piped up again: "Must be nice."

The woman in front of Nate turned. "That's Sarah Crawford, Lieutenant Governor of the State of New York."

"Well, excuse me," said the guy, which drew a dirty look from the woman. Nate moved aside a little to make sure she reached her intended target.

"She does a lot of good for the arts in this town," said the woman.

Vaguely, Nate realized that he'd heard of Sarah Crawford. She looked pretty young to be lieutenant governor but he kept that thought to himself, not wanting to spark more ire from the woman. The guy behind him kept quiet too.

When he finally made it to the door, Nate showed his invitation and was allowed inside where he was handed a program. "In loving memory" read the caption beneath a black and white photograph of Peter. It showed him, brush in hand, in front of a half-finished painting. He was turned away from his work looking directly at the camera, his eyes blazing as if he had just been rudely interrupted. Nate wondered idly who would have chosen that particular photograph for the program. Then again, Peter never smiled all that much. Nate took off his coat and left it at the coat-check stand then rubbed his hands together to warm up.

Elbow-tall conversation tables covered in white linen dotted the floor of the hall and from the back, strains of a viola and harp drifted over the buzz of the crowd. The lighting was subdued to the point of being dim over the center of the hall, but along the walls each of Peter's paintings glowed from the diffused light cast on them by specially focused, ceiling mounted portrait lights.

Nate thought back to his own low-budget exhibit that he'd put on in the village a couple of years ago where he hadn't even managed to draw in much of the leisure-suit crowd, much less the wealthy upper-crusters he saw around him tonight. Peter's exhibit had to cost a fortune in comparison. But look at them all, over-perfumed and over-cologned, they jammed the viewing areas and slowly circulated around the room from painting to painting. He took a place in line.

"Wine, sir?"

He grabbed a glass of red and a couple of tooth-picked cheese cubes. He put one in his mouth and followed it by a sip, savoring its flavors; good wine. Then he came to the first painting: *Thunder on the Mountain* according to the program.

Within a simple three by four-foot wooden frame, wild clouds of muted colors hung threateningly over a raging river of blues and whites. Beside the river a man and boy raced down the slope, their desperate faces directed straight through the canvas as if screaming for the observer to save them. The yellow-white flash of a lightning bolt in the foreground cast stark shadows behind them making it look as if they were being chased by demons. Rain streamed across the scene and trees tilted at a sharp angle almost giving voice to the howling wind. The effect was startling, combining the realism of Wyeth with the sensory overload of Munch and Duchamp. Here, the forces of nature battled the power of emotion and it was their imbalance that propelled the man and boy down the mountainside and made the observer an active participant in their fear. Nate couldn't take his eyes off it.

But the push of the crowd moved him slowly around the gallery from painting to painting. Another that made its mark on Nate was less dramatic but no less effective. Entitled *Alone*, it showed an old man sitting by himself on a park bench in the rain. Oblivious to the weather, he stared out of the canvas as if looking past Nate, as if imagining something in the distance that he knew wasn't really there now but had been at one time. His face was a study in despair and hopelessness. It made Nate think of Peter's father. And it made him think of himself, and what he might become years from now without a life's companion. He finished off his wine and moved on.

Each of the paintings pulled him in, the last being the erotic, *Woman in Winter*. Each had demanded such an intense emotional involvement that by the time he'd seen them all, Nate was breathless. He stepped back to the center of the room and grabbed another glass of wine and a few cheese cubes from a passing waiter. He found an empty table. His palms were sweating. After what he'd just seen, he wondered why he should bother to pick up an artists' brush again. The works of Peter Caruso had said all that needed saying and in comparison, the works of poor Nathan Parks were the creations of a child. He swirled the wine in his glass and took another swallow; a gulp this time. He felt himself slipping into one of his moods; questioning his talent, questioning everything. Then a glass clinked his.

"Hello Nathan, remember me?"

The red-gowned woman next to him took a sip of her own wine and leaned closer. "Coffee-spilling Cat; from the train."

"Cat, yes, of course," said Nate, hardly believing that this was the same woman who had bumped into him. Her diamond necklace sparkled and despite all the competing scents around him, her perfume woke up his senses – all of them. He absently tossed a cube of cheese into his mouth and attempted: "Good to see you again." The cheese caused him to mumble so he swallowed quickly. "Good to see you again, miss...?"

"Chaplin – Cat Chaplin." They shook hands. "You look good in a tux."

"You look...magnificent. It's borrowed – the tux."

She waved a hand over her diamonds. "Wealthy parents." She glanced around the room. "You knew him, didn't you? Peter, I mean—same home town, same school?"

"Do you study up on all the local artists?"

"Just the ones I like. I like you."

For some reason Nate felt relieved to hear that but then figured well, what else is she going to say? "Thanks, and I assume you like Peter's work?"

"The collection is fabulous, don't you think? Too bad he died. What was he like growing up?"

"He was a pretty average kid, nothing special." Something prevented him from telling her about Peter's weird streak. You didn't speak ill of the dead. Besides, that was just his opinion.

"Two artists growing up in rural Scranton, attending the same high-school, the same college, then both living in New York – were you close?"

Nate put an elbow on the table. "Yes, back when we were kids. At college we'd bump into each other every now and then but that was all." He wondered why she was so curious about Peter but he liked her company, and her brown eyes.

They talked for another ten minutes as the crowd thinned. He glanced at his watch, surprised to see that it was nearing midnight. The paintings had so absorbed him that he'd hardly noticed time passing.

"His father's over there," said Cat, pointing to Frank Caruso who sat at a table near the back of the hall, close to the harp and viola. He was formally attired with a white carnation in his lapel but his tie was crooked and his expression blank. "He's by himself now. Earlier he was surrounded by the press – you know, everyone wants to get the inside story on Peter. Do you know him? Peter's father I mean?"

"Not well. I was at the funeral. Before that I hadn't seen him since high school. He was pretty shaken up by his son's death; Peter was all he had. I never knew anything about Peter's mother. She was already dead and gone when I first knew Peter. Why are you so interested? You aren't a reporter are you?"

Cat smiled. "No. I'm not a reporter." She said this as if she was playing twenty-questions with him, divulging next to nothing about herself. "I'm really just curious to know more about the man who created all this beautiful art."

"You seem to know quite a lot already. But I was planning to speak to Mr. Caruso before leaving anyway. Come on, I'll introduce you."

"Oh, he and I have talked already, but I'll go with you if you don't mind."

Nate gave her his arm and they walked over.

"Hello Mr. Caruso, I thought I'd say hi before leaving." He extended his hand but Caruso remained seated and took another swallow of wine. Up close now, Nate could see that his eyes were red.

"Hello Nathan," – not Natey, or even Nate this time. His voice rang cold and hollow.

"Ms. Chaplin here tells me that the two of you met earlier."

Caruso gave Cat a glance. Her grip on Nate's arm tightened.

But Nate pressed on. "I know this whole thing must be tough on you, Mr. Caruso, but is there something else wrong?"

Caruso looked down into his glass and finished off the remaining wine. His eyes took on a fierce look that almost caused Nate to take a step back. "I'll tell you what's wrong, Natey boy. My mind isn't so sharp these days so maybe it's the wine that got me thinking but I remember now. I remember the argument you had with Peter and I remember your threat as clear as if it were yesterday." He stood up. "So tell me now and tell me the truth. Did you kill my son?"

Nate was stunned. Now he did step back and Cat dropped her hand. Had he heard him right? "How could you even think such a thing?"

Caruso's voice raised a level. "*I will shoot you dead.* That's what you told him in his own house – in my house. And now Peter's been shot dead."

The words echoed in Nate's mind and then he remembered shouting them and he remembered why. "Mr. Caruso, that was fifteen years ago. We were just boys."

"Peter didn't have an enemy in the world except for you." He stepped closer to Nate, his chest heaving, the smell of wine on his breath. "You were jealous of him because he was better than you. He was always better than you."

"Peter was my friend, Mr. Caruso, and I loved his work. I didn't kill him. I could never kill anybody."

Caruso gave him a shove but Nate stood his ground. Then the

old man seemed to waver. He wiped his hands over his face and went back to the table. "I need to be alone. I just want to be alone." He looked at Cat. "I won't be able to meet with you tomorrow morning. I'm feeling the need to sleep late. It'll have to be in the afternoon."

"The afternoon will be fine," said Cat.

Nate turned to her, wondering what they were talking about. "And give me a call first," said Caruso. He grabbed another glass of wine from a passing waiter and sat back down. "Now please, just leave me alone."

His mind clouded, Nate headed slowly toward the front of the gallery, Cat following. Then he stopped, suddenly curious. "Why will you be seeing him tomorrow?"

She hesitated. "My firm's been hired to investigate Caruso's art prior to its sale to Livingston. It's still owned right now by the estate. I have to meet with Caruso tomorrow to go over a few things."

"You're authenticating this art?"

"No, not me, we hired a guy for that. We almost hired you but they thought you were too close to the Carusos – you know, it might look funny."

"So who do you work for?"

"I'm with the Bradshaw Detective Agency. We do a lot of work with art stuff."

Nate shook his head. "You call all this *art stuff*?" He waved a hand toward the wall.

"I didn't mean it like that, Nate. I may not be as high-brow as you and all these people here but I do like art and I've got a job to do."

"You're a private investigator. When were you going to tell me?"

"I was working up to it. I was going to tell you, really I was. I guess I liked you thinking I was a wealthy socialite. This dress, this necklace, they belong to the agency. I'm really just Cat Chaplin from the Bronx."

Nate put his hands in his pockets and felt for his coat-check token. He didn't like being lied to and he wasn't sure he was comfortable around someone who invaded other people's lives for a living. It explained how she knew so much about him and about Peter. It also explained why she was being so friendly. She was just pumping him for information. "I should be going, give me your ticket and I'll get your coat."

He returned with her coat and helped her with it.

She thanked him then asked: "Did you really threaten to shoot Peter?"

More pumping. "I don't want to talk about it." He put his coat on. The doorman opened the door for him and he was back out in the cold.

It was snowing again. A few cabs waited by the curb, engines running, wipers slapping. There were people already waiting. He got in line and she got behind him.

He was unsure whether to be mad at Cat or to ask her out for coffee. He turned around. There were those brown eyes again. He opened his mouth to say something, unsure just what that would be but he was interrupted by the cab-stand guy.

"You're next sir. This way."

It was just as well. He stepped aside. "Here, you go first."

"Thanks." She gave him a glance and got in.

Nate watched the tail-lights fade through the falling snow then got into the next cab.

CHAPTER 4

In the morning, a wet wind from the snow-turned-rain blew Cat through the door. She had a garment bag folded over one arm. "Chaplin here," she called out as she always did, forcing the door closed behind her until it latched.

"Hey," came the response from the back office.

She tossed her baseball cap toward the coat-hook and missed. She draped the garment bag over a chair. "Goodbye Cinderella," she said to herself with a pat on the bag. She knew she had made a mess of things – not with Caruso though, she'd meet with him later today. With all the money he'd be getting from Livingston, he shouldn't mind jumping through the last few hoops that would put a lid on the whole Livingston job. Her final report would finish it off.

No, the mess was with Nathan Parks. She liked him and first she'd spilled coffee on him then she'd deceived him by wearing that stupid fancy-dancey dress and not telling him who she really was. Dumb, dumb, and dumb. It seemed like she could never click with nice guys and it was always her own fault. But then again, Caruso said that Parks had threatened to kill his son. Maybe Parks wasn't such a nice guy after all.

Her desk was the first in a row of three. The other two belonged to a couple of field investigators who were hardly ever there. This morning, as usual, it was just she up front and old Bradshaw in back. She removed her coat and shook off the rain before hanging it up then grabbed a cup of coffee that she thinned with some milk. On the way back to her desk she caught a whiff of pickles from Bradshaw's morning Rueben. How could anyone start the day with kraut, pickles and corned beef? She put her cup down on the corner of her paper-strewn desk and sat down. Only three cases to work on but the paperwork facing her was daunting. Actually, Cat found any amount of paperwork daunting. She flicked her computer on and waited for it to boot up.

It was probably the stronger than usual smell of Bradshaw's Ruben that took her back to her first job at Chaplin's Chapel, her family's grocery-deli on Katonah Avenue. The little store had been the social focus of a tight-knit Irish neighborhood where she grew up sweeping floors, canning vegetables and building tall sandwiches for customers who became accustomed to seeing her behind the counter. 'Hi Cat, how're the pickles today?' they'd ask right behind the tinkling of the bell over the door. 'The pickles are still pickles,' she'd always yell back. Did they think they'd turned into radishes overnight? After her parents died, she was stuck managing the place and got to be pretty good at it until a chain grocery moved in a few doors down. She and her out-of-state brother held onto the business as long as they could but it was a losing proposition and they eventually had to sell out. She missed the old place but she didn't miss working with pickles – she hated pickles.

By the end of the morning, Cat had boiled down her clutter into three file-folders, the thickest of them labeled Livingston. She stretched back in her chair and once again thought of Nathan—Nate, she liked the name. He in his tux and she in her red gown—it could have been a storybook romance but now he probably hated her. At best, he just resented her. Nice work Cat.

She called Frank Caruso and set up a time to meet that afternoon and an hour later glanced at the clock – close enough. She zipped up her jacket and picked her hat up off the floor. "Chaplin out," she yelled, pulling the door closed behind her. Great, still raining. Across the street, she grabbed a Quarter-pounder without pickles and a large diet to-go and took bites and gulps while running beneath the awnings on her way to the subway. It was a short ride to the Four Seasons and an elevator up to the fifth floor where she brushed off a few crumbs, assumed her professional investigator disposition and knocked on the door of room five-seventeen.

Mr. Caruso, in jeans and T-shirt opened up. "Hello Miss Chaplin, come in." He didn't look exactly pleased to see her but he did look more comfortable out of his tux. He pulled the door wider and let her pass. There was scotch on his breath.

He waived her onto a couch where she glanced around the

room. It was modest by Four Seasons standards but still plush, and paid for, she knew, by Livingston. She took off her cap and placed it and a pocket recorder on the coffee table.

"Mr. Caruso, we've nearly wrapped up our investigation into your son's art work."

"And this should finish it off, right?"

"I hope it will, yes."

Caruso picked up his half-finished drink and jiggled the ice cubes. "Can I get you something from the mini-bar?"

"No, thanks."

He sat down opposite her. "OK then, let's get this over with. Fire away."

She pulled out the three page letter she'd received from the Livingston lawyers which listed the fifteen questions they wanted her to go over. She had some latitude to ask a few of her own as she felt necessary. She flipped on her recorder. "I'll be recording this, you have no objections? I'm not too good at taking notes."

He shrugged.

"Sorry, I need you to actually verbalize your full name and that you approve of my recording this interview."

He did so.

Cat moved the recorder closer to him. "All right then, to get started, there are thirty-nine paintings in this collection. Do you know over what period of time they were created?"

"Roughly ten years dating from Peter's last year in high school, through his time at Columbia and up to his death."

"He painted some of them while still in high school?" Quite the wiz-kid, thought Cat.

"Yes, two of them, I believe."

"Are there any other Caruso paintings in existence that you're aware of?"

"Five were in his initial exhibit at Columbia but they're documented and were included in the exhibit. So far as I know, there are no others."

"And do you think you'd know if there were others?"

"After Columbia, my son was obsessed with the creation of this collection. He stayed in his apartment here in New York and did nothing else. Practically speaking, he could have painted others but yes, I think I'd know if he had."

"So from the time of the Columbia exhibit until the age of thirty-two, he was artistically occupied solely with the creation of this collection. Is that correct? Did he ever leave on extended trips to see anyone – visit you in Scranton maybe?"

"He never even left for groceries. He had an arrangement with a store across the street from his apartment. I visited my son once a year on his birthday. I'd stay for a couple of hours and we'd hardly talk. I took his picture once – the one they used on the program. He just about threw me out."

"So you and your son didn't get along?"

"My relationship with my son is my affair, Ms. Chaplin. Please, just stick to the script."

"Of course, sorry, but I have to ask, how did your son provide for himself all those years living by himself? Are you sure he didn't sell any of his art?"

"I'm positive of that. He lived off a trust fund that my wife and I set up for him years ago. It was supposed to go for his college but, as you may know, he had a full scholarship. He also lived very...frugally. I don't believe he ever intended to sell any of his paintings."

"Peter didn't sell anything at all from the Columbia exhibit?"

"He got some fantastic offers that I wish to God he'd accepted, but no. It was like he couldn't bear to part with any of them. I'm only selling them now because I need the money."

"What about sketches or drawings? Was there anything like that?"

Caruso put an elbow on his knee and pinched his lower lip. "There was his sketchbook from high school."

Cat looked up from her list of questions. "Where is that sketchbook now?"

"I haven't seen it in years. I don't have any idea where it might be. Peter used it to get into Columbia and to qualify for his scholarship. They may have some record of it. Why is that important?"

"The Livingston Gallery is offering to purchase all of your son's creative work. We can only exclude those he might have created as a child prior to the age of fifteen or so. The sketchbook would qualify as a creative work." Cat pulled another folded-over document from her purse. "It's all spelled out here in the draft of the contract." She found the relevant clause. "Here it is, section 5, paragraph two point two." She handed it to him but he waved it off.

"I'm not a lawyer, Miss Chaplin. I know I've agreed to sell all of Peter's work so just go on and let's get through this." He stood up and headed for the mini-bar.

Cat picked up the recorder and held it out, tracking him as he poured a single-shot over a few ice cubes and walked back. "I'll need your permission to obtain your son's entrance papers from Columbia, and to obtain the sketchbook if it's there. I'll fax you the forms for your signature."

"Fine, fine, I'll sign whatever you want." He took a gulp and started pacing.

Twenty minutes later Cat reached the end of her list of questions. She stood up, snapped off the recorder and put it back in her jacket pocket. "Thank you for your patience, Mr. Caruso. I'm sure you understand the need to cover all these details."

"I understand completely. There's a lot of money involved."

Cat nodded. "Will you be in town much longer?"

"Only until Livingston stops paying my expenses here." He laughed at that. "And there's the matter of the check for my son's paintings. Maybe you can see if you can move that along? I'm not a poor man, Miss Chaplin, but I could very much use the money."

The amount of Livingston's offer had been blacked out of Cat's copy of the contract but it was abundantly clear: if Mr. Caruso wasn't rich now, he soon would be. "We'll need to look into the sketchbook thing. And, just to clarify, you have no problem with it being included with the sale?"

"No, I don't."

Cat glanced at her watch. She really wanted to ask Caruso about his accusation last night that Nathan Parks had once threatened Peter but no, that would be going way off script and the Livingston file was thick enough as it is. "Okay then, that'll wrap things up for today. I'll send you the forms in the morning."

They shook hands and she left. It was at her apartment much later that night when she had an idea and picked up the phone.

CHAPTER 5

Nate's affair with Meredith Sinclair had advanced from the brown couch at his studio to the lumpy double bed in his apartment. He leaned his back against the loose headboard cradling Meredith's head in his arms. It was dark and both of them were out of breath. She murmured, half asleep as he brushed aside a strand of her hair then settled his hand on her breast. The phone beside the bed rang. He let it go to his machine but could hear the message.

Hi Nathan, this is Cat. Sorry about last night. I'd like to make it up to you – how about lunch tomorrow? I've got something else to talk to you about too. Give me a call. She left her number.

"Who's Cat?" asked Meredith with a yawn, eyes still closed.

"Just a girl, I don't really know her." He wondered how she got his number.

"You know her well enough for her to have done something that she has to make up for."

"It was really nothing. She spilled coffee on me."

"I noticed a stain on your trousers when we first met. It looked like coffee. But that was two months ago. This girl was talking about last night. Maybe that was somebody else who spilled coffee on you?"

"No, that was her."

"So it's something else she wants to make up for? She must be pretty clumsy. You said you hardly knew her - you've known her longer than you've known me."

Nate swallowed. Where was Meredith going with this? Could she be jealous?

"Do you like her?" asked Meredith. Under the sheets, her hand moved lower. "Has she done things to you yet?" She raised her head and pressed her lips lightly on his. "Have you done things to her?"

"We haven't done anything." This sounded more defensive than he'd intended. He had nothing to be defensive about. What did she expect him to say?

"But you want to do things with her, don't you?" she whispered, her tongue playing with his ear-lobe, her breath hot.

Nate pulled her closer, forcing his hips against hers and, thankfully, Meredith asked no more questions.

She left an hour later, consistent with her cover story to Teddy about taking in a show in mid-town. She didn't tell Nate if or when she'd be back. This got him wondering again, why would a rich and beautiful socialite want to have anything to do with him? Why would she want to make love in this dump of an apartment? From somewhere inside him the voice of Eduardo offered some guidance: *Never question good fortune*.

Nate didn't think about Cat until the next morning and he didn't call her until the morning after that when he agreed to meet her for lunch near Columbia. She'd said she wanted to talk with him about Peter.

When he entered *Mel's Burger Bar* he saw her from the back, the same way he'd first seen her. She wore the same jacket, no baseball cap this time and sat alone at a window table, pecking at her phone. She bore no resemblance to the stylish, diamond-decked woman from the exhibit.

Nate wore a scarred, brown leather bomber jacket. He walked over and, when she saw him, she put down her phone.

"Hi Nathan, glad you could come. When you didn't call yesterday I was afraid I'd really screwed things up with you."

"Not at all," he said, still standing. He had only agreed to come because of his curiosity over the Caruso paintings. All right, maybe Meredith's questioning if he'd ever done anything with Cat had something to do with it too. Looking at her now, she was as alluring as she'd been with her diamonds. He felt himself staring then caught himself. My God, he was turning into Eduardo, seeing every woman as a target for an affair. But was that a bad thing? Maybe not bad, he decided, but it certainly wasn't a Nate-like thing. He reminded himself that he was done with meaningless affairs – well, except for Meredith. But there was nothing meaningless about the way he thought about Meredith, was there?

His head was a little cloudy on that point. He took off his jacket and sat down.

"I keep mine on because I like to sit by the window – a little chilly," she said.

"I haven't eaten here, what's good?"

"Burgers are their thing - fifty different varieties."

He looked over the menu. "Fifty different ways to trigger a heart attack."

"Yup, that's what they're famous for. Not a good place for a vegan." Her eyebrows went up. "You aren't vegan are you?"

"No, a burger and beer'll be fine."

They ordered; his with Mel's secret sauce on the side.

"So, you wanted to talk about Peter."

"Yes, but before we do, I need to ask you about what his father said to you. Did you really threaten to shoot Peter?"

Nate looked out the window, remembering the look Peter's father had given him. "Why do you need to know?"

"I'm in a bind and I'd like to involve you with my investigation. But I can't bring you in if there's any suspicion that you killed Peter."

"Oh for God's sake, you can't believe I'm a killer."

"Caruso does."

"He was tired and he was drunk. He knows better. He said himself that it was the wine talking. When I saw him at Peter's funeral he was as cordial as he could be under the circumstances and didn't mention it at all."

"You said you made the threat fifteen years ago. Tell me what happened."

Nate folded his arms and looked out the window at the heavy foot traffic on Broadway. "All right. It wasn't a big deal really. We were in our junior year – high school. A girl at the school had died in a drowning accident. She was a senior, very popular and I knew her pretty well and liked her. The accident was a total shock to me. It was a shock to the whole town. On the day after the funeral I was at Peter's house. We were just goofing off like we usually did when he started making jokes about Patty – that was her name, Patty Harris. It was like he didn't care if she were alive or dead. He did things like that sometimes; if he knew something or someone was important to you he'd make fun of you for it. He liked getting a rise out of people – Peter could be very cruel that way.

"Well, he was getting a rise out of me and I nearly threw a punch but Peter went into one of his rages and I just decided to get the hell out of there. I was on my way down the stairs when he ran out of his room and yelled out: 'What would you do if you knew it wasn't an accident? What would you do if you knew I was the one who killed her?' He asked it in a sneering kind of way as if testing me to see if I'd stand up for her. So I yelled back up the stairs telling him that if Patty had been murdered and if he was the one who did it, I'd shoot him dead. I think I said that last part twice and maybe that was all his dad overheard. I didn't even know he was in the house. I remembered being so angry that I was shaking." Nate tapped a finger on the table.

"What happened after that?"

"Nothing. I left the house and the next day was just another school day."

"And Peter never mentioned the girl after that?"

"If he did, it wasn't to me. He knew better."

"He doesn't sound like a good friend."

Nate shook his head and took a sip from his beer. "He was normally a good kid and a good friend but he had moments where he just flew off like that. Like I told Mr. Caruso, we were just boys and boys say a lot of things – things they don't really mean."

Cat nodded. "You know that Caruso's going to mention the threat to the police – he probably already has."

Nate shook his head. "I can't stop him, but I've got nothing to hide."

"I know they don't have any good leads on the case. Right now the police think it was just a break-in gone wrong. If they call you, just tell them what you told me and you should be okay."

"You're giving me legal advice now?"

"You don't have to be a snot about it."

Their food came.

Nate dipped a fingertip into the little container of Mel's sauce then applied it sparingly to his burger. "So, am I clean enough to be part of your investigation?"

Cat put her beer down. "You done being a snot?"

"Maybe."

"Look, you're right, I'm not a legal person. But I do know a few cops and I know how they work. If they can't come up with any leads in a case they get pressure from the higher-ups. The higher the profile of their case, the more pressure comes down on them to show some progress. They'll jump at anything that's the least suspicious even if it happened fifteen years ago. You should be careful, Nate. That's all I was getting at."

"Okay, I'll be careful and I'll stop being a snot. So tell me why you need me."

They ate as Cat did most of the talking. She apologized for misleading him at the exhibit and told him about the Bradshaw Agency. "We do proprietary rights investigations, clear-title work, and lately have gotten into ownership issues on high-worth properties."

"Like works of art," he said between bites. The sauce was actually very good. He poured more of it on his burger and asked for more napkins.

"Yes, we do a lot of art, especially lately. Everybody's worried about investments these days. And the value of good art keeps going up."

"Even more so for artists who happen to be dead."

"That's right, but Livingston was interested in Caruso's paintings even before his death. Now that he's dead they want to make sure they've cornered the market on his stuff – sorry, on his creative works." She put down what was left of her burger and moved her plate aside. "Do you have anything going on this afternoon?"

He didn't. "I might be able to make some time."

"Good." She told him about her meeting with Caruso two days ago and about the sketchbook then checked the time on her phone. "I've got the authorization papers from Caruso and have a meeting with the chair of the Visual Art School at Columbia in forty minutes. Livingston's insisting that the sketchbook be included in the sale of the collection. One day it could be as valuable as one of the actual paintings."

Nate nodded, thinking about the famous sketches and renderings of da Vinci and Picasso.

"Anyway, I'm looking into it and I thought it would be good to have someone along who actually knew Peter and knew a lot about art, you know, to authenticate the sketchbook and to ask the right questions. You interested?"

"You said at the exhibit that it might have looked funny if I was the one authenticating the paintings. Are you sure Livingston will be okay with me working on the sketchbook—especially considering the threat thing?"

"They'll be fine with it and I just won't tell them about the threat. Besides, like I said, I'm in a jam. Our other art expert is already on his way back to Argentina."

"You hired him because of his Latin accent, right?"

"It wasn't my decision, but I understand it was a definite plus."

"Well, to answer your question, yes I am interested."

"Great, consider yourself hired, Mr. Parks. Now drink up, we've got an appointment with the art guy at Columbia."

An hour later Nate crossed his ankles and leaned back in a waiting room chair. Next to him, Cat was going over some notes, mumbling to herself. Opposite them a gum-chewing grad student sat behind a desk staring at a computer screen. Every now and then she'd smack her gum and punch out a few keystrokes keeping time with Cat's mumbling. Nate cleared his throat every now and then to remind them he was still there.

They had been advised by the chair of the school of visual arts that they would need to retrieve Peter's file from Professor Cyrus Gray, dean of registration and scholarships who had yet to return from a late lunch. It was two o'clock when he finally did. After hasty introductions, Nate and Cat followed him from the waiting area into his office. He closed the door behind them.

"Sorry to be late – these business lunches." He rolled his eyes and told them to have a seat. He put on a pair of glasses and picked up a folder from his in-box. "Ah, I see we have the file right here. Our retrieval system is hardly a model of efficiency but on occasion we get it right." He flipped through it then closed it again and leaned back in his chair, hands folded at his waist. He looked at Cat. "Based on the papers you've submitted, we have the elder Caruso's permission for you to view this file but you cannot make copies of anything nor can you take any portion of it from this room."

"We weren't notified of any restrictions," said Cat.

"Yes, well there you have it. It's the best we can do. Our procedures guarantee the privacy of our alumni many of whom have gone on to be leaders in their fields. I'm sure you can imagine how information of this sort might be misused." He handed the folder to Cat who flipped through it quickly then looked up.

"The sketchbook's not here." She handed the folder to Nate.

There had to be fifty documents in it. Glad to finally have something to do, Nate began going through them.

Gray waved his hand. "I don't know anything about a sketchbook, Ms. Chaplin. When Peter applied for admission here and for the scholarship..."

"The Murray Scholarship," interjected Nate, holding up the award document. He put it back then continued working his way through the rest of the folder. Grade transcripts, other awards, letters of commendation, then, a psych evaluation – two of them. He went through these more carefully, line by line only vaguely aware of the continuing conversation between Cat and Gray.

"The sketchbook," Gray was saying, "was submitted when Peter applied for the Murray Scholarship. Following that it would have been returned to Caruso – either to Peter or to his father. All work produced by the artist remains the property of the artist."

"His father has no idea where it is. He thought Columbia might have it."

"If Columbia doesn't have the original, maybe you have a copy," said Nate glancing up from the folder.

Gray looked bothered. "We may, down in the scholarship archives."

"Can you check?" asked Cat.

Gray slid his glasses up his nose and made a call and, after a five minute conversation, hung up. "You're in luck. We can get you into the archives. You're through with this file then?"

The question hadn't registered with Nate until Cat nudged him with her elbow.

"Nathan, are we through with the file?"

He was staring at the last page of Peter's psych report. Below a listing of clinical terminology which included the acronym *ADHD* and the term *obsessive/compulsive* was Peter's IQ: 192. He made a mental note of the psychiatrist – E. L. Wright.

Cat nudged him again.

"Yes," said Nate, closing the folder, "we're finished." He stood up and handed it to Gray.

At Gray's direction, the gum-chewer girl took them to a different building and down two flights below ground level. She pushed open a double-door. Lights came on in a long corridor with a tile floor and doors on either side.

"Motion sensing lights, not many people down here." She ended each sentence on an upward inflection so every statement sounded like a question; as if she was making sure that her listeners were *pickin' up what she was throwin' down*, thought Nate. It seemed to him that all students did this. He found it mildly irritating – right up there with the over-use of words like 'awesome' and 'really'.

"These are the art archives," she went on. "We're looking for Room B260." She had a key at the ready and used it about half way down the hall. She opened the door.

Inside the room more lights came on, illuminating rows of tall steel file cabinets.

"Don't you have this all on computer?" asked Cat.

"We like to keep hard-copy documents. Otherwise we

wouldn't have much use for this building."

"And no need for the energy-saving, motion-sensing lights," Nate pointed out.

"Really." She took them down an aisle. "Caruso with a C-A-R, right?" She found the right drawer and flipped to Peter's folder. "Oh, there are two of them. He must have been a big deal." Both were an inch thick. She handed one to Cat and one to Nate. "Table and chairs are over there. I'll come back to check on you."

"Thanks," said Cat and Nate at the same time.

They took the folders to the table, Cat already shuffling through hers as they walked and then sat down.

"This might be the sketchbook, Nate," said Cat, pulling out a thick stack of paper held together by a staple in the corner. "Yes, it's a copy of it." She set it down between them and shifted her chair closer to Nate's. The scent from her hair hit his nostrils and, as curious as he was about Peter, his mind drifted. He leaned forward so his shoulder touched hers.

Clipped to the copy of the sketchbook was a cover letter:

July 10, 1998
Attached is an authorized color copy of all the pages from a book of drawings submitted by Peter Lazar Caruso as part of his admissions application. The applicant has certified that the contents are entirely his own work and that it was created over the preceding two years while attending William Bennett Public High-School in Maysville PA.
The original sketchbook is bound with all pages pre-numbered.
On review of this work, our assessment of Mr. Caruso's artistic potential is entirely positive.
Respectfully submitted,
Harold S. Major MFA, PhD, Department Chair
Columbia University, School of Visual Arts

Nate had to smirk. Dr. Major would have probably given a young Caravaggio the same understated but 'entirely positive' assessment. He folded over the letter then looked at the first page from Peter's sketchbook. He was shocked.

Covering the page in blue ball-point were, in order of prominence, line drawings of a woman's large-eyed face, a race car, a knife and a boat riding the waves with the sun shining from above. Over all of this, three dimensional block letters spanned diagonally across the page: *Only the Brave.*

Nate leaned back in his chair dumfounded. At best, it was the

work of an ordinary high-school freshman – very ordinary.
"Obviously some of his early stuff," said Cat.
"I guess so," agreed Nate. He turned the page and saw more of the same. In fact the next ten pages were more of the same, then...

The change was stark. It was as if a lifetime of learning separated one page from the next. Here the lines and shadows flowed. Graceful images leaped off the paper: A bird in flight, the curvaceous figure of a woman's naked torso, a sketch of an elderly woman holding a bag of groceries her shoulders bent, her eyes sagging with fatigue.

"Whoa," said Cat. "All of a sudden, here's Peter the grand master. Is that normal for you artists? Pickleman one day, Picasso the next?"

"There must have been a time lag here. They have to be out of sequence." He flipped ahead to page after page of glorious sketches. Nate tried to remember the Peter he once knew – or thought he knew, from high school. What could possibly explain what he was looking at? While Nate had been busy learning light and shadow, Peter had been transformed into a young da Vinci.

Pages of practice sketches followed, each progressively more impressive. The last ten pages of the sketchbook left him truly astounded. Here Peter had sketched compositions in miniature, four, or as many as five to a page: seascapes, portraits and still lifes. It took a while for Nate to realize exactly what he was looking at. Yes, there was *Thunder on the Mountain*, much smaller and in black and white but none the less the same. *Woman in Winter* and all the others seemed to be there. On these pages, Peter Caruso had designed and composed his entire life's work! The complete Caruso collection was there.

Cat pulled out her phone. She went back to the letter that preceded the sketches and stood up. "You flip, I'll snap."

When they had finished, they went through the rest of the first folder, then the second, most of it college level class work, sketching and drawing exercises – all beautiful work.

Cat went back to the sketchbook. "This is what Peter did in high school? Why would he even bother going to college?"

Nate could only shake his head.

"Done?" The grad student had returned. "Hate to rush you but I gotta go - I've got a class coming up."

"Just finished," said Cat.

"What class is that?" Nate asked the grad student, only a little more snidely than he intended.

"AMB – Advanced Molecular Biology." She folded a fresh stick of chewing gum into her mouth. "It can be a little tough."

"Oh," said Nate.

Outside, the weather had turned balmy. As they headed down the brick walkway off campus and onto Amsterdam Avenue, Cat breathed deep and spread her arms. "Don't you love days like this? It feels like spring is about to explode – sun shining in a blue sky, people out for walks, birds chirping away, kids running around."

"It's a beautiful day. It's good that you don't let your work keep you from enjoying it."

"Work's work; but it's getting late, I suppose you have to go? No time for a hot chocolate?" There was a stand on the corner, steam rising from its kettles.

"Only if you let me buy," said Nate.

They found a bench.

"We still don't know where the actual sketchbook is," said Cat, wrapping her hands around her cup, her nose inches above it. "We've got pictures of each page though; that should be enough for Livingston to decide if they really need the sketches included with the collection."

"They'll want them, I've got no doubts about that," said Nate. "The notes and drawings from da Vinci and Michelangelo are masterpieces in their own rite."

"You put Peter up there with them?"

"I suppose that might be a stretch but, in his own way, Peter's work is every bit as revolutionary as the works of the old masters back in the early Renaissance. Art is a subjective commodity that's worth whatever people will pay. How much is Livingston offering?"

"They don't tell me those things but I've heard it's ten million."

"That's a bargain. And, with Peter dead, they will have all the Caruso works. There will never be more." The hot chocolate was good and Nate enjoyed being with Cat here on the bench, watching the traffic and the passers-by. "How did the Livingston group come to be interested in Peter?"

"I'm not sure about that. I do know that they asked us to investigate Peter a couple of years back. I wasn't with Bradshaw then but from what I understand, they just couldn't find the guy."

"He didn't want to be found," said Nate. "I think he just wanted to finish the entire collection of paintings that he envisioned from the start. They're all there in the sketchbook – every one of them. But you said they wanted Bradshaw to investigate not just Peter's art but Peter himself; why would Livingston want you to do that?"

"They're an art gallery; they like to know as much as they can about the artists they invest in." Cat's voice trailed off. She took another swallow. "They were interested in you once."

"In me? Well I could use ten million." He folded his arms. It was getting a little colder. Yes, ten million would be nice. He might even be able to afford Paris, and Meredith. Then another question occurred to him. "Is that why you came to my exhibit? Were you hired to be there?" Nate remembered all the hard work, time and money he'd invested in that one big event. It was supposed to have been the launching pad for his career. Instead it had left him deeply in debt with an inventory of unsold paintings.

"Yes, that's why I came to your exhibit, but it's not why I remember it. I was very touched by your work, Nathan."

"Evidently Livingston wasn't impressed."

"They liked you and they liked your art but the reviews were harsh; the turnout was low. They also thought your prices were out of line."

That brought Nate to a boil. "They thought they were too expensive? How...?"

She shook her head. "Your prices were too low, Nathan. You undervalued your work to the point where they lost interest. They want big-money art, ideally from artists who are either eccentric or dead."

"Peter was a reclusive eccentric when he was alive and now he's dead."

"That's right," said Cat, "two gold stars for him."

"I'm pretty normal and I'm alive – two big black ones for me." He stood up, finished his chocolate and tossed the cup in a trash container. "There was a heavy snow that day."

"Yes, I remember, and your exhibit was in the Village so you didn't attract many from the hoity-toity crowd. But I'll always remember my favorite piece. You'd painted a little girl in a yellow raincoat sloshing through the rain pulling a Red Flyer wagon behind her."

She smiled, it was a pretty smile but Nate watched it quickly waiver. "What's wrong?" he asked.

"Nothing's wrong. I just remember that one painting. It's been two years and every now and then I still find myself thinking about it." She ran a sleeve across the side of her face. "I was that little girl Nathan. It was as if you'd painted me, as if you *knew* me." She pulled out a Kleenex and wiped her nose. "Sorry, I'm a compulsive crier. I cry at everything – not a very good quality in my line of work."

"Emotion is everything in my line of work, Cat. I'm glad you liked that one, I did too."

She got up and they started walking toward the subway. He felt like holding her hand, but didn't. "We should talk more about Peter," he said. "I read the psych reports in his admission papers. There were two of them."

"Livingston won't be interested in them unless they contain something scandalous that they may want to quash."

"Cat, the first report shows Peter's IQ in high school at 122; a smart kid but nothing unusual and no behavioral issues. The next one diagnoses him as having obsessive-compulsive and ADHD issues and an off the charts IQ of 192 – that's higher than Einstein."

"Wow. But I guess it's consistent with the sketchbook – Pickleman one day, Picasso the next."

"I'd like to talk to the psychiatrist who wrote the report."

Cat scratched her head. "They won't be able to tell you anything – the patient confidentiality thing. Besides, that's beyond what I'm authorized to do by our current contract with Livingston. Mr. Caruso might have some objections too. I'll get the pics of the sketchbook over to Livingston and see what they want to do. I'll get back to you."

"Fair enough; do you mind if I follow up on the psych report? I've gotten very curious about Peter."

"Knock yourself out, but I can't get directly involved, not officially anyway," said Cat, stopping at the stairs down to the subway. "Thanks for coming with me today."

"It was fun, Cat. I enjoyed it." His stop was on the other side of the street. He turned to go then looked back. "Thanks for lunch."

She waved. "Mel's Burgers – they're the best."

CHAPTER 6

The following Tuesday, Nate sat across from Doctor Evelyn Wright who looked at him with deep concern over folded hands. He had called her office the day before and left a message. He hadn't expected a quick response but the good doctor had personally called him back an hour later with the same concern in her voice as he now saw in her deep-set eyes. Maybe worry was a better word. It made him worry.

"I was sorry to hear of Peter's death," she said. "What a tragedy."

Nate nodded. "It came as a shock to me too."

"You said on the phone that you knew him in high school and at Columbia. You were close to him? Did you know him well growing up? What was he like then?" She asked these questions in rapid-fire, like she was anxious to get to the bottom of something.

As Nate explained his relationship with Peter, he saw some of the tenseness drain from her face. She leaned back in her chair and rubbed a knuckle under her lower lip. "Peter Caruso was the most unusual patient I've ever had or ever will have. When you called, I thought that you could perhaps shed some light on his...extraordinary life."

"Sorry, I was hoping you could do the same thing for me, Doctor Wright. What can you tell me about him? How did you come to do the psych evaluation on him?"

"I want to be clear on something first. Normally we wouldn't be having this conversation about one of my patients. He's deceased and you aren't a family member, and you aren't with the police...are you?"

Nate shook his head. "Have the police talked to you about his death?"

"No they haven't, and there wouldn't be a need. I only met Peter twice and that was some time ago. But, getting back to you, you have no family relationship with Peter and no authority for even being here, so this conversation will have to be completely off the record. If asked, I'll deny it ever took place. Are we clear on that?"

"Yes, of course." Nate had been getting more comfortable, now he was back to being worried.

"Besides," she continued, "Peter was different, wasn't he? And he's dead now so what harm can it do?" It was as if she was talking herself into doing something she knew to be wrong. Nate detected a bit of role-reversal with him now being the shrink, she his patient. She folded her fingers under her chin and swiveled her chair to face her diploma-covered wall. "The evaluation was required by the scholarship committee at Columbia. Have you seen Peter's drawings from high school?"

"Yes, just a few days ago."

She swiveled back around. "Then you know what prompted his meeting with me – the abrupt change he'd gone through while still in high school. I remember his wild, piercing eyes. He had a nervous twitch in his facial muscles every thirty seconds or so. It was like a wink but there was nothing playful about it. That boy was wound up tight as a drum. Sitting across from him at our first session, as I am now with you, was like being in a room with a ticking time bomb. I'm a trained psychiatrist, Mr. Parks. I'm trained to detach and analyze these things dispassionately and to know what they mean, but I'll tell you honestly, Peter Caruso scared the living hell out of me. I think he resented me and he resented having to go through the evaluation. Maybe things would have gone better if we'd met in a more relaxed environment – who knows. Anyway, I spent the day with him, running tests and asking questions. His answers were always compact, given in an emotionless monotone. When we were done, he just stood and walked through that door and I was relieved beyond measure to be done with him. That was the last time I saw him. The next day the test results came in and I was not surprised – an IQ of one-ninety something. The highest by far that I had ever seen."

Nate crossed his legs. "The report mentioned ADHD and obsessive-compulsion."

"Yes, it did and he exhibited strong symptoms of both conditions, yet it would have been wrong to think of him as being impaired. Instead, he seemed enabled."

"Enabled to channel his genius into art?"

"Yes, that's a good way of putting it. Like a lens, he was somehow able to direct nearly all the power of his intellect into that single task." She leaned forward. "Do you know that Einstein did all his important work over a span of less than three years? Three revolutionary papers on atomic structure, space-time and the nature of light were all published in 1905 in what he called his miracle year. The rest of his life he spent marketing and proving his ideas, never duplicating or even coming close to his most towering achievements. Isaac Newton explored the heavens, developed the theory of gravity and invented calculus, in an equally short time while on hiatus from London where the Black Plague was raging."

"But Peter painted for ten years and may have painted for another ten if he hadn't been killed."

"Yes, that is a long time, and my point is that the human brain is an organ capable of towering achievements but it has a way of peaking-out and degrading over time. I worried that such would be the case with Peter but, as you say, his genius for art was evidently still with him right up until the time of his death. That is one unusual characteristic. The other is, of course, the suddenness with which the change took place in him. You saw his sketchbook. Peter seemed to be a normal kid one day and a genius the next."

She folded her arms. "The brain generally evolves in two ways, either through normal growth or through trauma. In the trauma cases, change happens, not because there's suddenly an increase in the number of synapses and neurons; it happens because the connections within the brain have been somehow rearranged. You've probably read about people experiencing brain injuries which resulted in their having extraordinary new abilities—especially in mathematics. Some call it acquired savant syndrome. Peter may be an extreme example of this."

"You think Peter had some kind of an accident?" asked Nate.

"It would be a possible explanation."

"Did you ask him about that?"

"Yes, and he denied that there ever was an accident or trauma of any kind."

"Are there any records of him being hospitalized around that time?"

"I don't know. It wasn't part of my evaluation to find out. It would be interesting to look into though."

"Do you know where his sketchbook is, Doctor Wright?"

She picked up a pen and clicked it a few times then gave Nate a thin smile. "I was hoping you wouldn't ask that. I have it. It was left with the original papers filed by the committee when the psych evaluation was requested. I sent a copy back and they seemed to be fine with that. And frankly, Peter seemed totally disinterested in it, like he had it all up here. You know what I mean?" She tapped the side of her head. "I'm sorry to admit it, Mr. Parks, but I hated to give the sketchbook up then and I hate to give it up now. It isn't often in this life that any of us is given the chance to hold in their hands the work of a true genius. I know that book forward and back. I'll hand it over, of course, but legally, it'll have to be to a surviving relative or an authorized representative of the family."

"Peter's father's in town to sell his son's paintings and it looks like the buyer will want it to complete the collection."

"I understand, of course." Doctor Wright put the pen down and handed him her card. "Have Mr. Caruso or his representative contact me."

Nate left and called Cat right away, filling her in on his conversation with Dr. Wright. She called him back a few hours later.

Cat spoke quickly. "I called Dr. Wright's office and set up a meeting there for one, tomorrow afternoon. Caruso and a lawyer from Livingston will be there. I'd like you to be there too, Nate. Can you make it?"

"Yes, but with Mr. Caruso being there, that may not be such a good idea. He might still be upset about me threatening Peter."

"It could be a good time for you to clear the air with him. You know, explain it like you did to me. Anyway, Livingston will need the sketchbook authenticated. That's something you can do, right? I've recommended you to them. They've given me one of their standard contracts. I'll bring it with me."

Reluctantly, Nate agreed.

Nate arrived on time back at Dr. Wright's office and found Cat, Mr. Caruso, and a young guy in a suit already there waiting.

"Dr. Wright called and said she was running late – shouldn't be long," said Cat.

The young suit stood up. "I'm Woolsey—like the Cardinal, part of the Livingston legal team. Pleased to meet you, Mr. Parks." They shook hands and Nate sat down.

Mr. Caruso gave Nate a polite hello then told him in a very casual way that he had informed the police of his threat against

Peter and that they may be contacting him.

Woolsey turned to Nate. "Did I hear correctly? You threatened Peter Caruso?"

"He told him he was going to kill him," said Caruso, turning to face Nate.

"It was fifteen years ago when we were boys," explained Nate. "A girl at our school had died and Peter was making fun of her. It got me mad. That's all it was."

"A girl who died?" asked Caruso.

"Yes, Patty Harris, she drowned. She was in the class ahead of ours."

"Oh yes, I remember now." Mr. Caruso straightened and turned back to face Dr. Wright's empty chair.

Woolsey made a note in his legal pad then asked: "Mr. Caruso, are you okay with Mr. Parks authenticating the sketchbook?" Caruso didn't respond right away. His eyes were fixed, staring straight ahead. "Mr. Caruso?"

"Yes, of course," he said finally. "Nate knows Peter's work better than anyone. Besides, Ms. Chaplin tells me it would take some time to find someone else who's qualified. It's time I haven't got. I just want this all to be over with and done."

"I understand," said Woolsey.

"I really wish you hadn't gone to the police," said Nate.

"I have a friend on the force in Maysville. It's him that I told. He said he'd get the information to the right people. They'll sort things out." He took a deep breath as if renewing his conviction. "Besides, it's still true that you were always jealous of Peter's work."

"That's not true..."

At that moment, Dr. Wright came in expressing her apologies for being late. She sat and Nate folded his arms.

"Something wrong, Mr. Parks?" asked Dr. Wright.

"No, everything's fine," said Nate.

After the introductions, Doctor Wright opened a desk drawer. "All right, this is why we're all here." She pulled out a worn, gray-covered booklet about half an inch thick. "As I told Mr. Parks, I had no intention of holding onto the sketchbook except as part of the records I keep for all of my patients."

"He wasn't a patient," corrected Caruso.

"That's true, I only saw him twice – both times as requested by Columbia. At any rate, here it is: The sketchbook of Peter Lazar Caruso." She slid it across the table to Caruso. "Here's a receiver document. Please sign and date it." She pushed a sheet of paper over to him along with a pen.

Caruso signed the receiver then, without even opening it, handed the sketchbook to Nate.

At his first touch of the outer cover, Nate was conscious of its age. Here was something that had been almost a physical part of Peter at one time. The woven black binding, the gray cover worn rough with use and a little frayed at the corners, were immediately familiar to him. Sketchbooks like this had been a requirement of Mr. Whitaker's art class and Nate had several just like it.

"You'll be authenticating it then, Mr. Parks?" asked Dr. Wright, her eyebrows slanting up.

Nate was getting used to these concerned expressions of hers. Maybe she always looked that way or maybe it was something that psychiatrists just did on reflex, like ballplayers spitting. "Yes, I've been retained by the Livingston Gallery with Mr. Caruso's consent. Is there a problem?"

"No, there's no problem at all. I just want to assure you that the book is exactly as I received it. I haven't made a mark on it and haven't tampered with it in the least."

"Thanks," said Nate, wondering why she'd felt it necessary to make that statement.

CHAPTER 7

After the meeting with Dr. Wright, Woolsey and Caruso grabbed a cab, while Cat and Nate headed for the subway.

"Don't worry about the police yet," she told him as they walked, sensing correctly that his mind was more on Caruso having gone to the police than on the sketchbook. "I know the guy on the case in Brownsville. Let me talk to him and see what's up."

"Tell him why I threatened Peter and that it was a long time ago."

"If Caruso just told his police buddy in Maysville, my guy might not even know about it. I won't bring it up."

Nate shook his head as he walked. "Caruso's a bitter old man, Cat."

"A bitter, soon to be rich old man," she agreed. They walked further. "Hey, how about me helping out with the sketchbook? I wouldn't mind taking a look at it."

"It's pretty meticulous work, I should really do it alone," said Nate. It wasn't like he didn't want her with him so much as he knew he'd need to keep focused on every line of every image that Peter had drawn. He'd need the sketchbook to pull him in and, just as when he was painting his best, that meant no distractions. "It'll take a while."

But Cat wasn't easily deterred. "Well, I'll just help get you started then."

"Great," said Nate. "I have a studio a few blocks from my place. We'll go there."

"I've never been to an artist's studio before."

Once there she took a three-sixty tour, followed by a visit to his bathroom, then plopped down on his brown couch. "Nice place," she said.

"It's a dump - cold in the winter, boiling in the summer."

"You're in a fine mood."

He ran his fingers through his hair then offered her a can of diet soda. He popped open a bottle of water for himself then walked to his desk. "I'll be working over here but you can look over my shoulder if you want."

On his desk he had positioned a blank legal pad, a few samples of Peter's writing, and a binder containing photographs of Peter's paintings. Centered on the desk was a circular magnifying glass lamp. Beneath this, Nate positioned Peter's sketchbook and opened to page one. He sat down and switched on the lamp then slipped on a pair of reading glasses as Cat took the stool beside him.

Having a woman in his studio or in his apartment was not a normal occurrence, and now Cat was the second one this month. He would have felt like quite the stud except that he felt so differently about Cat than Meredith – one a sexual temptress, always in control, the other more of a colleague and friend who might become something more.

Nate looked over page one. On the legal pad he recorded the date, made a note about the block wording, *Only the Brave,* the woman's face and the race car sketch then turned the page.

"That's all you're going to say?" asked Cat.

"Yes, that's all. I'm just authenticating its artistic content, remember?"

"He was a nervous guy. Did you see all the funny dots and doodles at the bottom? Looks to me like he was just trying to fill the page so he could go onto the next. Was he nervous like that? – Impatient? There was also that drawing of a knife, with blood dripping from it. Was he violent? Well, he was a jock; of course he was violent. I'll bet he liked horror flicks."

"Cat, this is not psychoanalysis, but you're right. I should have mentioned the knife." He modified his notes but did not go back to page one. "And not all jocks are violent."

"Most are."

Nate felt her leaning forward to get a better look at page two where Peter had drawn a jet plane firing off the page and onto the next where a spiked polygon surrounded the word 'BAM'.

"See," said Cat, pointing just below the jet, "there's another knife."

This back and forth continued for the next two pages, after

which Nate turned and looked at her over his glasses. "Sorry, Cat, but I think maybe it would work best me doing this alone."

Cat hesitated then stood up. "No, I understand perfectly. I'm no artist and I'm full of opinions that I have a hard time keeping to myself. My mother was like that – it drove my dad nuts."

"Normally it wouldn't be a problem. I really enjoy your company, but with this I have to pay attention to detail."

"You would have missed the knife if it wasn't for me."

"I know, thanks for that."

She put her hands on her hips. "All-righty then. Seeing as how I've been such a big help getting you started, how about I make you some coffee and leave you to it?"

"I don't drink coffee. I drink chai." He hadn't intended this to be snooty but it came out that way.

"You don't drink coffee? What kind of New Yorker doesn't drink coffee? Besides, you mean chai tea don't you?"

"Chai is Indian for tea. When you say chai tea, you're saying tea tea." Still more snootiness - he was self-destructing.

"Oh. I'll have to remember that." She turned toward the sink. "I don't know how to make chai."

Nate stood up. "Cat, that's okay, I'll be fine. I'll take a break and make some later."

"You sure?" She put on her jacket and took a few steps toward the door.

"Cat?"

"Yes?"

"Thanks for setting me up with the sketchbook work. I appreciate the opportunity, I really do. And I don't mean to be such a party-pooper but with work like this, I'm much better doing it by myself."

He got up and saw her out with a polite grasp of her hand that, as he closed the door, he immediately felt badly about. It wasn't enough. He should have kissed her – no, well...maybe just on the cheek. And that dumb comment about the chai—he was such an idiot - *dumb, dumb, dumb.*

Nate went back to his desk but found himself more distracted than ever. He made some chai. He was well into his second cup and the windows had gone from dim to dark by the time he reached the page where Peter's sketches turned masterful. Now he became entirely absorbed with the skill of this suddenly accomplished artist and the beauty he had created. In this, Peter's original sketchbook, the effect was even more jarring than with the copies he'd seen at Columbia. The shading, the subtle and the bold alterations of lights and darks, made each page come alive. Going through these first pages of Peter's practice sketches down through each page containing his composite miniatures, Nate felt as if he was a diver swimming in dark waters that grew richer with life as he went deeper. And with the greater depth, the greater the mystery his one-time friend became. Who was Peter? What happened to him? Why was it important to him that he create these particular paintings? Nate studied them as a group, in the order in which they appeared in the sketchbook. They seemed to go from themes of violence and emotion to the more tranquil and sublime, the more primitive to the more refined. He laid out the titles of each work in a column. Could there be a pattern? Maybe a play on words if arranged just so? But if there was a pattern, he couldn't see it.

It was odd, Nate thought, that Peter didn't have the sketchbook in his possession over the years it took to create his collection. It had been with Doctor Wright all that time, yet each of his paintings and the titles he chose were faithful to the concepts in the miniatures. Like she'd said, he had it all locked up in his head.

Nate's notes became more detailed and more complex. He went to bed at two then resumed work early the next morning, comparing the miniatures in the sketchbook to the photographs of the actual paintings. He saw now that there were subtle differences in detail and in some of the shading, but the layouts and visual effects were the same in the sketchbook as in the paintings themselves.

When he finally closed the sketchbook, Nate was exhausted, much as he had been at the exhibit. He called Cat to let her know he'd have the report to her the next day. They arranged to meet in the morning.

After hanging up from Cat, he went for a long jog. He watched some TV over dinner then went to bed early. His dreams were haunted by thoughts of Peter and by thoughts of him laughing at Patty's death. Then, still in his dream, he thought about something else – something he'd forgotten about entirely.

The next morning, after a short ride on the subway, Nate picked up two large to-go cups—one filled with chai from Panera's, the other with coffee from McDonalds. He met Cat on Seventh Avenue where she was seated on a curbside bench, dressed in her usual cap and North Face jacket. As the wind picked up, he sat down and handed her the coffee. "As I remember it, you like this brand. I took a chance, large with two creams."

Cat smiled. "Thanks, yes, that's perfect." She held it in both hands and took a sip.

"I felt bad about throwing you out of my studio the other day. I didn't mean it the way it may have seemed."

"You didn't exactly throw me out, and no, I understand you needing to work alone."

"Sometimes it's the only way I can really get into what I'm doing." He took a sip from his chai. "You chose a cold place to meet."

"Yeah, sorry about that. I'll explain later." The wind caught her hat and she tugged it straight. She pointed to the large envelope, now in his hand, that he'd been using as a drink-tray. "That your report?"

He handed it to her. "It's all there, sketchbook too. I didn't see any problems with the sketchbook. Everything in it is Peter's work, which is the important thing."

Cat hefted the envelope. "And the legal form from Livingston?"

"In there too, all filled out."

"Great, thanks," said Cat. She put it in her purse with the top sticking out. She was quiet for a while then said: "I talked to the police, Nate."

It was the way she said it that raised the red flag for Nate. "And?"

"They don't know about your threat and I didn't tell them about it but they may be in touch with you. They think there might be something to you and Peter being boyhood rivals and, as adults, being professional rivals. Something like that thing with Mozart and what's his name...?"

"Salieri."

"Right, him." She put a hand on his knee. "I'm sorry to say it, Nate, but you're the only person they know of with a motive for wanting Peter dead. If they...when they, find out about your threat, things could get a little dicey."

Nate was speechless for a moment. "You can't be serious. I'll just go in and tell them how ridiculous they are for even thinking I could have done such a thing." He got up off the bench, his left hand balled up in a fist.

"Nate? Now wait a minute, just stay calm. They haven't called you in yet so they know they haven't got much on you. The big problem is that they don't have anything on anybody else."

Nate glanced down the street. Cat was right, he had to stay

calm. "So the only way to get the heat off me is for the cops to find a better suspect?" He turned back to Cat. "Or for *me* to find a better suspect."

"Well yeah, that's the best way I suppose. You got some ideas about that?"

"No, I don't, but I thought of something last night, Cat. It's something the police may have missed in going through Peter's apartment. As a boy, Peter had a hiding place in his bedroom. It was a spot under the floorboards that he had cut out with angled seams so that, with the wooden panel in place, everything in the floor blended in. You could be looking right at it and not see it. Maybe he had a place like that at his apartment. Maybe the police missed it."

"Those guys are usually pretty thorough, but there's always a chance...You haven't been there, have you?"

Nate took a long sip and set the cup down on the bench. He sat back down and folded his arms. "No, I haven't been there. But I'd like to have a look around."

"On your own? What do you think you'll find?"

"I don't know, maybe drugs or something. If Peter was into drugs that might explain why he was murdered."

"You should tell the police. They should be the ones doing the search."

"It may be nothing, Cat. It's just a hunch. Besides, I know what I'm looking for and where to look for it - they don't."

"They'd know if you told them. They may even want you to go with them," said Cat.

"And if we didn't find anything I'd look like a desperate fool. It'd make me look even more suspicious. I should go there myself."

Cat gave her cap another tug and squinted. The sun was just peaking over the tops of the buildings across the street. "It's in a crummy neighborhood, but it's been a few months now. All the crime scene restrictions should be off." She said this as if she were thinking aloud. "Are you sure this is really what you want to do, Mr. Detective?"

"No, but I've got to do something."

"You're going to need some help, and a witness in case you find anything."

"I was hoping you would come with me."

"You sure I wouldn't be too distracting? – you know, make you lose focus?"

Nate guessed he deserved that. "I need you to come with me, Cat. You're the detective, not me."

She took another sip of coffee. "We could talk to the building manager. Maybe they haven't rented the place yet. You know, we could be prospective renters."

"Good idea."

She poked his overcoat with her thumb. "You can't go like this though, not in that neighborhood. You got any tough-guy clothes? – Jeans, sweatshirt, tennis shoes, a pull-over cap to hide that stylish hair-cut. You shouldn't shave for the next few days. And it'll have to be after hours - maybe Friday night?"

"I'll call the landlord and see if I can set it up."

"You mean the building manager. The actual landlord's probably someone down in Florida. I can get a name and number for the manager – I'll text it to you. When you talk to him, don't use any big words."

"I'll try to remember. Thanks Cat."

"You're welcome, Nate."

Cat suddenly straightened; she'd been looking directly across the street.

"Something wrong?" he asked.

She relaxed, then shook her head. "I thought I saw something. Actually, if you must know, I'm working another case - rich guy, thinks his wife's cheating on him. I'm hot on her trail."

Nate swallowed and tossed a disturbing thought out of his head before it had a chance to take root. "What do you mean? Like you're following her right now?"

Cat pointed across the street. "She's in that hair salon over there and will be for another half-hour or so. She's there every other week, Wednesdays usually. That's how I knew I could meet you here without losing her."

Nate tried to peer inside the salon but couldn't see past the elderly woman seated nearest the window. "How do you keep up with her? Does she have a driver?"

"She usually takes a cab. But it doesn't matter. Either way, I've got a deal with the cab guys." She patted her phone. "They'll be here in a flash if I need to tail her. Not only that, if I lose her, the cabbie who picked her up will let me know where he dropped her off. Pretty cool huh?"

"Yes, cool," said Nate running his hand through his hair.

CHAPTER 8

With Cat preoccupied by her adulteress, Nate left and took a long lunch at the Starbuck's on Flatbush where he spent half the afternoon correcting essays written by his students. Only a couple were borderline-good and he left there feeling like he was wasting his time trying get those kids to share his passion for art. At best he might be getting through to two out of twenty; not a good track record.

He picked up a few groceries and walked back to his apartment. Even before reaching the door, he heard the TV on inside. Then he remembered that he'd given Meredith his extra key. The door was unlocked. He had been tired, but now...

She lay on his plaid couch, knees up, her back propped by a few pillows. She wore a bright yellow, long-sleeve blouse and white pants. Her feet were bare, toes freshly polished. But what really caught Nate's attention was her hair.

"Where have you been?" she asked. "I tried your cell but couldn't get through."

Nate put down his bag of groceries. "I had some work to do, I must have flipped it off," he said, unstrapping his messenger bag and taking off his jacket. He bent over and gave her a kiss while running a hand through her hair. There was a stiffness to it and a peach fragrance he hadn't noticed before – she'd just had it done.

"Something wrong?" asked Meredith.

"No, no, nothing wrong," he straightened then walked over to the front windows scanning the other side of the street, half expecting to see Cat standing guard. But there was no one there. He took a breath, deciding he was just being paranoid. "I had to check something out."

"Well, if you're done over there, come back over here and check me out."

Nate pulled the shades and walked back to where she lay. He kissed her again, this time forcefully – hungrily. She wrapped her arms around him and pulled him down.

"Teddy's in Europe this week," she explained afterwards. She lay naked next to him on his bed, letting her lips brush against his as she spoke. "We could do something more...overt."

Nate was lost in the fog of her perfume, entranced by the touch of her lips, her tongue. "I can do overt," he said, his eyes half closed. She had things all planned out, starting tomorrow afternoon, and everything she said sounded good.

After she left, Nate began to have second thoughts. He glanced at the key on his night-stand: Room 508 at the Hilton. Maybe she just didn't like his apartment. The windows were drafty – dirty too. He'd never been good at keeping things clean and neat. But Meredith evidently liked him, and what else mattered? In the bathroom, he looked at himself in the mirror. He drew in his stomach. He squeezed the sides of his nose to make it narrower. What on earth was it that she saw in him? And what about Cat? What if Meredith *is* the one she's tracking? The hair thing made him worry. Should he warn Meredith? Should he call off things with Meredith and tell Cat about her? One of these women was his wildest, most sensual fantasy come true and he knew it couldn't last; the other could turn out to be the most meaningful relationship of his life. The old wing-walker's theory hoisted itself in his mind like a big, red, white and blue political banner: *Don't let go of one thing before you take hold of something else*. That seemed to apply here – right? For the time being, he had to keep a hold on both Meredith and Cat, otherwise he risked losing them both. He shook his head wondering how his simple life had suddenly gotten so complicated.

The next morning he headed upstairs and knocked on Eduardo's door. Over orange juice and croissants he gave him an update on his women issues, this time telling him about both Meredith and Cat. "Why question your good fortune?" he said, just as Nate had predicted. "Most men would kill to be in your position."

"Meredith's a ten. At best I'm a five. Why is she interested in me?"

Eduardo hmm'd from his side of the table. "You're a four, no higher," he said as if he had a precise way of measuring such things. He took two bites of his croissant. “Women can be irrational sometimes. Or maybe you’re just very good in bed.” He gave him a sly glance that made Nate uneasy. “But, either way, why question it?”

“And what about Cat?” He hadn’t mentioned that she was a private detective.

“Do you think she might be the Miss Right you’re after?”

Nate thought about the hot-chocolate they’d had together and what she’d said about his art. There was no pretense in Cat and that’s what he liked best about her. Meredith, on the other hand, was all about pretense and mystery and temptation. “I don’t know her well enough to say. We haven’t even been out on a date.”

“So, go out with her and get to know her better. But I tell you, this Meredith sounds like exactly my type of woman – sensual, mysterious,” he lifted an eyebrow, “maybe a little depraved? You have trouble keeping up with her, yes?”

“Well I...” The truth was, Nate *was* having trouble keeping up with Meredith and had secured a Cialis tablet which he had slipped into his pocket along with the hotel room key.

“I would not have this problem.”

“You want me to introduce you to her?” asked Nate. “You think she would choose you over me?”

Like a magician completing a trick, Eduardo just spread his hands.

“Women like artists,” countered Nate.

“Women like actors – especially Latin actors, this is a known fact.” He raised his hand and extended a finger. “I am Eduardo Goya and I am ready to take this woman to the top of Mount Eduardo. How could you deprive her of that? Don’t you see? Everyone will be happy. Meredith will have me, you will have Cat, and this rich husband fellow can always buy himself another bride.”

Nate thanked Eduardo for his advice and left. For the time being, Meredith would just have to be satisfied with Mount Nate.

He was back in his apartment a few hours later when Cat’s text came in giving him the name and number of the manager of Peter’s building. He called him. Yes, the room was for rent and yes, he and his ‘wife’ could see it tomorrow night. He made the appointment for seven and texted Cat telling her he’d meet her there. Nate slipped his phone back into his pocket. He checked to make sure the key to Meredith’s hotel room was in his other pocket, then for a moment, just stood there contemplating what he was about to do. He felt like he was standing at one of those forks in the road, where, once he'd made his choice, there'd be no turning back. He took a deep breath knowing already that he'd be taking the path most-traveled. He packed a bag, swallowed the Cialis and went to Room 508 at the Hilton.

The next twenty-four hours were a blur of alcohol, beluga caviar, and hot sex in variations that tested Nate's limited repertoire. He and Meredith left the room only once for dinner. Had he been in touch with all of his faculties he might have been worried about Cat and her phone-cam lurking somewhere in the dining room but no, for the whole time he had only been in touch with one of his faculties.

It was now, Friday noon. He had a terrible headache and he hated himself for being deceitful to Teddy. He felt deceitful to Cat, too.

"We shouldn't leave together," said Meredith from the bathroom over the sound of running water.

"Right." He pulled his pants on and sat on the edge of the bed. The room was a mess. Clothes lay on the floor and over the backs of every chair. The remains of breakfast lay on a room service cart near the window. The mini-bar was half empty. The bill for this was going to be enormous. But that wasn't his problem. This was Meredith's little fling and he was just a part of it, like the caviar and the whiskey. He was a kept man, here for her pleasure, bought and paid for by the pleasure she gave him. But oh, what pleasure that was – almost enough to staunch his guilt and regret—almost. He pressed his fingers over his eyes and sat still, then finished dressing. He gathered his things and stuffed them into his duffle bag. Before he left, Meredith gave him a kiss good-bye like he was an off-to-work husband and he'd be back that night. But it was Teddy who'd be returning to her. His plane was scheduled to land at eight-ten and she'd be there to meet him; there to say how much she missed him.

Nate went home. He spent an hour under the hot shower, took three aspirin, slept for three hours then woke up and took three more. It was five o'clock and his head was beginning to clear. He got himself back in character, no longer Nate the gigolo. Then he remembered he had to meet up with Cat in a couple of hours. Tonight he had to be Nate the tough-guy.

In a worn jean-jacket and scruffy hat, Cat was waiting for him outside Peter's apartment building. "That's the best you could do?" she asked when he got out of the cab.

He pulled up the collar of his leather bomber jacket and stuffed his hands in his pockets. "Better?"

"Your tennis shoes are gleaming white. They're brand new, aren't they?"

He stepped over to a trash pile and gave it a few kicks with each foot. "How's that?" He gave her his best Rocky Balboa with a few right and left jabs into the air.

She rolled her eyes. "I suppose it'll do. Now remember, we're married. Mr. and Mrs. Parks but I'm still Cat, okay? – not Adrian."

He ran a fist under his nose and sniffed. "Sure thing," he said, then he looked around. Up the street a few ragged men were gathered outside a liquor store. Across the street an old man with a limp was walking his dog. It was a big dog – a German shepherd with a hungry look on its face. Nate turned and glanced up at Peter's building. A few windows were lit but most were dark.

"You ready?" she asked.

"Sure."

They walked up the stairs to the front door, announced themselves into an electric speaker and were buzzed inside to a small foyer where they faced another locked door.

"It's like a security air-lock. Keeps the riff-raff out," said Cat. She pointed up to the ceiling where a video camera was mounted. Its red light was on.

Nate stared up at it.

"Camera's new, sorry," said Cat, reading his thoughts. "The cops told me there was no video from the night of the murder."

Well, that would have been too easy. "The place looks clean at least," said Nate. Mail-boxes lined one wall. Only about half of them had names.

"There's Peter's," said Cat, pointing to the one marked 48B.

From beyond the locked door, they heard footsteps then the latch turned. The door opened to reveal a bent, bearded man with silver-gray hair, dressed in a broad-knit, brown cardigan. Age spots covered his sallow cheeks. He spoke with an Eastern-European accent. "Mr. and Mrs. Parks, I assume?"

"Yes, that's us, Mr. Novak. I'm Nate and this is Cat." They shook hands and he brought them through the door where a hallway extended like a dark tunnel back into the building. To the right was a staircase leading up.

"Cat? Odd name."

"Short for Catherine."

"Ah, like Cat Ballou, I get it, yes, good name," he nodded then coughed his throat clear. "Novak's my first name – like the tennis player - so no need to use the mister. I like to get right to the point. Two years minimum, fifteen-hundred a month."

"Best we can do is a grand and one year," said Cat, "if we like the place."

"Sorry, can't help you." Novak didn't move. He took a wheezing breath and waited, expressionless.

"We might be able to do better," said Nate. "Can we at least see the place?"

"Eighteen months at twelve-hundred," said Novak.

"Done – if we like the place," said Nate.

"Security deposit, first and last month up front. You don't have pets do you? Kids?"

"Nope, just us," said Cat, hands in her pockets.

The old man turned back to Nate. "You mentioned 48B on the phone. Why is it you're specifically interested in that room?"

Nate had been expecting that question. "I know that Peter Caruso lived there for over ten years. He was a friend of mine once. We grew up together, went to school together. He was an exceptional artist. The room's got some sentimental value to me."

"Are you an artist? You don't look like one."

Cat spoke up. "We both liked Peter's art."

Novak lowered his voice. "You know he was killed there."

"Yes."

Novak gave a shrug. "Okay then, follow me." He talked to Nate as he walked down the hallway passing closed, numbered doors spaced every twenty feet or so. "I keep things dark to keep costs down. Electricity is terrible. I'd go back to candles but then the fire department would be after me. The police finished up their investigation into Peter's death a month ago. I had the place cleaned and fumigated and painted. It was expensive. Everything's expensive. Peter may have been a great artist, but he was messy and he hardly ever went out. He was a strange man. Then again, we have a lot of strange folks here, you should fit right in – oh, I didn't mean that in a bad way." He gave a little snicker at his joke then stopped at 48B. He inserted his key then looked at Nate. "Mr. Parks, where is your wife?"

Nate looked, no Cat. "I have no idea, I..." Then he heard her walking fast up the hallway to catch up.

"Here I am, sorry, I was looking for a restroom – couldn't find it but that's okay, I can wait."

"You can use the one in here," said Novak, bending over the lock again then opening the door. "Everything works." He snapped on the light switch and nothing happened. He waited then hit it again and the lights went on. "Yes, everything works." He took a breath. "Four rooms, living room, kitchen, bathroom, bedroom, everything you need. Cable hook-up, phone hook-up, stove, fridge, everything you need."

The living room had two windows. Nate walked to the spot between them. "This is where he would have painted, with the light coming from both windows."

"Disposal?" asked Cat.

"Of course," said Novak shuffling off toward the kitchen.

While she occupied Novak with questions, Nate ducked into the bedroom which was the room he really wanted to see. He turned on the light. Starting at the door, he stooped low, carefully checking the floorboards and the edge molding testing for loose sections as he went. The woodwork seemed new for such an old building.

"If you're looking for signs of mice, you won't find any," said Novak entering the room.

"Never hurts to check," said Nate, from down on his knees. "We're pretty thorough. If you want to go back to your place, we'll let you know when we're done."

"No, no, I'll stay." Novak glanced at his watch. "I'll give you another fifteen minutes, how's that? Jeopardy's coming on and I hate to miss it." He went back to the living room, apparently not the least concerned about Nate's checking for loose floor-boards or Cat's tapping at the backs of cupboards for a panel that might conceal a hollow in the wall.

A short time later, Novak checked his watch again. "So, what's the verdict? Great place, isn't it?"

"Yes, everything's great," said Cat with a glance at Nate, "but the bathroom's too small."

"Yeah, I just don't think it's right for us," said Nate, heading for the door. "If we change our minds, we'll get back to you. Thanks for showing it to us."

Novak grumbled, then after they'd brushed past him into the hallway he turned out the lights in the apartment and locked the door. Someone was coming up the hallway.

"Hey, Mister Novak," said a teenage boy walking toward them from the front door. He carried a brown paper sack.

Novak stuck up a hand. "Hello Benny, how's your mom?"

"She's fine – says hi." Benny gave Cat and Nate a glance as they passed by, heading out.

Once outside, Nate closed the door behind him and followed Cat down the stairs to the sidewalk. He couldn't imagine living inside that building, and for years, not once leaving. But apparently, that's what Peter had done. What kind of a life was that? And if he'd led such an isolated life, why would anyone want him dead? At the curb, he took out his cell and called for a cab. He then turned to Cat. "Well that was a dead end."

"Maybe, maybe not." She flashed him the inside pocket of her jacket.

Nate's jaw dropped when he caught site of a small stack of white envelopes. "You stole Peter's mail? While you were looking for a bathroom, you stole Peter's mail."

"Nate. I wasn't really looking for a bathroom."

"You're good."

Cat shrugged and patted her jacket. "It may be nothing, but you never know."

Nate heard the building door open behind them. It was the kid, Benny, trotting down the stairs toward them – empty handed this time. He was a good looking black kid and wore an army field jacket. Nate figured him for about fifteen.

"You deliver groceries here?" Cat asked him.

"Yeah, that and other stuff." He obviously did not want to hang around. He started stuffing in his I-Pod ears and began walking off.

"Did you know Peter Caruso?" asked Cat.

The boy stopped and looked back. "The cops have asked me all about that. I don't know anything."

Nate realized that except for Novak, this kid might have been one of the few visitors Peter had. "Are you the one who brought him his groceries?"

"Yeah, I did. Look, I gotta go." Then he hesitated. "You with the cops?"

"No," said Cat, "we're just friends of Peter's."

Benny stared at Cat. "Are you his girl?"

"No, I just knew him from his art."

"Yeah, he painted a lot. That's all he did."

"Peter had a girl?" asked Nate.

Benny smiled. "One day a few months ago he added some chocolate covered cherries to his grocery list. He said they were for his girlfriend, but I never saw her. Maybe he just wanted them for himself."

"Yeah, maybe," said Nate.

"Well, I gotta run." Benny turned and walked off.

"So Peter had a girlfriend. That's interesting, don't you think?" said Cat.

Then Nate remembered something. "There was a woman in the back of the church at Peter's funeral. My folks didn't recognize her. I don't think she was a local."

"There you go," said Cat, hands spread, "maybe that was his girl. Would you recognize her if you saw her again?"

"No, I only glanced at her and she was gone before the ceremony ended." Nate tried to remember more about the woman – dark coat, with a beret type hat but he hadn't really seen her face.

Nate put his hands in his jacket pockets and shifted his weight from one foot to the other. His tennis shoes weren't much good at keeping the heat in. On the other side of the street, the man with the German shepherd was walking back the other way now. The dog gave Nate a snarly look.

The cab finally arrived and they got in. "Rigoletto's, on Forty-third," Nate told the driver. "I'm buying you dinner," he said to Cat.

"Mmmm, Italian," she said, sliding close to him. "Are you sure we can get in, dressed like this?"

"I'll bribe them if I have to." They rode in silence for a few miles before he asked, "How's your other case going?"

"The rich cheater? Still tracking her. She gave me the slip a few days ago, probably shacked up somewhere, but I'll catch up."

Nate almost gave a sigh of relief. Then he wondered - why was he so worried about Cat finding out about him and Meredith? He was unattached. It was a free country and affairs were the most natural thing in the world; well, at least in Eduardo's world. But Nate knew the answer. The more he was around Cat the more he liked her and the more he cared about what she thought of him. It was one thing to have an affair, it was another to be a free-loading, two-timing gigolo and that's exactly what he was. He had to fix things. Then he wondered if Cat was seeing anyone else. The cab pulled up at the restaurant. It was only half full and he didn't have to bribe anyone to get in.

When they sat down at their table Cat pulled out Peter's mail – four white envelopes and a grocery flyer. She sliced into the first envelope with a small pocket knife. "Hey, Peter just won a free membership to a dating service – lucky guy." She went onto the next. "A past-due bill from his credit card." She gave Nate a glance. "Two more to go, not looking good here." She picked up another. "This one's from some kind of delivery service." She slit it open. "It's a certified mail receipt."

"What's the date on it?"

"It gives an address and a signature: David O'Neal. Yes, here's the delivery date: two-ten. It says it was a package – thirty pounds. That's pretty heavy." She handed him the note and pulled out her phone.

"That was about a month after Peter's death." He scanned the page then focused on a few lines written by hand in the 'Special Instructions' box. He looked at Cat. "It says here that Peter had asked for the package to be held for thirty days here in New York then shipped to an address in...Maysville PA. That's where Peter and I grew up."

"Do you know David O'Neal?"

Nate shook his head. "The name's not familiar."

"Since moving to New York, did Peter ever go back to Maysville?"

"He could have. Like I told you before, we lost touch with each other after Columbia. I'll give my parents a call tomorrow. They should know who David O'Neal is. Maysville's a pretty small town."

"What do you think Peter might have sent him?"

"I have no idea." He reached over and opened the last envelope - more junk mail.

Cat leafed through the grocery flyer. "Big sale on tuna salad this week," she said then picked up her menu.

The waiter came over and they ordered.

"And you'll be having wine of course?" the waiter asked Nate. He picked up the wine list and scanned it as if he knew what he was looking at – he didn't. He glanced at Cat. "Do you have a preference?"

Cat didn't bother looking at the list. "A Pinot Grigio would be nice, 2007 if you have it."

The waiter nodded. "Indeed we do, *signora*, a good choice with your entrées - bottle or glass?"

"Bottle," said Nate handing him the wine list, not wanting to know the price.

After the waiter left, Cat smiled tentatively at Nate. "I know wine pretty well, and cheese. It's from working in my family's grocery store. It was really a grocery-deli. We did sandwiches too. I can make bang-up sandwiches. Just don't get me near pickles. I hate pickles."

"I'll remember that," said Nate with an easy smile. "What else should I know about you?"

"Sorry but you'll have to find out about me as we go along. Or do you like your women to come with a list of ingredients, like cans of soup?"

"That would sure simplify things." He asked her if she'd been to this restaurant before—she hadn't. She asked him about growing up in Scranton and he told her about his parents and the farm and how he'd gotten into art.

"You sound like a regular country boy, swimming and fishing in the summer, helping out on the farm. And here you are in the big city. Ever want to go back?"

"Someday maybe, but the city's where the money is."

The wine arrived and Nate deferred the taste test to Cat. At her approval the waiter diplomatically filled her glass first.

Nate touched his glass to hers and they each took a sip.

"Most men are put off by my wine thing," said Cat, "and they get tired of hearing about the store or my detective work – too blue-collar for them, I think. And I've never been to college..."

"And you spill coffee on the subway."

"Yeah – that's me. I'm just a mess."

"And I can be a real snot and I'm not good at being a tough-guy."

She leaned over and whispered: "I don't really like tough-guys."

Dinner arrived, followed by espresso, his second choice after chai.

"So what do you want to do about David O'Neal?" asked Cat.

"I'd like to know what Peter sent him. It may have something to do with his murder. That's a funny thing, isn't it?—the police not thinking to check Peter's mail."

"Not from the date on the envelope," she picked it up, "February thirteenth post-mark. The cops were probably monitoring the mail for about as long as they had the crime scene sealed off. After that, they wouldn't necessarily have picked up on it. Still, if we can't find this O'Neal guy, it won't make much difference."

"My mom should know him. I'll let you know what she says."

"Ask her about the woman in the back of the church, too."

"Right."

When they finished, Nate picked up the check and rode with her in the cab to her apartment in Harlem.

"No, don't get out," she said as they pulled up. "It's tough finding cabs around here. I'll be fine. I had a good time, Nate. Thanks for dinner."

He put an arm around her and gave her a kiss, liking Cat more and more. "Let's do this again," he found himself telling her.

"What are you doing Tuesday night?"

She smiled as she got out of the cab. "Going out with you – how about Chinese?"

"Great."

Nate had the driver wait until she was safely inside then rode back to his apartment.

In the morning he called his mother and asked her about David O'Neal.

"You remember him, don't you, dear? Oh, maybe you wouldn't. But you remember his niece Patty. Mr. O'Neal was her guardian after her parents died in that awful plane crash. It happened when you were still pretty young."

"I don't remember a plane crash," said Nate, "but I knew Patty Harris, the girl who died."

"Yes, that's her. She was in the class ahead of you. Poor girl, dying just two months before graduation, such a terrible thing. I think she was the same age as you. She skipped a grade, maybe two—smart girl." She paused for a moment. "What makes you ask about her uncle?"

"Well, something just came up. I can't talk about it now but I might be making another trip down there."

"We'll be glad to have you, but I'd hate to see you bothering Mr. O'Neal about Patty. I remember how upset he was. Did you know there were some who thought she'd been murdered? Now who would do such a terrible thing to such a nice girl?"

CHAPTER 9

At his mother's words, Nate felt a chill run through him. Except for Peter's cruel teasing, he hadn't heard any rumors about Patty being murdered. He quickly wrapped up the conversation then went into his bedroom. From the top shelf of the closet he pulled down a cardboard box he'd packed when he left home for Columbia years ago. He rifled through it and near the bottom, found the high school yearbook from his junior year. In bright white letters on a blue hard-cover it read:

CELEBRATE THE CLASS OF 1997

Maybe it was the feel of the old book or the musty smell of old things, but his mind flashed back to the day he'd found out about Patty.

It had been nearly ten o'clock when they'd called an all-school assembly in the gym. Students filled the bleachers and the basketball court. Everyone wondered what was up and there was a wave of whisperings going on when Principal Jenkins walked onto the stage and made the announcement: "We regret to inform you of the death of one of your classmates – Patricia May Harris."

The gym fell immediately silent. Then a few girls screamed out, "No, oh no." Nate remembered them sobbing, bent over with their hands covering their faces.

He'd liked Patty and had worked with her on a few class projects. She was the pride of William Bennett High – always got the best grades, class president, a born leader. She was going to go far, but not now. Classes were dismissed for the rest of the day and black armbands were handed out the next day.

Everyone attended the funeral. The mayor spoke and her uncle—Nate remembered him now, gave a tearful good-bye speech. If there had been a murder investigation it must have been kept pretty quiet.

Nate opened the yearbook and flipped past the few hand-written notes he'd been able to collect from friends, past the listing of the class song and the class motto, stopping at the page that read: *In Memoriam, Patricia May Harris*. Behind these words, her high school picture was printed as a faded water-mark. She was a pretty girl, Nate thought, with a nice smile and curly red hair. The next three pages showed her in various activities at the school. The mayor's eulogy was there too, printed in full, and there was the picture of her and Peter. He was hard ball, the ace of Scranton and Patty was fast-pitch softball. The picture showed them standing together on a pitcher's mound back to back in full uniform, she with a light-hearted smile; he with a face of dead seriousness.

Nate closed the book and called Cat. He told her about David O'Neal and about him being Patty's uncle. "I'm going to call him," he said.

"Don't call him."

"Why not?"

"It's easier for people to say no over the phone. It's also easier for them to lie."

"Why would he lie?"

"People lie for a lot of reasons. People lie all the time just to shake off someone they don't know, or to shake off someone who wants to talk about something they'd rather not talk about. Look Nate, if you really want to know what's going on, you'll catch him off guard, unsuspecting, like you just happened to bump into him."

"Like you bumped into me on the subway?"

"Hey, I never planned that, and anyway, you don't have to spill coffee on the guy. Look, Nate, today's Saturday. You head out to Maysville. There's still plenty of time left to get there yet today. This guy O'Neal probably attends church, that'll be tomorrow. You'll be there too. You'll bump into him, make a little conversation and bring up Peter's death. Then you lead him casually into telling you about the package Peter sent him."

"I don't even know what he looks like."

"Have your parents point him out. Gees, Nate, do you want me to write this all down for you? Oh, I've got to go. My rich-bitch is on the move. Good luck. Let me know what you find out."

Nate put the phone down. He had to admit, Cat's plan made sense. He checked the time and started packing. He was half-way along when there was a knock at the door. He opened it and Meredith walked in hurriedly, carrying a suitcase.

Her hair was disheveled, her eyes red. She sat down on the couch and looked up at him. "I've left Teddy."

Nate was speechless for a moment. "Why would you...?" no, he didn't want to go there. "What happened?"

"We had a fight. He thinks I'm cheating on him. I denied it. Oh Nate, I don't know how he could have found out."

Nate knew at least one way.

"I need a place to stay," she went on. "He cancelled all my credit cards. I've got no money. I'm poor, Nate. I'm back to being poor Meredith Sipriano." She dabbed her eyes with a Kleenex and blew her nose.

It dawned on Nate that he was finally seeing the real Meredith that had been hidden for so long under her stunning good looks and the insatiable sexual passion. He felt sorry for her. He sat down beside her and kissed her cheek. "Does he know about me?"

"No, he doesn't know about you... I don't think he does."

That wasn't very reassuring. "Did anyone follow you here?"

Her eyes suddenly flared. "You're still worried about what he might do to you – you and your precious career. What about what he's done to me?"

"You're right; he's been awful," said Nate, thinking it best to be agreeable.

"I need some coffee," said Meredith, looking around.

"I have chai. It's tea, Indian tea." He made her a cup and had some himself. He glanced at his watch.

"Do you have to be someplace?" she asked.

"I'm going to Scranton today to visit my parents."

"You're from Scranton?"

"Maysville, a small town outside of Scranton. They have a farm there – my parents do. But you can stay here while I'm gone. It'll just be for a few days. There're groceries in the pantry and stuff in the fridge." He realized he was starting to talk fast.

"I need coffee," she said, putting her cup down. "This stuff is terrible."

He went to the donut shop on the corner and got some coffee provisions keeping his eyes straight in front of him, afraid he might see Cat. Then he went back up.

"How long will you be gone?" she asked as he finished packing.

"Until Monday – maybe Tuesday. I'll call you."

When he was ready to leave, she gave him a long kiss. "I'll be ready for you when you get back."

Nate caught his breath in the hallway, relieved to close the door behind him.

The drive to Maysville was far easier than the last time and it was still daylight when he approached the Caruso house on the way to his parent's place. He noticed there was a large dumpster in the drive and beside it, a Ford pick-up. Mr. Caruso's Chevy was nowhere in sight. Nate slowed down. He pulled in and parked half-way up. There was no one around. He walked to the dumpster that was filled with junk: a ragged purple couch, a few tables, a few lamps, a mattress and a box spring and a lot of paper-backs and magazines. He remembered the couch from when he and Peter were kids and he remembered the kitchen table where they'd have a quick bowl of Cheerios on summer mornings before hustling off to the ball-diamond.

A scraping sound came from the front porch and Nate saw a man in jeans and a Penn-State sweatshirt pulling a love seat out through the door. He had it half way out before he stopped and noticed Nate.

"Hey friend, would you mind lending a hand?" the man asked, out of breath.

With Nate's help, the love seat found its way off the porch and into the dumpster. The guy turned out to be young, maybe just out of high school. Sweat covered his shirt. He took off his baseball cap and wiped a sleeve across his forehead as he leaned against the dumpster. "My partner took off a couple of hours ago. Don't know how I would have gotten that damn thing in there without your help. Thanks. I'm Jake by the way." He gave Nate a fist-bump.

"No problem. I'm Nate. I was passing by and saw the dumpster. I used to know the Carusos. So I guess he's moving is he? – the old man."

"I'm just helping out here, making a little money. I don't know anything about the owner, but I do know I wouldn't want to live in this dump. It's all falling apart—kind of creepy, you know? Probably really creepy at night."

Nate nodded and glanced up at the old place. From close up, it looked even more run down than when he'd seen it from the road two months ago. Boards along the side were warped, and overhead, part of the gutter had detached itself and was drooping down. It swung slowly from side to side in the late afternoon breeze. So Peter's father wasn't wasting any time in getting out. He couldn't blame him.

"They're going to bull-doze the place but needed it emptied out first – some kind of land-fill regulation I think. I'm just about done. This was the last of the heavy stuff."

The house sat on a small rise and Nate turned to look across the road and beyond the forty-acre tillage over to where he knew the river ran. Leafless trees lined its banks. There was a trail leading down to it along the wind-break between the fields. He and Peter used to race along it. He turned back to the house. "Mind if I have a look inside?"

"Be my guest. There's not much there now."

Nate climbed back up onto the porch. It gave him an immediately eerie feeling, opening the door and crossing the threshold. He stepped inside. If the house hadn't been bare and empty it would have been like entering a time machine, going back to his boy-hood. Here was the living room and down the narrow hallway was the kitchen with the big bay window. And there were the stairs. He grabbed the railing and slowly walked up to Peter's room, stepping lightly, trying to be quiet without knowing why.

The sun beamed in through the cracked front window. The room was empty. There was no zebra painting on the wall. Nate walked to the wall opposite the window, to the spot he knew well, and knelt down. He grasped the edge molding in a way he'd seen Peter do years ago and lifted up. The floor-board panel came up easily. He placed it to one side. Inside the cavity he expected to see something familiar, a baggie of marijuana or maybe an old Playboy, but he didn't. Instead, a switch-blade knife lay by itself in plain sight on a dirty bed of yellow insulation. Its blade was folded into the bone-grip handle that measured maybe five inches long. Nate was about to pick it up when he thought better of it. He pulled out his handkerchief and blanketed it over the knife, then picked it up by one end. It was heavier than it looked and by mistake, he pressed the blade release button. The mechanism made a scrapping sound and the blade nudged its way out only a little. Through the handkerchief Nate pulled it out the rest of the way and it locked in place. He took a closer look. The blade was tinged dark brown. He ran his thumb cross-wise over the cutting edge – still sharp. He turned the knife over and saw that something had been scratched over the brown stain into the surface of the blade. They were perfect block letters engraved in a perfectly straight line. He angled the knife to catch the light from the window and read the three words: *Only the Brave*.

Nate nearly dropped the knife. His hands were shaking. His mouth had turned dry.

He folded the blade back and, with his handkerchief still wrapped around it, stuffed the knife into his pocket. He checked Peter's stash again for anything else that might be hidden further back or maybe under the insulation, but it was empty.

Carefully, Nate repositioned the floor-board and went back outside where Jake was busy tossing more odds and ends into the dumpster. The sun was just catching the tree-tops. In the short time he'd been inside, the temperature had dropped. The wind was picking up and the hanging gutter had started thumping against the side of the house.

"Seen enough?" asked Jake.

"Yeah, I think I'll be going. Thanks for letting me go inside."

"Hey, it ain't my house."

Nate was about to get into his car when a thought occurred to him. He walked part way back to Jake. "Say, did you used to go to Bennett High?"

"Still do. I'll graduate in June."

"Good for you. Do you know if Mr. Whitaker is still there? He teaches art."

"I'm not much into art, but the name's familiar. Yeah, I think he teaches history too. Yeah, I remember him now. He's still there – old guy."

"Okay, just wondered. Thanks."

It was a short drive to his parent's. Before getting out, Nate pulled the wrapped knife from his pocket and put it in the glove compartment. When he entered the house, Sal ran up and gave him three big slurps as if he hadn't seen him in years. He took his parents out to the newest of the town's three restaurants. It had opened for business more than ten years ago but they still called it the *new* place. Over dinner he explained how he hoped to casually bump into David O'Neal at church the next day.

Mom smiled. "So we'll all be going to Mass as a family; how long has it been?"

"Long time," said Dad, chewing, well focused on his steak.

"Do you think he'll be there?" asked Nate.

"Mr. O'Neal's there every Sunday, just like us. You'll let us know what it was that Peter sent him, won't you dear?" She smiled at Dad. "We like to know these things."

Nate said he would.

The next morning Nate drove to church separately from his

parents. Once there they sat together in one of the back pews and his mother pointed out David O'Neal. He was a tall man, slightly bent, who walked with the assistance of a cane. After Mass, Nate broke off from his parents and caught up with O'Neal in the vestibule. He'd just gotten a church paper.

"Mr. O'Neal?" asked Nate.

The old man had a long, thin comb-over, dyed black. Strands of it fell across his milky-blue eyes when he jerked his head around. His brows slanted up. "Yes?"

Nate introduced himself and they shook hands.

"Yes, I know the Parks—your mom and dad, not well but I hear they're nice folks. So you're back for a visit, are you? Where are you visiting from?"

"New York City. I was in town a couple of months ago for Peter Caruso's funeral." Nate watched for a reaction to the name but didn't see one.

"Is that right? Yes, I know the Carusos." O'Neal adjusted his hair and started walking toward the door, encouraging Nate with a wave of his hand to walk along with him. The rest of the congregation was already out in the parking lot, most of them, Nate supposed, heading off for Sunday breakfast. He felt his stomach rumble.

"You were a friend of his?" asked O'Neal. "Yes, I suppose you would be—he lived in New York too."

They walked outside and down the steps then stopped as Nate explained how they were friends growing up but didn't see much of each other in the city. Then Nate tried to take on a casual tone.

"I understand that Peter sent you something before he died."

O'Neal's eyes narrowed and met Nate's. "Maybe he did, but I'm not sure that's any of your business." He began walking again across the gravel parking lot, stopping at a dusty old Buick. He pulled out his keys.

"Peter didn't have many friends, Mr. O'Neal, but I was one of them once. He was an incredibly gifted artist but his life was cut short and the police have no idea who killed him. As his friend, and as someone who loves the art he left behind, I want to find out more about him. A short time before his death he sent out a package addressed to you. He'd instructed the delivery service to hold onto it for a month before routing it on to you. I was thinking that maybe there was a connection between Peter's death and whatever was in the package."

O'Neal opened the car door and got in. He sat there for a while with the door opened and the key in the ignition. The day was bright and sunny and pleasantly crisp. He pulled the key half out to stop the interior chimes. His eyes were directed straight ahead through the windshield as if fixed on something at the distant horizon. "Do you remember Patty?"

"Yes, Mr. O'Neal, I do."

"That poor, bright, promising girl, my niece, died two months before her high school graduation. She wasn't even eighteen. It was *her* life that was cut short, not Peter Caruso's. Patty never had a chance to live. And now, fifteen years later, this 'gifted artist,' as you call him, sends me a wooden crate nailed shut. There was a note along with it." He paused and took a breath, then just continued to stare as if he'd lost his train of thought.

O'Neal collected himself. "His note said, 'A Life for a Life,' that was all." A tear ran down the old man's ruddy cheek then he turned to face Nate directly, his eyes glassy. "He killed her. He killed her as sure as I'm sitting here. Why would he do such a thing? What kind of a monster was he?"

Nate backed away. Peter really had killed Patty? He felt his hand shaking and a knot tightening around his stomach. He grabbed onto the car door. "Mr. O'Neal, I thought Patty drowned. I thought it was an accident."

The old man shook his head. "That's what I wanted everyone to believe and that's what I still want them to believe. Maysville is a small town, Mr. Parks. People talk and I didn't want Patty's death sensationalized. The police and the local paper cooperated and Patty was laid to rest quietly, like her mom and dad would have wanted." He drew a deep breath. "The truth of it was that Patty had died that night before her body ever hit the water. Her throat had been cut."

The image of Peter's stained knife flashed through Nate's mind. Could he really have killed her? Then he thought of the note from Peter: *A life for a life*. O'Neal was right, it sounded like a confession.

Nate leaned a little closer. "Mr. O'Neal, what was in the crate?"

The old man swallowed hard. "I honestly don't know. When I read the note I didn't want to open it. I was afraid of what I'd find. It took me years to get over Patty's death and now Peter Caruso was trying to taunt me into reliving the agony I'd felt when I first learned she was gone. I let the crate sit in my living room for two days before carrying it out to the garage – I was going to throw it out or burn it, I wasn't sure which. It'd serve that monster right, me not even looking at whatever it was he sent."

"So what did you do?"

O'Neal dried his cheek with his sleeve. "I would have burned it, but then, just a couple of days ago, a fellow came by the house and asked me about it – just like you're asking about it now. He said he was with the Caruso estate and was authorized to give me a thousand bucks in compensation for it. I know Frank Caruso – I haven't talked with him in years but I do know he's a good man. Back when she was alive, he'd taken a real shine to Patty – you know, like a second father. I figured Frank wanted to keep things quiet just like I did, so I let the fellow have the crate." O'Neal pulled out a cigarette, lit it with shaking hands. He took a long drag. "I'll be using the money to buy a better head-stone for Patty."

"How big was it? - the crate."

"Flattish – maybe three foot square, six inches high."

"Did the man show you any ID? Did he have you sign anything?"

"He said his name was James Bridgeman, but I didn't ask for any ID and there was nothing to sign. He seemed to know a lot about Frank and his family so I took him at his word. He just counted out ten, one hundred-dollar bills right there in my living room, then left. I watched him load the crate into his trunk. I was glad to be rid of it."

Nate's hopes fell. God only knew where the crate might be now. "Can you describe him?"

"A youngish fellow – your age maybe, dark hair. One thing did bother me about him though: when he pulled out of my driveway I saw that he had New York plates, which seemed odd for someone helping Frank Caruso out here in Maysville. But then, that's where Peter had lived so I thought it might make sense."

"Do you remember anything else about him?"

"No, he was a pretty average guy – good manners. But I did have my suspicions about him. I wrote down his plate number and have it back at the house. You figuring him for a crook or something?"

"Not sure if he's a crook, but yes, the plate number could be useful. I can use it to check him out. I'll let you know if he's on the up and up."

O'Neal started the car and had Nate follow him back to his small Cape-Cod home not far from the church. They went inside and O'Neal gave him the plate number.

Nate decided to press his luck. "Would it be too much trouble for you to show me Peter's note?"

"Burned it," said O'Neal, his hand tightening into a fist. "I didn't want any part of it or the crate. I'm glad to be rid of them both." Then he looked at Nate more closely. "I'm being very open with you, young man, because you're a local boy. I hope you won't take advantage."

"You can trust me, Mr. O'Neal. I won't do anything to disrupt your life or Patty's memory." It was a promise Nate hoped he could keep.

CHAPTER 10

Nate left the O'Neal house and took the long way back to his parent's house. He tried to remember more about the Peter Caruso he knew in high-school. Bits of conversation and flashes of disjointed images from those days flowed through his mind. He remembered Peter's taunt: *What if I was the one who killed her?* How could he kill Patty and then make fun of it just a few days later? How could the Peter Caruso he knew be a cold-blooded killer?

Nate hadn't told O'Neal about Peter's knife, but the more he thought about it the more he realized that maybe he should have. He wondered if the police file on Patty's murder was still open - probably not after all this time, but he knew cases could be re-opened. He'd seen TV shows about tireless detectives finally solving old cases and bringing the perps to justice. But if Peter was the killer, what difference did it make? Peter was dead and that was all the justice Patty would ever get. Besides, the old man didn't want the truth to be made public. Nate had to respect his wishes, didn't he? Then Nate thought about the brown-stained knife in his glove compartment and shrank within himself at how Peter might have used it on Patty.

Maybe he'd driven her up to the lake that night. There were desolate spots all around the shore and it was a popular place for high-schoolers to make out. Maybe Peter had planned to go all the way with her and she tried to stop him. But he wouldn't have stopped. Nothing could stop Peter when he set his mind to something. Nate could see him forcing himself on her, thrusting, then hitting her again and again, until it was done. Still caught in a rage as if he were a madman, he would have pulled out his knife. He would have waved it in front of her, wanting to see the fear in her eyes. Then he would have sliced deep in a single violent stroke. In his mind the scene had played out in an instant and suddenly Nate was sure of it - Peter *had* killed Patty.

His palms were sweaty on the wheel. Sleet began to fall and he turned on the wipers as he negotiated a turn in the gravel road. His parent's house rose up in the distance.

He didn't tell them about the painting and he didn't tell them about the knife but over dinner, at which he scarcely ate, he asked about the woman in the back of the church.

"Yes, I saw her too," his mother said. "I didn't recognize her though, so she probably wasn't a Maysville resident. And I don't remember seeing any out-of-state plates on the cars in the church lot before going in – except for yours of course." She was a little miffed that Nate hadn't given her any details about the conversation he'd had with O'Neal.

Nate left early Monday morning but had one more stop to make in Maysville. He pulled up to William Bennett High. It was a sprawling new building, much larger than the old one he remembered. He went to the office and introduced himself and asked if Mr. Whitaker was in.

"Do you have an appointment?"

"No, I was a student in his art class and am in the area visiting my parents. I just thought I'd stop by and say hi."

The woman at the desk smiled then glanced at the clock on the wall. "He has a class in fifteen minutes, so you'll have to be quick – Room 202, up the stairs and take a right down the hall."

Nate made his way through the noisy rush of students and found Mr. Whitaker seated cross-legged behind his desk, reading the paper. His back was to Nate but even from that angle he recognized his old teacher - black with a slim build and close-cropped hair that was almost entirely gray now. He held a half-filled cup of coffee at chin level, about to take a sip.

"Hello, Mr. Whitaker," said Nate.

The teacher put down his cup and the paper, abruptly swiveling his chair around, ready to confront whoever had been bold enough to bother him during what was probably his pre-class relaxation ritual. When he had Nate in full view, he scanned him up and down. "Who are you?" he asked.

"Nate Parks, class of '98."

His expression remained blank, but only for a moment. Then

a big grin took over his face as he got to his feet. He put on his glasses. "Nate Parks, my God. But these days it's Nathan Lido Parks, the artist – isn't that right? Wow, it's an honor to have you back, Son. You were one of my best students. How the hell are you?" He shook Nate's hand with vigor.

"I'm doing all right, Mr. Whitaker, doing all right."

"I think you're old enough to call me Chuck now. What brings you back here?" But before Nate could answer, the old teacher's expression changed. "Say, can you stay for a bit? My kids," he waved his hand toward the gathering storm of students just taking their seats and he lowered his voice, "most of them don't give a damn about art – just an easy grade, you know. But you, you're an accomplished artist in New York." He clamped a hand on Nate's shoulder. "Can you talk to them? It doesn't have to be for the whole class period, but it would be good for them to hear from you about your art. What do you say?" He checked his watch and grabbed his pointer, smacking it on the desk like a gavel. Nate jumped. Mr. Whitaker shouted: "Seats people, seats now," and the room quieted.

His old teacher didn't give Nate much of a choice. After an embellished introduction, he turned the class over to him.

Nate talked to them about how art had affected his life and how he used his own art to affect the lives of others. The class listened politely, some with blank expressions but a few with interest. He took some questions, some about style, and some about technique. The last question came from a boy with wide-rimmed glasses and stringy black hair: "How much money do artists make these days?" he asked.

Nate hesitated. He didn't want to dissuade the boy from going into art but he wasn't going to lie to him either. "Between teaching gigs, speaking engagements and commissions, a top artist in New York City can bring in six-figures. If you're not one of the, say, top five, then it can be a struggle."

"Are you one of the top five?"

Nate smiled grimly. "I'm still working on that. Look, if painting is your passion as mine is to me, it's what you have to do. The money is secondary."

The boy nodded but Nate could see he wasn't buying it. Thankfully, the class bell rang cutting off any follow up discussion.

Mr. Whitaker's next period was open, so he and Nate went to the faculty lounge where Nate explained why he was back in Maysville.

"Ah, yes, Peter Caruso," said Whitaker seated across a table from Nate. "I was shocked to hear of his death. I would have been at the funeral had I not been on vacation down in Florida that week. We were on winter-break then. That kid was...exceptional."

"But he wasn't always that way, was he? I was involved in the evaluation of his collection after his death. I saw his high school sketchbook."

Whitaker cupped his hands under his chin. "If you've come to me for an explanation of just where Peter's talent came from, you're wasting your time. I have no explanation. He certainly didn't get it from me. One day he was the most ordinary of art students and the next...well, you've seen his sketches. You saw the change. I wouldn't have believed it had I not been looking over his shoulder as he effortlessly rendered drawing after drawing. I'd say, draw a horse, and he'd draw the animal in a fierce pose, muscles bulging with true to life detail from hoof to mane. It was as if a brilliant light had just been turned on in Peter's head. It was extraordinary."

"Do you remember when exactly that was?"

"The actual date? No, but it was sometime in the spring of, let's see, it would have been 1997. Yes, spring of '97."

"Maybe April?"

Whitaker's eyes met Nate's. "Why the need for specifics?"

Nate hesitated. "I haven't exactly thought this through yet, but I know there've been instances of people who've experienced violent trauma, usually physical but sometimes emotional, who have exhibited unusual abilities afterwards. They suddenly become a whiz at math, able to perform fantastic multiplications in their head. Or their memory has become photographic. Or..."

"You think something like that happened to Peter? It's as good an explanation as any, but Peter was a strange kid to begin with, didn't you think so? Very withdrawn and shy, yet somehow volatile and," he held up a finger, "gregarious enough and skillful enough to be the best pitcher on our baseball team for two years running." The old man shook his head. "After he turned to art, Peter never pitched again. It was all very odd, but I can't think of any particular incident that might have caused the change in Peter. We had one girl who died that year. It was tragic; I suppose that might have affected Peter..."

"Patty Harris, you mean."

"Yes, that's her. But I don't know if she and Peter were connected at all. You may know that better than me."

Nate he glanced down at the Formica table-top. "No. There was no connection that I knew of."

They talked for a while longer then, after promising to stop by the next time he was in the area, Nate left.

On his way out of town, he drove slowly past the police station fighting the urge to pull in, to show them Peter's knife and to tell them what he knew about the death of Patty Harris. But going to the police would be a direct betrayal of Mr. O'Neal's trust. He couldn't do it. Still, he had to tell someone. He hit the interstate then called Cat.

After a ten-minute conversation, she summed things up pretty well: "So Peter kills a girl when he's seventeen, gets away with it, then fifteen years later and only days before his own death, he sends the girl's uncle a box along with a note admitting to the murder. Then, only two days ago, a guy shows up at the uncle's house and buys the box from O'Neal."

"There's something else," said Nate. "I went to Peter's old house - they were emptying it out, getting ready to tear it down. I found his knife, Cat. It was right under the floorboards where he used to hide things. I didn't tell O'Neal about it."

Cat was quiet for a moment. "So you actually have the knife? Did you touch it?"

"No, I didn't touch it. It's in my glove compartment, wrapped in a handkerchief." Nate waited for a response from Cat. There was none. "I should have gone to the police with it, right?"

"You think?"

"I couldn't do that, Cat. I promised Mr. O'Neal I'd keep quiet about Patty. Turning in the knife would just re-open the case. Besides, Peter's dead now. What good would it do?"

"You think his killing the girl is what triggered it, don't you – the change in Peter?"

"I guess I do. I don't have a better explanation."

"Did you find anything out about the woman you saw at the funeral?"

"No, my mother didn't know her and she says she didn't remember seeing any out of state plates on the cars in the lot."

"Your mom's pretty observant."

"That's one word for it. And that's the other thing: O'Neal said that the car this James Bridgeman drove had New York plates." He gave her the number.

"Well, just get back here, Nate. In the meantime, I'll have the plate run and see what I can find out about Bridgeman."

"See if you can get the sketchbook back too," said Nate. "I want to take another look at it."

After hanging up from Cat, Nate drove a few more miles then

thought of Meredith. Was she still upset about leaving Teddy? Was she was still at his apartment? Part of him hoped she was and part of him didn't. He called her but couldn't reach her. At the next rest-stop, he sent her a text that he was on his way back.

A couple of hours later, he collected his mail at the front door and was climbing the stairs up to his apartment. The door was unlocked. He opened it part way. "Meredith? It's Nate. I'm back." He walked in a few steps then saw a note on the kitchen counter:

Thanks for putting me up.
Stayed two days and got bored out of my head.
I'm trying to patch things up with Teddy so don't call me.
I'll call you when I can.
M.

Nate sat down on the couch and tried to decelerate the thoughts racing through his head. Life without Meredith would certainly be simpler, but could he really give her up? Dumb question - what choice did he have? She didn't need him. Like she'd said, he was simply her man of the moment – good for the moment, but it was time to get real. His ride on the Meredith express was over.

Nate turned on the TV and started flipping through channels, but only found the late afternoon talks. Then he remembered his mail and started going through it. Bill, junk, junk, bill, and a letter from an outfit he didn't know somewhere on Thirty-Eighth Street. He opened it and saw it was from a financial consultant advising him that he should have a 401K and that he should be planning for his future. He was invited, with a guest of his choice, to a free dinner at which a guy named Donald with a few important looking initials after his name, would explain his strategy for building wealth.

Nate had no 401K and he didn't have a spare dime to start one. He tossed the letter onto the coffee table and pulled out his phone. He had fifteen paintings out on consignment at various galleries around the city. He had an auto-deposit arrangement so that, when any of them sold, the money, less forty percent to the gallery, would be sent directly to his account. He punched up his bank info – there was the check from Teddy for Meredith's painting and there was the last deposit from Manhattan College which reminded him that he needed to apply for a summer adjunct spot.

There were no other deposits. None of his consignments had

sold. But there'd been plenty of auto-withdrawals: rent, utilities, car, and credit card. Something had better sell soon or he would be in trouble. He knew he had to get back to painting and he remembered the still unfinished baker at his studio. What on earth had prompted him to paint a baker? He needed to get more commercial with his art. Portraits of famous people always sold well but he didn't like doing them. He stretched out on the couch and closed his eyes. He thought about the faces of the kids in Mr. Whitaker's class most of whom clearly saw the field of art as a dead-end career with no chance of a comfortable, financially stable life. Why hadn't he seen that same thing years ago? He should have been a stock broker, like Donald.

Cat called in the morning.

"I've got the sketchbook," she told him, "and there are something like thirty James Bridgeman's in the New York phone directory."

"What about the plate?"

"I've got a DMV guy running it now. I should hear back in the next day or two – he has to do it on the side you know – un-official-like."

"Thanks Cat."

"We're still on for tonight, right?"

"Of course, Chinese." Nate had forgotten but now found himself really looking forward to seeing her again.

"Great," said Cat, "I'll bring the sketchbook."

They met in the lobby of the restaurant at seven. Cat wore a bright blue dress.

"You look wonderful," said Nate, tieless in his sport coat. "I feel a little under-dressed."

"Are you kidding? You look great." She took his arm as they were ushered to their table.

After ordering, Cat handed him the sketchbook. "How come you wanted it back?"

He didn't answer right away. He went immediately to the last page. He felt along the binding and looked closer.

"Care to tell me what you're doing?"

"I was dumb to have missed it Cat." He showed her the inside binding. "Do you see? Here, go like this, you can feel it." He ran a finger along the inside spine of the sketchbook.

Cat did the same then winced, "Ouch, almost got a paper cut." Then she understood. "There's a page missing. It's been sliced out."

"That's right. Not ripped out, but sliced out very carefully. It's a missing page. I have a hunch about what Peter sent to O'Neal."

Cat put up a finger. "It's a painting – right?"

Nate took a sip from his water glass. "Yeah, I think it's a painting."

"Oh, I stole your thunder on that one, I guess. I wouldn't have thought of it, though, without just now finding out about the missing page thing. That was a good pick up on your part. But why would Peter have cut the page out?"

"Maybe he didn't; maybe someone else did."

Cat continued to look at the sketchbook. "Here's something, I think." She showed him the back-side of the last page where thin streaks of graphite speckled the paper. "This must be residue from the missing page. Like somebody's dirty footprint."

"Can you see an image?"

"No, but I'll bet a hi-res scanner could."

"And I suppose you know how to get one."

"Sure do. I know an engineering guy at Manhattan College. You know where that is?"

"Cat, I'm an adjunct there. I thought you studied up on me."

"Guess my info's a little dated." As she handed the sketchbook back to Nate, the waiter came with their egg rolls and plum sauce and two cups of tea. She doused the egg roll and savored the first bite. "I love egg-rolls."

"Have you found anything out about Bridgeman?"

"Frank Caruso doesn't know anything about a James Bridgeman or about Peter sending something to O'Neal, so the guy's cover about somehow working on behalf of the estate doesn't hold water. I still haven't heard back about the plates. That's the thing that should really tell us something. Anyway, I'll try to get the info tomorrow. I'm still on other cases, you know; have to pay the bills."

Nate took a swallow of tea. "How's your rich adulteress thing going?"

"Ah, that, yes, you want to hear a good one? You won't tell anyone will you? I could get in trouble."

Nate ran a thumb across his closed lips. He tried to look unconcerned but his heart was thumping.

"Turns out she's a lesbian. She confessed to him that she's been cheating on him with another woman, and, now that he knows, he thinks it's a real turn-on, so everyone's happy again. Guess she's one of those switch hitters." She shook her head. "It's a crazy world, let me tell you."

Nate conjured up an image of Meredith having torrid lesbian

sex, then added a naked Teddy to the mix. He looked down at his half-eaten egg roll.

"You okay?" asked Cat. "You look like you just swallowed a gold fish."

"No, I'm good." He cleared his throat and moved his plate to one side.

"You're not going to finish that?" she asked.

He slid it over to her.

So that was it then, whether Meredith was or wasn't a lesbian, the important thing was that she and Teddy were back together. Nate felt suddenly free. No more sneaking around, no more worry about Cat finding out that he was a two-timing, wife-stealing scum-bag. All of that was behind him. But Meredith a lesbian – *really*?

When their entrées came, he found himself enjoying the food and enjoying being with Cat more than he ever had. They finished dinner and left the restaurant. It was a brisk, early spring evening with a half-moon peeking between the tall buildings. They took a stroll, talking and window shopping and, at a stop light, Nate pulled Cat close and kissed her. Her arms wrapped him in a warm embrace. Her lips moved with his and when the light changed, Nate nudged her along, more purposefully now.

"Where are you taking me, Mr. Parks? Remember, I'm a good Catholic girl."

"You trust me, don't you?"

"Not entirely."

He laughed, "Well you may be disappointed then. Our destination is straight ahead."

They walked another half-block then stepped down into a small, below-street-level restaurant.

"Best apple pie in the city," he said.

"Oh boy, oh boy," she said, heading down the steps in front of him.

Inside, the aroma of freshly baked pies and pastries filled the air. They shared a piece of apple pie with two scoops of ice cream. Glancing behind the counter, Nate saw a baker rolling out the dough for tomorrow's pies. He told Cat about his unfinished painting.

"What made you decide to paint a baker?"

Nate shook his head. "I don't really know. I must have been hungry at the time. But it wasn't just the baker, it was all his creations with him - the colors, the smells, the taste of the pastries and pies. I wanted to capture it all."

"But you're stuck?"

"Yes. Something's missing and I'm not sure what." Nate watched Cat take the last bite of pie with a small mound of half-melted ice cream.

She held it in her mouth, eyes closed, savoring its flavors before swallowing. "You're right, this is the best pie ever."

Two days later, Nate met Cat in the Manhattan College office of Professor Allen Bryce, a short, totally bald man who wore a white lab coat. Perched near the tip of his nose were a pair of silver, wire-rimmed glasses. After the introductions, they all sat and, from behind a paper-strewn desk, Professor Bryce spoke first, looking at Nate. "I believe I've heard of you...oh no, that was someone else." He waved his hand as if erasing the comment then folded his hands. "Cat here said you had something you needed scanned."

Nate pulled the sketchbook from a folder and opened it to the last page. "There's a page missing. We think these smudges may tell us what was on that page." He handed it to Bryce who studied it for a moment, holding the book at different angles in the sunlight that streamed through a window.

"Yes, I can see the markings. I think we might be able to help." He stood up and, taking the sketchbook with him, stepped through a door to his left. "This won't take long," he shouted back, his voice muffled by the door that had already closed behind him.

"He seems a little scattered," said Nate.

"No, he's good. I bring him stuff like this all the time. Not always for the scanner. He's got a complete lab back there."

Bryce returned five minutes later. He handed Nate the sketchbook, then turned his computer screen so Nate and Cat could view it.

At first there was just the Manhattan College splash-screen. Then Bryce hit a couple of keys and an image of the sketchbook page appeared, blank except for a few dark streaks and dots.

"There's your page," said Bryce.

"It looks no clearer than it did to the naked eye," said Nate, disappointed.

"That's because you're seeing it one-to-one, no magnification." Bryce grabbed his mouse and drew a one-inch square on the screen. He double clicked. The screen changed to show a pitted, fibrous surface of random lights and darks. "That's about ten-to-one. We can go much higher but I think you get the point – we're talking gigs of pixels here. Can you see a pattern?"

Nate and Cat both shook their heads.

"Neither can I, but fear not. This is where pattern-recognition software comes in." He punched more keys then sat back in his chair.

The screen changed more slowly this time until it showed the entire page again with thin red, computer generated lines connecting some of the streaks and dots. The red-lined image showed a rectangular frame of the same size Peter had used for his miniatures in the preceding pages. But inside this box there was no detail that showed the concept for the actual painting.

"It's just an empty frame," said Nate.

"What's this here?" Cat pointed to some computer generated lines beneath the empty frame. "It's writing I think."

Bryce saw the spot, outlined it in a red rectangle then double-clicked. The rectangle enlarged to fill the screen with the reversed image of four words.

"It's in Peter's hand," said Nate.

"You might want a mirror so you can read it proper," said Bryce. "I think the software can do that but I'm not quite sure how to pull it off."

"Don't bother," said Cat, not taking her eyes off the screen. "I can see what it says."

"Yes, I see it now too," said Nate. A chill ran through him as he stared at the words written by the seventeen year old killer, Peter Lazar Caruso, and conceived by him to be the title of his last painting:

Death of the Artist

CHAPTER 11

Before they left, Professor Bryce gave them a thumb-drive with the screen-shots. He shook Nate's hand. "Over the phone, Cat told me a little about this artist friend of yours. He must have been a tormented soul. He should have enrolled here instead of that mill-of-commerce across town. We might have been able to help him. We Catholics are good at extricating inner daemons. You might say we wrote the book on it." He chuckled. "Anyway, come back if you need anything more."

Nate said he would, then followed Cat out into the hall. "We need to talk," he said as Bryce's door closed behind them.

"Yeah, I was going to suggest that."

They ducked into an empty classroom. Nate took the instructor's chair and Cat took a seat in the front row.

"Is this some kind of a private lesson Mr. Parks?" she asked, fluttering her eyelashes just a little.

But Nate was entirely preoccupied with Peter. "So the painting that Peter sent to O'Neal must have depicted Peter's own death. How did he know he was going to die? How could he have known *how* he was going to die?"

"He wouldn't have known fifteen years ago when he drew that blank frame – that's why it was blank. But he might have known in the weeks or months leading up to his death. People who have cancer have a good idea of how they'll die. People who commit suicide know how they'll die."

"But he was murdered – shot three times."

"Maybe he knew he was going to be murdered," said Cat. "Maybe he knew it was going to happen because he set it up – he made it happen."

"He arranged his own murder? Assisted suicide?" Nate rubbed the bridge of his nose then leaned back in his chair contemplating what Peter's last days might have been like. "He was accepting justice – a life for a life, his for Patty's. A little like Jesus accepting his fate in Gethsemane."

"Well, I think you're giving him too much credit there, but all this does point to a connection between Peter's death and the death of the Harris girl." Cat frowned. "That reminds me Nate, I don't care what you might have promised O'Neal, you need to talk to the police about the knife. Concealing evidence, especially when the evidence happens to be the probable murder weapon, is a crime all by itself. Did you know that?"

Nate shook his head. "Let me worry about the knife. I made a promise to O'Neal and I want to keep it." His mind shifted back to his conversation with O'Neal about Bridgeman. "What about the plates?"

"So you're just going to keep the knife in your car—right, good plan, wish I'd thought of it." She folded her arms. "The plates, yes, I did make some progress, that's what I wanted to talk to you about. The car's one of the fleet of cars owned by the state of New York. Its home base is in Albany but any one of a hundred state employees would have had access to it."

"Any of those hundred named James Bridgeman?"

"No. There's no one by that name who works for the state."

"Shouldn't there be a log somewhere in Albany showing who signed out the car? And besides, if a New York state official had Peter's last painting, maybe he's already sent it onto the police."

"I suppose the police could have it," said Cat, "but they aren't in the habit of paying for evidence in a murder case. Bridgeman gave O'Neal a thousand bucks for it. If Bridgman had been acting officially on behalf of the state he would have had to get a warrant for it. Even then, state warrants don't extend beyond state lines. He would have had to involve the local police in Pennsylvania. As far as I've been able to find out, none of that happened. As for the car log in Albany, supposedly that particular car hasn't been signed out for three weeks."

Nate tapped the desktop then glanced back at Cat. She raised her chin just a little and he stopped tapping. "You know something else too - something about this Bridgeman guy, don't you?"

She smiled. "No, not about Bridgeman, but I think I might know who he was working for." Nate raised his eyebrows as Cat continued: "Of all the state employees in Albany who would have had access to the car, there were three who attended Peter's last exhibit."

"Good idea to check that, so you narrowed it down to three. Who are they?"

"It's better than that, Nate. I looked up some old records. Of those three, there was only one who also attended Peter Caruso's first exhibit, the one at Columbia five years ago."

"So who is he?"

"Sorry, I'm getting to that; oh, and it's a she." Cat reached into her inside jacket pocket and pulled out a folded sheet of paper. She handed it to Nate.

It was a black and white print-out of a web page with slick, professionally designed, graphics. It showed the image of a young woman standing on the observation deck of the Empire State Building looking out over a scene doctored to stretch from the congested streets of Manhattan out to the pristine Finger-Lakes upstate. A caption, in bold letters spanned the page: *Sarah Now!* Nate shook his head thinking back to when he was standing in line outside the Park Avenue exhibit – it was the woman in tennis shoes with the VIP limo. "You can't be serious."

Cat held up her hand. "I said there was nothing firm about this."

"But Sarah Crawford? She's the lieutenant governor of the state. Hell, she's running for governor."

Cat nodded. "She's the favorite too. She's also high enough up to be able to jimmy the car log in Albany."

"What could she possibly have to do with Peter?"

"She liked his art. Maybe she even liked him."

"You think she's Peter's girlfriend, the one the kid mentioned?"

Cat shrugged. "That might be a little far-fetched, but who knows."

"How would she have known about the missing painting?"

"Hey, I don't have all the answers here, not yet anyway. I look for facts, and I go where they point me. Right now they're pointing me to Sarah Crawford. Maybe next week they'll point to her kid sister or to Joe Shmo."

"Right, sorry," said Nate. "Good work connecting Crawford to Peter. What do we do about it though?"

"That's a tough one," said Cat. "If you knew her, you could just bump into her like you did with O'Neal and casually ask about Peter – see how she reacts, then go from there. But I checked her schedule. She's having a fundraiser dinner here in the city next week – a thousand bucks a plate."

Nate made a choking sound.

"Yeah, I don't have that kind of money either. You don't have any rich democrat friends, do you? You need to find a way to get in."

Nate immediately thought of Teddy who was well known for being active on the democratic side of state politics. He was almost certain to be at the dinner. But did he dare contact him? How would Meredith react? It wasn't worth the risk, was it?

Cat evidently saw his wheels turning. "These things fill up pretty fast so you don't have much time, Nate. If you do know someone, you need to talk to them now."

Nate rubbed the back of his neck. "It's a long shot, but I'll see what I can do." He handed the print-out back to Cat along with Peter's sketchbook then glanced at his watch. "I'd better get up to my class."

They stood to go.

"I was meaning to ask you," said Cat, on the way out, "what is it you teach? I mean I know it's art but..."

"This class is: *The place for realism in contemporary art.*"

"Oh, I'll have to catch it sometime. No, I'd like to, really. No time today though. I'll call you tomorrow."

That night Nate decided to see what he could learn about Sarah Crawford. He flipped on his old desktop and went to her website. There she was, on the observation deck: Bright auburn hair, roundish, good-looking face, hazel eyes. She wore a blue winter coat and the photo had caught her with what he would call an expression of hopeful concern. If he were to paint her, he might well have chosen that same tilt to her head, the same angle to her brow, the same sweep of her lips that suggested youthful vigor, intelligence and honesty – no hidden agendas here. Below the picture were bullets of her recent accomplishments: four years in the state house, two years as Lieutenant Governor, champion of senior rights, champion of organized labor, champion of small businesses and of infrastructure improvements. The list went on and beside each bullet there was a link for more details.

He went back to the top of the page and clicked on her bio.

She had grown up the daughter of a middle class couple in Albany and from there her list of accomplishments was impressive: President of her senior class in high school where she graduated at fifteen; active in student politics at Cornell where she was valedictorian with a degree in political science. She received her JD at twenty. For a year she practiced law in one of the poorest neighborhoods in Rochester after which she became an elected representative in the state house where she completed a four-year term with the highest possible performance rating among the independent polls. Then came the Lieutenant Governor's spot and now her run for governor – and she had just turned thirty.

Nate clicked on a video that showed her speaking from a podium. Her voice was strong, her inflections and pauses well timed with hand-gestures and facial expressions that lent a natural force to her words. This woman was polished. The three-minute video ended with the serious, no-nonsense white on black words taking up the full screen: *Sarah Now!* Although he was a staunch Democrat himself, Nate pitied the poor Republican running against her. But, then again, you'd expect her own website to show her in the best possible light.

Nate searched other sites looking for a more objective or even a negative view of Sarah Crawford. He wasn't able to find much and it was nearing midnight when he landed on a story from the *Albany Chronicle* dated only two weeks ago. The headline read: Sarah Pregnant? There was a side-profile of her showing what it claimed to be a possible baby-bump. The article ended by stating: *When asked about the possible pregnancy, the un-wed gubernatorial candidate had no comment.*

Too bad, thought Nate, a scandal like that could be a real set-back for her. Still, social mores about out of wedlock pregnancies weren't what they used to be. He took a last look at the picture of her looking out from the Empire State Building then flipped off the computer and went to bed more convinced than ever that a woman like Sarah Crawford couldn't possibly have had any interest in Peter Caruso—in his paintings, maybe, but not the man.

He slept well and in the morning went to his studio and got back to work. Like a novelist, Nate always named the imagined people he painted and gave them a back-story. For him it helped to personalize and give character to the image. His baker's name was Joe Brody – married, two kids, struggling to make ends meet. His painting showed Joe kneading a mound of dough behind the counter wondering if he'd have enough customers today to pay the bills. Attentive worry was the right facial expression for Joe, and for himself, Nate thought as he worked, wondering if this painting would ever find a buyer.

Time flew by and it was already two in the afternoon when he thought about the Crawford fundraiser. A connection between the lieutenant governor and Peter was a real long-shot but it was the only shot he had and, if he was going to call Teddy, he should do it now. He washed the paint from his hands, and picked up the phone.

"Nathan, good to hear from you again," Teddy responded in his usual boisterous way. "I want you to know that we've got your painting of Meredith hanging in a very prominent place here at the house and I enjoy it every time I see it. It gets a lot of good comments from visitors. I always tell them about you and I wouldn't be surprised if you got some commissions out of it. You're doing well I hope."

"Never better," said Nate.

"You know you ought to have an exhibit of your work. Have you thought about that? Something fancy, first class; I'd consider being one of your sponsors. Let me know if you ever need my help."

"Well, Teddy, that's sort of why I'm calling. I'm not doing an exhibit, not right now anyway, but I would appreciate your help in getting me into a fundraiser next week. It's a political thing."

"Fundraiser?" The phone became muffled for a moment then Teddy was back on the line. "You mean the one for Sarah Crawford? Yes, evidently I'm supposed to be there. I didn't know you were political, Nathan. Well good for you. I think everyone should be involved in such things, damned Republicans being what they are."

Nate felt it best to be agreeable. "Yes, they've certainly made a mess of things and I think Sarah Crawford can make a big difference. I've been an admirer of hers for some time now and I know she likes art."

"Yes, she's well known for that. Well sure, I'll be happy to get you in to see her. It could be a good boost to your career."

"Yes, it could."

"Meredith and I have tickets and we were wondering who to go with. I'll pick up two more. A man like you, I expect you have a young lady you'd like to bring along?"

"Oh, I wouldn't want to bother you for *two* tickets."

"It's no bother at all. In fact I insist on it. It'll give Meredith and I a way to learn a little bit more about you and your art. They say you never really know a person well until you meet their closest friend."

"The woman I'd take doesn't know me all that well. We only met a few weeks ago."

"Well then maybe we'll be able to fill her in on a few things about you that she isn't aware of yet. At any rate, I'm sure we'll all have a good time of it."

Nate swallowed. There was no way out of this one. "Sure then, yes, I'll bring her. Thanks, that'll be great."

"Terrific, I'll have the tickets sent over to you and we'll meet at the event – it's at the Hilton I think, Sunday night."

Nate hung up with a sinking feeling. Not only had he just asked for and received a two-thousand dollar favor from the husband of the woman he had been carrying on an affair with, but now he'd be double-dating with them along with Cat, a woman he was beginning to really care about and who might well have been employed by Teddy to investigate his cheating wife. What the hell had he just done? He sat on his couch and went over the possible scenarios for just how disastrous Sunday night might be. He should take someone other than Cat, but who would that be? It couldn't be someone he'd already broken up with. Then he looked at the brighter side, maybe there wasn't a problem at all. Maybe Cat had never been following Meredith at all. Or maybe Cat was doing something Sunday night. Maybe she wouldn't be able to go. He called her.

"Great, sure I'll go," said Cat after he'd told her about the tickets. "Never been to a grand-a-plate dinner; wonder what they'll be serving."

Nate tried to sound enthusiastic. "There's a website for the event, they probably have the menu posted."

"Who'll we be going with? – they must be pretty rich."

"Teddy and Meredith Sinclair; he's a big investor type. We'll meet them there."

"How do you know them?"

There'd been no hint of recognition from Cat at the Sinclair name. Maybe this was going to work out all right. "I did a painting for them a few months back. They're nice; you'll like them." He arranged to meet Cat at the Hilton.

Nate had just hung up from Cat when Meredith called.

"I heard you'll be joining us Sunday night and you're bringing a friend. It'll be good to see you again."

He'd expected her to be angry but her tone was actually pleasant. "Yes, I'm looking forward to it too. I was glad to hear you patched things up with Teddy. How did you manage that?"

She laughed. "I can get pretty creative when I need to be. Yes, we're tighter than ever these days. Now, tell me about this friend of yours, I assume it's a she? Is she the coffee-spiller?"

"Her name's Catherine – Cat for short."

Meredith's tone suddenly changed. "Is she a pretty serious

thing for you Nathan? Have you banged her yet?"

Nate knew she liked to put him on the spot, to see how he'd react. He found himself hating her for it. He didn't say anything.

"So now you're two-timing me, Nathan? Have I got that right?"

Nate felt the blood rush to his head. "You're the one who's married, Meredith, not me. I've made no promises to anyone."

"Well, you've got me there, I suppose. Anyway, tell Catherine that I'm looking forward to meeting her. I'm sure we'll have *lots* to talk about."

CHAPTER 12

It was Sunday night.

"Over here Nate," he heard Cat shout when he entered the crowded lobby at the Hilton. She waved to him from the wall near the portable bar. She held a glass of wine and looked radiant, in a blue dress accented by the same diamond necklace she'd worn at Peter's exhibit. He worked his way over to her.

"You look spectacular," he said, giving her a kiss.

"Bradshaw has two in my size, one red; one blue. The diamonds, they're not real, go with either one."

"I was talking about you - your face, and your hair," said Nate. "Those are both real, and they're not from Bradshaw are they?" He thought he saw her blush.

"No, those are me. You're looking pretty snazzy yourself."

He took off his overcoat and handed it to the woman at the coat-check. "Same borrowed tux as last time." He gave her his arm and her touch felt good – somehow reassuring as if tonight wasn't going to be the disaster he feared. Still, his heart was pounding like a steam engine.

"I thought blue might be best among all these Democrats. Did I tell you I'm a Republican?"

"No, you didn't." Nate scanned the room for Teddy and Meredith.

Cat took a sip of wine. "Don't worry, I'll keep my political views to myself."

Nate spotted them next to the cheese-cube tower. He grabbed a glass of red then pointed them out to Cat.

She stood up a little on her toes. "Can't see, let's just go over."

They took a few steps in that direction before she pulled back hard on Nate's arm. "Oh, my God, Nate, oh my God - it's her."

Nate's heart shifted into a higher gear. Meredith turned in his direction. Their eyes locked. She smiled but Cat continued to tug at his arm.

"It's her, Nate, the rich-bitch-lesbo. What are the odds of that?"

Nate wondered the same thing. "I thought you said you didn't know the Sinclairs."

"I don't, not by name. I wasn't the lead investigator on her case. I was just a field tracker. We're not supposed to know names. We're just supposed to follow and report. She sees us, doesn't she? She's looking right at me." She took a breath then displayed a suddenly composed smile directed at Meredith. In a gulp, she finished off her wine and set the empty glass on a passing platter. "I'm okay. We can go over."

"You're sure?"

"I'm sure. It'll be like I'm under cover. I do it all the time – piece of cake – might actually be fun."

Nate doubted that.

They headed over.

Teddy and Nate shook hands and Nate introduced Catherine.

"Call me Cat," she said with a laugh that didn't sound the least bit strained. "Thank you for the tickets to this wonderful event. We're excited to be here."

Meredith twirled a cheese cube on a toothpick. "Nate tells me that you spilled coffee on him the first time you met." She put the cube in her mouth and drew out the toothpick through pursed lips.

"Yeah, that's me, always trying to get attention. Don't worry though, I have no spills planned for tonight."

"And what do you do for a living, Cat?" asked Teddy.

"I'm in wine and cheese," she said.

"An importer?"

"An investor actually," said Cat. "I'm also in distribution."

Her cover story rolled off her tongue as if it were the gospel truth. Nate hoped she wasn't about to overplay her hand. He held his breath.

"Is this good cheese?" asked Meredith twirling another cube.

"I prefer an aged cheddar or an imported Swiss. What you've got there is a processed cheese, one step up from Velveeta, no flavor to it, no character and every bite you take ends up right here." Cat patted her stomach. "I'd stay away from it."

"Thanks for the advice." Meredith put down the cheese cube.

"Anything else you'd suggest I stay away from?"

"No, that's about it. I did check the menu for dinner though and, if you go with the beef tenderloin, they're serving an excellent Cabernet Sauvignon. I think it's a 2002 – good year."

"And with the salmon?" asked Teddy.

"You should definitely go with the Pinot Noir. It brings out the flavor of the fish and combines it with a subtle yet distinct flavor of its own. I know it's a red but you really ought to try it."

"Well, Ms. Chaplin, you're a handy person to have around."

"I try to be, when I'm not spilling things." She smiled and gave Nate a glance.

They talked about Nate's portrait of Meredith and about the art scene in general while nibbling on crackers and broccoli flowerets dipped in ranch dressing. Nate wondered if Cat had made up her thing about the cheese. He didn't have any. At eight-thirty the doors to the dining room were flung open and a maître d type requested that everyone take their assigned seats.

Fifty flower-decked, round tables were spread across the giant room. Nate quickly did the math: ten plates per table at a thousand each, times fifty rang up a cool half-mil. Teddy led the way single file up to table number five, just one row back from center-stage where a lone podium stood unattended. In the far corner a band played Glenn Miller.

"We ladies will sit together if you don't mind," said Meredith taking a spot next to Cat.

Nate was glad not to be sitting between them.

They introduced themselves to the others at the table who were already seated. Teddy seemed to know everyone there on a first name basis and the evening got underway with a discussion of the prospects for the Yankee's over the Red Sox in the upcoming season.

"Pitching will be our problem," Cat interjected into the thick of the conversation. "We haven't got a closer – Boston does and good pitching always beats good hitting. We should do a trade."

"For whom?" asked a man from the other side of the table.

"I like Baxter with the Reds. It'll take a lot to get him here but he's one of the best in the majors."

When the conversation drifted onto other subjects, Nate reached under the table and gave Cat's knee an admiring pat. She leaned over and whispered into his ear: "Told you I was good at this."

Nate glanced at Meredith. She hadn't said much and looked like she'd much rather be somewhere else.

Appetizers were served then festivities were called to order by a flourish from the band followed by the introduction of the mayor who was given a mixed reception. More speakers followed through dinner then, as post-dessert coffee was brought out, up stepped the sitting Democratic Governor who gave a short speech then introduced "...the next Governor of the State of New York, the honorable, the indomitable Ms. Sarah B. Crawford."

The band burst out with *New York-New York*, the crowd got to its feet and sang along, then as the applause and the cheers reached a deafening level, out strode Sarah Crawford in her trademark tennis shoes and, there was no mistaking it, a bright blue maternity pant suit.

The applause faltered and cameras flashed but the band kept playing and Sarah Crawford kept waving and smiling broadly as she stepped behind the podium. She had to have heard the reaction, thought Nate, yet he couldn't see the slightest blink or waiver, not the slightest loss of poise in the face of this determined looking young woman who now, with both hands raised, quieted both the band and the smattering of applause that remained. Everyone took their seats and the large room went silent. Even the waiters and waitresses had stopped what they were doing, all eyes on Sarah Crawford.

"Good evening, New York City," she began in a conversational tone. "Thanks to our governor, to the mayor and to the many other dignitaries here tonight for this wonderful dinner held to promote my gubernatorial campaign. I am grateful and I am emboldened by your support and yes, to dispel all doubt, I am happy to announce that I am indeed pregnant."

The crowd remained silent.

"You know me. I am younger than many of you. I am part of an age demographic that makes up thirty-eight percent of our state. I am a woman in that demographic, so cut that percentage in half, to nineteen. I am white, I am single and I am pregnant, so cut that percentage down to two. Now I could go on selecting parameters like religious persuasion, political leanings and so on and pretty soon the percentage of the people in the State of New York who are exactly like me would shrink to zero and the truth would be self-evident: I am an individual, just like you. I have my hopes, my dreams, my talents and my faults. Like each of you, I am unique and I am not perfect. But as I said, I'm proud of who I am and I'm proud of what I've accomplished over the short time that I've been alive. I have great hopes for my future and for the future of the child forming within me. And who it will be who will make this future? It won't be just me and it won't be just you. It will be all of us, together with all our differences and all of our similarities, all our strengths and all of our weaknesses."

Like the rest of the room, Nate listened, almost spellbound by her words and by her frank honesty. He looked at Cat, then Meredith, both sat perfectly still with their eyes fixed on Sarah Crawford who spoke for another thirty minutes in a tone she might have used if she were talking across the breakfast table with an old friend. Interruptions for applause, Nate realized, would have seemed out of place and there were only a few.

Then Sarah took a breath and turned her head slowly from one side of the quiet room to the other. She placed her hand on her chest. "I am a candidate for the office of Governor of this great State of New York. I am running under the banner of the Democratic Party but if I am elected, I warn you right now, I will be everyone's governor. I will unite this state like never before and I will move us forward with vigor and determination. I will not rest until we have molded a practical and ambitious vision of prosperity and self-determination for ourselves. I will not rest until we, all of us New Yorkers, have laid down a fertile, rich soil in which to plant that vision and grow it to encompass the hopes and the dreams of our elderly, of our vigorous retirees, of our strong, working-age people and of all of our sons and our daughters who will learn from us that this world can always become a better place and that it's the challenge and the responsibility of each generation to make it so. Our great state *will* be a better place for our children for one reason only: because we choose to make it that way.

"If you believe in that vision, and if you believe that together we can make it a reality, then vote for me to be your next governor." She raised both hands. "Thank you, New York City."

The room remained silent for three long seconds as if everyone was hungry for her to say more. But Sarah seemed unperturbed. She collected her notes from the podium. One man in the back of the room stood up and shouted "Way to go, Sarah!" Then, suddenly, everyone was standing and cheering. After a full minute a chant rose up: Sarah! Sarah!

Nate clapped with enthusiasm as, on the stage, Sarah took a few bows before being joined by the mayor, by the governor and by an older man with a cane who gave her a hug – maybe her dad, thought Nate. Balloons fell, the band again belted out *New York - New York*. The applause and cheers continued until finally, Sarah left the stage and the lights in the auditorium came on.

Teddy grabbed Nate. "Wasn't she something? Come on, I can get you back there to meet her."

Nate glanced at Cat who gave him a nod that told him not to worry, she'd be fine alone with Meredith. He followed Teddy to a door beside the stage where a burly security woman stood guard. Teddy flashed his gold badge and she let them inside. He led the way through a hallway where the noise from the crowd became muffled, replaced by the sounds of excited conversation and exuberant shouting from further down the hall. Teddy set a quick pace toward a small gathering of press people, each of them seeming to have a camera and a recording device. Everyone was facing the two arms-folded guards who stood in front of a closed blue door. Someone switched on the bright lights from a TV camera.

"She usually comes out and says a few words then takes questions," explained Teddy as they joined the group. "You'll have to do battle with these guys if you want to get a word in."

In his head, Nate formulated his question and got ready to shout it out. They waited ten minutes. The light from the TV camera was turned off. They waited another five then the door opened and the guards pushed back the crowd to make some room. But it wasn't Sarah Crawford who appeared at the door.

"Ladies, gentlemen, I'm Colleen Logan, Sarah's campaign manager." The tall middle aged woman, wearing glasses and green dress, spoke in a booming voice with her hands raised. "She'll be out shortly and will take some questions, but just a few. Please be patient with us and have your questions ready."

The TV light came back on. "We'll do the TV spot first," said Logan. "Are we live?"

"We are live in...ten seconds," said the TV guy, forcing the issue.

"Okay, we're just about... yes, we are ready." She looked behind her, then stepped aside. "Ladies and gentlemen, our next governor, Sarah Crawford."

There was polite applause.

Sarah Crawford was shorter than she'd looked on stage, thought Nate, giving the appearance, up close, of being only a few years out of high school. She smiled at the group and shaded her eyes momentarily when she moved into the bright light.

"When are you due, Sarah?" someone shouted.

"I'm about half-way along now," she said.

Then the TV guy took charge. "Political campaigns can be grueling. Do you expect your pregnancy to limit you in any way?"

"When I actually have the baby, I'll have to take a little time off, otherwise no. I'm fit and I expect no complications but, if it comes down to it, I'll do first what's best for my baby, and second, what's best for the campaign."

"We've got you live on the air now Sarah. What can you tell our viewers?"

She looked directly into the camera. "Only that I'm happy to be the Democratic Candidate for Governor and I hope to earn your vote."

"And about your pregnancy?"

"I'm happy to be pregnant too."

"Who's the father?" someone shouted from the back.

She didn't flinch. "That's a private thing between him and me. Maybe one day we'll let you all know, but not now."

"Any plans to marry?"

"No, I have no plans to marry."

There were a few softball questions asked and answered then the TV lights were turned off and Nate saw his chance. "Ms. Crawford, I'm a friend of Peter Caruso. Do you know anything about his last painting?" He thought he saw the slightest twitch from the corner of her eye at the mention of Peter's name and, there was something else.

"You are...?"

"I'm Nathan Parks—an artist. I grew up with Peter."

"I knew Peter Caruso's art, Mr. Parks, but I didn't know him. I wish I had. He was a wonderful talent and his death was a great loss." She nodded to her manager who immediately stepped in front of her like a human shield and announced: "Sorry, that'll be all the questions for now. Thanks to you all for coming."

The door closed and the reporters that remained quickly dispersed.

"I thought you were going to offer to paint her portrait," said Teddy. "Why would you ask her about Peter Caruso?"

"I thought she knew him. I thought it might be a way to gain her trust – you know, start a conversation. I didn't feel comfortable just outright asking her if I could paint her portrait."

"Comfortable or not, that's what you should have done. You're a good artist Nathan, maybe even a great one, but you have a lot to learn about what it takes to sell yourself. Come on, let's get back to the ladies."

The auditorium was nearly empty of guests when they returned. The janitorial crew was busy stripping each table of dinner-ware, center pieces and table cloths and toward the back, a vacuum cleaner was going. Cat and Meredith were nowhere to be seen.

Nate and Teddy checked the lobby and found them on opposite ends of a bench looking to Nate like a pair of bookends on a shelf waiting for some thick books to fill the gap between them. Well, he hadn't really expected them to get along.

Cat's shoes were off and she was holding a nearly empty glass of wine which she finished off when she saw Nate. She put the glass down and grabbed her high-heels from beneath the bench. She and Meredith stood at the same time.

"I didn't expect you to be so long," said Meredith to Teddy.

"Sorry, it was my fault," said Nate. He hurried over to Cat who was looking a little unsteady. He linked an arm with hers and supported her discreetly.

She whispered in Nate's ear: "That last glass of wine might have been a mistake."

They got their coats and Nate thanked Teddy and Meredith who then left in a waiting limo.

Still in the lobby, Nate helped Cat get her shoes back on. Once outside, the fresh, cool air seemed to revive her. "How'd it go with Sarah?" she asked on the cab ride back to her place.

"I think I blew it," said Nate. "She wouldn't give me the time of day. She did react a little funny when I mentioned Peter."

"Funny how?"

"I don't know, she kind of twitched, like she'd been caught off guard." He saw Cat's eyes were only half-open. She looked like she was about to nod off. "You seemed to get along with Meredith."

"She's not too talkative but she's okay," said Cat through a yawn. "She seems to know Sarah Crawford well enough from when she ran for Governor."

"Lieutenant Governor, you mean."

"Yeah, Lieutenant Governor – she and Teddy were big contributors. There's something about her though, like she's hiding something, you know? But I suppose that's natural for an adulterous rich-bitch lesbo. That's a lot of heavy baggage. Still, I sort of like her."

Nate put his arm around her. "You're drunk. You like everybody when you're drunk."

"How do you know? You've never seen me drunk. Besides, I'm not *that* drunk." She rested her head on his shoulder and closed her eyes. "Meredith likes you, says you're a sweet guy."

"I am a sweet guy."

She snuggled closer, running the palm of her hand toward his belt buckle, then lower. "I know you are. Everybody likes Nate. Who do you like, Nate?"

"I like you Cat. In fact, I'm liking you a lot more right now," he whispered.

Cat's breathing slowed and her hand slowed in mid-caress then suddenly she turned rigid. She pulled back her hand and sat up straighter. "Whoa, guess you're right, I am drunk." She called up to the driver and had him pull into a McDonald's where she ordered a large black coffee. She took a sip, then a swallow. "That's better, I'll be okay now. Sorry."

"I'm sorry too," said Nate, loosening his tie.

"Oh, Nate, I don't mean to be a tease. I get that way when I'm drunk. I get sexually uninhibited then I fall asleep. You don't want me to fall asleep when we're..."

"No, I wouldn't want that," he said, taking a deep breath. Her perfume mixed gently with the aromas of wine and coffee.

When they pulled up to her building, he walked her to the front door where they kissed.

"Are you okay?" asked Nate. "Do you need help getting up to your apartment?"

"Don't be silly," she said, using her key. "I probably won't get much sleep tonight thanks to all this coffee but I'm perfectly fine. She kissed him again. Thanks Nate - it was a fun night."

He watched her get safely inside then got back into the cab. On the way to his place he thought about her, beautiful, smart, fun and frustrating Cat. He realized that he loved being with her. Did that mean he loved her? He leaned his head against the window and closed his eyes. He was tired and glad that the night that could have gone so wrong, was over.

The cab ran over a pothole and jarred him from his thoughts. He stared out the window. His mind went back to Sarah Crawford. Again he saw her reaction to his question – more specifically, to the name Peter Caruso. There'd been a subtle flick of her eye and then there was that something else, what was it? - a slight jerk of her shoulders – one up and one down as if she was in a car bracing for an abrupt change of direction. The reaction seemed familiar to him. He'd seen it before; but when? The answer eluded him until much later that night as he lay in bed waiting for sleep to come. His eyes were closed and, as if in a dream, he recounted more vividly that day in the gym years ago when he'd first learned about Patty.

He remembered standing there along with the rest of the student body. Peter, who was a few inches taller, stood in front of him so when the principal walked slowly to the microphone Nate had to shift his position to see. Then came the announcement that Patty Harris was dead and even as he had absorbed the terrible news himself, Nate remembered Peter turning back, away from the stage, his face agitated. The image was as clear to Nate as if he was looking at him here and now. He saw Peter's eye twitch and he saw a sudden shift of his shoulders. It may not have been the same reaction he'd seen tonight from Sarah Crawford, but it was close.

CHAPTER 13

The next morning Nate slid out of bed and wiped his hands across his face. Outside, rain was falling. The wind rattled the window in blowing gusts. It was a good day to stay inside. His mother would have said it was a good day for a hot bowl of her stormy-day bean soup. He had, several times, made the soup himself and remembered the rich homey smell that had filled the apartment. He wondered if he had any bay leaves. The sounds of a truck revving through its lower gears out on Vanderbilt Avenue carried over the storm.

Nate shook his head trying to clear his thoughts. Had he dreamt it? Had his mind conjured up a connection between Sarah Crawford and the Peter Caruso of fifteen years ago? And even if there was a similarity in their mannerisms, so what? It didn't mean there was any meaningful connection at all.

But he couldn't shake the image of Peter's expression in the gym. Was that the look of a killer whose victim had just been discovered? Had Peter really killed Patty Harris? His life for a life note said he did; the stains on his knife said he did. Then he remembered the knife was still in his glove box. Cat was right, he should turn it into the police. Even if it meant some tough times ahead for Mr. O'Neal, he'd get over it and maybe the whole tragic case would be closed the right way as it should have been years ago.

He showered and thought of Cat. He'd been proud of her last night and the way she held her own with Meredith. And then there was the cab ride to her apartment. He could still feel her hand and smell her perfume as she cuddled with him in the back of the cab.

She was sweet, sexy, fun and smart all rolled into an energetic, surprise-filled package.

Nate was in his bedroom getting dressed when he heard a knock at the door. He zipped up his cut-offs and pulled on a T-shirt then saw that a red envelope had been slipped under his door. He knew immediately what it was; his rent was past due. The last auto-withdrawal must have been rejected - insufficient funds. The color of the envelope indicated that this was his second warning. One more and he'd be out on the street. He picked it up and threw it on the coffee table. Any thoughts about Peter and Sarah, Cat and the bay leaves would have to wait. He had something much more basic to worry about - money.

Teddy was right, he didn't know how to sell himself and he had missed a chance last night to land Sarah Crawford as a high-profile client. Why hadn't he just offered to paint her portrait? After seeing the way she owned the crowd last night, he knew she had a brilliant future and he knew he could capture her vitality and charisma in a way that a photograph never could. It couldn't hurt to have the portrait of the next governor of the state of New York in his portfolio. Then he thought about the local galleries where he had paintings on consignment. He hadn't had a sale in months and he imagined his art languishing in their back rooms, unseen and gathering dust. Now *that* was something he could do something about right now.

He spooned down a bowl of corn flakes then changed into a dress shirt and pants. He put on his coat and hat and grabbed his umbrella.

Nate's first stop was a twenty minute walk and he kept his umbrella angled against the rain the whole time. Approaching the Brady Gallery, he saw five paintings in the display window, none of them his. He closed the umbrella and stepped inside, stomping off the rain, hooking his umbrella over a railing.

Chamber music played in the background. There was no one behind the granite-topped counter on which a ring-for-service bell sat. Nate ran his fingers through his wet hair and looked around. From where he stood, two walls no more than ten feet apart ran forty feet to the back of the gallery. Paintings, poorly lit from above by track mounted halogens, covered every square foot of each wall. A banner on the back wall announced that Brady also offered custom framing and restorations. As far as he could tell, there was no one in the store. He did a quick tour of the place and spotted his works near the back, a good two feet below eye-level.

They were both medium sized paintings. One depicted a

pastoral scene with an old farm house and tall barn with fields of corn stretching into the distance behind. On the porch of the farmhouse an old man sat in a rocker, eyes heavy as if he was falling asleep. High above the farm a bird soared with wings extended against a clear blue sky.

The other painting, the same size, showed another pastoral scene from high above, the fields trailing into the distance. An astute observer would have recognized that it was the same farm as in the other painting seen this time from the bird's perspective and that there, on the lawn of the farmhouse, a young girl sat cross legged, shading her eyes against the sun, watching the old man on the porch. Nate remembered his own family farm and Andrew Wyeth's *Christina's World* as having been his inspiration for this pair of paintings.

"Can I help you sir?"

Nate jumped and turned to see a short, mid-twenties man dressed in a navy-blue suit, shiny from wear at the shoulders. Below the man's roundish face, a yellow-checked tie hung loose. "Where's Mr. Brady?" asked Nate.

"He's out of town. I'm Tom, Is there something...?"

Nate told him who he was and why he was there.

"Your paintings are very nice but things are slow these days – except for frames, that is. We do well with frames. I have nothing to do with the consignment side of things or with how the paintings are displayed. I just handle sales." He then added, "I do framing too."

"You have a background in art, do you?"

"Two courses in art-history," said Tom.

"Good for you," said Nate. He could feel his face reddening. No wonder his paintings haven't sold. "I've decided to pull my paintings from your gallery. By the terms of my contract, I'll be back for them in thirty days. Please inform Mr. Brady."

"Of course, Mr. Parks, I'll let him know. Like I said, things have been a little slow. We're hoping that things pick up when the weather turns warmer."

"I hope you're right." Nate left and spent the rest of the day getting much the same story from four other galleries. He decided to pull all his paintings. He decided that Teddy was right. It was time for an all-out, first rate, Nathan Lido Parks exhibit.

At the studio, he had eight completed paintings and three more in the works. For a major exhibit he would need maybe ten more which would take him at least three months. That would put the exhibit sometime in July. What would he do for money in the meantime? For one thing he'd reduce expenses. He'd close the studio and work in his apartment. His neighbors and his landlord wouldn't like the paint smell but they could put up with it for three months. He hoped Teddy had been serious about his sponsorship offer.

It was six by the time he walked up the hill on Vanderbilt then turned down his street to his building. The wind had subsided and the rain had stopped but he still felt the moisture and chill from earlier in the day. Bean soup would have been good right now – he ought to get one of those crock-pots. He wondered what Cat was doing for dinner. Once up in his apartment, he called her but there was no answer. He left a message then texted her to call him. He ended up that night with a bowl of pasta and a vegetable marinara which he gobbled up quickly while sketching out an idea for a new painting. At nine he called Cat again. He was excited about his decision to go ahead with the exhibit and he was excited to tell her. Again, there was no answer. He left another message.

Nate didn't hear from her for three days and he was starting to worry. He'd been working to finish up the baker painting and as much of the rest of his in-process work as he could before moving back into his apartment. He was at the studio when she finally called. She got right to the point.

"Meredith told me about you and her."

Nate was stunned. In the awkward silence he couldn't think of a thing to say.

Cat went on, "So while I was tracking her, she was cheating on her husband with you while you were coming on to me. And you knew I was tracking her. Is that about it?"

Nate's head spiraled. "I didn't plan it that way, Cat. I'm not like that. Really I'm not. And I didn't know it was Meredith you were following. I mean, I suspected maybe it was but I wasn't sure until the other night."

"I'm not blaming you Nate. She's a beautiful woman. What man wouldn't fall for her? But you're supposed to be Teddy's friend – right? What kind of man does something like that to his friend?"

"I only met Teddy a few months back. He's more of an acquaintance than a friend. Besides, he and Meredith are back together again and my thing with her is over."

"Not according to Meredith."

"It's over as far as I'm concerned."

"So if she were to knock on your door right about now you'd just tell her to leave?"

Nate swallowed. "Yes, I would."

"Look out your window, Nate."

What was she up to? Nate hurried over to the window and pulled the curtains aside. There was Cat across the street, leaning against a light pole. She waved and gave him a put-up smile. He jumped at the knock on the door.

"Tell her I said hi," said Cat, ending the call.

Could it really be Meredith at the door? Was Cat still tailing her?

He opened the door slowly.

"Delivery for Mr. Parks?" said a uniformed UPS guy. He held out a small arrangement of flowers in a glass vase.

Nate took a breath. "Yes, that's me." He signed for the flowers and closed the door. From between the blooms he pulled out a card. It read:

Sorry – Cat.

He jumped again at another knock. Now what? He put the flowers down and opened the door a crack. Cat pushed it opened the rest of the way, then slammed it closed behind her. She wasn't smiling.

"Did I scare you? You thought the flower guy was Meredith coming up, right? Maybe you're disappointed?"

"You had me going, but no, I'm not disappointed." He stepped closer and put a hand on both her shoulders but she shook him off.

"I liked you Nate. Why'd you have to go and be such a sneak?" She straightened her hair. "I hate sneaks."

"What are the flowers for?"

"I was feeling bad about the cab ride the other night – leading you on. I was drunk."

"The card said you're sorry. You don't look sorry."

"I'm not. I ordered the flowers yesterday before I really thought about what might be going on between you and Meredith. It was a moment of weakness. I don't have many of those. If I'd known the truth, I would have written something else."

"Meredith didn't tell you a thing, did she?"

"Nope, I figured it out myself, and you filled in the blanks."

"It really is over between her and I."

"Just can't get past the lesbian thing huh? Not very open minded of you Nate. I'd have expected lots more from a liberal Democrat."

"It's you I can't get past, Cat." He really wanted to get off the subject of Meredith. “I bought some coffee, would you like some? I know you don’t care for chai. It’ll only take a few minutes. Or are you on another case, tracking some poor schlep?”

“Now you’re making fun of me.”

Nate reached for her shoulders again. She didn’t resist this time but her face held an expression of stony resolve. “Meredith and I are done, Cat, and I’m glad you found out about it. I didn’t like keeping it from you. I’m not a sneak.” He looked into her eyes and he could tell that she was trying to believe him.

She pulled away, gently. “Coffee, chai, either would be good – anything warm. It was pretty cold out there waiting for the UPS guy to show up.”

Nate made coffee as Cat took off her coat and looked around. The whole time, neither of them said a word. He poured then mixed in some milk and handed it to her. She accepted it then put it down right away.

“Oh, Nate, I so wanted you to be a good guy.”

“I am a good guy, Cat, but I’m not perfect – nobody is.”

She looked away for a moment. Nate could tell she was struggling to hold back tears. Finally she picked up her cup and took a sip. She walked over to his still unfinished baker painting.

“It’ll be finished in a few days,” he said. “In fact, this studio will be finished in a few days.” He told her about his need to cut back and about his plans for the exhibit.

“An exhibit’s a good idea,” she said quietly. “When will it be?”

“Sometime this summer – July maybe. It’ll be a lot of work putting together enough paintings and lining up sponsors.”

“Teddy’ll be one – as long as he doesn’t find out about you and Meredith. Don’t worry, I won’t tell him. Do you have any others lined up?”

“Not yet. I figure I’ll need about twenty-thousand dollars to do it right.”

Cat shrugged. “That should be easy for a talented guy like you. You can raise a lot of money on line for a good cause you know.”

“Do you think I’m a good cause?”

She took a couple more swallows then put her cup down. Her hands were shaking. “Give me a week Nate. I’ll let you know then.” She picked up her coat.

“Do you have to go?”

“No, but you have to get back to work and, like I said, I need some time to think. There’s also the Peter thing. I told Livingston that there might be a missing painting – they want it as part of the deal. And you really have to do something about Peter’s knife. Still in your car, right? You have to turn it in."

"Yes, it's still in my car. But I can't take the time to go back to Maysville. And we have no idea where the painting is."

"Well, maybe it's time I gave Crawford a call to see what she really knows about the painting. You said she reacted oddly to Peter's name. It's a pretty slim lead but it's all we've got. As far as the knife goes, you can turn it in here, to the NYPD." She rummaged through her purse and pulled out a card. "I know a guy at the Seventy-Third Precinct in Brownsville – he's got the Caruso case." She handed the card to Nate. "Give him a call, drop off the knife and he'll take it from there. Tell Mooch, Cat says hi."

Then she left.

CHAPTER 14

Nate spent the next four days in non-stop work, wrapping things up in his studio. He completed the Baker painting and one smaller work. Moving out of the studio wouldn't take long, maybe three or four carloads which he could do over a weekend. He was relieved that he hadn't heard from Meredith over this time but if she'd called or even if she'd have come over he would have just told her that it was over between them and that would be that. And, if she didn't call, well that would be even better. But what would he do if Cat didn't call? What if she couldn't get past his affair with Meredith? Well, he would just have to find a way to win her back – but how? He needed time to sort things out. He decided it would be a good time to get some air and pay a visit to the NYPD in Brownsville. He called and set up an appointment for the next day.

On arriving at the Seventy-Third Precinct on East New York Avenue, Nate was kept waiting for twenty minutes before being escorted to the detective's desk for his ten AM meeting. It was ten-ten.

Detective Moochakouski was a big man, middle-aged, rumpled black hair, black mustache, and bushy black eyebrows that edged over the top of his black-framed glasses. He wore a white shirt and a narrow sixties-style black tie.

Nate waited for him to look up from his computer screen and, when he didn't, he decided to take the initiative. "Detective Moochakouski? I'm Nate Parks." He stood beside the detective's desk on which was a fold-out family picture poised to topple over the back edge – two sons, happy looking wife. "I'm a friend of Cat's."

Mooch pecked out a few more strokes, then sat back in his chair. "You're early Parks." He took a swallow from his coffee cup, made a face and put the cup back down.

"I'm late actually," said Nate.

From his chair Mooch eyed him up and down then looked at the clock. He reached over and cleared some papers from his side-chair. "Sit. How do you know Cat?"

Nate sat. "She and I are friends. I worked with her to authenticate some of Peter Caruso's art."

"And now you're here about the Caruso murder, and about this." He held up a plastic baggie. Inside it Nate could see Peter's knife which he'd turned over to security when he'd entered the building. There was a custody log imprinted on the surface of the baggie which contained two signatures. The second of these was Detective Moochakouski's. "This is a knife," continued Mooch. "Caruso was shot. Or weren't you aware of this fact?"

"No, I was aware of that - from the news reports. The knife is from Peter's old house near Scranton."

"And what does it have to do with Caruso's murder?"

"Nothing, directly, but it may have been used in a murder fifteen years ago."

Mooch's eyebrows went up. "There's a second murder? I thought you were here to help."

"A girl named Patty Harris was killed fifteen years ago. She was a classmate of mine and Peter's. This knife may have been the murder weapon."

"You're saying Caruso killed a girl fifteen years ago?"

"I don't know for sure that he killed her but it looks that way. Before his murder, Peter sent Patty's uncle, her only living relative so far as I know, a package along with a note. It said: *A life for a life.*"

Mooch looked unimpressed. "And what was in the package?"

"It was a crate really," said Nate. "From its size and shape, I think it was a painting. It would have been Peter's last painting: *Death of the Artist.*"

Mooch punched a few keys on his computer then turned the screen so Nate could see. "Do you think the painting might look anything like this?"

Nate wasn't prepared for what he saw. His body stiffened and his mouth went dry. He forced himself to lean closer to the image of the police photo of the Caruso crime scene. There was Peter, lying on a bare wooden floor with both legs and one arm splayed out, the other hand clutched his chest like he was trying to stop the blood that was flowing around his fingers. His eyes were closed but his face with a passive expression - neither fear or pain or hate - was turned as if he'd been staring at something or someone as he died.

Nate swallowed and looked at the detective. He could tell he'd been watching his reaction to the photograph. Nate looked back at the screen. "The painting may look like that, I don't know."

"So you think Peter knew he was going to die?"

"The name he gave to his last painting, *Death of the Artist*, was in his sketchbook. I know it sounds far-fetched but..."

"It sounds nuts. *You* sound nuts." Mooch sighed then moved his computer screen back into position. He folded his arms. "Where's the crate now?"

"I don't know. O'Neal sold it to someone. He never opened it." Nate sensed that it was time to cut his losses with this Mooch guy.

Mooch reached for a notepad and picked up a pen. "This uncle of the girl who got killed, I'll need his name and address."

"He's David O'Neal. I don't know his address but he lives in Maysville just outside of Scranton. He's probably the only David O'Neal there."

Mooch wrote that down. "Okay, we'll find him. Now, just to sum things up: Peter Caruso was a boyhood friend of yours who may have killed a girl back in high school. I know that you and he graduated together, you went to college together, and you both became artists. Then Peter gets murdered but before his murder he paints a portrait of his death and sends it to the uncle of the murdered girl with the note: *A life for a life*." Mooch scratched his head then picked up the plastic bag with the knife. "How do you know this is Peter's knife?"

"I found it in his room in his house down in Maysville. I knew the place where he hid things."

"Was anyone with you when you found it?"

"No."

"Was there anything else in this hiding place of his?"

"No."

"When you found the knife, did you handle it at all?"

"I was careful not to touch it but I did open the blade – there are brown stains on it."

"Could be from chocolate brownies."

"I think it's blood. It could be Patty's blood."

Mooch put the knife down. "Are you aware, Mr. Parks, that

you were a suspect at one time in Peter's murder?"

Nate shifted in his chair and crossed his legs. "Yes, Cat told me."

"You were one of the few people who knew him."

"We grew up together."

"You went to his funeral."

"Yes, I did," said Nate. "So did a lot of other people."

"Not a lot," said Mooch. "We had a guy checking it out."

"Was it a police woman? I saw her there, in the back of the church."

Mooch shrugged. "We thought she'd blend in better than a guy. She said she didn't see anything suspicious – except for you."

Nate blinked. "A murderer wouldn't go to his victim's funeral."

"You'd be surprised what people do," said Mooch folding his arms. "You were both artists - rivals."

"I never competed with Peter Caruso."

Mooch stared at him for a moment. "It turns out Peter was killed about the same time you were teaching your class at the college. We checked your class schedule."

"Yes, I teach at Manhattan College twice each week," said Nate. He hadn't realized that the murder had been on a class night. That meant he was in the clear, didn't it? He started to feel a little better.

"Yeah, there. Looks like a good alibi."

"I just came here to turn in the knife."

"Why didn't you give it to the cops down in Scranton?"

"I promised O'Neal that I wouldn't tell anyone about the possibility that Peter killed Patty. It happened so long ago and with Peter dead, what good would come of it? He didn't want Patty's name to be dragged through the mud. Everyone there thinks it was just an accidental drowning."

"Do you think Peter was killed as revenge for the Harris girl?"

"Could be I suppose, but I don't think anyone suspected him of killing her."

"The girl's uncle did. *You did.*"

Nate swallowed. He hadn't expected this to turn into an interrogation. "O'Neal didn't get Peter's note until after Peter was already dead. And he doesn't know anything about the knife. I'm turning it in as evidence that's all." His foot started tapping.

"Just being a good citizen."

"Yes." Nate stood to go. "Is there anything more?"

Mooch took another swallow of coffee. "Except for you, we

have no suspects and no leads in the Caruso case. Whoever did it was smart enough to wipe down anything he might have touched. He collected the shell casings and, if there had been a struggle, he took the time to straighten things up. We have no witnesses. The neighbors and the landlord who lives just up the hall had to have heard something but they've all clammed up. The only thing we do know is that there was no forced entry. That tells us that Peter Caruso knew his killer and since he was a hermit kind of guy, the field of possible suspects is pretty limited." Again he stared up at Nate through his thick glasses. He leaned back in his chair. "He knew you and you knew him. That's why you're still in the mix."

"I thought you said I was no longer a suspect. I was teaching a class at the time of the murder." Nate had had enough of this over-fed desk-jockey who liked playing games: first he was a suspect, then he wasn't, then maybe he was.

"Yeah, well sometimes the lab guys get things wrong. Time of death can be hard to pin down. Anyway, we'll be in touch if we need anything else. I have you at..." He hit the keyboard again and read off Nate's address. "Is that right?"

It was.

When Nate finally left the building, his head was spinning. He stood on the sidewalk for a moment not quite believing that he really was a suspect in a murder investigation. How in the world could that be? He thought about the detective's bushy-browed eyes, staring him down as if he'd do anything for a break in the case. Nate felt good to be rid of Peter's knife but he wasn't so sure it had been a good idea to turn it over to this particular detective. He started walking then called Cat and told her about the interrogation.

"Yeah, I guess I should have warned you about Mooch. He can be a real prick and he's getting a lot of pressure on the Caruso case. It makes sense him asking you some tough questions. He's just doing his job."

"Cat, I felt like I should have had a lawyer with me. This buddy of yours came after me like a bulldog."

"Oh, come on now. You'll get over it. It was the right thing for him to do and now it's over. You can get back to your painting."

"I told him about the missing painting."

"Why'd you do that?"

"I don't know, it just came up. He wanted to know where it was."

"Did you tell him about Sarah Crawford?"

"No."

"Good. I called her office yesterday but couldn't reach anyone."

"When can I see you, Cat?"

"This has really got you rattled hasn't it?"

"I've never been a suspect in a murder investigation. Of course I'm rattled."

"What are you up to this week end?"

"I was planning to move out of my studio. I need to save the money. I'll be painting in my apartment from now on." There was silence on Cat's end of the line. He waited.

"I suppose you could use some help...with the move."

"Are you offering?"

"All right, I guess I am. But I won't be getting serious about you again for a while, maybe not ever." She ended the call.

Well, at least she hadn't given up on him entirely. Nate took a cab back to his studio where there was a missed call on his landline. The "return call" prompt was flashing. Whoever it was hadn't left a message. He was about to hit the erase button figuring it was just a telemarketer when he saw the 518 area code - Albany. He wrote down the number on the back of a business card then erased it from the machine. At the studio on Saturday morning he showed it to Cat.

"It's not the number I have for Sarah Crawford if that's what you're thinking," she said in a flat tone. She was dressed in jeans and a sweatshirt, ready to help with the move.

"I don't know anyone in Albany."

"You should call it." She handed the card back to Nate then looked around the cluttered room. "I thought you said you were ready to move. You need more boxes and you should have some more help – it's just you and me?"

Nate looked at his watch. "I have a friend, he should be here anytime. It's just a few blocks – three car loads, tops."

"More like five."

Eduardo showed up thirty minutes later as they were taking down the first load. "What's this? You started without me?" He glanced at Cat, who was carrying a large box out the door. "And you must be Mer..."

"This is Cat," said Nate quickly. "Cat; Eduardo."

"A pleasure my dear," said Eduardo, "may I take that from you?" He grabbed the box from her and struggled with it down the stairs.

"Thanks," said Cat with an unsmiling glance at Nate. "Even your friends have a hard time keeping up with your love-life." She went back for another box.

They continued working, loading, driving, unloading, driving then loading again. The bulkiest of the furniture they strapped precariously to the roof of Nate's car. It took six loads in all. By two o'clock, they were done and were sharing beer and pizza in Nate's apartment.

"You should have gotten anchovies," said Eduardo picking at his pizza, holding up a slice of an objectionable topping. "What is this?"

"Pepperoni," said Nate. "You don't like pepperoni?"

"There should never be meat on pizza. What do you think Cat?"

"I like it, the cheese is a little gummy though." She licked the tip of her finger looking at Nate. There was nothing sexual in her expression.

"All right, next time I move I'll take your orders in advance."

"Beer's good though," said Cat.

"Yes, the beer is good," confirmed Eduardo who clinked his longneck with Cat's.

They took swigs in sync, then, from her spot on the brown couch, Cat looked around. "This may not have been a good idea Nate. You've got a regular Salvation Army store here. Where are you going to work?"

"I don't need much space, and I'll be saving five-hundred a month."

"So, that's only fifteen hundred by the time your exhibit rolls around. It'll pay for the wine – maybe. You've got two of everything here. You should have sold some of it."

"You're having an exhibit?" asked Eduardo, "An art exhibit?"

"July," said Cat, "big event, mucho dinero."

"How exciting, you must tell me how I can help."

"I only just decided," said Nate. He was about to go on when the phone beside him rang. He checked the caller ID – no name but it was an Albany area code. He glanced at Cat and, after the third ring, picked up.

"Are you Nathan Parks, the artist?" It was a female voice.

"Yes, this is Nathan Parks. Who is this?"

"I'm Colleen Logan, Mr. Parks. You and I met after the New York fundraiser for Sarah Crawford. I'm her campaign manager."

"Yes, I remember. If you're looking for additional contributions I'm afraid I can't help you."

"No, no, nothing like that. The Lieutenant Governor would like to meet with you Mr. Parks. I'm just calling to make the arrangements."

Nate glanced at Cat as he spoke into the phone. "Why would she want to meet with me?"

"I believe she may be interested in commissioning a portrait – something for the campaign, you know, something dynamic."

"I don't do billboards, Ms. Logan." Nate bit his tongue – that was a stupid thing to say. Well, he couldn't take it back. There was silence at the other end for a moment like she'd covered up the speaker at her end. He could hear a side-bar going then Logan came back on. "I'm sure the concept would be artistic and tasteful. You would have complete say over the actual work, of course. Besides, I'm just arranging the meeting right now. You'll be able to discuss the details directly with her."

Nate covered up the speaker on his phone. "Sarah Crawford wants to meet with me," he said to Cat.

"That's good, tell her I said hi."

"You'll need to come alone, Mr. Parks," said Logan. "And this meeting will be off the record - strictly confidential. Is that agreeable?"

Nate said it was. They worked out the logistics which Nate wrote down, then he hung up.

Eduardo's eyes were bugging out. "You have a meeting with Sarah Crawford? I love that woman. Powerful and dynamic, but in a sensual way, she..."

"You can't tell anyone – either of you. They want it kept secret and they want me there alone."

"We've got her spooked about Peter," said Cat.

"Who's Peter?" asked Eduardo. "You mean Peter Caruso, the dead artist? The guy whose exhibit I got you an invitation to?"

"She just wants a portrait," said Nate.

Cat shook her head. "She wants to know how much you know about Peter's last painting. She's got it Nate, I know she does."

"Well, that may be, but right now I'll just be happy to get a commission out of it. I'll ask her about it though."

"When's the meeting?" Cat grabbed the last slice of pizza, corralling with it a long thread of cheese that was stuck to the bottom of the cardboard box.

"Day after tomorrow," said Nate sliding back into his chair. Then he looked around the room at the mess of boxes and furniture. He could hardly see the floor. Cat was right; abandoning the studio may not have been such a bright idea.

CHAPTER 15

On Monday, Nate got up early, found the quickie version of his portfolio and was on the road by seven but there was no beating the heavy morning traffic. His meeting with Sarah Crawford had been set up for eight at the airport in Linden which he learned she often used when she wanted to avoid publicity. Logan had told him there would be someone to meet him in the private charter area.

He parked short-term, grabbed his portfolio and hustled into the terminal where he saw a big guy in a black overcoat holding a sign that said: *Parks*.

"I'm Parks."

"You're late," said the man, hatless, with a trim, military style haircut. "Follow me." He strode off, ditched his sign and turned down a long corridor and didn't bother looking back to see if Nate was keeping up.

Nate felt a little like he was going under-cover, like he was in some kind of a low budget spy movie. They passed gray metal doors with labels on them: maintenance, security, janitorial then things got a little more up-scale. The man stopped and opened the next door, this one paneled wood - Conference Room 3. He waived Nate inside then shut the door without going inside himself.

The only person in the room was Sarah Crawford. Again, Nate thought she looked small and very young – a college freshman – sophomore tops. The room was well lit with a single table stretching its length – nothing fancy. She sat on the opposite side of the table dressed in a brown pant suit, her fingers bouncing away at her tablet. A slim black briefcase lay flat beside her. She ignored him for five seconds then put the tablet aside and stood up. She extended her hand. “Mr. Parks, good to see you again.”

Bright green eyes and a fearless stare were his first impressions which seemed inconsistent with her limp handshake. “Sorry to be late, Ms. Crawford – traffic.” He struggled to keep his eyes on hers, to keep them from shifting down to her bulging stomach. He blinked then they both sat down.

“Do you know why you’re here, Mr. Parks?”

“Colleen Logan said you might want a portrait. I brought my portfolio.” It lay in front of him. He double-tapped it with his hand.

“Yes, that’s what I told her to tell you and we may have a word or two about that one day. Is there any other topic we should discuss?”

“Peter Caruso?”

She was obviously the one at the wheel of this conversation. If this had been a courtroom he would have expected her to take a few steps now toward the jury and maybe shoot a knowing glance at the judge. He tried to remember from her website if she’d had a background in criminal law. Well, she was the Lieutenant Governor and she had a JD. If she hadn’t been a practicing attorney herself, she was probably the next thing to it. Her green eyes continued to stare. Had she even blinked since their handshake?

“That’s right, you asked about him the other night and my office received a couple of calls since about him from someone else. Do you know a Catherine Chaplin?”

“Yes, she was involved in the sale of Peter’s collection to the Livingston Gallery.”

“As were you?”

“Yes, but only minimally.”

“Why did you ask me about him?”

Nate could think of no reason to lie. “One of Peter’s paintings is missing – one that wasn’t shown at the exhibit. It’s his last painting Ms. Crawford, and I have reasons to think that you may know something about it.”

“I don’t.”

“But you don’t deny knowing Peter.”

Crawford sat back in her chair and turned her gaze to the wall which was a relief to Nate. He felt as if a bright light shining right at him had just been redirected.

“Peter Caruso was a genius, Mr. Parks. I’m sure you can appreciate that better than anyone. You grew up with him, you went to school with him; you tried to emulate him." She turned to face him again, her gaze more intense than ever.

"I never tried to emulate him."

"Oh really? You should look a little more closely at your work and his. In particular, compare your quite good *Lady in White* with his soaring *Woman in Winter*. His was from the Columbia exhibit and pre-dates yours by two years. They're very similar don't you think? Even the titles suggest it."

Nate felt his blood pressure rise a notch. "At that time I was still working to find my own style."

"After Columbia, Peter Caruso became reclusive. For five years nobody heard from him – no exhibits, no commissions that I know of - nothing. Why was that, Mr. Parks? As someone who knew him best, why do you suppose he'd go underground like that?"

"I don't know. I had no contact with him after Columbia."

"Apparently no one did, until his death. And now the question is: Who killed him? At the time of his murder no one really knew him or much remembered him – oh, but you would have, wouldn't you? Tell me, after seeing Peter's works in all their glory at his second exhibit, what did you think?"

"I was impressed. His paintings are remarkable."

"You felt intimidated, didn't you? Peter always intimidated you."

"That's not true. I was Peter's friend and if he were alive today I would still be his friend."

"You're lying. You haven't been his friend since the day you threatened to kill him."

Nate felt the blood drain from his face. "How do you know about that?"

Sarah Crawford smiled ever so slightly. She pushed her chair back from the table but remained seated. "The police have no idea who killed Peter Caruso and right now they have no clues to go on. They were considering you a suspect at one time but then they learned you were teaching your class at the time of the murder – a good alibi but one the police might find a little flimsy if they looked closer. And I don't believe they know about the threat yet. You told Peter you were going to shoot him, isn't that right?"

"You're being ridiculous," Nate fired back, rising from his chair. "I didn't kill Peter and you know it. I don't even own a gun and I didn't come here today to be intimidated by you."

"Take your seat Mr. Parks. Maybe you killed Peter Caruso, maybe you didn't. All I want is to be left alone. Do you think you can help me out with that?" Her eyes were calm now, as if a dimmer switch had just been throttled back. Now she was just having a friendly conversation.

"You're blackmailing me. But I've got nothing to hide – nothing." He sat back down.

"You've got your threat against Peter to hide; that's something. You've got your shaky alibi to hide; that's another. But I can see that you're not too experienced in these matters. The things I mentioned so far have nothing to do with blackmail." She snapped open her briefcase and pulled out a folder. She slid it over to Nate. "This, Mr. Parks, is blackmail."

Nate opened the folder and was shocked by what he saw. It was filled with photographs of him and Meredith, most of them taken in the dining room at the Hilton. There was a three by five card with *Room 508* scrawled across it. There was even an itemized copy of the hotel bill.

"Teddy Sinclair is a good friend of mine, Mr. Parks. He's very generous and he's very influential. He will continue to be a good sponsor for you or he could be your worst enemy. I'd hate to see all this end up in the wrong hands – wouldn't you?"

Nate went numb.

"Just something to think about," she said pleasantly, grabbing the folder, putting it and her tablet back into the brief case. "Sorry to leave you so abruptly but I've got a plane to catch. I have quite a busy schedule these days. Good-bye, Mr. Parks." She stood up and walked out, letting the door close softly behind her.

Nate remained motionless, listening to the squeak of her tennis shoes fade down the hall. He wasn't sure what had just happened but he knew it wasn't good. Then he realized that all he had to do was to leave Sarah Crawford alone and he would be all right. There was really no problem. He would go on with his plans for the exhibit and Sarah Crawford could go to hell for all he cared. And so could Peter's last painting.

He got to his feet and picked up his portfolio. In the restroom down the hall he splashed cold water on his face, which he dried with a wad of abrasive brown paper towels. He hit the drinking fountain then walked back out into the terminal where a few morning commuters were milling about.

The freeway got him back to his place in half the time of the outbound trip. He closed his apartment door and with his foot, shoved aside a few boxes. He had to close his eyes if only for a few minutes. He plopped down on the brown couch and was just starting to doze when Cat called.

"So, how'd it go? Did she know about the last painting? Are you going to paint her portrait or did you screw it up and say something snotty like 'I don't do billboards'?"

Nate hesitated.

"Nate?"

"Yes, everything's just fine. There's no problem. She just wants us to leave her alone."

"Was she mad?"

"Well, she wasn't very friendly. Cat, I'm sorry, I can't talk about it right now. Maybe tonight. Can you come over? I'll get some Chinese."

"Nate, I'm not really..."

"It'll be just business. You have to get the painting back for Livingston. We'll keep it strictly business."

There was silence at Cat's end, then: "I'll be there at six."

"Six is good, thanks Cat."

He ended the call and laid back, letting his mind clear. He must have slept because it was mid-afternoon when he looked at the clock. He broke off a banana for lunch then started tidying the place up a little. At five-thirty he walked down to the corner and picked up dinner. When he got back, Cat was at his door.

She smiled tentatively as they went in. "Food smells good." They ate side by side on the brown couch and he told her about his meeting with Sarah Crawford, leaving out the part about her photos of him and Meredith.

"What a bitch," said Cat, chop-sticking expertly over her white cardboard carton. "And she claimed not to know anything about the missing painting?"

"Right."

"Do you believe her? She sure seemed well informed on everything else. Did she look surprised when you told her about it?"

"She's got a real poker face. I don't think anything surprises her." Nate took a sip from his Diet Coke.

"So what do I tell Livingston about the missing painting?"

"Tell them you're still looking for it. It's the truth. But leave Sarah Crawford alone for now. She's out to screw me Cat. She'll tell the cops about my class being cancelled on the night of the murder – I remember that now – they called it off because of the snow. Cat, this could get serious."

"But you didn't kill him. Besides, the police will find out about your class being cancelled anyway. That wouldn't be enough for them to bring you up on charges."

"She also knows about my threat."

"Oh." Cat took another mouthful and chewed thoughtfully. "Can you patch up your alibi? Was there anyone with you that night?"

"I was alone."

They ate in silence for a while. Then he told her: "She also has photos of me and Meredith. She's threatening to turn them over to Teddy. She can ruin me, Cat."

Cat finished the last of her food and dabbed her lips with her napkin. She spoke slowly. "Were the pictures that incriminating? What were you two doing in them Nate?"

"We were just having dinner."

"Must have been a very friendly dinner."

Nate put down his carton. "We were shacked up at the Hilton. Sarah Crawford has all the evidence of it including our bill and room number. It was something I did that I'd just as soon forget."

"Don't lie to me Nate. I've seen Meredith. How could any man say he'd want to forget her?"

"You still aren't past this are you?"

"That was the night before we went to Peter's apartment wasn't it? You were with her that morning. That's why you asked me about my rich-bitch in the cab. You were worried that I was onto her and onto you." She stood up and started putting on her coat. "No, I'm not past it. I'm not even on my way to getting past it."

"Cat, I just have to work this out." He stood up. He didn't want her to go, not like this. "There's nothing between Meredith and I now. Don't you believe me?"

Cat finished buttoning her coat. "Oh, Nate, I guess I believe you, sort of. I just don't like being played. Can't you understand that?"

He met her eyes. They were brimming, tears about to fall but before that could happen, she turned away and walked out the door. "Good-bye, Nate."

Nate had his hand on the door knob ready to open it and race after her, but didn't. What more could he say? Almost robotically, he walked back to the couch and cleared away the drinks and the cartons tossing them into the trash under the sink. He noticed that it was beginning to smell. He'd have to dump it soon. He straightened and looked out the window.

Across the street he saw a man jogging. Further down, a man and woman walked hand in hand. He watched them until they turned the corner then he straightened and saw his own reflection, hair rumpled, a brown blotch on his sweatshirt, and his hands limp at his side. Here was the famous artist Nathan Lido Parks, a self-portrait in doubt and self-pity; eyes maybe not as crazed as Peter's but crazed in their own way. He thought about Tolstoy's first line in *Anna Karenina* and suspected it held for individuals as well as for families. He was unhappy in his own way, and his world was threatening to come apart because he had ceded control over it. Teddy, Meredith, Sarah Crawford, detective Moochakouski, Cat and maybe even Peter from the grave - they were the ones in control, not him.

He broke his gaze with his reflection and started to pace as much as the clutter would allow. He walked slowly at first, then more purposefully. Things were not going to get any better unless he himself made them better. It wasn't up to anyone else. It was all up to him. So what should he do?

He pondered that question then decided that Sarah Crawford posed the most immediate danger. She had to be his first priority. He got a pad of paper and sat down at his desk. He wrote down what he knew about her, then he wrote down what he didn't know. Three pages later he put down his pen. He had made some progress and he felt better. He took out the trash. Next priority: Cat Chaplin.

He slept well that night. In the morning, he got in his car and headed to the Bradshaw Detective Agency.

CHAPTER 16

As soon as Nate walked through the door, he saw her look up from behind her desk. Her jaw dropped, but she recovered fast. She stood up.

"What are you doing here?" she asked, walking quickly toward him, keeping her voice down.

"I want to talk with you - now. We could do it here, or you could have a late breakfast with me across the street – your choice."

There were two other people in the room. Cat looked back at them. "Chaplin out - early lunch," she yelled back. She jerked her coat off the rack and put it on, heading out the door with Nate following. They jaywalked to McDonalds where she ordered a large coffee then grabbed a seat in the corner. He joined her a moment later with a breakfast sandwich, a hash-brown patty and an orange juice.

"You're not hungry? Here have this." He slid the hash-browns to her side of the table. She ignored it and him.

He took a bite from his sandwich then pulled out his pad of notes. He read from it: "Sarah Crawford: What's her connection to Peter? Why is she blackmailing me? Does she have the missing painting? I have other questions about her but those are the main ones." He took another bite, then a swig of juice. "Well, Ms. Detective?"

Cat remained silent for a moment arms folded then took a sip of coffee. "She liked Peter and she likes his art."

"That's the connection?"

"She liked his art a lot, okay?" Her eyes met his. "What do you want from me Nate?"

"We'll get to that. Right now we're talking about Sarah Crawford."

Cat stared out the window. He waited. He could see she was thinking.

Nate decided to prompt her: "She went to his first exhibit at Columbia. She would have been just out of college herself. That's a long way for a Cornell girl to go just to look at art. How would she even know about Peter? He hadn't made a name for himself yet."

Cat shifted her eyes to the food tray. "Maybe she was in town for another reason. People come to New York for all kinds of things. Maybe she visited Columbia trying to get a job and just happens to come across Peter and his exhibit. The only thing we know is that she was there and took the time to sign the registry."

She picked up the hash-brown patty and took a couple of bites. "And five years later she attends the posthumous exhibit. There may have been some contact between them over that time. Maybe she eventually became his cherry-chocolate girlfriend but we have no way of finding anything out about that. We need to focus on something more recent."

"More recent, like what?"

"Like how did Crawford know about you and Peter? Why would she put a tail on you before your dinner with Meredith? That was well before her fundraiser when you first made contact with her."

"She must have known that I hadn't really been ruled out as a suspect in the murder. It wouldn't be difficult for the Lieutenant Governor to have well placed contacts with the police."

"So she was having you followed because you were a suspect? Why would she do that?" Cat reached for her coffee then suddenly stopped. "Oh my God."

"Oh my God, what?"

"She *does* know about the missing painting and she found out from us, Nate."

"What are you talking about?"

"The letters that I took from Peter's mailbox at his apartment, we opened them in the restaurant, remember? The guy who took the pictures of you and Meredith was still following you. He could have been at the next table over from us. A directional mike would have been all he'd need to pick up everything we said. Maybe Crawford didn't know about the painting at that point but she would have known that Peter had sent something to O'Neal. All she had to do was send someone down there to pick it up. Yes – I'll bet you twenty bucks, she's got the painting."

Nate was struck by the simplicity of it, then he looked around the inside of the McDonald's – it was half filled. He started checking faces but none looked familiar.

"Yeah, her guy could be here right now, still following you. Of course with his mike and with my big mouth, if he is here, he knows we're onto him. Man, I screwed this one up all over the place." She ate the last of the hash-browns and looked through the window toward Nate's car. She stood up. "Let's go for a ride."

They left the restaurant and piled into the car. "Where to?" he asked.

"Doesn't matter, just drive for now. And use your mirrors to see who's behind us. I don't think he'd be stupid enough to follow us now but, you never know."

They headed south.

"Okay, let's sort this out," said Cat. "Back to your original question: What's the connection between Sarah and Peter?"

"Obviously, they both like art."

"Maybe Sarah mostly liked Peter and his art was just part of the package. She really could have been his cherry-chocolate gal. "

"So Peter was sexually involved with the Lieutenant Governor of the State of New York?"

"Why not?"

Nate stopped for a light. "Peter wasn't the loving type – at least not the type that would attract a smart woman like Sarah Crawford. He loved his art. I think that was all he loved."

"Okay, put that on the back-burner for now. How about this; they're both brilliant, he in art, she in politics – crazy brilliant wouldn't you say?"

"And both young, just about the same age."

"Both grew up in rural settings, he on a farm outside of Scranton, she on a farm outside of Albany – said so on her website."

They drove in silence for a while. Nate thought back to his conversation with Crawford, the intensity in her eyes, the mechanical way she'd completely dismantled him. Peter had eyes like that and he had a kind of a herky-jerky, mechanical set of mannerisms, as if every movement had a thought process behind it – nothing quite natural. And then there was that funny twitch in her shoulders.

Cat pointed to the golden arches just ahead on the right. "Pull in here – the drive-through. All I had was that little hash-brown thing of yours. Want anything?

He didn't.

She got a quarter-pounder and wolfed it down over the next two miles with the rest of her coffee. She wiped her lips and checked herself out in the mirror behind her visor. "You're watching for a tail right?"

"Nobody's back there Cat," said Nate. They were in a run-down part of the city now, boarded up buildings, teens roving the streets in groups of five or six. "What if Peter's somehow related to Sarah Crawford?"

"Related how? Like blood related? I've only seen a couple of black and whites of Peter but from what I remember, he looks nothing at all like Sarah – both have high cheekbones maybe. I suppose it's possible. The Livingston casebook is still open so it's billable time. I'll check on Sarah's genealogy. Maybe she's got family in the Scranton area."

"Good, I'll see what I can find out about Peter's ancestry. Maybe they're cousins or something."

They drove for a while longer, then Cat looked at her watch. "I should be getting back. We should turn around."

Nate pulled onto a side street intending to go around the block and head back the way they came. There were three burned out houses on the left and the ruins of a tenement on the right.

"Not a good spot, Nate. I'd be quick about it."

From the porch of one of the houses two hulking high schoolers stared - one of them bouncing a basketball. Nate turned into the drive, gave them a wave and pulled back out. A quick right turn got them headed back into the city.

"I thought you private investigators were supposed to be rough and tough," said Nate.

"That's nothing to tease about Nate. I had a bad experience once. It's nothing to tease about."

"Back at Peter's building in Brownsville you didn't seem to have a problem."

"Just get me back to Bradshaw's." She sat stiff, eyes straight ahead.

"Sorry," said Nate. On the center console, he put his hand on hers, feeling her tremble. Quickly, she pulled her hand back and folded her arms. "Forget it."

Nate hesitated, wanting, yet not wanting to learn about Cat's raw nerve that had just been exposed. He sensed that if he'd been able to hold her in his arms at that moment, she might soften but he was driving and they were still on the bad side of town. Twenty minutes later, he pulled in front of Bradshaw's. He reached back and picked up his note-pad from the back seat. “Well, we didn’t answer many of my questions.”

Cat had her hand on the door but didn’t get out right away. “I wasn’t fair to you last night Nate, about the Meredith thing I mean. When you were shacked up with her you barely knew me. I had no right to make demands and I still don’t. You’re not married, you can do what you want about her and about me. Just let me know, that’s all I ask.”

Nate turned to her. “Are you seeing anyone else right now?”

“No.”

“Neither am I. There’s only you, Cat. This seems like a good place to start - fair enough?”

She got out of the car. “Okay Nate, fair enough.” She closed the door and walked into Bradshaw’s without looking back.

When he got back to his apartment, Nate hopped on the internet but soon learned that, while he could get all the info he wanted on his own genealogy, getting that info on others was much more difficult. He tried to remember if the Columbia file had birth records. It probably did but he’d need Peter’s father’s permission to look through it again. Then he thought about Dr. Wright’s file on Peter. There was probably a birth record in it somewhere: Date, place, full name of each parent and maybe more. It would be a start.

Nate spent another futile hour on the internet then called Dr. Wright’s office. She agreed to meet with him the next day after-hours which, for her, meant three.

He arrived on time and she saw him right away. She was at her desk; at her elbow was Peter’s file.

“So, Mr. Parks, what is it that has come up with Peter?”

“As one of the few people who knew Peter well, I’ve been asked to do an informal biography on him.” It was as good a cover story as he could concoct. He hoped she’d swallow it.

“Ah, I thought you might be here because of the page that’s missing from the sketchbook – or hadn’t you noticed?”

“Do you know something about that?”

“I know that Peter’s father sliced it out – he admitted he did, but didn’t say why.”

“His father?” Nate thought about that for a moment then decided to tell Dr. Wright what he knew about the missing page thinking that it might put her into a reciprocating mood. “There was residue in the sketchbook from that page. We had it checked out and found that only an empty frame had been drawn on the missing page. It was to be Peter’s last painting and evidently he had yet to compose it. But he did have a title: *Death of the Artist*."

Dr. Wright nodded. "Very appropriate. Mr. Caruso probably didn't want Columbia thinking his son was susceptible to fits of depression – as if that were his biggest problem." She leaned back in her chair and brought her finger-tips together. "But that's not why you're here. You want to do a bio on Peter - you're a writer as well as an artist?"

Nate knew she wasn't buying his story but he pressed on with it. "It'll only be a few pages long," he said, "and I'm sure they'll tweak the thing before publishing. It's to be part of a pamphlet on Peter that will accompany the future exhibits of his work." He was making things up as he went along but it sounded plausible to him.

"So this is for Livingston?"

Now this was a hard fact she was looking for. His answer would be easily confirmed or refuted by a call to Livingston. He decided to play it half-way. "I'll be offering it to them, yes."

She leaned forward again. "You knew him as a boy, Mr. Parks. When exactly did the two of you meet?"

"Fifth grade maybe - something like that."

"Did you know his parents?"

"Just his dad."

Dr. Wright rubbed her chin. "Officially, I can tell you nothing - not without Peter's father's permission. And you certainly cannot include anything of a confidential nature in your pamphlet without his permission." She put her hand on Peter's file. "I know of nothing in this folder that you couldn't find out about elsewhere if you looked hard enough. Maybe you'll find some of it useful."

She shoved the file closer to Nate and stood up. Nate stood too.

"I'll leave the room for ten minutes, Mr. Parks. When I come back, I want the file here, with nothing missing, nothing out of place, and everything exactly as it is now and I want you gone. You can consider this a one-time professional courtesy."

"I know I shouldn't ask this, Dr. Wright, but why are you helping me?"

She stared at him for a moment. "I'm a psychiatrist Mr. Parks. I'm tightly bound by ethics to honor the secrets of my patients." She placed her hand on the file. "What you'll find here, if you look hard enough, is the hint of a secret that goes back more than thirty years and it involves more than just Peter. In fact, it's a secret even he might not have been aware of. I don't know where it might lead you but I hope you'll find that hint, and I hope you'll know what to do with it." She left the room.

Nate had no time to question what Dr. Wright had just said. He checked the time and pulled out his phone, putting it in camera mode. The file was easily an inch thick. He opened it and hoped his batteries held out.

Quickly, he flipped through page after page sometimes snapping both sides. As he went, he skimmed what he could. There were health exam records. There were legal documents and boiler-plate disclaimers that he didn't bother copying. He was only at the halfway point when he came across an eight by ten black and white photograph, yellowed and creased with age. It was the picture of a naked baby lying inside a clear plastic incubator. It looked like a hospital photograph.

This had to be baby-Peter. Nate snapped it then noticed some writing on the back. There was the number sixty-eight followed by two words Nate didn't recognize – they weren't English. He photographed them and his phone warned him that he was down to ten percent. He flipped through more legal papers. No birth records yet. He glanced at the clock. It was going on twelve minutes since Dr. Wright left the room. She could be back any moment.

He ran through the rest of the papers, snapping what looked interesting then came across the last set of documents in the folder. They were forms from the US Department of Immigration and Naturalization. As Nate hurriedly photographed each of them, a single word on one of the forms caught his eye and he realized that this could be the hint to the secret Dr. Wright had mentioned.

There, in a box labeled Place of Birth, was typed the name of a clinic with an address in Bucharest, Romania.

CHAPTER 17

Nate didn't stop to think things through. He continued on and photographed the last document, finishing with his phone at five percent. Then he straightened the papers, closed the file and left Dr. Wright's office. He caught the subway, heading back to his apartment.

So Peter had been born in Romania and must have been adopted by the Carusos – interesting he supposed, and something that the Carusos had chosen to keep private, but by itself it couldn't qualify as the secret Dr. Wright spoke of. He remembered reading about the huge number of orphaned babies born in Romania back in the eighties. Peter could have been one of them. And instead of a name, he'd been given a number – sixty-eight according to the note on the back of his baby picture.

He wondered what Cat had found out about Sarah and he called her from his apartment.

"Nothing new, no surprises," she told him. "All the info in the bio on her website checks out. She's got two younger siblings, both respectable but not what you'd call over achievers. Same with the parents."

"They still alive?"

"Her mother died a few years ago but her dad still lives in Albany - into insurance it looks like. How about you, any luck on Peter's side?"

He told her about the adoption papers. "There might be something else in the photographs I took so we'll have to go over those. How about your place tonight?" They agreed on Mexican. Cat furnished the food and Nate brought the Corona's.

They ate first, cleaned up, then sat on the floor, shoes off with their backs against the front of her sofa, and started going through the photos on Nate's phone. Cat had a notepad and wrote things down as they went.

Cat squinted. "What are these?"

"Oh, that's personal stuff – a few of my paintings. There's my mom and dad. There's Peter's house. I took that on my last trip down there."

"Spooky," said Cat, "his house, not your parents."

He scrolled further. "Here are the shots from Peter's file." They both looked closer, trying to make out the details of what looked to be a medical form. Nate enlarged the image but, in doing so, ruined the context with the rest of the form.

"Your screen's too small." She got her tablet and connected it. "Better, but this picture's fuzzy." They scrolled to the next one – same thing.

"I was in a hurry."

"I can make out some of it. Wow – Peter had twenty/twelve eyesight in both eyes. That's impressive."

"That's from high school," said Nate pointing out the Bennett heading on the form. "I told you he was our best pitcher. There are some records from Columbia that we've already seen. Those will have his other stats – IQ, verbal skills, math skills..." He kept scrolling.

"Here they are," said Cat, "off the charts, slacked off in verbal but still high."

They came to the hospital baby picture and then to the notation on the back of it:

Baiu anormalitate.

"It must be Romanian," said Nate, noticing the initials D.C. beneath the note.

Cat took the tablet and shifted to the internet. In less than a minute she had the translation. "Looks like it means 'No abnormalities,'. Funny way of saying 'healthy' don't you think? Like abnormalities had been the norm rather than the exception."

They got to the immigration and adoption papers. On the lines for the adoptive parents the form read: Mary Margaret Caruso and Francis Albert Caruso. The date on the form was October 8th, 1982.

"Here's something," said Cat, enlarging the image of a

signature with a typed name beneath it. "This is probably the guy on the Romanian end of the adoption." She wrote it down: Dmitry Cavianski.

"D.C. from the baby picture," said Nate.

"Says he's with..." Cat slid her finger over, shifting the view to the next box over. "Darvos Pharmaceuticals," she wrote it down, "that ring a bell with you?"

"No, but I think it's odd that a guy working for a drug company would be involved in an adoption."

"Maybe it's not odd in Romania."

"I think it's odd anywhere."

"Let's check them out." She did searches on *Darvos* and on *Dmitry Cavianski* but came up empty on both.

Since the documents pre-dated the internet Nate wasn't surprised by that. They went over the rest of the photos and Cat added a few more items to the list on her notepad. When they'd finished, she put it and the tablet aside and drank the last of her Corona. She closed her eyes. "Bet he was named after Sinatra."

"What?"

"Peter's father – adoptive father, Francis Albert. Sorry, just trying to lighten the mood." She shook her head. "So what now? I suppose we should summarize what we know and see if we can put any of it together."

"I'm tired of talking about Peter, I want to talk about you, Cat." He moved closer.

She yawned. "All right, let's talk about me."

"Cat, I want to make things better if I can." He paused and he could hear her breathing quicken just a little. "You seemed really bothered about something when we were going through the bad side of town yesterday."

Cat shook her head. "That was nothing. I'm okay - really."

"Your hands were shaking, Cat. You were deathly afraid. It was almost like a panic attack. Sometimes it helps to talk things out."

She forced a laugh. "Now that would be a real mood lightener."

Nate didn't say anything. He waited patiently, sensing that she wanted to talk but maybe just didn't know how to begin. From where he sat on the floor he began to notice things around the room. Neat as a pin, photographs on the walls – one of an older couple standing in front of a grocery store - probably mom and dad. A Don Quixote poster hung on another wall and beside it a picture of Cat with some friends at the beach. She looked good in a swimsuit. As his eyes shifted casually around the room, sounds of the building floated randomly – footsteps overhead, the soft hissing and occasional clank of the steam heat, a car horn from outside. He thought for a moment that Cat might have gone to sleep but then she spoke quietly.

"Have you ever been afraid for your life?" she asked.

"No."

"It's something that stays with you. You can't talk yourself out of it. You can't ever feel really safe again, not when you know how fragile things are; how quickly things can turn on you."

"What happened, Cat?"

She breathed in, deeply. "I was twelve when our store got robbed. It was mid-afternoon, summertime, school was out. Mom and dad had gone out for something, leaving me to manage things alone. That wasn't unusual, they knew I could handle the few customers that might come and go. I remember it being really hot that day and business was slow. I was sitting on a stool behind the counter. There weren't any customers in the store when the two guys came in, one with a gun. One of them stayed by the door. The guy with the gun came right at me and told me to take all the money out of the register and toss it in a bag. He pointed the gun in my face. I was a little jerk back then so I thought I'd be cute. I got off the stool. 'Paper or plastic?' I asked.

"The guy didn't like that. He smacked me with the barrel of his gun right across the cheek. I could feel the whole side of my face give way, like maybe something had cracked. There was blood, a lot of it – I could taste it. I fell and he jumped behind the counter. He didn't know how to open the register so he pulled me up. 'Open it,' he shouted, holding me. I could barely see but I opened it then stumbled back against a rack of canned goods.

"As he was pulling out the money, I grabbed a can of something – diced tomatoes I think – a thirty-two ouncer." Cat paused and shook her head. "I'd watched too many TV police shows I guess. I wanted to be the hero and I didn't want to let my mom and dad down. I was about to hit the guy over the head with the tomatoes when he saw me. He grabbed my wrist and twisted and I dropped the can. Then he smacked me again. I fell again and must have blacked out. When I came to, my parents were there and so were the police. I had no idea what was going on. My head felt as big as a beach ball and throbbed like a base drum. With every beat I thought it was going to burst. They loaded me onto a stretcher and into an ambulance and I spent all of the next week in the hospital. My jaw and arm were both broken.

It was on my second day there that I learned something else. While I was unconscious, lying there on the floor behind the counter, blood everywhere, the guy raped me. I was twelve years old – what kind of a guy does that?"

Nate put an arm around her, holding her close, kissing her hair. He felt her body tremble.

"It was my mom who told me. The doctors thought it would be better coming from her and I suppose they were right. I got better though. Everything healed okay, everything good as new. September came, school started and that's when the dreams started. It was like I could remember things now, you know, things that had happened to me on the floor. I could feel him on me, pulling up my skirt, holding me down with two strong hands, one on each shoulder. I could feel...oh Nate, I could feel him inside me, pounding again and again and again. And all I could think was – stop, stop, you're killing me." She started shaking again, then buried her face in Nate's chest and cried.

They lay there for a while, Cat's tears flowing freely. Then she got up, came back with some Kleenex, and sat down on the couch.

"And that was my bad experience," she said, blowing her nose. "Aren't you glad you asked?"

"I'm sorry to have put you through it but, yes, I'm glad I asked."

"I was lucky not to have gotten pregnant. And, by the way, the docs say I'm okay to have kids – nothing broken but I've got to tell you Nate, I'm not good with sex. I've tried. I can get excited about it no problem, like that night with you in the cab, but then I chicken out."

"You didn't chicken out. You just didn't know me well enough. You were apprehensive, that's normal."

"You're beginning to sound like a shrink."

"Too much time with Dr. Wright." Nate got up and used the bathroom then came back and sat beside her on the couch. "Paper or plastic – what were you thinking?"

"I told you, I was a jerk back then. I still can be when I want to."

He picked up Cat's notepad. "Yes, I know."

Cat let that slide, blew her nose again then foul-shotted the box of Kleenex across the room onto the kitchen counter. "I figure it's my turn to decide what we talk about now." She got up and walked to the fridge and came back with two more Corona's. She handed one to Nate. "My suggestion is that we put Peter and me on the shelf for tonight. I want to talk about the new Nathan Lido

Parks exhibit. If I'm going to be your marketing manager we need to get to work now. July isn't that far off." She retrieved her tablet and re-took her spot on the floor, back against the sofa. She thumbed over to a blank spreadsheet. "We have to work out the details on what you'll need for your big bash and take a stab at a rough cost."

Nate slid off the couch and sat on the floor beside her, touching her stocking foot with his. "You sure you want to do this?"

"Yeah, Nate, I'm sure. But this is my last beer for the night. You know how I get."

They worked for an hour discussing what would be needed and how much each thing might cost. Cat made the entries. Finally she showed him the number at the bottom of the spreadsheet.

Nate shook his head. "Forty-three thousand for a single night – I can't do that Cat. There's no way I can borrow that much money. I'm having trouble just making rent payments."

"You won't have to borrow it. You'll have to hit up some sponsors. That's the way this is done. Teddy already said he'd help, and he's got friends. Maybe you could get Manhattan College to kick in a few bucks. You're a Columbia alum, they should be interested. You have lots of Democrat friends, right? They always seem to have money for the arts. We've got to get the ball rolling on this; we don't have a lot of time." She got up and took her tablet to her desk. She sat down and started punching the keyboard.

"What are you doing now?"

"Putting together a timeline," she said. "It'll be pretty rough, just like the spreadsheet, so we'll have to do some fine tuning as we go along."

They talked as she worked and when Nate looked over her shoulder he saw the milestones in her timeline: Preliminary publicity complete, funding lined up, venue set. Her last entry was at the four-month milestone: *Nate becomes a world famous, independently wealthy artist.*

"You really think this'll work?" he asked, his hand caressing the side of her face. He wondered if that was where she'd been hit by the gun.

She held his hand there for a moment. "Nate, you're a great artist, of course it'll work."

The next morning he received an email from Cat with the spreadsheet and her timeline attached. There was a long list of to-do items organized by date. He saw that his task for today was to call Teddy and any other potential sponsor. His mission – to raise money.

Over the phone, Teddy was immediately excited and they set up a lunch meeting for later in the week. Teddy insisted that he bring Meredith with him and volunteered her help for whatever he needed.

"Oh, I hate to bother you both over this," Nate protested mildly.

"Nonsense, she'll love it," Teddy assured him.

They met at a restaurant, two days later.

"We'll have a fundraiser at our place," Teddy announced after they'd been seated. "I know a lot of folks with money – big money. They like me and they like art. They'll love you."

The last time Nate had seen Meredith had been at the Sarah Crawford dinner. Today she was dressed casually in a bright orange dress that seemed to hug her in all the right places. He found his gaze wandering then thought it might help to imagine her in a dumpy burlap potato sack. He'd always been good at visualizing things and he saw in a flash just how that might look with her bulging out on both sides of the Idaho Potatoes logo. No, that didn't help at all. He took a drink from his water glass and thought about Cat's brown eyes – there that was better.

Meredith told him how good it was to see him again. "We're both very excited about the exhibit but I was hoping you'd bring Cat with you."

"Too busy, couldn't make it."

"All that wine and cheese – tough job." Meredith gave him an understanding nod.

The waiter handed out the menus and took the drink orders. "Of course," Teddy continued, "you'll have to have a sampling of your paintings there, at our fundraiser I mean, and you should have a brochure with a quick bio. Can you manage that?"

"Yes, I can get that together," said Nate. He remembered seeing the word 'brochure' somewhere on Cat's to-do list.

Teddy turned to Meredith. "When do you think we can manage it my dear?"

"We'll keep it exclusive, maybe thirty couples. Contacting them shouldn't take long. It's not quite proper but we'll do it by email with a link to the Nate Parks website. You do have a website, right Nate?"

"I have a Facebook page."

"That'll do. We could make it for mid-May, that's three weeks from now. Does that sound about right? It won't have to be a full blown dinner; maybe just drinks and dessert? Something casual." she looked at Teddy then at Nate.

"That'll be great," said Nate to both of them. "I really appreciate your help."

"You're a great talent, Nate," said Teddy, "we're just happy that we can play a small part in your success. Aren't we my dear?"

"Yes, we are. It'll be our privilege," said Meredith. When her eyes met Nate's, it was as if they spoke louder and, in a voice only he could hear, they warned him: *I'm not quite through with you yet, Mr. Parks.*

Nate decided it was time for her to meet Eduardo.

The three weeks went by quickly with Nate focusing on his paintings and Cat polishing up his Facebook page and putting a fold-out bio together. In the back of his mind he knew he should be researching *Darvos* and *Cavianski* and the other information from Dr. Wright's file on Peter but there just was no time and, the truth was, he was starting to get excited about his exhibit. He wondered how much money they'd be able to raise. On the night of the event he arrived early at the Sinclair house along with Cat and Eduardo.

"Nice house," said Eduardo from the back seat when they pulled up. "He's in real estate you said?"

"Commercial properties," said Nate as the valet opened the car door for him.

"Good evening Mr. Parks," said the valet as, on the other side, another man opened the door for Cat.

Nate wore a white dinner jacket, Cat a black dress with elegant lines. He gave her his arm then strode into the house with red-scarfed Eduardo following. They were ushered into the great-room where a roaring fire blazed away. Easels placed around the room displayed Nate's paintings. *The Bakers* was on display just beside the fire where the flickering of the flames gave it life. He had re-titled the painting after adding the image of the baker's young daughter beside him, her eyes closed as she savored a bite from the pastry she held. On the opposite side of the fire was his painting of Meredith.

"Nate, it's all beautiful," said Cat, squeezing his arm.

"Ah, here's the guest of honor." Meredith came up behind them in a ruffley blue cocktail dress. She shook his hand. "We're just pouring the Champagne now. Good to see you again Cat." They brushed cheeks. If Cat said anything to her, Nate didn't hear it.

He introduced Eduardo as his Broadway actor friend rattling off a list of his more prominent roles. Eduardo took Meredith's hand in both of his and kissed it in a low bow, managing to hold her eyes with his the whole time. "So you are the mistress of this beautiful house? How fitting that is. I am so pleased to meet you." Nate smiled to himself but if Meredith was the least affected by this Latin charm she didn't show it. He sensed a tour de force in the making and his money was on Eduardo.

"Please make yourselves comfortable," said Meredith, "our guests should start arriving soon. If you'll excuse me, I've got a few things to check on."

"This is fabulous," said Eduardo after she'd left. He extended an arm and swept it around the room, his pirouette coming to a stop neatly in front of a waiter who'd just approached him from behind holding a silver platter of filled glasses.

"Champagne?" asked the waiter.

Eduardo took one. "Fabulous," he said again after taking a sip.

The other guests arrived in a constant flow that kept the waiters busy with their drink trays and Nate busy with introductions and conversation. Some of the names Nate recognized as prominent New Yorkers closely connected with the arts and some closely connected to politics. The couple who'd sat opposite he and Cat at the Sarah Crawford dinner were there and he was about to be embarrassed that he couldn't recall their names – but Cat stepped in and saved him. They were Dave and Margaret Gillespie, mid-sixties both with silver-gray hair. They each held half-empty wine glasses.

"Have you heard the latest about Sarah Crawford?" asked Margaret.

Nate's ears perked up. He shook his head. "No, we haven't."

Margaret glanced over her shoulder then spoke in a low voice. "I don't know if there are any of the press around, but the word is, she's in a private clinic. There've been complications with her pregnancy."

"That's terrible," said Cat, "maybe it's just a precaution though. She's not due until September right?"

"Yes, that's what she told everyone, but there seems to be a lot of hush-hush about this latest thing. Her office won't say much except that she's on an extended period of rest, preparing for the campaign ahead."

"It sounds like you spent some time looking into this. How do you know she's at the clinic?" asked Cat.

"Well, you can never be too sure about the political people you contribute to, so we check up on them from time to time. I'm not thrilled that she got herself pregnant but she's a strong woman and you have to admire that, don't you."

Her husband explained further: "We found out about her complications from a niece of ours who's a doctor at the clinic. She's not treating Sarah herself, she just knows that she's there. You're right, it may be nothing and she could be out soon."

"Let's hope so," said Nate, "she's a courageous woman and she'd make a great governor."

A shout from the other side of the room followed by laughter derailed the conversation. Nate looked over to see a group of couples gathered in a half-circle around Eduardo, who had apparently just finished one of his theatrical stories. He saw that Meredith wasn't part of that group. He scanned the room and found her. She stood beside Teddy but she had her eyes on Eduardo. He took that to be a good sign.

About an hour into the evening, Teddy tapped his wine glass with a dessert fork and got everyone's attention. He walked up and stood in front of the fire as some of the guests scrambled to grab a spot to sit, most remained standing.

He spoke in a loud voice. "My friends, thank you all for coming. As you know, we're here tonight to honor and to assist a rising young star, a true genius in the world of art. Here in this room, you see all around you a small sampling of his work." This elicited some applause. "My wife Meredith and I first came into contact with Nathan Parks when he graciously agreed to paint the portrait of Meredith you see here." More applause.

Nate stood in the back of the room listening with Cat beside him. As Teddy went on, she put her arm around him. He had poured his soul into his art and had spent countless hours perfecting his ability to see the world through the tip of his brush. Never in that time had he received such accolades as he was receiving tonight from Teddy. He felt humbled but at the same time, felt guilty of being a poor friend to Teddy. He promised himself, never to let that happen again. He was glad Cat was there to share this moment with him.

When Teddy finally finished his introduction, everyone clapped. Nate gave Cat a kiss and weaved his way up, feeling a little like he was on a TV awards show. He shook hands with Teddy. Eduardo shouted "*Hear-hear!*" as the applause died out.

Nate thanked Teddy and he thanked everyone for coming. "As many of you know, I was raised on a farm outside of Scranton. I was close to nature and learned at a young age that nature is art and art is nature. It's a phrase probably coined by someone famous so please ignore the plagiarism. As an artist, I pursue beauty but not at the expense of what's real. It's through my art that I seek to provoke thought and I seek to inspire. It's unfortunate that I can't ignore the practical considerations that are necessary to overcome obstacles and to realize a worthy goal. To help me out with these practical considerations I am grateful for whatever you can donate." He held up his brochure. "For this event it seemed like a good idea to put down in writing something about me and my background, my training and my artistic credentials. You can read it if you like, but it's not where you'll find me. You'll find me in my art."

Nate put down the brochure and extended his hand. "I'm here in this painting of our beautiful hostess this evening, Meredith Sinclair. I am here in this baker who loves the creative toil of making breads and pastries but is worried about the day's receipts. If you're wondering who Nathan Parks is, just look around."

He stopped short, and scanned the faces around the room. There was Eduardo, there was Teddy and Meredith and there in the back, with a Kleenex in her hand, was Cat. Nate smiled at her. "If you like what you see here tonight, if you believe that realism and honest emotion have a place in art today then I thank you for that belief and I thank you for believing in me."

The room burst into applause and as Nate stepped away from the fire he was surrounded by well-wishers who shook his hand and slapped him on the back. Their faces were a blur until a round-headed man with curly hair and a pink bow-tie stepped up. He carried a pen and note pad and waited patiently until the hand-shaking and back slapping was done before grabbing Nate's attention.

"Hello Mr. Parks, I'm Joe Briggs. I'm a feature reporter with the *Times*."

Nate was immediately pleased but put his guard up. Be careful what you say, he told himself. "Glad to meet you, Mr. Briggs."

"I have some questions for you if you don't mind – actually, just one in particular." His probing gray eyes met Nate's.

"Ask away."

"Is it true that you're a suspect in the murder of Peter Caruso?"

Nate was struck numb. He opened his mouth then closed it right away. Briggs hadn't bothered to lower his voice and nearby conversations stopped abruptly. Nate was conscious of heads turning in his direction. "No, that's not true. Peter and I were close friends growing up, and I've always admired his work."

"But you were a suspect at one time, isn't that right?"

"I don't think I was ever seriously considered. The police never even questioned me about it. I consider it a closed issue." Now the room was completely quiet.

"Do you have any idea who killed Peter Caruso?"

"No, I don't. And if I did, I'd certainly let the police know about it before sharing that information with you."

Briggs was unfazed. "Mr. Parks, do you know a Patty Harris?"

Nate hesitated. Who was this guy and how did he know these things? "She was...she was a girl that Peter and I went to high-school with. She died in a swimming accident."

"It's my understanding, Mr. Parks, that she was murdered and that, until recently, you were in possession of the murder weapon. Is that true?"

There was an audible gasp from somewhere in the room. The floor seemed to sway under Nate as he tried to gather himself. "I don't know where you get your information from Mr. Briggs but it's not true – none of it is true." But Nate knew better; it was all true and he suspected Briggs knew it too.

"Thank you Mr. Parks," said the reporter with a breezy expression on his face. He turned around. "Might I have my coat please?" he asked. He put it on and found his way out.

The door closed with a thud and the room stayed quiet, all eyes on Nate. He didn't know what to say, so he said nothing. His stomach was churning. He steadied himself with a hand on the back of a chair. Then, from the back of the room, Meredith stepped forward and waved her hand over the table of food that had just been set up. "Dessert anyone?" she asked.

CHAPTER 18

There was an awkward silence in the car as Nate drove out through the gates.

"I liked your speech," said Cat.

"Yes," agreed Eduardo, stretched out on the backseat, "it was very good."

But Nate was focused on one thing. "Your friend Mooch told him," he said to Cat. "The bastard. I never should have trusted him and I was a fool to turn in the knife."

"What knife?" asked Eduardo.

"Mooch wouldn't do that, Nate. I know him and he just wouldn't."

"Well he told somebody and now everyone in that house back there thinks I'm mixed up in two murders when I haven't done a damn thing. Fat chance them offering any money for the exhibit now. And tomorrow it'll be in all the papers. Nobody will give my art a second look. I'm ruined, Cat." He stomped on the accelerator and took a turn a little too fast. The tires skidded onto the gravel shoulder and Nate cut the wheel, pulling back onto solid pavement.

"Stop the car, Nate," said Cat, "let me drive."

"I'm okay." He tightened his two-handed grip on the wheel.

"No you're not Nate. Come on, stop the car."

Nate took a breath, realizing she was right. He guided the car to the side of the road and pulled to a stop where he rested his forehead on the steering wheel. He felt like screaming. He balled his hand into a fist then he got out of the car to switch places with Cat. His heart was pounding, he needed to hit something. Cat met him in the headlights halfway around.

"This isn't over Nate, and you're not ruined," she said, taking his hand. "You're being set up and we're going to find out who's behind it. Come on now, calm down. We need to work this through."

"I can't think, Cat, not now."

"Tomorrow then. Just put it out of your mind for now. Tomorrow's Saturday. We'll try and figure it out tomorrow, all right?"

He went around to the passenger side and got back into the car, slamming the door. As his mind whirled, reliving the best and the worst night of his life, Cat drove back into the city.

Nate woke up the next day to a phone call, it was from *The Post*: Had he seen the *Times* article? Did he have any comment? He hung up and rolled over, wishing the previous night had just been a bad dream. The phone rang again, the *Daily News* this time. He let it go to voice-mail and covered his head with the pillow. Two calls later he threw on some clothes and went down to the corner drugstore and bought a paper and a large black coffee - he was done with chai. He went back up to his apartment. At the top of page two was a stupid looking photo of him and below it the headline: *Local Artist Tripped up at Big Money Soiree*.

Nate read the two-column piece then crumpled the newspaper and threw it across the room. That's it, he thought: forget the exhibit, forget selling another painting in New York, forget being an artist. He might as well throw the last ten years of his life out the window.

He got into the shower and let the hot water run over his face. Through the steam and over the water-spray he could hear his phone ringing in the other room. He felt like a criminal being chased through the bayou and the hounds were almost on him. He closed his eyes, forcing his mind to clear a bit. Cat was right, he was being set up. But who would do this to him? Who knew enough to do this to him? The answer was easy: Sarah Crawford. An image of her piercing eyes flashed through his mind. She knew everything, and as high up in the system as she was, she'd be able to influence any active police case. But why would she care about him? What would she have to gain? The answers had to be wrapped up with her connection to Peter and with her connection with his last painting.

He was toweling off when the phone rang again. At the same time there was a knock at the door. Why couldn't people just leave him alone? He ignored the phone and threw on a pair of pants then opened the door – it was Cat and Eduardo.

"Don't you answer your phone?" asked Cat. "We called to let you know we were on the way but you didn't pick up. We would have been here sooner except we had trouble finding a breakfast sandwich place that sells this stupid chai stuff."

Eduardo held up the white bag and a drink carrier with three white, hot-cups. He put them down on the coffee table.

Cat sat on the couch as Eduardo handed out the food.

"I'm not complaining or anything Nate but are you going to put on a shirt?" asked Cat.

Nate looked down at his bare chest, still wet from his shower. "The phone's been non-stop this morning, different papers asking for my comments on the *Times* article. Have you seen it?"

"Yeah," said Cat. "They didn't use your best photo – makes your nose look funny."

Nate went into the bedroom and put on a shirt then joined them.

Cat handed him his chai and a sandwich then said: "I filled Eduardo in on what we know about Peter and his sketchbook and the Harris girl."

"Did you tell him about Sarah Crawford?" asked Nate, taking a bite. It tasted good. He didn't realize how hungry he was.

"I thought I'd let you handle that. You think she's behind all this don't you?"

"I do, but I have no idea what she has to gain." Nate told Eduardo about his meeting with Crawford but didn't say anything about the photos she had of him and Meredith. "She's ruthless. This is out and out blackmail and I don't think she's above tipping off a sleaze ball reporter like Briggs."

"He's not exactly a sleaze ball, Nate" said Cat. "I checked him out. He's been with The *Times* for over ten years; has a regular column. Teddy must have invited him because he thought he'd give you some good PR."

"How would Crawford know about your plans to have an exhibit?" asked Eduardo.

"It wasn't a secret," said Nate. "And she's been tracking me pretty closely. I would have been surprised if she hadn't known about the exhibit and the fundraiser."

"I played a lawyer once," said Eduardo. "Off-Broadway, not a big production but I remember a line I had." He raised the hand that held his sandwich and extended a finger. "There are only three things of utmost importance in criminal law: motive, motive, and motive.'"

"There's a real show-stopper," said Cat.

Eduardo shrugged. "The point is – we need to discover her motive. What does she have to gain by publicly incriminating you in Caruso's murder?"

Cat put down her coffee. "Maybe she's protecting someone, Nate. Maybe she knows the real killer and she's protecting him by trying to frame you."

"Our next governor protecting a murderer? That's a little extreme don't you think?" said Nate.

"Or maybe she's just convinced that you killed Peter," said Eduardo.

"And all she wants is to see justice done?" asked Nate. "That doesn't explain her blackmail stunt."

"There's something that bothers me," said Cat. "Why would she try to blackmail you with her inside information then leak that information to the press? Now that everyone knows about it, she's lost most of her leverage on you."

"Most of it?" asked Eduardo. "You mean there's more evidence against you?"

Nate just shook his head. He didn't want to go into his threat against Peter when they were boys or into the fact that he had no alibi for the night of the murder. And he certainly didn't want to talk about the photos of him and Meredith. No, Crawford may have given up some of her leverage over him but she still held him firmly by the balls.

He got up and walked to the window and pulled aside the curtains letting the sun stream in. He lifted the window, filling his lungs with cool air. The sounds of chirping birds, the barking of a dog and the passing of a few cars told him that life was still going on out there. The world hadn't slowed a bit because of his little crisis. He left the window open and went back to his chair. "I want to talk to Crawford again. Last night somebody said she was at a hospital – pregnancy complications."

"That was Margaret Gillespie," said Cat. "She said Crawford was in a private clinic, not a hospital and that her niece works there. I can check to see what facility Gillespie's niece is tied into."

"So you're going off to see Sarah Crawford? What are you planning to say to her?" asked Eduardo.

"I don't know yet."

"Want me along?" asked Cat.

"Yes, that would be good."

"We'll do it this afternoon," said Cat as she started tidying up the breakfast mess. "Right now I'm going to pay Mooch a visit."

"He's a bastard," said Nate.

"It's Saturday. He works on Saturday?" asked Eduardo.

Cat grabbed her coat and her half-finished coffee. "I know where he lives, and he's not a bastard. I'll check back with you later Nate."

"When you're done, I'll pick you up," said Nate. "Just let me know when and where."

"Roger that," said Cat, on her way.

"Is she always like that?" asked Eduardo after she'd left. "Like she's on a mission?" There was no cynicism in his voice.

"Once she sets her mind on something, yeah, it's like a mission with her." Nate thanked God she was on his side.

Nate picked up Cat two hours later. "So where're we headed," he asked as she buckled up.

"Postman Clinic—Gillespie's an intern there. I have it on GPS." She gave her phone a few pokes and its female voice started giving directions.

"What did Mooch have to say?" Nate asked as he drove.

"He says there could be a leak somewhere in the precinct but it wasn't him."

"Does he know Briggs?"

"No. Briggs is an art critic and wouldn't normally have anything to do with a homicide investigation. Nate, the last thing Mooch wanted was for the press to find out about you and Caruso. Now the heat'll really be turned up for him to make an arrest. Good thing it's Saturday; we have some time before the shit hits the fan."

"Did he say anything about the knife? He was going to send it to the lab."

"The knife's with the Scranton PD. No lab results yet, but the word is they've re-opened the Harris case and have questioned her uncle."

Nate shook his head. "Poor guy, I'm sure he blames me for dredging it all back up."

"You had no choice, Nate." She stared at the windshield for a while. "You know, revenge is a pretty strong motive. Maybe O'Neal killed Peter."

"He didn't suspect Peter until he got his note."

"That's just what he told you."

"Okay, suppose he had suspected Peter in Patty's death, why would he wait so long to go after him?"

"Yeah, that's a problem," she agreed. "Still, who else would want Peter dead?"

"Just me, according to the police."

They grabbed some lunch on the way and it was mid-afternoon by the time they pulled up to the clinic. Postman wasn't a big place but the building had a fancy look to it and a good view of the ocean suggesting that its services were reserved only for the very well to do, or for the very well insured. Nate parked between a Cadillac and a Lexus and, in his Columbia sweatshirt, led the way through revolving doors into the lobby.

"We're here to see Dr. Gillespie," said Nate, knowing he'd get nowhere if he'd asked for Sarah Crawford. When the stern-faced receptionist learned they didn't have an appointment she got more stern-faced and told them to have a seat. They spent twenty minutes in the otherwise empty waiting area then a white jacketed twenty-something woman walked up to them. She had 'Dr. Gillespie' embroidered in blue above her breast pocket and a lanyard around her neck from which hung an ID with her smiling picture.

"Doctor Gillespie, thanks for seeing us," said Cat shaking her hand. "We're good friends of your aunt and uncle, Margaret and Dave, and we're also good friends of Sarah Crawford who I understand is a patient here."

Gillespie winced at the mention of Sarah's name. She held up her hand and glanced back at the receptionist who was preoccupied with her computer screen. "Let's go outside, shall we?"

Well that's a little odd, thought Nate with a glance at Cat. They followed Gillespie back out.

"I knew I shouldn't have said anything about Crawford. My mom's such a blabbermouth, she must have told Aunt Margaret."

"Can we see her?" asked Nate. "Crawford I mean."

"No, I'm afraid you can't. And she wasn't my patient anyway."

"Doctor Gillespie," said Cat, "we're not with the press or anything, we're just good friends of Sarah's and we're concerned about her. We understand there've been complications with her pregnancy. Can you tell us anything about that?"

"Look, I'm not even an obstetrician. I just know she was brought in three days ago, stayed the night and then was taken somewhere else."

"She's not here?" asked Cat.

"No, she's not, and I don't know where she is now, but I can tell you that, while she was here, her condition was classified as serious."

"Life threatening?" asked Nate.

"That's usually what serious means. There was a big commotion when she left – a lot of security people."

"Suits or police uniforms?" asked Cat.

"Suits, no police. People were scurrying around. She was taken away in a private ambulance. They were all in a big rush." A cold breeze kicked up and Gillespie's lanyard ID flew back over her shoulder. She pulled it back where it belonged.

"Is that pretty common for high-profile patients – private ambulance and all?" asked Cat.

"The private ambulance wasn't unusual, but the sudden transfer was. And there's something else - even though she's no longer here, she's still listed as a patient and her room is still assigned to her."

"Maybe just an insurance thing," offered Nate. "Her dad in Albany must know where she is. He's probably with her now."

Gillespie nodded. "You're probably right. Now if there's nothing else, I've got to run."

They thanked her for her time and walked back to the car.

"Looks like you won't be able to talk to Crawford for a while," said Cat scooting into her seat. "What now?"

Nate had both hands on the wheel and the keys in the ignition. What now? How should he know? Then he had an idea. He started the car and pulled onto the main road.

"Where're we going?" asked Cat.

"We're going to see Colleen what's-her-name, Crawford's campaign manager. Maybe she knows what's going on. Maybe she's even the one Crawford's protecting. I figure she's based in New York, wherever the campaign HQ is."

"Good idea. You're starting to think like a field detective – that's a little scary." Cat pulled out her phone. "I'll get us an address."

They found the place on the lower eastside. Not the best of neighborhoods. Nate looked around at the abandoned stores that sandwiched the double-wide frontage that sported red, white and blue bunting over a sign that ran its full length: *Sarah Crawford for Governor*.

"You going to be okay here?" asked Nate.

Cat got out of the car. "Sure, you're my tough guy – right?"

"You bet."

They walked in and asked for Colleen Logan.

"Not here," said a young girl bent over a 'Sarah Now!' poster. She finished stapling it to a wooden stick then looked up. Nate wondered if she was even old enough to vote.

"Do you know where we can find her?" asked Cat.

"She tries not to work weekends, not yet anyway. Later in the campaign she says things'll get to be non-stop. I haven't been through the whole process before but I know you've got to pace yourself. That's what she says all the time, and she should know."

"Do you know where Sarah Crawford is?" asked Nate.

"Nope. Look, I'm just a volunteer. They don't tell me anything. You're best off coming back on Monday. Ms. Logan's normally in by eight."

Unable to think of anything else to ask, they thanked her and left.

"Can't get much done on weekends," said Cat. "You ought to just go back to your place, get some rest; do some painting. You can talk to Logan on Monday – sorry I can't go with you, I'll be tied up at work." He dropped her off and went back to his apartment.

The rest of the day and all of Sunday dragged by. Nate didn't feel like painting and he wondered if he ever would again. The passion inside him seemed to have just dried up. Over and over, he relived his shining moment at the Sinclair's and then his immediate fall from grace when he was thrown into the dumpster by that sleaze-ball reporter. He could still see his round face and his gloating expression. Nate even thought of going to see him but he knew the reporter would never reveal his source and meeting with him would just give him more garbage to write about. No matter what Nate did, Briggs was going to pump the story for all it was worth then move onto his next victim.

Finally, Monday came and Nate drove back to the Crawford campaign headquarters. The girl he and Cat had seen on Saturday was there, still doing her stapling. She looked up and recognized Nate. He gave her his card and she ducked into a back office then back out again.

"She'll be with you in a moment," she said.

Five minutes later Colleen Logan stepped out. "What can I do for you Mr. Parks?" Nate thought she looked a little more harried than the last time he'd seen her. It was her eyes he decided – deep set, the whites tinged with pink.

"I need to speak to Ms. Crawford," said Nate. "It's important."

"She's not accepting any new appointments this week. I'm sorry."

"I know about her complications."

"Then you know why she can't see you. And besides, from the papers I understand you have complications of your own."

Nate decided to ignore that comment. "Do you know where she is?"

"I do and that information is confidential."

"She's not at Postman."

Now she *was* irritated. "I don't need you to tell me where she is or where she isn't, Mr. Parks. Here's my card." She handed it to him. "You'll be best off sending me an e-mail. If I think you are someone Ms. Crawford should see, I'll forward it to her. Thanks for stopping by. Be sure to vote." She walked back into her office and shut the door.

Stapler-girl glanced up and gave her head a tilt. Nate left.

On the drive back, he got a call from Cat. "Mooch wants to see you – two this afternoon," she said.

Nate's stomach turned. He was getting tired of it doing all these flip-flops and now he was more angry than anything else. "Is he arresting me?"

"No, just questions for now." Cat was silent for a while then added, "I think you should call your lawyer, Nate."

"I don't have one, I don't know anyone who... I don't have much money, Cat."

"I can help you there. Not with the money but I know a guy. He's good and he's cheap."

Nate stopped at a light. "Will I need him today?"

"No, I'll come with you today. I'm no lawyer or anything but between you, me and Mooch maybe we can keep this thing from getting out of hand."

"It's a little late for that," said Nate as the light turned green.

They met at the Brownsville station house and were put in an interrogation room and told to wait. They sat in folding chairs at a wooden table. A third chair leaned, folded against the wall.

"Just like the set on a TV police show," said Nate looking around. There were dark stains on the floor. He pointed to a closed curtain on the wall. "Two way mirror, I bet."

"Good guess, Brainiac," said Mooch coming through the door with a bundle of newspapers under his arm. He closed the door and put the papers down then dragged the other chair over. "Nobody's watching today though. It'll be just us." He sat down.

"You won't be recording this?" asked Cat.

"Well, there is a cam up there," said Mooch with a glance.

"Nobody ever looks at the tapes though. I don't even know if it's working."

Nate looked up at the black box.

Mooch folded his arms. "Now, let's get to it. As you know, we have a problem. Your story's been picked up by all the city rags and I wouldn't be surprised to see things go national – it'll be the whole Nancy Grace thing: Artist suspected of killing a fellow artist – that's a story you don't see every day. Plus, now we've got the unsolved murder in Scranton that you were nice enough to put us onto. The news-creeps are really salivating."

"I thought I was cleared by my alibi."

Mooch twisted a little in his chair. "Yeah well, it turns out we had a big snowstorm on the night of the murder. The class you were supposed to be teaching that night never happened. I'm thinking you knew that but hoped we wouldn't find out – can't blame you there. But now that we found out, you're number one again. Actually you were always number one seeing as how we don't have a number two. Can you come up with another alibi? Do you have anyone who can vouch for your whereabouts that night?"

Nate's heart sank. He shook his head. "I remember now that I'd just gotten off the subway near the collage when I got the text that the class was cancelled. I grabbed the next train back and spent the rest of the night in my apartment."

"Anybody there with you?"

"No."

"You still don't have any evidence against him, right Mooch?" asked Cat.

"He had motive and now, without his alibi, he had opportunity, that's pretty much all we've got – except for the knife."

Nate shook his head in frustration. "The knife has nothing to do with Peter's murder."

"It just reinforces your motive. Maybe you and Peter were both involved in the killing of the Harris girl. With Peter dead, you're free to pin that entirely on him. Is that why you turned in the knife?"

Nate wanted to scream. "You're making all this up. You're just scrambling for any theory that might fit with the little you really know. I had nothing to do with Patty's death and I didn't kill Peter."

"I believe you, really I do," said Mooch. "The real killer wouldn't have done something so stupid as to turn in the knife. On the other hand, most murders are committed by stupid people who think they'll somehow get away with it, so you being stupid doesn't really work in your favor."

Nate raised his eyes to the ceiling but didn't say a word. This guy was starting to sound like Inspector Clouseau.

Mooch continued: "The bottom line is, you're still the only suspect and now, with all this publicity about the case, I can't clear you without having someone else to take your place."

"So you just ruin my life because you can't think of any better ideas?"

"Yeah, that's about it. But I'm open for suggestions, believe me I am. You don't happen to have any alternative theories do you?"

Mooch stared at Nate through his thick glasses looking like an overweight, late-middle aged Harry Potter, except not as smart. Nate glanced at Cat whose expression told him: *go ahead, not much to lose now*. He took a breath. "The missing painting I told you about last time, we have an idea who has it."

Mooch slid his chair closer to the table. "The painting Caruso made that shows his own death? We talked to the dead girl's uncle – well the Scranton PD did. He wouldn't tell them a thing. He was pretty upset when he found out you'd told us about it."

"He never opened the crate that Peter had sent him. He sold it to a guy who said his name was James Bridgeman. O'Neal got suspicious when he saw he was driving a car with New York plates. He took down the number."

"Oh?"

"Yeah," said Cat, "and I traced it to the state owned fleet up in Albany."

"State owned? So this guy Bridgeman's a state employee up in Albany? He's got the painting?"

"We think he's working for someone higher up," said Cat.

Like a gun-turret on a battleship, Mooch turned his head from Cat back to Nate. "Higher up, like who?"

"Sarah Crawford," said Nate.

Mooch blinked. "Sarah Crawford, the Lieutenant Governor of the State of New York? You think she has the painting?"

"Yes."

"Do you want to explain why you think this?"

"She met with me last month about Peter and warned me to stop looking into any connection she may have had with him."

"She warned you how?"

"She threatened to expose Nate as a suspect in Peter's murder," said Cat.

"Well that cat's already out of the bag," said Mooch scratching his head. "But what made you suspect Crawford in the first place? No wait, I have a better idea." He flipped to a blank page and slid his notepad and pen to Nate. "Write it down, all of it. Take your time. Knock on the door when you're done." He stood up. "Cat, you'll have to leave the room while he does this. We need to have this story be all his."

"I want a public statement from the police that I'm no longer a suspect," said Nate.

Mooch shook his head. "Just because Sarah Crawford bought a painting doesn't make her a suspect and it doesn't take you off the hook. I admit it'll be interesting if she has it, but that's all. And we'll want to bring in the painting – it could be evidence." He pointed to the notepad. "Just write it all up and we'll take it from there."

Cat stood and put a hand on Nate's shoulder, then left the room with Mooch.

Nate rubbed both hands over his face, feeling light-headed, unsure if he'd done the right thing in drawing Sarah Crawford into this. He knew she'd react by exposing his affair with Meredith, but that was a small price to pay if it took him off the hook for Peter's murder. He cleared his mind, then started writing.

CHAPTER 19

It was raining when Nate and Cat left the station house. They grabbed some food and ate it in the car as Nate drove, heading back to the Crawford campaign headquarters. It was Nate's idea to go there.

"You said she refused to see you this morning," said Cat. "Why would she talk to you now?"

"I've got a different approach in mind."

"You going to offer her some fries or something? I can save some back if you want." She dipped one in some catsup and popped it into her mouth.

"I'm going to tell her what we just told the police."

Cat shrugged. "That should get her attention. Just remember to be tough with her – you know, cop an attitude."

Nate turned his intermittent wipers up a notch and pulled into the left lane. "I can be forceful when I need to be."

"Good. That's what you need to be - forceful."

The rain had stopped by the time they walked into the Crawford HQ. Inside, a CD player set up near the window blared the *Black Keys* latest. Stapler girl had a couple of helpers. She was now stuffing, sealing and stacking envelopes. "Ms. Logan is in but she's tied up," she told them before Nate even asked, "and we close in twenty minutes."

"Tell her that the police might be here soon so there's not much time. This is important." Nate spoke loudly enough, he thought, to be heard over the music and from behind Logan's closed office door.

The girl looked like she was about to hyperventilate. "The

police? Why would...? Look, I just work here. I'm sorry I can't..." She rambled on for a while, then the office door opened.

"It's okay Marcy," said Colleen Logan from her doorway. "I'll speak with them. Turn that thing off would you?" The room went quiet. Marcy and her helpers watched as Cat and Nate walked into her office.

Logan closed the door. Her office had no windows and the lighting was dim. She sat down at her desk behind a computer screen that she now shoved to one side. She motioned them into a couple of upholstered side-chairs and didn't bother with handshakes or introductions. "What do you want and what's this about the police?"

"We just came from there," said Nate. "They know about Sarah Crawford's involvement with Peter Caruso and they know about the painting she has. This could all be very damaging to her campaign."

"I don't know what you're talking about," said Logan. "The first and last time I heard the name Peter Caruso was when you asked her about him after the fundraising dinner a couple of months ago." Her expression hardened. "Of course that was before you made the papers. You're a suspect in Caruso's murder and now you're somehow trying to weasel your way out of that by tarnishing the good name of Sarah Crawford. I have no idea why you think she's involved with Caruso but I and millions of New Yorkers know Sarah to be an honorable forthright person. You'll have a tough time proving otherwise. You may be a competent artist Mr. Parks, but from where I sit you're looking a little shit-faced. You are way out of your depth." She turned to Cat. "And I don't know anything about you."

"I'm with Mr. Parks, that's all you need to know," said Cat, her voice cold, intimidating.

Part of her attitude thing, Nate thought as he pressed on: "Sarah Crawford's not as honorable as you think. A month ago she met with me at the airport in Linden and tried to blackmail me. I think that she also used fraudulent means to obtain Peter Caruso's last painting."

"Like I said, I have no idea how she could possibly have anything to do with Caruso and I don't know anything about a painting. I know she likes art and always has been a generous contributor - that's all." She took off her glasses.

There was a soft knock at the door and Marcy opened it a crack. "We're about to leave, Ms. Logan. Is everything all right?"

"Yes, I'm fine. You can go, I'll lock up." When the door closed she turned back to Nate. "Mr. Parks, I don't know why you're here. I can't do anything for you."

"We want to see Crawford," said Cat.

"She's unavailable right now."

"We know she was at a clinic – The Postman Clinic - up until two days ago."

"Her being at Postman is private information but, yes, she's having trouble with her pregnancy. It's just a precaution. She hasn't delivered yet and, as far as I know, she and her baby are both fine."

"She was transferred somewhere," said Nate. "Can you tell us where?"

"No, I cannot."

"Can you tell us why she was transferred?"

"That's private information."

"We'll just wait for the police to get involved then," said Nate, standing. Cat stood too.

"The police have no reason to suspect Sarah of anything and if they show up here, I'll just tell them the same thing I told you."

Nate put his card on her desk. "Here's my number. Give it to Sarah Crawford and tell her to call me as soon as she can. Believe me, I can save her and her campaign a lot of trouble."

"Good-bye, Mr. Parks," said Logan.

Nate and Cat left.

Over the next two days, through the papers and TV, Nate watched the story of Peter's murder go national. The case was being called *The Mozart Murders*. They'd lumped the Harris killing in with Peter's. The press loved it and went after Nate like a pack of dogs, calling him at all hours of the day, or even showing up at his door trying to get a statement.

And out in Maysville they went after David O'Neal too. A TV reporter had ambushed Patty's uncle at his home and now a video of the old man acting confused and emotional was making the rounds on the major networks. Nate had seen it: "Patty was a good girl. Just leave her be," O'Neal said tearfully over and over into the microphone that the guy stuck in his face as he'd asked his probing questions.

Nate knew it was his fault that the reporter and his camera were there at all. He was the one who'd connected Patty's death to Peter's; he was the one who brought the police into it; he was the one who had found the knife, and he was the one who'd broken his promise to a poor old man who had already been through so much.

Nate decided that the only thing he could do was to lay low. He'd either be arrested or somehow the whole thing would blow over. It was all out of his control. He'd gotten into the habit of ignoring the phone but the caller ID of a late night call caught his attention. He picked up. "Mr. Parks? This is Colleen Logan. I need to talk to you. It's urgent, can you meet me at the office?"

"Now you mean? Yes, I can be there in thirty minutes." He'd been watching TV. He flipped it off so he could hear her better but she only said, "Good," then hung up. He called Cat and asked her to call a cab and meet him at Crawford's HQ.

When they arrived, everything was dark and looked closed up. He tried the door – locked. He knocked. He could see a dim light coming from the direction of the interior office and a moment later Logan unlocked the outer door. After ushering them inside, she re-locked the door. "I made coffee, grab some if you want." Both did, then met Logan in her office.

Nate wondered why she was being so nice.

"I'll tell you what I know," she said from behind her desk.

"Have the police contacted you?" asked Cat.

"Yes, they called and I played dumb like I did with you. But they aren't my most immediate problem."

"Look, all we want to do is to talk with Crawford" said Nate. "That should not be this difficult."

Logan took a sip from her mug. "You're right, it shouldn't be. But, at this moment, Mr. Parks, I don't know where Sarah Crawford is."

Nate wasn't sure he heard her right. They were talking about the lieutenant governor. How could her campaign manager not know where she was?

Logan continued: "She was in town last week for a state conference. It was nothing to do with her gubernatorial campaign so I wasn't involved. She experienced some pains, shortness of breath, a little tightness across here," she patted her waist. "It didn't look like it was anything to be too concerned about. Sarah was actually very calm as I understand it but obviously everyone wanted to do the safest thing and we didn't want a lot of publicity. She was ambulanced over to Postman. That part you already know.

"When you saw me the other day and said she was no longer there, that was news to me. After you left, I called Sarah's cell but went straight to voice-mail. I called Postman. At first they said she was still there resting comfortably but wasn't allowed to receive any calls or visitors. I told them who I was and that I'd heard she'd been taken somewhere else. They put me on hold. Then the head of obstetrics came on the line and said yes, she had been transferred but he couldn't say where. He told me Sarah herself had requested the move and her father had signed off on the transfer papers. I asked again where Sarah had been taken and that's when he admitted that he didn't know. He told me that right now she needs rest more than anything. Then he advised me to 'Just leave her the hell alone,' and hung up."

"So her father was okay with the transfer?" asked Nate.

"I got the impression that he was the one who requested the transfer. He's connected to the medical field – an insurance consultant I believe."

"He's just being a protective father," said Cat.

"Maybe so. I called him yesterday and left a message asking him to call me about Sarah when he had a chance and that's where I was going to leave it. But tonight, just a few hours ago, I finally got a call from Sarah. I was in the shower so it went to voice-mail. She said she was all right but she didn't sound like herself. It was almost like she was in a panic state, yet with an overriding fatigue as if she'd been sedated. She mentioned something about Livingston doctors. I wasn't sure what to do but I didn't want to call the police – not right away. You know how easily these things can get out of hand. I'd done some earlier checking on you two and I remembered that a Livingston outfit had been involved with the Caruso paintings. That's why I wanted to see you."

"Is her call still on your phone? Can you play it back for us?" asked Cat.

Logan pulled her cell and the voice of a very exhausted Sarah Crawford came out on speaker:

"Hello Colleen, this is Sarah. I'm calling to let you know that everything's okay - nothing to worry about. No need to call or come looking for me." There was some background noise in the recording and Sarah Crawford seemed to hesitate before continuing, almost in a whisper. Nate bent closer to the phone. *"It's the Livingston doctors. They wanted me here. They're worried about my baby. I...I'm afraid."* There was a pause and a stifled cry. *"But my dad's here and I know everything will be all right. So, don't worry. I'll call you in a few days."*

"I tried calling back, but couldn't get through," said Logan.

Nate shook his head. "Why would The Livingston Gallery have

anything to do with Sarah Crawford's medical condition?"

"They're owned by a bigger company," said Cat. "They're international. Maybe they have a division that..."

"You're right," said Logan, turning her computer screen toward them. "While you were on your way here, I looked them up. Livingston Pharmaceuticals is a small outfit based in Sweden. They're owned by the same parent company as Livingston Galleries."

Cat leaned closer to the screen, reading the fine print on the company's website. "So someone from Livingston is in charge of Sarah Crawford's care?"

Logan shrugged. "Must be, I don't know why else Sarah would have mentioned them."

"Has her father done any work for Livingston?" asked Nate.

"I can check." She turned her screen back around. "We have bios on everyone with connections to Sarah – just general stuff so we're not caught off guard by any family scandals. Here it is." She ran her finger down the screen. Say's here he's in health insurance with a well-known firm like I thought. No mention of Livingston. Look, maybe we should just concentrate on finding out where she is. Let me put this on the big screen." She changed the connections to her computer. Suddenly, a large, wall mounted flat screen lit up behind Cat and Nate. They turned their chairs to see the smiling face of Mr. Crawford with his bio alongside.

"Nice looking guy," said Cat, "a little George Clooney-ish. Much older though. I remember him now. He came out after Crawford's speech."

Nate remembered the fatherly hug he'd given Sarah.

"I'm sure everything's all right, I just want to be sure." Logan went back to the Livingston website and scrolled down. "I don't see anything about them owning any medical facilities."

"Go to Google," said Cat. "Search hospitals owned by Livingston."

Logan did but came up empty. They tried variations with the same result.

"Here," said Logan, clicking away on a few password entry screens. "We have some powerful demographic software on this computer. We use it for polling and political stats."

The screen went to a bright white logo on a sky-blue field.

"Wow, *PoliSoft*," said Cat. "I've heard of this. It's the latest big-brother tool to control the masses."

Logan pressed a few more keys. "I'm going to pull up a map of the city." A familiar black and white web of roads appeared with a dialog box in the lower right corner. Logan spoke as she typed. "I'll bring up medical facilities." Red dots popped up across the screen; ten then twenty then more.

"That's a lot," said Nate.

"This includes doctor's offices, small clinics and all the hospitals," said Logan. "Now we can do a search on the listing of active patients. Wherever she is, they're probably keeping her name off the list but it's worth a shot." All the red dots disappeared.

"Enlarge the search area," said Cat.

Logan did so, a little at a time. One red dot appeared. "That's Postman," said Logan. "Officially, she's still there."

"Narrow the listing to obstetrics patients, then enlarge the search area. Do the entire state," said Cat.

Logan did so but there remained only the one red dot at Postman.

"Go back to just New York City," said Cat. "It sounded to me like there was a thunder-clap in the background on the recording so, wherever Sarah is, it was raining then. What time was the call?"

"Just after seven."

"Bring up all the medical facilities again but with an overlay of the weather conditions at seven."

Nate glanced at Cat, impressed but she just shrugged as if any moron would have thought to do that.

"This'll take a little time, hold on," said Logan. She pulled up a menu, made a selection then a few more. Five minutes later a spotty blue-shaded area appeared over the city map. "This shows the weather pattern at the time of her call."

"So we can rule out all the medical facilities where it wasn't raining," said Cat.

Logan made the dry-area dots disappear. "That's still a lot," she said. They had narrowed it down to fifty or so.

"We can also rule out those that don't do obstetrics," said Nate trying to be helpful.

Logan made the modification and about half the dots went away.

Cat spoke first. "Well, there are three of us, and maybe what, thirty dots? Ten calls apiece? It's do-able."

Logan nodded, folding her arms. "All right then, we've got five land lines into this building. Be sure to identify yourselves as being with the Crawford campaign – give them my name if you have to." She stood up and turned on the lights in the outer office area. "I'll use my phone from in here. You two can use the ones out there."

"There's nothing to keep them from lying to us about her being there," said Nate, standing.

"Right, that's the hell of it," agreed Logan. "We'll just have to be insistent."

Nate stopped when he saw that Cat was still staring at the map on the screen.

"Does this thing have access to past patient listings?" she asked.

"I don't know, I think so," said Logan. "What did you have in mind?"

"She may be at a clinic or hospital that she's been to before. They're keeping her name off the current list of patients but maybe she's on an old listing."

Nate shook his head. "If she was somewhere familiar she would have said so in her call."

"Maybe so, but it's easy to check," said Logan, back at her desk working the keyboard. "If she was sedated while being taken to the new place she wouldn't have seen where she was going."

"And once inside, every hospital room looks the same," added Cat.

The screen went blank for a moment then came back on with a single red dot. "That's Postman again." Logan expanded the search area to the entire state and a few dots appeared in Albany along with one straight north of Albany, half way to the Canadian border. "Okay, these are the places that Sarah has been to before, they do obstetrics, and it was raining there at seven."

"Let's try one more thing," said Cat. "I want to check on another past patient."

"Who's that?" asked Logan.

"Peter Caruso."

Nate saw what Cat was onto. If the connection between Peter and Sarah was through the pharmaceutical division of Livingston then maybe there were other medical-related connections. He walked closer to the screen as Logan punched in Peter's name.

The screen changed with only a single red dot now – the one north of Albany.

Logan clicked on it. "Leyland Medical," she read. "Never heard of it."

"What was Sarah there for at her last visit?" asked Cat. "Can you pull up the hospital log?"

Logan typed away and Nate watched the information pop up in a separate box next to the Leyland dot. "Wow, so much for privacy."

"Yeah, how can I get a program like this?" asked Cat.

"You can't, it's governmental. We're only able to do all this because I'm using Sarah's governmental access code." Logan read off the hospital log: "Tonsillectomy when she was a kid and three more times after that for...GS. Most recent, in o-six."

"What's GS?" asked Nate.

"Pull up the log for Peter," said Cat.

Peter's log came up in a box beside Sarah's and the hairs on the back of Nate's neck stood up as Logan read the results. "Except for the tonsil thing, the dates are a match. Peter and Sarah were there together three times in the past; each time for GS. Okay, so what's GS?"

"Gastro-something?" guessed Cat.

"It could be an abbreviation unique to that hospital. Or it might just be the attending physician's initials," said Logan shaking her head. She picked up her phone and placed a call. After being bumped around by an auto-attendant system, she finally reached a human being. "This is the Lieutenant Governor's office calling to confirm that Sarah Crawford was transferred there two days ago." She waited then answered a few more question followed by a "Yes, yes. Thank you very much." Logan listened, asked some questions, listened again then thanked the person for their time. She put her phone down. "She's there, but she hasn't been officially admitted so she has no medical status. The guy at the night-desk was a little confused, like he wasn't sure if he should have told me anything."

"I'm heading out there," said Nate, picking up his coat.

"Me too," said Cat.

Logan backed out of the software and flipped her computer off. "We'll take my car," she said, rounding her desk. "I'll drive."

By the time they arrived, the sky was just starting to brighten over Leyland Medical. Its narrow red-bricked tower rose eight stories above an open field surrounded by tall pines. The sparsely filled, paved lot that ringed the building was spotted with puddles. Logan parked and they got out of the car.

"Funny having a place like this way out here," said Cat in the lead, approaching the door.

"I'll do all the talking when we get inside," said Logan.

"All right by me," said Cat.

Nate trailed behind. Stretched out in the back seat, he'd been able to catch some sleep but not much. There hadn't been much conversation during the drive but he picked up that Logan had handled the last campaign of the current governor who wasn't running this year. It made her the natural choice to lead Crawford's team. She'd known the candidate for less than a year.

Logan had driven the entire way yet managed to look fresh as a spring daisy. Once inside, she strode purposefully across the lobby to the information desk. An older man sat there, dressed in the red sport coat of a volunteer. The gold nametag on his lapel identified him as Fred Howard. He looked up.

"My name is Colleen Logan, I'm the campaign manager for Lieutenant Governor Sarah Crawford. We're here to see her." She handed him her card.

Fred glanced at her card then checked his patient listing on the clip-board beside him. It was only two pages long – not many patients Nate thought, for a place this size. "I don't show a Sarah Crawford here, sorry," said Fred.

"Which floor is obstetrics?" asked Logan.

"Seventh."

"Thanks," said Logan looking around. "Where are your elevators?"

"Oh, you can't go up there, not without a visitor's pass."

"Where are your elevators?"

Fred pointed, "They're just past those turnstiles but you can't get to them and they won't operate without a pass card."

Logan lit into Fred with both barrels but the old guy stood his ground until a burly, black-tied security man with a holstered side-arm came over. Nate had never seen a hospital with visibly armed guards. What kind of place was this?

"Looks like we're done here folks," said the guard calmly. "Come with me please." He walked them out of the building and, without another word, left them standing by the curb.

Logan had her head angled up to the seventh floor as if she was considering scaling the building.

"Well, we tried the direct approach," said Cat. "They won't let us in to see Sarah Crawford because, officially, she's not there. All we need to do is to say that we're visiting someone who actually is there – someone on Fred's list."

"He'll be watching for us though," said Nate, "so will the guard."

"We might be able to finesse that," said Logan. She pulled out her phone. "Low signal, I'll have to plug in." She took a few steps, heading back to the car when she stopped in her tracks staring at a tall man with a cane walking toward them from the parking lot. He carried a small vase of flowers. On seeing Logan, he slowed and his expression went from passive to sour.

"Hello Mr. Crawford," said Logan.

"You shouldn't be here," said Crawford, still heading for the entrance.

"Sarah called me last night. It sounded like she was in trouble."

Crawford stopped. "That was a mistake. She was in a lot of pain. She's better now, no thanks to you. Can't you see that she's here to get away from you and to get away from her job? She needs rest, especially today. The best thing you can do for her is to stay away." He gave Nate and Cat a fiery glance as a slow drizzle started up and a cold wind began to blow. "All of you, just stay the hell away!" He resumed his walk.

"How is she doing?" Logan yelled after him but he was already pushing through the revolving door.

Cat turned her collar up against the wind. "She must be all right then, if he's here watching out for her. There's not much more we can do. At least we know where she is."

Logan didn't respond. Nate could see the worry in her face. "You don't trust him, do you?" he asked.

"No, I don't," she said.

CHAPTER 20

Sarah Crawford forced her eyes open. She remembered the excruciating, radiating pain in her belly. She remembered the sudden feeling of panic she'd felt that prompted her to call Colleen and she remembered trying to hold onto the phone as it was being torn from her grasp. Someone had shouted for more medication and she remembered the pain floating mercifully away, then nothing. Except for the hum and occasional beeping of the electronics around her, it was quiet now, she was alone and it was dark. The window blinds were closed but they were framed in light. It might be the same day or maybe the next, she couldn't be sure.

She shifted her head. Her cell was gone but the hospital phone was still there – probably disconnected, she thought. She closed her eyes again then felt the blood-pressure cuff around her around her arm inflating. More beeps. When she opened her eyes again, the blinds had been raised but all she could see was a gray sky dotted here and there with black storm clouds. She placed her hands on her swollen stomach and moved them over the hospital garment covering her drum-tight skin. The pains were gone. Her baby was still alive in there, she knew, and she would do everything she could to protect him. She took comfort in that. She was going to be a good mother.

This place had an emotionless laboratory feel to it. It was all part of the great experiment that had been so important to her only a few days ago. How could she have been so wrong-headed? Or maybe she was being wrong-headed now. She knew her father thought so.

"How are we feeling today?" asked a nurse.

"Fine," she said. Her voice cracked from not speaking in so long.

"Let's sit you up and get you some water."

The bed hummed, raising her into a sitting position. She sipped some ice water through a straw then looked out the window. She could see the tips of some trees in the distance. "Where am I?" she asked.

"You're here at Leyland Medical," said the nurse. "Didn't you know that?"

"No, they wouldn't tell me."

The nurse paused then busied herself with jotting down vitals and fluffing up her pillow.

"I'm hungry," said Sarah.

"I'm not sure you can have anything just yet, but I'll check." She left.

Sarah struggled to move her arm. She reached over and picked up the phone – dead, just like she thought. She put down the receiver. Her head was starting to clear and the fear was coming back. No, it was more of a feeling of dread as if something very bad was about to happen, something she had to stop. But what could she do? She looked around the room and took stock of her situation.

To her left stood an instrumented I-V pole with a clear plastic bag and a long plastic tube that ran to a bandaged port on her wrist. On the wall facing her, a white grease-board announced in neatly printed, bright red letters, that her nurse today was Linda M. The outer door lay open to a hallway. She stared through the doorway for a long while but saw no one pass by. Slow day, she thought. She had to use the bathroom and was about to ring for help when she decided she could handle this herself.

She shifted her covers and swung her feet around so she sat on the edge of the bed. When her head stopped spinning, she touched a toe to the floor then placed both feet flat. She grabbed onto the I-V pole and stood up. Good, no problem. Wheeling the pole alongside, she shuffled into the bathroom and relieved herself, allowing only a glance in the mirror at the haggard, sunken-eyed, bent-over, fat woman she'd become. She then shuffled back to the bed and sat down, exhausted but satisfied that, despite the medication, she still had her mobility.

It was probably the drugs from yesterday that were making her so weak, but it was a small price to pay if it kept the pain away. She checked the labeling on the I-V bag—the clear fluid was just saline but she couldn't be sure. A soft knock startled her.

"Good morning, Sarah. Are you better?" Her father stood in the doorway. His full head of wispy gray hair was a little disheveled but his weathered face combined with his bright blue eyes to sustain the powerful memories she'd always had of him since she was a child. Here was her solid ground and she felt like running into his strong embrace but couldn't. He walked in and placed a vase of flowers on the window sill.

"I'm all right daddy," she said. "I'm sorry about yesterday. I know how important this is to you."

He smiled and nodded. He gave her a kiss on the forehead then sat down on the bed beside her and spoke quietly. "They're taking the baby this morning."

Sarah felt a shudder of fear course through her and folded her arms over her belly. She felt her eyes fill then spill over. "I don't think he's ready, daddy. I can feel it. It's too soon."

He put his arm around her. He kissed the side of her head the way he did when she was little. "It'll be all right. Everything will be all right," he told her, pulling her closer. "They've run tests. It's best to do it now; for your sake and for the baby's. You have to trust me on this."

Sarah closed her eyes and rested her head on his shoulder, the only loving shoulder she'd ever known. Yes, of course everything would be all right, she told herself. She was just being silly. She waited for the nervousness inside her to pass then lifted her head and took a deep breath. "I do trust you. You always know what's best."

"The doctors here are good and they understand your situation better than anyone. They'll take good care of you." He handed her a Kleenex.

Sarah wiped her tears then looked out into the hallway where three men in pale blue scrubs were standing. At a nod from her father, they came in.

They asked her to lay back on her side and to assume a crouching posture. "A little poke," said someone and she felt a needle at her spine. Then she was floating again – not asleep but not awake. Hands rolled her onto her back. She could feel herself being wheeled out of the room and down a long hallway then into another room. There were more people and more talking. "Stay awake, Sarah, deep breaths," someone said and she forced her eyes back open.

Time passed, she wasn't sure how much. Then she felt a release of pressure from her belly and from beyond the blue sheets tented over her lower body she heard a healthy cry. "He looks perfect," said the doctor whose voice seemed to be fading in and out. Sarah felt like she'd been standing on the top ledge of a tall building and now she was falling. She tried to call out but couldn't make a sound. She felt her eyes go wide but she was having trouble seeing. Someone gripped her hand. "Breathe deep, Sarah, breathe deep. You're okay. Do you understand?"

She gasped for breath but seemed unable to draw in enough air. The sounds in the operating room faded. She felt a mask being placed over her mouth and nose then she felt her lungs inflate and then release of their own accord. The cycle repeated again and again until finally she was breathing without distress.

Slowly, the room drew back into focus. She could hear again. The grip on her hand loosened and her father, she recognized him now in a surgical cap and mask, looked down at her. "That's my girl," he said. "We have a beautiful baby boy."

Sarah met his eyes and from behind her breathing mask, she gave him a nod. She knew her father was just trying to calm her down; to let her know that she was safe. She had done her part and now there was nothing more to worry about.

She knew she should feel relieved and her thoughts should be on her baby but, at that moment, with the danger and fear behind her, all she could think about was Peter.

After the run-in with Sarah's father, Nate, Cat and Logan drove to a diner a few miles back up the road they'd come in on. On the way Logan called Marcy at her office and asked her to use the *PoliSoft* program to get the name of an active patient at Leyland and to call her back with it.

"That high-school kid has access to a program like that, and knows how to use it?" asked Nate.

"She's bright for her age."

"Let's hope she hasn't used it to take over the world by the time we get back," said Cat.

Nate's croissant was stale. He put it down on his saucer and took another gulp of coffee then started pealing a banana. "Even if we get a name, they'd ask if we were family then ask for ID."

"Yeah, we'll have to find a way around that," said Cat. "What bothers me is why they have such tight security anyway. These days you can walk into any hospital and visit anyone you want. Here they have armed guards – like a prison. What makes this place so different?"

"Maybe they just have the high security while the lieutenant governor's in the building," suggested Logan.

Cat shook her head. "It looked to me like Fred was following SOP. I'll bet it's like this all the time."

"We also need to find out what the GS thing is," said Nate.

"Right now I just need to know that Sarah's okay," said Logan. She put down her empty mug. "Let's get back to Leyland." At that moment, her phone dinged. "Hold on," she said, reading a text. "It's from Sarah's father. He says: 'Baby delivered, mom and son doing well. Will meet you in lobby at noon.' Well, that's good news."

"Yes, good news," said Cat, checking her watch. "The bad news is, we still have two more hours to kill." She signaled the waitress for more coffee.

When they finally returned to the hospital they sat and waited in the lobby under Fred's wary gaze. It was just before noon when Mr. Crawford stepped out of the elevator and walked through the turnstile toward them.

Logan walked up to meet him. "Congratulations, Mr. Crawford. We were so happy to get your text that all was well." They shook hands.

"Four pounds, three ounces" said Crawford in a matter of fact way. "It's a bit light, but they say it's not bad for a preemie. He's healthy and Sarah's resting now in recovery. I just emailed you some general information. You can put out a press release but please don't mention this hospital by name. Just call it a private facility. Sarah still needs to rest up."

"Of course, I understand," said Logan.

Crawford then glanced at Nate and Cat. "And who are you? – Not the press I hope."

Logan introduced them and Crawford shook their hands politely. "They wanted to see Sarah but obviously that's out now."

"And what business do you have with her?" He looked directly at Nate.

"It's a personal matter," Logan was quick to say, "nothing to bother you with now."

But Nate decided he'd waited long enough. If he couldn't talk to Sarah Crawford, her father would have to do. "I've been accused of a murder I didn't commit, Mr. Crawford. You might have read about it in the papers. I think your daughter may have evidence that can clear me. It's very important that I speak to her."

Crawford's face transformed itself into a scowl. "Sorry, but it's not as important right now as Sarah's rest. You'll just have to wait."

"She met with me last month, she..."

Crawford stepped closer to Nate. "Sarah meets with a lot of people, Mr. Parks, and every one of them wants something from her. The stress of it all caused her to have her baby prematurely. It put her life and the life of my grandson in jeopardy and I won't put up with it any longer." His nostrils flared. "Sarah might speak with you when she's ready, that'll be up to her. If I hear that you try to contact her before that, I'll make sure you *never* talk to her. Is that clear?" Without waiting for an answer, he turned and walked back toward the elevators.

Nate took a step in that direction but Logan stepped in front of him. "What are you planning to do - pick a fight with an old man? Now is *not* the time, Mr. Parks. I'll take your situation up with Sarah when she's back on her feet. Two weeks – just give us two weeks."

"She's right, Nate," said Cat, her hand on his elbow. "I don't like it either, but we'll have to wait."

Nate shook them both off. "Sarah Crawford and the painting are the keys to all of this. I'm glad that she had her baby and I know she needs her rest but I might be in jail in two weeks. What will I do then?" He watched Crawford step into the elevator. He had missed his chance.

Five miles into the drive back Cat, spoke up from the back seat. "GS is Genetic Screening."

"How do you know?" asked Logan.

"I asked Fred. He doesn't know much but he knew about that. He says it's something of a specialty at Leyland."

Nate dredged himself up from his depression and forced his mind to start working again. "So maybe Peter and Sarah were part of some kind of a study?"

"Could be," said Cat. "And I'll bet it was a study sponsored by Livingston. When we get back, I can check to see if there's any record of that."

"Odd that the two of them involved in the same study," said Logan.

"Maybe not," said Nate. "Maybe the study was focused on the genetics of people who'd been child prodigies – an adolescent prodigy in Peter's case."

Logan maneuvered the car around a curve. "From what I know of her, Sarah had been an average student up to the age of twelve or so. Then the fireworks happened – aced every test, IQ off the charts, topped off by a perfect SAT and her admission to

Cornell at fourteen."

"Triggered by puberty maybe? You can see why someone might be interested in her genetics - Peter's too," said Cat.

"Peter was adopted," said Nate. "He was born in Romania. Info about his bio-parents would be hard to come by, even for Livingston."

"You met Sarah's father," said Logan, "He's a smart guy but I don't know if you'd call him a genius - might have decent genes though."

Nate watched the scenery for a while. "So Sarah Crawford meets Peter at Leyland. Maybe they form some kind of a bond. She likes his art and that's it – that's their connection. No big deal. She just wanted his last painting as a keepsake of some kind. But why would she blackmail me over it?"

Nate watched Logan re-grip the wheel but she didn't say a word. She'd been without sleep for a long time now.

Cat leaned forward, toward Logan from the back seat. "She wasn't blackmailing Nate because of the painting, was she? She was trying to keep a secret of her own. She was having an affair with Peter. He's the father of her child."

It was something Nate had always considered too far-fetched to be true. He waited for Logan to reply.

She merged onto the interstate and stayed in the right lane. "I don't know who her affair was with. I do know that there had been times maybe a year ago that I'd seen her with heavy make-up that didn't quite cover the bruises on her face. Whoever her relationship was with, it was a violent one."

"Did you ever ask her about it?" asked Nate.

"I was new to her team back then and besides, Sarah and I were never that close. She was all business with me – never anything personal. That's why I was so surprised when she called me."

Cat stayed on the offensive. "She was having an affair with Peter. It turned ugly and she killed him."

Logan shook her head. "That's ridiculous. She's not a killer."

But Nate jumped at the implications. "Maybe there's something in Peter's last painting that would incriminate her or whoever the killer is. And even if Crawford's innocent of the actual murder, her ties to it would create a scandal that would cost her the governor's seat."

"That's a convenient explanation because it would clear you," said Logan to Nate. "You're just guessing. You have no evidence."

"A paternity test would be a good first step," said Cat.

Nate wondered if Peter's body would have to be exhumed for that, then remembered he'd been cremated. Was a paternity test even possible?

But Cat was a step ahead. "Leyland will have DNA samples from Peter from his previous genetic testing so a paternity test shouldn't be a problem."

"You'd need a court order," said Logan. "That'd mean you'd have to put a case together against Sarah and right now you have no evidence for that." She massaged the bridge of her nose then re-adjusted her glasses, all the while keeping her eyes on the road. "Look, I'm her campaign manager. Of course I'm going to be on her side. But at the same time, I think I'm being objective. You've come up with a wild theory that'll clear you but that's all it is – a wild theory."

They stopped for fast food. Cat and Nate both offered to drive but Logan insisted that she was okay and, a few miles later, Nate closed his eyes and the sounds of the road faded.

Logan dropped them off at the Crawford HQ where Nate's car was still parked. She thanked them for their help in finding Sarah and told Nate that she'd do what she could to arrange a meeting with her for him. Then she drove off.

Nate snatched a parking ticket from under his wiper. His car was warm inside from the hot sun. It felt good.

Cat got in but didn't buckle-up right away. "Nate, I didn't want to mention it earlier - you needed your sleep. I got a text from Mooch on the way back."

Nate sat behind the wheel and braced himself. From the sound of her voice, he knew this wouldn't be good.

"They've got some new evidence – he didn't say what. He said you should come in again as soon as you can."

Nate sank lower in his seat. "I almost wish he'd just arrest me."

"No, you don't Nate. But I need to send him a reply. I think you – we, should go there in the morning. Can I tell him that?"

It was all a sick joke, thought Nate, it had to be. It was something Peter might have pulled on him when they were kids. He could almost hear him laughing as the whole thing unfolded while he watched, eating his Snickers, sitting on that rock beside the stream. Nate couldn't believe any of it was really happening. By this time tomorrow, he could be in jail. He put his hands on the wheel and started the car. "Sure, I'll be there," he said. "I've got nothing better to do."

He pulled out into traffic and Cat sent the text.

CHAPTER 21

The next day they sat across a table from Detective Moochakouski. He had his eyes fastened on Nate's. "I got it from the DA that you threatened to shoot Peter."

Nate's heart skipped a beat but this wasn't really a surprise. Information about his threat had finally filtered down from Frank Caruso's police buddy in Maysville to the NYDA and then to Mooch. "Peter and I were just kids," said Nate. "The girl, Patty Harris had just died and he was teasing me about it asking what I'd do if I knew he'd killed her. I didn't really think he'd done it but I got mad and I threatened him. That's all there was to it."

Mooch showed no reaction. "Right now the background doesn't matter. The fact is, you made a threat and that fact has just turned up the heat. And then, there's the knife."

Nate couldn't believe he was bringing that up again.

Mooch held up a hand. "I know you're going to tell me it doesn't have anything to do with Peter's murder, not directly anyway, but the lab results came back. The brown stain on the blade was blood from the Harris girl. No fingerprints though – blade or handle."

Nate felt his hands shake and moved them under the table. He knew he had to keep his cool.

Mooch continued: "From the DA and from what you just told me, you threatened to shoot Peter because of the Harris murder. But it was you who had the murder weapon. Maybe you had it all along. It's only your word that says you found it in Peter's house."

"We can go back there. I'll show you where I found it."

"No we can't. The house has been torn down."

Nate could hear Peter in his head, laughing, *Man, you are so fucked!* He folded his arms, every muscle drawn tight.

Cat fired back. "You've got two murders separated by fifteen years and you're trying to pin them both on Nate? You'll never swing a warrant with this circumstantial shit."

"The DA doesn't consider the knife to be circumstantial and they do think the murders are connected, one motivating the other – revenge or cover-up, they're looking at both angles."

"What about Peter's 'life for a life note'?" asked Nate. "That was him confessing to the first murder. And what about Sarah Crawford and the missing painting?"

"The Scranton PD is handling things with the uncle. It doesn't help that he destroyed Peter's note – that makes it hear-say. We're still trying to contact Crawford."

"She just had her baby," said Cat. "She'll be out of commission for the next couple of weeks."

"She and Peter knew each other," said Nate. "They were both part of a genetics study,"

"Oh, yeah?" said Mooch making another note. "Was that recently?"

Nate looked at Cat, trying to remember the Leyland records from Logan's computer. "About nine years ago, I think."

Cat nodded. "Yeah, and two times before that." She told Mooch about the Leyland clinic. "It was at the same place where Sarah just had her baby. She's there now."

"Okay, we'll check that out."

"We think she and Peter were having an affair that turned bad," said Nate.

Mooch put his pen down. "I thought you were accusing the lieutenant governor of stealing a painting. Now you're saying she's guilty of murder?"

"Her own campaign manager said she'd been involved in an affair that turned violent. Colleen Logan's her name. Ask her about it."

Mooch wrote down the name then spread his hands. "Look, there's only so much I can do. I just wanted you here today to give you a heads up that things are not looking too good. I also wanted to tell you that I might be booted off the case."

"Oh yeah? Why's that?" asked Cat.

"The word is that the DA wants to handle this one directly. They're not telling me why and I'm not asking, but this is not good news for you. I'm thinking they're going to move quickly on this."

"Arrest me you mean?"

"Yeah, that's what I mean."

Nate's stomach knotted up, the blood draining from his face. He couldn't take any more of this. He stood up. "We've got to go."

"I can't stop you," said Mooch. "But don't go very far, they could show up at your door anytime. If they find that you've left the area, believe me, it won't look good. You should find yourself a good lawyer."

"Thanks for the tip, Mooch, but you're full of shit," said Cat from behind Nate who was already halfway out the door.

Another day went by before Cat was able to arrange a meeting with the lawyer she knew. She warned him: "He's not from the classiest of firms but he's competent and cheap."

His name was Sam Bellows and, to Nate, he could have been Mooch's twin brother. They caught up with him in a hallway at the courthouse downtown where Sam was handling another case. Cat filled him in on Nate's predicament and added a few words about their Sarah Crawford theory. Sam seemed unimpressed. "Lay low for now," was his suggestion. "See what the cops come up with. If they arrest you, give me a call and I'll come right down."

"That's it?" asked Nate.

"That's the best legal advice I can give you and, for now, it's free of charge."

Late that night, Nate sat across from Cat in his apartment, toying with his food. "There must be something we can do. I can't just wait around here until they come and get me. I know I keep going back to it but we need to find the painting. We need to put some solid evidence together against Crawford."

"What do you want to do, Nate, break into her house and steal it? We don't even know for sure that she's got it."

"She lives in Albany, right?"

"I guess so, and I would assume that she's got all the latest security gismos wired in. Even if we could jimmy the front door, we wouldn't get two feet inside before the sirens started going off and the police showed up – bad idea Nate."

"So we just lay low like your guy says?"

"We're going to see Sarah Crawford as soon as she's out of the hospital, remember? That's our plan."

Nate got up and started pacing.

Cat turned on the TV and began flipping channels. "Rats, just basic cable? No HBO?"

Nate didn't answer and, half an hour later, he walked Cat down to her cab. Appropriately, it was raining again.

He tossed and turned for most of the night then in the morning he got a phone call from Tom at the Brady Gallery with one piece of good news: two of his consignment paintings had sold. "People know your name now," Tom explained over the phone, excited. "You're the *Mozart Murder* artist, maybe soon to be the Rembrandt of Riker's Island. People eat that stuff up." He asked when he could get more of his paintings. Nate said he'd get back to him.

In the morning paper, Nate saw the press release about Sarah Crawford's new baby: *Mother and son doing well but staying at a private clinic for further tests and observation* – all routine said the article on page three. He wondered how long it would be before he was able to confront her - he itched at the chance. In his mind he had rehearsed the questions he'd ask and he'd be sure to ask them with his own eyes blazing just as hers had been at their last meeting. The stakes were higher now - he wasn't fighting to get a commission or to gain information; he was fighting for his life.

He called Logan – no answer, he left a message.

The morning dragged on. He tried to paint but his heart just wasn't in it. He'd been losing sleep. He had to get this Caruso thing behind him before it drove him nuts.

At two o'clock that afternoon, the police struck with their warrant. It came with a knock on his door and an insistent shout: "Police. Open up, Mr. Parks."

He was allowed to use the bathroom then the lead cop read him his rights as he was frisked and "cuffed" with a plastic zip-tie. The detective turned him around. "Mooch says that he called your girlfriend and she's calling your lawyer. They'll meet you at the station."

Nate nodded. His throat was sandpaper-dry. He was in a daze and said nothing as he was led out of his building. Outside, a knot of people were gathered on the sidewalk. A few cameras clicked. Somebody asked if he had anything to say. He just shook his head as he was lowered into the Crown-Vic police cruiser. There was also a second car – probably a back-up in case he went ape-shit or something.

He found himself thinking about the scene. It would make a good painting - lots of human interest. He'd call it: *The Arrest of the Artist*, or maybe *My Arrest*. It could be the start of a series to be followed by, *My Trial*, *My Sentencing*, *My Imprisonment* and then, many years later by *My Release*. He pictured himself a withered, gray-haired man standing beside a uniformed cop who maybe hadn't even been born yet. Nate's world was coming undone. As his cruiser pulled out, he looked up at his apartment building, wondering how long it would be before he'd see it again.

Cat got out of the cab, tossed the driver a couple of bills and sprinted into the station-house. She passed through security. "Visitor for prisoner Parks," she shouted to the desk clerk. She was ushered through a door and down a hallway then through another door. She stopped abruptly when she saw Nate alone in a holding cell sitting on a bench with his elbows on his knees. His hands were folded and he was perfectly still until he looked in her direction. He stood up as she hurried over.

"Nate, I came as quickly as I could. I can't believe they're doing this to you."

He was pale and expressionless; looking ten years older than the last time she'd seen him. He attempted a smile. "Hi Cat." He stepped to the bars that separated them.

She reached in and grabbed his hand. "Sam's on his way. We'll get you out of this. There'll be a bail hearing in a few hours I think."

A guard shouted, "No touching of prisoners, ma'am," but she ignored him.

Sam arrived a few minutes later, briefcase in hand, tie loose at the collar. He glanced at Cat then gave the guard a fierce look. "Open up," he ordered, "I need to speak to my client."

Cat entered the cell in front of Sam and pulled Nate close. He felt unsteady, as if all his strength had left him. "It'll be all right, Nate, it's going to all work out," she told him. She jumped when the cell door clanged shut. "We can get him out on bail, right Sam?"

Sam sat down on the bench with his briefcase open, and began going through some papers. "Bail isn't normally allowed in a murder case," he said without looking up. Then he handed some papers and a pen to Nate. "Here, you need to sign these – by the yellow highlight. It's just officializing me representing you."

"No bail?" asked Nate.

"It's not that they think you're a flight risk," said Sam "but murder's murder. It doesn't get more serious than that."

Nate sat down and signed the papers. Sam put them in his briefcase and snapped it closed.

"So what happens now?" asked Nate.

"Now, you get put into the system, mug-shots, finger prints, cell assignment, that'll all be done today. You'll probably be transferred to the county jail downtown. Tomorrow we go before the judge and enter a plea – not guilty of course. After that a trial date is assigned. We usually have a couple of months to go over the facts, put together a strategy and prepare for the trial but it could be longer than that depending on the backlog of cases. Or they might fast-track us because of all the publicity – you know, everyone talking about it in the papers and on TV, it makes it hard to find jurors who haven't already made up their minds about you.

"We've got a good shot here, Nate. This is a high-profile case and I think they jumped the gun with your arrest because of all the shit they were getting from the politicos at City Hall. Their evidence is weak but there's enough of it to cause us some trouble." Sam stood up and signaled the guard, then turned back to Nate. "Just remember, you're innocent so you've got nothing to worry about. This is just a minor inconvenience – consider it a vacation. I hear the food's okay at county. I'll see you there tomorrow." They shook hands and Sam left.

"A vacation," said Nate. "Is this guy serious? He's good you said?"

Cat nodded. "He's not the most polished but yeah, he's good." Still, she didn't feel quite as confident about Sam as she had a few days ago. The truth was that she had simply heard a few good things about him but hadn't seen him in action.

Nate put his hands in his pockets. "I never thought it would come to this, Cat."

"Me too, but don't lose faith. We're going to get you out. Me and Sam, we're going to get you out."

The guard, who'd been holding the cell door open since Sam had left, opened it wider. "You really can't be in there, Miss. You need to go." Nate and Cat both stood up.

Nate spoke fast. "We need to get hold of Crawford. I called Logan this morning and left a message. And can you give my parents a call. Let them know what's happened and tell them I'm okay." He gave her their number.

"Right, Nate. I'll do it. Now, buck up. Innocent people get accused of bad things all the time. Have a little faith in our justice system, okay?"

Nate nodded and attempted a smile. "I know I'm being a wimp but I've never been arrested before. I don't even *know* anyone who's been arrested. I had jury duty once but that's the closest I've been to any of this." He took a deep breath. "Okay, I'll buck up, don't worry."

Cat looked into his eyes that seemed a little calmer now. She gave him a kiss and left, more worried than ever.

She'd hoped to catch up with Sam but instead was waylaid by Mooch in the outer lobby. He grabbed her elbow. "Let's have a talk," he told her, matching her pace, guiding her through the outer doors.

Out on the sidewalk she shook off his grip. "Why would I want to talk to you? How could you guys arrest him? You don't have a case and you know it." The flow of pedestrian traffic forced them to move along with the current. It was a bright sunny day in May, the kind she would have normally enjoyed.

Mooch looked at her sideways. "You like this guy don't you?"

"What do you care?"

"Come on Cat, we go back a long way. You know I care. Angie does too. You're like family."

Cat thought about the last time she'd had dinner with Mooch and his wife - spaghetti and homemade garlic bread – it was one of Angie's specialties. "Sorry, I wasn't being fair. Yeah, I do like him. He doesn't deserve this Mooch. He had nothing to do with the murder." They stopped for a light at the corner. "So what did you want to talk about?"

"After talking with you and Parks the last time, I tried to contact Sarah Crawford. We got Logan, her campaign manager who didn't know anything. Then I talked with old man Crawford."

"He told you that Sarah was still in the hospital and was still recovering and couldn't talk – right?" They started walking again, faster this time.

"Yeah, that's what he said. Then I mentioned the painting and he got all upset – really upset. He let go a few f-bombs and hung up. Then, a short time later I was booted off the case like I told you I would be. I had nothing to do with the warrant."

"You think Crawford got you pushed out?"

"I don't know for sure. The DA's playing it pretty close to the vest. You should know that they do have a reasonable case but it's starting to smell funny." Mooch was keeping up but was huffing and puffing.

Cat slowed down and stopped when they reached the stairs leading down to the subway. She leaned against the railing.
Mooch caught his breath. "The point is, the painting was a hot button for the old man. You might want to follow up on that."

"Wouldn't the DA follow that angle?"

"I don't think they even care about that angle. Right now

they've got a suspect in custody and they intend to go after him with everything they've got. You're a good investigator, Cat. The best way to help your guy is to find that painting. That's all I wanted to tell you."

Mooch was a tough cop, always interested in finding the truth, and maybe that's what Cat liked most about him. She pointed to a street-vender. The smell of kraut and mustard was in the air. "Can I buy you a dog?"

"Naw," said Mooch, patting his belly with both hands. "Angie has me on reduced gluten and low-carbs - makes me weigh myself every night. Some women check their husband's shirts for lipstick smudges, mine checks for mustard and catsup stains. Nothing gets past her. Besides, I've got to get back."

She leaned over and kissed him on the cheek, his skin rough with stubble reminding her of her dad. "Thanks for the info, Mooch. I'll see you around." She headed down to the trains.

As Sam predicted, Nate was transferred downtown and the plea hearing took place two days later. Halfway back in the courtroom, Cat sat with Nate's parents, who had taken the train up the night before. She filled them in on what to expect.

Nate was one of maybe a dozen accused prisoners who would be run through the courtroom, one at a time. The charge on the arrest warrant would be read, the plea entered and a court-date set. And that was it. Nothing else would happen today.

The courtroom was jammed by ten when the judge entered and got the cattle-call started. From a door on the left, the first prisoner was escorted in. He wore loose-fitting, bright orange prison garb and was met by his lawyer who stood beside him in front of the judge. As the clerk read off the case number and the charge, Cat spotted Sam who sat to one side with the rest of the lawyers. He had his brief case open, using it for cover as he munched on an apple and leafed through some papers.

She glanced at Nate's parents thinking how hard this must be for them. They sat straight and taut with grim, *American Gothic* expressions.

Nate was fifth to be called and there was a commotion in the gallery as he entered the room. Cat strained for a better look. He seemed oblivious to his surroundings. He kept his eyes straight and his walk was mechanical but he didn't seem afraid. Sam, who had finished his apple by this time, joined him in front of the bench as the clerk read the warrant.

"How do you plead?" asked the judge.

"Not guilty, your honor," said Sam, "and we petition the court for bail your honor."

The prosecutor was half out of his chair, but the judge waived him to sit back down.

"This is a murder case, Mr. Bellows, you know better. There'll be no bail." He looked to the clerk and set a trial date for June thirtieth then pounded his gavel and shouted, "Next." As Nate was guided out, half the courtroom emptied. Cat led Nate's parents out and flagged Sam down in the outer hallway.

"Nate told us there was nothing to worry about," said his mother not waiting to be introduced. "He's on trial for murder. How could they think he'd do such a terrible thing?"

Cat looked around at a few reporters who were edging closer. Sam saw them too. "Come on," he said, "we can't talk here."

Sam took them into a small conference room where they all sat. He closed the door. "They don't have much of a case," he told Nate's parents, "but there was so much publicity, the DA was pressured into making an arrest. You saw them out there. They're all fighting for a story."

"Does he really have to stay in jail until the trial?" asked his father. "That's a long time."

"Not as bad as some," said Sam. "And they treat prisoners awaiting trial much better than convicts up at the state prisons. No hanky-panky here if you know what I mean. They're afraid of getting sued by guys who are found innocent."

Cat put her elbows on the table. "So your strategy is to just let this go to trial; the jury will see how flimsy the evidence is and all this will go away?"

"Yeah, that's about it."

"You're not going after Sarah Crawford?" asked Cat. She had explained the lieutenant governor's possible involvement in the case to Nate's Parents.

Sam folded his hands. "I'm a lawyer, Ms. Chaplin. I'm not with the police and I'm not a private detective like you. I stick to what I'm good at. If you can dig up anything useful from Crawford, be my guest but you might want to take a look at this first." He reached into his coat pocket and handed her a brown envelope.

She went through the pages inside.

"It's a Cease and Desist Order," explained Sam. "It prevents me or anyone associated with my office or with this case, from contacting or going anywhere near Sarah Crawford or her father. I guess you and Nate tried to see her in the hospital? Her father's also gotten calls from the police about the case."

Cat looked up from the papers. “So the state’s protecting them.”

“Yeah,” said Sam. “Protecting them from what they consider to be harassment. It’ll take some new evidence to get the order rescinded. Until that happens, we can’t touch them.”

“But I can’t get the evidence if I can’t talk to them,” said Cat.

“Right, Catch-22. That’s why our best strategy is to just let the DA’s case fall apart on its own.”

Cat shuffled through the five-page document and reached the last page that granted power of attorney to Sarah’s father while she was in the hospital. There, on the bottom of the page was Sarah’s signature and just below it the signature of her father, David Lucas Crawford. The image of it jarred her memory. She stared, wondering if she might be imagining what she thought she saw.

“Mind if I take a photo of this?” asked Cat, reaching for her phone.

“Knock yourself out. What is it? Did you see something?” Nate’s dad held the document flat while she took a photo of it. “Maybe,” she said, putting her phone away calmly. But her heart was thumping as she gave the papers back to Sam.

“When can we see him? We were told we could see him,” said his mother.

Sam stood up. “Right now.”

They all took the elevator to the third floor. The desk clerk recognized Sam and took them into a waiting area. “Two at a time, you know the drill, Mr. Bellows.”

“The two of you should go first,” said Sam indicating Nate’s parents. “Stay as long as they let you.”

The clerk showed them through a door then closed it behind them.

While Sam sat, Cat remained standing, leaning against the wall, her mind churning, her fingers drumming the cinder-block.

“All right, let’s have it,” said Sam. “What did you find?”

“I can’t say yet. It’s almost too outlandish to be true so just let me keep it to myself for a while.”

“Yeah, right, I’m only the guy’s lawyer here, why would I need to know?”

“Just give me some time, Sam. I’ll get back to you tomorrow.”

When they left the courthouse Cat had lunch with Nate’s parents, trying to be leisurely and encouraging but all the while dying to get back to her apartment where she could see whether or not her memory was playing tricks with her. She made sure they were settled in at their hotel, then hurried home.

Inside her apartment, she tossed her keys on the table and found her tablet. With her power at only five percent, she wasted a few minutes finding her charge cord and plugging in, then pulled up the photo's Nate had taken of Dr. Wright's Caruso files. She swiped through them quickly then came to Peter's adoption papers. There it was at the bottom of the page. She enlarged the area she was interested in then pulled out her phone tabbing over to the power of attorney document she'd just taken a photo of. She enlarged David Crawford's signature and held it next to her tablet.

"My God!" she said in disbelief studying the sharp corners of the 'D' and the smooth curve in the 'C' of both signatures. She leaned back in her chair, thumbing the table top then made a call, nearly dropping her phone. After completing the call, she sent an email with two attachments.

CHAPTER 22

Cat had to wait until the next morning to pay a visit to Hiram H. Foster, a legal consultant and handwriting expert. He worked out of his apartment and only on weekday mornings. Bradshaw had used him before and she knew there were some Bradshaw-bucks left untapped from a previous retainer.

"So, what do you think?" she asked him, sitting at his kitchen table. The guy lived alone and was definitely not the outgoing type, but he knew his shit and right now, that's all that mattered.

Hiram showed her a printout of two signatures side by side; one of David Crawford, the other of Dmitry Cavianski, the man in Romania who'd signed off on Peter's adoption papers thirty years ago. Then he showed her a printout of just the D and C superimposed from each document – one in red, one in blue. "Same slant, same size ratios, same curvatures," he said, raising a finger, "not just close, but identical. It's a little odd, seeing as how you said that there were thirty years separating the two samples. You know, arthritis hits the fingers, it can change the character of the writing. But, apparently that's not the case here."

"So, same guy right?"

Hiram nodded. "With ninety-five percent certainty, yes, same guy. Of course I could do better if I had a larger writing sample to work with."

"No chance of that," said Cat, her thoughts whirling. If Sarah Crawford's father was really Dmitry Cavianski, the man in Romania who'd signed off on Peter's adoption papers thirty years ago then *he* was the real connection between Sarah and Peter. There was no telling how this was going to play out but she had a good hunch it would work in Nate's favor. "Can you put your results in writing?"

He slid his already prepared report across the table: Three pages with diagrams and analysis and a professional concluding statement. Yes, Hiram knew his shit.

"By my records," he said, "this fulfills the obligations of my old retainer." He handed her his invoice.

Cat took a breath at the amount. "Yup, looks like we're all square."

"I'll need more if you need me to testify."

"I'm hoping that won't be necessary." Cat would have some explaining to do with Bradshaw about the money but it had been worth it. She shook hands with Hiram and left. Next stop - Sam's place.

His two-room office sat over a Jewish deli where, even on this rainy day, the smells of pastrami and rye filled the air for a half-block in all directions. From the street below, Cat tilted her umbrella back to read the red neon sign in his window: *Law offices of Sam Bellows*. She had called him on her way over to see if he had time to meet with her and he'd reluctantly agreed - big favor, she knew he didn't have anything better to do. Lawyers could be a pain in the ass sometimes.

Once inside, Cat shook off the rain and climbed the stairs. "Hey, it's Cat, I'm here," she yelled out, entering the outer office where she would have expected a secretary to be posted. The desk was empty. Guess Sam wasn't doing as well as he liked everyone to think.

"Enter," said Sam from behind the inner office door.

She hung up her coat and gave the door shove. "Hey Sam," she said, walking in and taking a seat as if they were old buddies. She put her purse down on the bare wooden floor.

Sam watched her as she did this then snuffed out his cigarette and lit another. That done, he leaned back, his chair almost touching the window behind him. "All right, what's your big secret?"

"Sorry, I couldn't talk about it yesterday, I had to be sure."

Sam's head bobbed side to side in a let's-get-on-with-it kind of way.

Cat pulled a file-folder from her purse. "Peter Caruso was born in Rumania. He was adopted by Frank Caruso and his wife. The adoption process and the immigration process were both handled at the Romanian end by a guy named Dmitry Cavianski."

Sam stared at her blankly.

"I have good reason to believe that Sarah Crawford's father, David Crawford, is really Dmitry Cavianski."

Sam's brows went up a little. Cat showed him Hiram's report, and Peter's baby picture and his Romanian birth certificate.

He studied these for a while then tapped his ashes. "Combined with what you told me earlier, you've got quite a story here. Tell me if I've got this right: Peter Caruso was born in Romania. Somehow his parents were out of the picture but there's this Cavianski fellow who takes responsibility for him. He arranges for Peter's adoption by the Carusos of Maysville, PA. Peter grows up a typical American kid until one day in high school he somehow turns into a young Rembrandt. At about the same time, a girl in his school is murdered. Then, fifteen years later, after leading the life of a hermit, Peter is murdered. But a few days before his death, he sends a painting to the dead girl's uncle along with the life for a life note." Sam had said this all in one breath; he took another. "Good so far?"

"Yeah, good so far."

"Okay. While all this is going on, Cavianski has a daughter, born roughly around the same time as Peter. They come to the U.S. where he changes his name to David Crawford and probably forges U.S. papers. He then gets married and has a couple of other kids and they all live, happy as clams, in Albany. Sarah grows up the all American kid then, in her early teens, somehow turns into a mental genius. She goes to Cornell, aces everything, gets her J.D. and gets into state politics where she becomes a regular female Machiavelli. She gets to be lieutenant governor and now, barely thirty, is running for governor.

"This is where your buddy Nate gets involved. Because the cops don't have any better ideas, he becomes a suspect in Peter's murder. In trying to clear himself Nate tries to learn more about Peter. He comes up with the blood-stained knife that killed the high school girl and finds out about the painting that had been sent to the girl's uncle but then was sold to an intermediary guy who's driving a State of New York vehicle. You and Nate jump to the conclusion that Sarah Crawford's involved since she's with the state and she's shown an interest in Peter's work in the past. Nate confronts her and she goes nuts, threatening to blackmail him if he tells anyone about her and Peter. But – she denies having the painting."

Cat broke in at this point. "Her father got agitated when a detective asked about the painting. Sam, the painting is evidence in Peter's murder and this new info about David Crawford really being Dmitry Cavianski proves that he's the link between Sarah and Peter. It should be enough to get a warrant to search the Crawford place don't you think?"

Sam rubbed his jaw. "Maybe, but do you see how complicated your story is? Juries like to keep things simple. *I* like to keep things simple. And, even if the old man is who you say he is, that doesn't directly support your theory that Sarah and Peter were having an affair and that she killed him. Besides, if the painting really does implicate her as you're hoping it will, why wouldn't she or her father just destroy it?"

Cat stared down at the floor. "Yes, they may have destroyed it. That would have been the smart thing to do. But right now that painting is Nate's only hope."

"That and the for-shit case the DA has against him." Sam snuffed out his cigarette. He drew his chair closer to his desk and handed her documents back to her. "Look, Cat, you've done some good work here. Do me a favor - I've got a copy machine out there, go make me three copies of your stuff. I'll see what I can do. Maybe Crawford's connection with Peter and Sarah will be enough to swing a warrant."

Cat got to her feet. "Thanks Sam."

"Yeah, yeah." He stood up and turned to the rain-spackled window, a hand in his pocket jiggling some loose change.

From Sam's, Cat took the subway to the jail making it just in time for visiting hours. She waited by the Plexiglas window until they escorted Nate in. His sullen expression brightened when he saw her but she could see that his smile was strained. He sat down and picked up the phone receiver.

She tried to sound as positive as she could. "I've got some good news, Nate. I found the real connection between Peter and Sarah. It's Crawford - the old man."

Nate shook his head. "I'm not following you."

"Yeah, it's pretty incredible. The signature of Dmitry Cavianski on Peter's adoption papers from Romania is a match for David Crawford's. I had them analyzed. It's ninety-five percent certain that Crawford really is, or was, Cavianski. How about that?"

Nate pulled back from the window, his eyes widening just a bit. "You're right, Cat, that's incredible. How did you ever think to look into that?"

"Hey, just using my every day, normal, detective instincts."

She watched Nate's face. "So, what do you think?"

He ran his fingers through his hair. "I'm not sure what to think. But, like you said, that's the link we've been looking for between Peter and Sarah – that and the GS testing at the Leyland Clinic."

"I'm hoping Sam can use this new info to get a warrant issued to search Crawford's home for the painting. He's on it now."

"They probably wouldn't have it at their house. They might have even destroyed it."

She nodded. "That's what Sam thought, but we have to try. Even if we don't find it, they should at least be able to pull Sarah's father in for questioning. That might lead to something."

"Yes, yes, that's good." Nate leaned closer. "Have you talked with Logan? We need to talk to Logan."

Cat watched Nate's hand flexing into a fist every ten seconds or so. "Don't go buggy on me Nate. I told you I tried to get hold of her yesterday. I left her a message. I'll try again today."

"Call her now, Cat, we need her to get to Sarah Crawford. Tell her you need to talk to her right away."

"I'm not sure that's a good idea, Nate. If we can get a search warrant, we don't want to tip them off about it."

Nate paused. "Yeah, I guess maybe your right about that." He nodded and leaned back in his chair, looking up to the ceiling.

"You *are* going buggy aren't you? Nate, it's only been a couple of days. You've got a few weeks before the trial. Try to put things out of your mind. Trust me and Sam to work things out. I thought you said you were going to catch up on some reading. Are you doing that?"

"I'm into Russian novels now. Just about half way through *Crime and Punishment*," said Nate.

"Ha, good one," said Cat. Then, seeing Nate's dead-pan expression she wasn't so sure. "You're joking, right?"

His face broadened a little. "Had you going, didn't I?"

It was good to hear at least an attempted joke from Nate.

The days dragged by and each time Cat visited Nate she grew more conscious of the hopeful look on his face when he'd first catch sight of her – like maybe she had some good news for him. But there wasn't any good news, and she began to feel that her visits were just making things worse.

A week passed. Nate's parents, who'd also visited him faithfully, took the train back to Scranton planning to be back for the trial. Cat told them she'd keep them updated if there were any new developments. At their leaving, she felt relieved that she was no longer charged with keeping their spirits up, as well as Nate's, as well as her own. She called Sam every day but he'd still not heard back from the judge who was considering his search warrant request.

There were only two weeks to go before the trial and Cat was at her desk at Bradshaw's when Sam called.

"The warrant's been issued," he said. "They conducted the search this morning but didn't find a thing."

Cat took a breath. "Whose house was searched? Sarah's or her father's?"

"Both. And the local cops are interviewing them."

"Locals? Anybody from Brownsville there?"

Sam said he didn't know who was handling the searches or the questioning. "We should get a report on the interviews sometime tomorrow but you know Cat, unless the Crawfords say something really stupid, the cops will have no reason to hold them. Besides, Sarah was just released from the hospital two days ago and her baby's still undergoing some kind of treatment there. Without some very good reason, they aren't about to haul her off for a formal interrogation."

So it was more bad news for Nate. Cat ended the call and leaned back in her chair. She was alone at Bradshaw's, a stack of folders piled on the desk in front of her: divorce cases, slander, assault, dregs of the earth type stuff. She started wondering how or why she'd ever gotten into the detective business. It was all so depressing. Then she thought about her next visit with Nate. After she told him the bad news about the search, his first question would be about Logan? She decided to try her one last time. This time she answered.

"What do you want?" she asked when Cat told her who she was.

"Nate's in jail. I need to talk with Sarah."

"Can't help you there even if I wanted to. I'm off her campaign. I've been fired because of you and Parks. The Crawfords didn't take kindly to being questioned by the cops or to the search warrant you had issued. They're blaming me for all of it."

"I'm sorry for the way things turned out," said Cat with genuine regret. Logan was silent but she was still on the line. Cat tried her luck with another question: "I hear the baby's still at Leyland – Do you know why?"

"No I don't."

"Is he okay?"

"I think so. The doctors are probably just being cautious. Sarah's staying in a place near the hospital."

"Is she accepting visitors?"

Logan laughed. "There's no way you're going to see her now. All her security people have your pictures – you and Parks. They'll stop you before you even get out of your car."

"She still running for governor?"

"Oh, yeah. There's no stopping Sarah Crawford once she gets her mind set on something. She's like a Sherman tank. She and her tyrant father will probably be handling the campaign directly now. She never needed me anyway. Strategy? Spin? Tactics? Her ideas were always the best anyway. She'll be president someday, I honestly believe that."

Not if she was born in Romania, thought Cat. "Do you have any idea why she called you that night from Leyland?"

"It was probably the drugs that got her scared. That and the hormones from the pregnancy. She just wasn't thinking straight."

"Is she thinking straight now? Is she under any sedation?"

"Don't know; I haven't talked with her."

"She didn't call you when she fired you?"

"She fired me by text – real classy huh? Look, I'd just as soon forget I ever met Sarah Crawford."

"I really am sorry about things."

"Hey, I'm just another victim of hardball politics – happens every day." Logan ended the call.

Cat knew that gubernatorial campaign managers easily pulled in six-figures with incentives and cancellation clauses so she didn't feel too bad for Logan.

Sam called an hour later.

"I got the transcripts from the cops on their questioning of the Crawfords," he said. "They denied everything – Romania, Cavianski, the painting – everything."

"How did they get around the handwriting analysis?"

"They said your handwriting guy must have just gotten it wrong."

"Did the cops believe them?"

"Well they didn't arrest them, so yeah, I guess for now they believe them. But we've got both the Crawfords on our list of people that we may want to have testify in the trial, so that's a plus."

"Yeah, big plus," said Cat, already dreading her next visit to Nate still with nothing good to tell him.

"There is one thing though," said Sam. "Sarah Crawford and

her baby are back in Albany, staying at the old man's place. The baby was released this morning."

"About time. I was wondering why they were keeping him there so long. Say, can you send those transcripts to me? I'd like to take a look at them – oh, and the report from the search."

She was at Bradshaw's when the email from Sam arrived half an hour later. She printed out the attachments and spent the rest of the day studying them, highlighting certain sections and making notes in the margins. Sam was right – they denied everything. Sarah even denied ever having met with Nate, much less blackmailing him. Cat was sure the questioning of Sarah and her father had occurred separately yet their answers to certain questions were surprisingly similar, down to the use of the same phrasing. Had he coached her or had she coached him? Who was the puppet master here? She tapped her pen against her notepad and glanced at her watch almost glad that it was too late to visit Nate yet today. She had an idea to work out.

Cat saw Nate the next day and broke the news to him straight out. "They did the search at the Crawford's yesterday and questioned them both - no painting and they denied everything." She watched his eyes deaden as she spoke. She hated to see him like this. "Sorry Nate."

He just nodded and, for a while neither spoke.

Cat tried to sound casual when she asked if she could use his car for the next few days.

"Giving up, leaving town, right?"

"Leaving town, not giving up."

"You aren't going up to Albany are you?" Nate asked showing concern from behind the glass.

"Well, yeah, I'm going to pay a visit to the Crawfords – hopefully both of them."

"You're just going to knock on their door and expect them to talk with you? The old man has seen you Cat; he'll never talk to you. He'll just slam the door in your face. With that Cease and Desist Order back in force, he could even have you arrested."

Cat tried to read Nate's expression. He spoke forcefully enough but his eyes were a dull blue – glassy even, like an old man's. He hadn't shaved in a few days and his hair was starting to flap over his ears. His mouth was drawn tight and straight, his lips were thin, more bluish than pink. She was afraid to ask what it was like to sit in a cell, waiting to be put on trial for murder. She could see he was having a tough time and it was all she could do to keep the tears from her eyes. This was a good man in front of her and she had to stay strong for him.

"I've got a plan," she said.

"You're going to break in and search their house on your own?"

"Come on Nate, I'm not stupid. But it's only ten days until the trial. I have to do this. Are you going to let me take your car or do I have to go to Avis?"

He finally relented. "Eduardo has a key to my apartment. The car keys are on a hook beside the door." He placed his hands closer to the glass. "Be careful, Cat," he said as she left.

Once outside, Cat called Meredith.

CHAPTER 23

They met at a forty-second street diner. Meredith's hair was tied back in a ponytail and she wore a bright yellow and white pant suit with long sleeves. As she slid into the booth opposite Cat, she flicked the strap of her white leather purse off her shoulder. "How's Nate?"

"Not great but he's doing okay." Cat filled her in on the latest as the waiter came over. Her stomach growled for a burger and a diet but she ordered a salad with iced-tea, the same as Meredith.

"The trial's next week, right?"

"Yes."

"You said on the phone you thought I could help. What did you have in mind?"

"I want to clear up something first," said Cat folding her hands on the table. "I know you and Nate had an affair."

Meredith drew some ice-water through her straw. "Did he tell you that?"

"Yes, and he told me about the two of you shacking up at the Hilton."

"Well, so much for gentlemanly discretion." Meredith wiped down her silverware then placed her napkin on her lap. There'd been no shock or embarrassment in her voice.

Cat watched her eyes. "Sarah Crawford had a private detective there at the hotel. He snapped some pictures of the two of you. She tried to blackmail Nate over it."

Meredith winced at this, as if bitten by a mosquito, but only a small one. "Why would she do that?"

"To get Nate off her back about Peter. She threatened to tell

Teddy."

"Oh."

Their salads and drinks came.

"I like Nate," said Cat, adding a packet of sugar to her tea then stirring. "I like him a lot. He says his thing with you is over but I want to hear it from you – is it over?"

Meredith sat silent for a time, staring down at the table. Then she locked eyes with Cat. "I almost thought that he'd be worth leaving Teddy over but I just couldn't bring myself to do it. When a man like Nate comes to you in your home and paints you so beautifully, so sensuously..." She took another sip of tea. "I'm telling you it was almost like we'd already made love even before he first touched me. I've never had that feeling before. It was an experience somehow beyond the flesh."

Cat wasn't sure if Meredith was being corny for her benefit or if she really was that emotional. She lowered her voice. "Do you love him?"

"You know, at that time in our relationship I really did, and it was a more intense, more intimate feeling than I've ever had." She shook her head as if reacting to her own comment. "I'm a fickle woman, Cat. I like using my beauty, my sex, to control men. Teddy's easy. His money's easy and he makes my life easy. Nate was easy too but there's more to him than I ever got to know." She took a fork-full of salad and chewed quickly. "Nate has this thing about an old Eagles song, *Lying Eyes* – do you know it?"

Cat nodded.

"He knew right away that I was that girl – rich old husband, pretty young wife lonely for love – the whole bit. And he was right, I'm that girl. And for a time, Nate was my blue-eyed boy on the other side of town."

"Not anymore?"

Meredith shook her head slowly as if deciding the matter just at that moment. "No, not any more. He deserves better than me. The two of you look good together – you really do."

Cat wondered if she should believe her. Well, there wasn't much of a future in not believing her was there? She picked up her plastic cup of thousand- island dressing and poured it over her salad. "We won't be together too much if he's stuck in jail."

"You're not really in the wine and cheese business, are you?" asked Meredith.

"No, not as much as I used to be." Cat handed her one of her Bradshaw cards. She wanted to tell her that she was the one who'd tailed her while she was having her fling with Nate but thought better of it - no sense rocking that boat.

Meredith tucked the card into her purse. "Okay, now that we've got all that out of the way, why did you want to meet with me?"

"If you're interested, I think there's a way we can get Nate out of this mess." Cat took the intrigued look on Meredith's face as a good sign.

Two days later, there was a cold-snap in Albany and a chill ran through the Crawford home, but it was warm in the great room where a gas fire blazed and Sarah held little Noah to her breast. She felt his warmth through the blankets and felt the warm flow of milk leaving her body. It was the most pleasurable experience of her life. It was her love that was feeding him, continuing to give him life even now that he was no longer inside her. She watched his eyelids droop then finally close. His lips kept up their suckling motion for a little longer, then stopped, then gentle breathing.

From behind the couch, her father leaned over and kissed the top of her head. "He's a beautiful creature, Sarah."

His use of that word bothered Sarah, as if Noah was more of a medical specimen than he was his own grandson. She knew of course that he wasn't really his grandson just as she wasn't really his daughter.

In actuality, both she and Noah were medical specimens of his – products of the terrible chain of events he'd set into motion thirty years ago with all his noble, good intentions. She knew now that those intentions had been nothing more than a shield that he'd hidden behind as he forced his un-natural, un-holy work on the most helpless and most innocent of victims. What kind of man would do that? And what kind of person would condone such a thing? Well, the brilliant Lieutenant Governor Sarah Crawford had condoned it and had even participated in it. No longer the helpless victim, she herself had become an accomplice in the crime. Now it was little Noah's turn to be the victim.

Sarah shrank from herself just as she shrank from the touch of the old man behind her who she'd called "Daddy" for so long.

She dried, then covered her breast and got up with an effort, carrying Noah from the living room into the nursery where she laid him down. She tucked the blanket around him and left the door open a crack on the way out. "He'll sleep well tonight," she said, sitting back down on the couch, knowing there'd be another feeding at two in the morning, four hours from now – she could hardly wait that long.

Her father sat in a chair closer to her than to the fire with an open book on his lap and a reading lamp beside him. "Do you wonder if it was all worth it?" he asked.

"I wonder about that all the time. Don't you?"

"What's done is done, Sarah dear. This is a new beginning." He marked his place and closed the book. "You should start thinking about getting back into things."

Sarah had left Leyland without her baby nearly a month ago. Noah had stayed behind for what the doctors called important tests but Sarah knew what those tests were and she'd let them happen. The whole time, she'd been desperate to have Noah back and now that he was back with her, they were inseparable. Sarah never left the house. "I'm afraid," she said quietly, staring into the flames. "I've never been afraid of anything before but I'm afraid now. I don't know if I can function any more. My drive is gone and my confidence is gone. I feel like I can no more run for governor than I can fly to the moon. I'm not sure I *can* get back into things."

"You're just in one of your moods again. Your hormones are still coming back into balance. The doctors warned you about this." Her father leaned forward. "You've got people depending on you, Sarah. What are you going to tell them?"

"The same thing I just told you."

He got up and closed the glass doors to the fireplace then eased himself back into his chair. "We're going to have a visitor tomorrow, you know her, Meredith Sinclair."

"Teddy's wife."

"Yes. As you know, the Sinclairs have been very generous contributors in the past and they have many friends. I think they're a little concerned about you being out of the public eye for so long. Meredith is in Albany visiting a friend of hers. She wants to stop by and see you."

"Teddy won't be with her?"

"No, it'll just be her. Will you be up to it? Will you do it for me?"

Sarah reached down and pulled up an old, loose-knit afghan. She wrapped herself in it, putting her feet on the ottoman. It felt good – nice and cozy as Daddy would say when she was little, back when she had no idea of the way things really were. "Yes, I think I can manage it."

It was warmer the next day and it was mid-afternoon when Sarah heard the doorbell ring. From where she sat, next to a sun-filled window in the nursery, she heard a grunt and a rustle of newspapers as her father walked to the front door and opened it. She couldn't quite make out the exchange of pleasantries but she knew it must be Meredith. She put on her slippers and as she rose she glanced at Noah, sleeping peacefully. She closed the door gently behind her then walked toward the foyer where she saw her father guiding Meredith into the great room.

"Meredith, so good to see you again," said Sarah.

Meredith gave her a warm embrace. "Good to see you again, Sarah. How are you feeling? You look great."

"I'm feeling well," said Sarah thinking that Meredith was being a little over the top with her greeting. She had known Meredith only through Teddy's money and, though they'd always been genial to one another, they were hardly best of friends. She glanced at her father.

"Have a seat, both of you," he said. "I've got some tea brewing. I'll be back in a moment."

"Tea would be nice," said Meredith, taking a chair by the window. "It's cooler here than in New York."

"It was actually cold yesterday," said her father from the kitchen. "I'm glad to see it getting warmer today. It is June after all."

"My father's been doing everything for me," said Sarah to Meredith. "I've only been back a few days."

"We'd been afraid there were complications, you being in the hospital so long and then the baby staying even longer. Are you sure you're all right?"

"They just wanted to run some tests. Noah was three months premature you know."

"Yes, I know, but they ran tests on you too?"

Sarah was feeling more herself today and her instincts were kicking in. Meredith was asking too many questions. She decided to be truthful, at least with this answer. "Hormonal instability, they called it. The doctors just wanted to play it safe. I'm fine now."

"Great. And where is little Noah? I hope I get to see him?"

"Afternoon nap, we can look in on him before you go, unless he wakes up sooner."

Her father came in with the tea service along with some shortbread biscuits. "High tea," he said to Meredith, "the best thing the Brits ever gave the world. How do you like yours?"

"Light with two lumps, thank you."

He passed her the cup then fixed one for Sarah and himself.

Meredith took a sip. “I hope you don’t mind my saying, Mr. Crawford, but you would have made a wonderful English butler.”

He laughed, sitting down. “Guess I missed my calling. Please call me David.”

“I understand you’re here visiting a friend?” asked Sarah.

“That’s right. I’ll be staying at her place tonight then back home tomorrow – old college pal.”

They talked about Teddy and then about the campaign.

“So, David, I understand you let Logan go?” asked Meredith, biting into a biscuit.

Sarah shot him a glance, curious to hear how he’d handle this question.

“That only just happened,” he said. “Do you mind my asking how you found out?”

“The important thing is that the press will ask about it. Who’s handling the campaign now?”

“I am. Well, Sarah and I together are.”

“Big job.”

Sarah watched Meredith cross her legs and lean back in her chair, giving the impression that her interest was only casual – but Sarah knew better. Nothing about this visit was casual. She decided it was time to get to the point. “We can count on your support, I hope?”

“Of course you can,” said Meredith. “Teddy wanted me to make that quite clear. In fact,” she reached into her purse, “Teddy wanted me to give this to you personally and to tell you there’s more to come.” She handed Sarah a white envelope.

Sarah looked at the check inside and saw the dollar amount. “Thank you ever so much. This is very encouraging.”

“Teddy also wanted me to express his concern over your recent complications with the local police. There’s some question about a missing painting? Is that right? He wanted to make sure things haven’t gotten out of hand.”

Sarah’s father cleared his throat. “We’ll be issuing a press release on that in a few days. The best way to deal with things like this is quickly and directly. It was all just a colossal misunderstanding.”

“You don’t have the painting?”

He shook his head. “Never even seen it. Sarah’s been to a couple of the deceased artist’s exhibits and the police just jumped to the strange conclusion that we must have one of his paintings. They even came here looking for it.” He said this last part with a laugh.

Sarah watched Meredith's eyes shift to her then back to her father.

"I'm sure Teddy will be happy to know about your press release," said Meredith. "We'll watch for it." She finished her tea then excused herself to the restroom.

Her father let out a sigh that told Sarah what she already knew: they needed to get the painting issue settled and she would have to get back on the campaign trail, fast. He glanced at the envelope, the question on his face. She mouthed the amount and he responded with a shrug again telling her what she already knew - ten thousand wouldn't even buy a thirty-second TV spot.

Meredith returned from the bathroom but did not sit down. She asked if she could look in on Noah.

"Oh, of course," said Sarah. She showed her into the nursery.

"He's beautiful," said Meredith, smiling.

Meredith left a few minutes later but Sarah could hear her having a few words with her father out on the porch. "What was that about?" she asked after he'd shut the door and walked back into the room.

"Nothing, my dear. Meredith was just concerned about you and about the campaign."

Sarah could feel her old intensity rise—funny thing, hormones. She glared at him. "She told you something she didn't want me to hear."

He sat down. "Meredith says that a private detective has been hired. He'll be coming up here in a few days."

"Looking for the painting?"

"I'm going to get rid of it, Sarah, right now, tonight! I know how you feel but we can't go on risking your political future, or worse."

Sarah nodded, remembering the painting. She'd actually cried when she'd first seen it but then again she'd been three months pregnant at that time – another hormone thing. Now, with everything on the line, it was all coming back into focus. She felt her fist close, almost as if there was someone else controlling it. "You're right, we should destroy it."

Auburn Lakes was a quiet neighborhood located only three miles from the capital building in Albany. Here, where the Crawford's lived, big stately houses sat three to a block along curving, tree-lined drives. Sidewalks ran white, without cracks and long front lawns rolled lush and green like fairways.

Cat was parked two doors down from the Crawford's and from

behind the wheel of Nate's car, she watched Meredith walk casually toward her, toe directly behind heel. In her bright, springy outfit she fit in well with her surroundings, thought Cat. She got in the car.

"How'd it go?"

"Don't know. They say they don't have the painting and with Logan out of the picture, they sound pretty shaky about taking on the management of the campaign. What do we do now?"

"Now comes the hard part," said Cat. "We wait." She passed her the half bag of Cheetos left from the drive up then stared through the windshield. Though it was farther off than she would have liked, they had a clear view of the Sinclair house. Cat checked the time: four o'clock. "They'll wait until dark before doing anything," she predicted. "Or, they may do nothing at all." At four-thirty, the garage door, built into the frontage of the Crawford house, went up and a black Cadillac pulled out. "Whoa, here we go."

Cat started the car and followed, keeping a safe distance through the subdivision and out onto a main road. She wasn't used to tailing a car but she was pretty sure that Crawford wouldn't be suspicious enough to spot her. She just had to be careful. Two blocks down, he pulled into a Seven-Eleven and went inside.

Cat parked in the far corner of the lot and kept the motor running. "Probably a diaper run," she said.

"Isn't this where you get out and stick a GPS tracking device to his bumper?" asked Meredith.

"I wish. Those things are expensive and Bradshaw's too cheap. Some of our guys bust out a tail light to make someone easier to follow in the dark but I've never been a big fan of that. Something in me just hates to hurt a pretty car like that, you know what I mean?"

"Besides, Crawford might see you do it, then we'd be stuck." Meredith tossed some Cheetos into her mouth.

"Glad you agree." Eying the near-empty bag, Cat grabbed a handful.

Crawford reappeared five minutes later carrying a box of diapers and a plastic grocery bag. He drove back to the house and pulled into the garage. Cat parked back in her spot.

Meredith, crumpled the empty Cheetos bag.

"There's more stuff in the back -Twizzlers, candy bars, a six-pack of Mountain Dew, a few Cokes too, check it out – sorry I don't eat too healthy on these gigs. You need a lot of sugar to stay awake. There's a thermos of coffee there too but it might be stale by this time."

"What if I have to pee?"

"Better wait until dark for that," advised Cat.

So they waited.

It was two in the morning when Cat felt something at her shoulder. She jerked her head up.

"Hey, wake up," said Meredith, her hand on Cat, "I think we've got something."

"I wasn't asleep." Cat stared through the windshield and saw a light in Crawford's garage. Then the garage door went up. She rubbed her eyes and opened them wider. "Okay, okay, I'm good. Here we go." She started the car, lights off for now.

"You were too asleep," said Meredith.

Cat kept her distance from Crawford's car as he drove onto the main road, past the Seven-Eleven and picked up speed, heading out of town. She flipped on her lights. There were only a few other cars on the road and she was able to keep her eyes glued to Crawford's distinctive tail-lights from a few hundred yards back. Before long, the drive became more rural with businesses appearing in clumps only every now and then along the road. A few times Cat lost sight of Crawford from around a curve or behind a hill and she'd have to speed up until she got him in view again. She watched her odometer: five miles out, then ten.

"He's making a left," said Meredith.

"You sure? I didn't see it."

"I'm sure. It was up here somewhere."

"Okay, okay, I'll pass that spot and continue on just to be sure, then we'll double back." Cat slowed a little, approaching a dim lamppost that lit a cluster of derelict businesses.

"This is where he turned."

"I don't see his car."

"Me neither," said Meredith after they'd driven past. "There were a couple of places he could have turned into - a dirt road too." Cat stared at the road ahead - no sign of Crawford. She sped up and kept driving through a curve then another mile further. "Okay, guess you're right, he must have turned." She turned around and headed back. She squinted, seeing the lamppost in the distance, on the right this time. She slowed to a crawl and cut her headlights, tightening her grip on the wheel.

"There's the dirt road," said Meredith as they passed it. "No sign of him there." She read off the businesses as they passed: Gas station, Equipment rental place..."

Then they heard a low, rising hum.

"Car behind us," shouted Meredith, looking over her shoulder. "He's coming fast around the curve. Turn your lights on."

Suddenly, the brights of the car behind them filled the mirror, blinding Cat. "It's Crawford. He must be doing eighty." She sped up, looking for a spot to pull over; there was none - just a drainage ditch. A chill ran down her spine. "He's running us off the road."

"For God's sake, Cat, it's not Crawford," shouted Meredith.

Cat sped up and veered right. The tires bit into the edge of the ditch, spraying gravel. She braced for a rear-ender but the other car suddenly jerked left, its horn blaring as it flew past, its taillights different than Crawford's. Cat caught her breath but she wasn't out of trouble yet. They were half in the ditch, doing fifty in the dark.

Tall weeds pounded the front bumper. Cat had to keep the car moving or they'd be stuck. She floored it and tried to steer left.

"You're still in the ditch," yelled Meredith over the din.

"No shit," said Cat. Then she got lucky. Her front tires caught a rise and the car bounded up onto level ground. She swerved around the light pole then hit the brakes, tossing up a cloud of gravel, skidding to a stop five feet from an unlit portable roadside sign. With big black letters and a giant red arrow, it announced that *Phil's Storage* was just ahead and to the right.

Cat swallowed, her hands still gripping the wheel. "I think this is it." She glanced at Meredith and saw that she was digging out from the garbage that a few seconds earlier had been on the floor of the back seat. Cat lowered her window and shifted into neutral then gunned the engine lightly. "Car seems all right." She pulled forward a few feet. "You okay?"

"Yeah, except for all this crap. I've got your Mountain Dew all over me."

"Hey, at least we're not stuck back in that ditch."

"Or lying dead in the road. You should have kept your lights on. And that wasn't Crawford. It was just some poor schlep in a hurry who didn't see you."

"Okay, okay, you were right, I was wrong." Cat took a breath then pulled out her phone and placed a call that didn't connect. "Damn. No cell coverage out here."

"Who you calling?"

"The cops. I got a friend of a friend on the Albany PD. He knows what we're up to. He can bust Crawford legally - we can't." Meredith tried her phone – nothing.

"Looks like we're on our own," said Cat. "You don't happen to have a gun on you do you?"

"You're the private detective, don't you have one?"

"Too dangerous, maybe I'll have to re-think that." Cat pulled ahead, lights still out.

The storage sites were laid out in rows, parallel to the road. She drove to the far end of the lot then turned right, driving slowly, looking through Meredith's window down the first row. A security light on a pole halfway down gave her a good view – no one there.

She drove onto the next, then three more – each row deserted.

"When we find him, what are we going to do?" whispered Meredith.

"We're going to take the painting. I thought you knew that."

"Yeah, I did, right."

They were nearing the fence at the back of the lot. Cat cut the engine. "We'll do the rest on foot. He can only be in this row or the next."

They got out quietly.

"Should have worn my ninja outfit," said Meredith, easily visible in her bright yellow pant suit.

Cat realized she wasn't much better in her sky blue outfit. She wondered if Crawford had a gun – no, he wasn't the type, was he?

A sound reached Cat from the next row. She gave Meredith a nod and moved in front, peering around the corner. There was the Cadillac, pointed away from them. The trunk lid was up, there was no one around. She was too far away to see anything more but she could hear a dull, pounding sound that continued for a moment, then stopped. "Follow me but stay a ways behind."

Meredith nodded.

At a sprint, Cat took off for the Cadillac, passing closed garage doors on both sides, keeping her footfalls as quiet as she could. She then slowed and lowered herself into a crouch, ten feet from the Cadillac. In its trunk she spotted a red gasoline can. So he was going to burn the painting. The garage door to the storage unit beside the car was closed but there was a sliver of light below it. The pounding resumed. It was coming from inside.

Cat steadied her nerves and took up a position at the center of the door, where she grabbed the handle and readied herself to lift it up.

Meredith moved to the side.

Cat tested the weight of the door, lifting it slightly, then counted silently: one, two...

In a single violent motion, she jerked the door upward. In an instant, her eyes adjusted to the light. There was Crawford, on his knees, facing away from her, bent over a flat wooden crate. He held a claw hammer. He turned, his fiery eyes glaring back at Cat.

"Something I can help you with in there, Mr. Crawford?" she asked. "Or should I call you Dmitry?"

Crawford got to his feet and raised one hand as if he was a cop halting traffic. "This is private property. Stop where you are."

"Or what? Are you going to throw your hammer at me?" Cat took a step inside.

Crawford dropped the hammer and reached inside his jacket. He pulled a gun and aimed it at her.

Cat froze.

"I'm within my rights protecting my property. Now just back up and get the hell out of here."

"Okay, okay just keep your cool," said Cat, heart thumping. She raised her hands and took a step back. "No one has to get hurt over this."

"It's too bad, but I think that's unavoidable now," said Crawford, both hands on the gun now.

Cat felt like she was back in the grocery store, powerless to do anything. Her mouth was dry. Was he really going to shoot her? Without thinking, she dove for cover behind a steel barrel.

The gunshot was deafening in the enclosed space and Cat landed hard on the concrete floor, her elbow twisting, taking the brunt of the impact. Pain tore through her shoulder but it didn't feel like she'd been shot. Had Crawford missed? From behind the barrel, she raised her head. Crawford still held his gun but he was shifting his aim now, bracing himself against a threat from a different direction.

With a scream, Meredith plowed into Crawford. He fired wildly, the bullet smashing a side window in his car. He tumbled back and his gun clattered to the floor.

Cat got to her feet, her left arm hanging limp at her side, pain still blazing. She ran for the gun, grabbed it and pointed it at Crawford who was in a tangle with Meredith. Right now he was getting the worst of it.

Cat fired a bullet into the air which ricocheted off the metal ceiling then imbedded itself in the floor two feet from where she stood. All right, that wasn't so bright. She cocked the gun and aimed it at Crawford. "It's over Crawford. Stop, God damn it."

Meredith staggered off him and backed away. Hands on knees, she struggled to catch her breath, then straightened. Her lip was cut and she had a bluish lump over one eye. She was gasping for breath.

"You okay? Were you hit?" Cat asked her.

"No, yeah, fine...I'm okay."

"You duplicitous bitch," shouted Crawford, glaring at Meredith, wiping his sleeve over the stream of blood pouring from his nose.

Cat kept the gun steady. "Meredith, go get the car, the keys are inside." Cat glanced at her and saw that, except for the lump, her face was painted white as a ghost, her eyes zoned-out. "Meredith? You with me?"

She stared at Cat as if not registering the question. Then: "Right, yeah, I'll get the car." She straightened then headed off.

Cat looked down the barrel of the gun at Crawford. "I see this thing's adapted for a silencer. I bet if the police do some ballistics they might find a match for the bullets they dug out of Peter Caruso. Would that be a good bet? Is it registered to you?"

Crawford didn't say a word. The splintered but still unopened crate lay on the floor beside him.

"Good plan, you keeping quiet. I never memorized the Miranda thing but I think a court of law is somewhere in your future."

Meredith drove up and was able to get the crate into the trunk of Nate's car. She slammed it shut.

"Just so you know," Cat told Crawford, "we're taking it to the police. We're taking your gun too. You and your daughter should be hearing from them later today."

Meredith stooped to pick up her purse. Beside it lay a nickel plated Smith & Wesson. She picked that up too.

"You mind driving?" asked Cat, "my arm's a little busted. Just a bad sprain I think."

Color was starting to return to Meredith's face. "Yeah, I can drive."

Meredith got into the driver's seat while Cat circled to the passenger side keeping her gun on Crawford until she got in. Meredith hit the gas and was peeling off even before she closed the door.

"That was you firing the first shot," said Cat, once they were on the main road headed back into town – lights on this time.

"Teddy insisted I have a gun. I trained with it but never had to use it. I never liked having it." Her voice was raspy. She shook her head. "Dumb thing jumped out of my hand when I fired. All I wanted to do was scare him. I nearly shot you instead."

"That's when you decided to rush him."

"You had him distracted. He was an old guy, I figured I had a pretty good chance."

"He was an old guy with a gun and what you did took guts. You saved my life – probably both our lives." She put a hand on hers. "You're okay for a duplicitous bitch."

It was five in the morning and the sky was just starting to brighten when they stopped at an all-night diner where they got cleaned up and had breakfast with plenty of hot coffee. From there, Cat was able to make a call. She arranged to meet at a police station house with the detective Mooch had set her up with. Her name was J.D. Lawrence.

JD was short for Janet Deloris, an African-American of moderate height, a little rotund with short black hair, straightened so that it curled toward her chin on both sides. It bounced when she talked. "So, where's the painting?" she asked.

"Downstairs in the property room, we just checked it in. The gun's there too," said Cat.

"Crawford's gun?"

"Yeah. You'll find his prints on it, mine too."

"Tell me what happened."

"Not much to tell," said Cat with a glance at Meredith. "We happened to be in the area and thought we'd check out the Crawford place. You know, see how the other half lives."

"And when exactly was that?"

"About two this morning," said Meredith.

"We were going to stop in but we saw Crawford's car heading out. We followed him."

"Just wanting to say hi," interjected Meredith.

"We found him in a storage garage going at the painting with a hammer. He had a container of gasoline in his trunk. He was going to burn it."

"We saved it."

"Then brought it here."

JD folded her arms. "You know we went out on a very thin limb getting that search warrant issued for the Crawford's and when nothing turned up we looked like shit. Now you two show up and steal the evidence we were looking for. I could say; 'nice work' but we've got a problem. As we speak, the gun and the painting are stolen property and the two of you are suspects in a robbery."

Cat was about to object but JD raised her hand. "It's not a big problem and I'm sure Crawford isn't about to register a complaint regarding a painting he assured us he knew nothing about just a few days ago. We do need written statements from both of you though; then you'll be free to go."

"We'd like to see the painting before we leave," said Cat. "It's still in the crate but some of the boards have been removed where Crawford was prying it apart."

JD shook her head, her bangs bouncing. "Can't help you there. It's evidence and will be in lock up until we get it down to the Brownsville PD. It'll be up to them if and when you can see it."

Damn, thought Cat, they should have checked it out earlier when they had the chance, but then again the court might consider that to be tampering with the evidence. It was probably best this way, but it sure didn't satisfy her curiosity. She'd been itching to see it ever since learning of its existence. Did it identify the real killer? Would it be enough to exonerate Nate? Well, she'd have to wait a little longer to find out.

JD handed them each a yellow pad and took them to separate holding rooms to write out their stories. It was mid-afternoon by the time they were on the road driving back. Cat drove the first leg. She'd taken some extra-strength aspirin which helped with the throbbing in her arm. She could bend it a little but there was no strength in it. They switched off with the driving.

"Get some sleep, you look awful," said Cat when she pulled up at the Sinclair house. "And you smell like Mountain Dew."

"Thanks, you're looking pretty bad yourself," said Meredith getting out and grabbing her bag from the back. "You're seeing Nate tomorrow?"

"Yeah, I'll bring him up to speed. I'll tell him how you saved the day."

"Tell him we're pulling for him – me and Teddy both."

Meredith tried to talk her into staying the night but Cat wanted to get home and sleep in her own bed. It was dark by the time she found a parking spot near her place and a little too close to a fire hydrant. She hoped it wouldn't attract a ticket. It reminded her why it was dumb to own a car in the City.

CHAPTER 24

For Nate, the morning started off as usual with the breakfast march from his cell to the cafeteria for cold cereal with OJ and coffee then back again to his squeaky-spring cot and the too-hard pillow that was starting to smell. The weeks had gone by slowly – reading and sleep spotted by visits from his folks and Cat and by meetings with Sam.

He decided he didn't like Sam. In the first week he seemed lazy and uninterested, like an overworked doctor who had much more important patients to worry about. But lately Sam began to meet with him more often. He wore his tie a little straighter and had gotten a hair-cut. Nate suspected the more frequent meetings were Sam's way of justifying a higher fee and for him to get more camera time with the media which he told Nate "were all over this one."

Sam always began these meetings the same way. "So how're you holding up?"

"Like shit," was always Nate's reply which he was sure Sam paraphrased for the press-folk into something like: 'My client's holding up as well as can be expected.'

And the meetings weren't about legal strategy. They were more like pep talks: "Keep your chin up, we've got a good chance, they barely have enough evidence to keep you here much less bring their shit-case to trial." The meetings were a waste of time. But then again, Nate had a lot of time to waste. Today he wondered how Cat was doing up in Albany with the Crawfords. He hadn't seen her in four days now. He missed her, but more than that, he worried about her.

Nate sat up on the bed and leaned his back against the rough plaster wall. He grabbed his latest in a series of paperback thrillers and opened to his last dog-eared page and tuned out the shouts and clangs of prison life that echoed through the cell-block. The hero of the story, a fellow named Jack of course, had been backed into a corner by some gunmen who were secretly working for his new father in law who was actually a mob boss. Nate was glad he wasn't Jack.

His cell-door clanged open. "Visitor," said the unsmiling Hispanic guard who Nate had seen before. Conversations with guards were not allowed and instead of name-tags, they had numbers. This was one-twenty-one.

Twenty-eight paces to a locked gate; fifteen to a stairwell and seventeen steps down, brought him to the visiting area door. One-twenty-one opened it and Nate shuffled through. It was early so Nate and his visitor should have the place to themselves. He hoped it was Cat and not Sam. He sat down behind the smudged window opposite an empty chair.

Then Cat came in, her eyes wide and bright like he hadn't seen them in a long time. He stood up with relief and high expectations. She didn't even bother to say hi. She hurried over and sat down in the chair opposite him. They each picked up their phones.

"Nate, the police have the painting and they have Crawford's gun."

Nate felt like he'd just been blown back by a gust of fresh air. This news couldn't have been better. He wanted to jump over the glass and squeeze this wonderful woman in front of him. "My God, Cat, how did you manage that? Have you seen the painting?"

Cat shook her head. "No, I haven't seen it yet. Meredith was a big help, Nate."

"Meredith? You and Meredith got the painting?"

"Yup, me and Meredith. We were a regular pair of super-heroes but she was the one who knocked Crawford down."

"There was a fight? She knocked down Sarah Crawford?"

"No, not Sarah, her old man. He was trying to burn the painting. Meredith was great, Nate. I really mean that. She still cares a lot for you but not in the way she once did – we talked a lot."

Nate sat back in his chair, visualizing Meredith bowling over the old man. She was one of the two most determined women he knew. The other sat across from him. "You're amazing, Cat. You risked a lot for me, both of you did. Where's the painting now?"

"We left it with the police up in Albany but it should be here in town by now. The whole case is about to explode. Somebody already tipped off the papers." She held up a copy of the *Times*: *New Mystery Evidence in Mozart Murders*.

Nate shook his head, a little bothered that everyone seemed better informed about his case than he was himself. Then he noticed the way she was holding the paper. "Something wrong with your arm?"

"Yeah, I fell when Meredith was doing her take-down thing on Crawford. It's just a sprain: stiff, can't move it so well." She winced when she demonstrated her range of motion. "It's better now than yesterday though."

Nate nodded, feeling helpless. Everyone was going the extra mile to help him but he couldn't lift a finger to help himself.

Cat read the article to him then flipped to where it was continued a few pages back under a snazzy picture of Sam. "It's on the TV too. They've got everyone wondering about this 'startling new development.' Can you believe it?"

"Any word on Crawford's gun?"

"Ballistics might take a few days. I'll check with Mooch on that."

"I thought he was off the case."

"According to the police in Albany, he's their primary contact. So, I guess he's back on it. That's good for us Nate. He's pulling for you."

An image of the bug-eyed Blues-Brother detective flashed through Nate's mind. He hoped Cat was right about him.

When their time was up Nate was led away, back through the door to the visitor's area. As he walked, he glanced back at Cat, who was standing, watching him through the Plexiglas. Her face wore the determined expression of a football coach about to lead the winning drive.

"Good news?" asked One-Twenty-One after they'd left the room.

Nate smiled. "Yes, very good news." He knew the guards treated you better when they knew you were going to get out.

From the jail Cat headed over to the Seventy-Third to talk to Mooch.

He came down to meet her. "Good work on getting the painting for us. It was grossly illegal, but we're working to get your actions covered by our original search warrant." He took her into an interrogation room. "Don't worry, no guys behind the mirror."

She sat down as the door closed. “Guess I can have my way with you then?”

“As long as it doesn’t involve catsup or mustard. How’s your boyfriend doing?”

“He’s better now,” said Cat crossing her legs. She wore her cowgirl boots today and saw Mooch give them an admiring glance. “Have you seen the painting?”

“Yeah. The word is that we’ll be pushing back the trial a couple of weeks while we re-figure things.”

“Are the Crawfords talking?”

“We’ve asked them to come in and make a statement. It’s voluntary for now but we can force the issue if we have to. The painting contains some things in it that seem to fit with what you and Parks have been telling us about Crawford – the old man I mean.”

“Dmitry.”

“Well maybe, yeah. Tell me again where you got that info.”

Cat didn’t want to mention Dr. Wright’s files. Nate had warned her that doctor-patient confidentiality could get her into trouble and it could taint the evidence they’d already given Mooch. “I have my sources, Mooch. I like to keep them safe, you know that. You just focus on the Crawfords. I’ll bet they’ll tell you everything you need to know.”

“Do you think they know anything about the Harris girl?”

“I almost forgot about her,” said Cat. She uncrossed her legs. “But that has nothing to do with Nate, you know that.”

“He had the knife. It had her blood on it.”

Now she was more angry than worried. “Come on Mooch. He found the knife and he turned it in – that’s all. Besides, Nate’s convinced that Peter killed her. He’s the one who knew Peter best. He found the knife in Peter’s room. He just knew where to look.”

“So he says,” said Mooch nodding. He stared at her for a while then gave her a thin smile. “The guys in Scranton are saying that they won’t be bringing charges up against Parks for the Harris murder unless something else turns up. Still, it’d be nice to put both cases to bed.” He leaned back in his chair and folded his arms. “So back to my question: Do you think the Crawfords know anything about the Harris murder?”

“I have no idea. You should ask them about it. I’ll bet they know a lot of interesting things.”

Sarah had been holding Noah in her arms when the police came to the door. Her father let them in. The police were polite and respectful and made no comments about the bruises on her father's face. She and her father were required to sign papers acknowledging that they were suspected of withholding evidence and evidence tampering. They agreed to appear voluntarily at the Seventy-Third Precinct in New York the following week. When the police left, Sarah sat back in her chair and resumed her slow rocking. Noah hadn't even woken up. He was a good baby and she smiled down at him. It wasn't fear she felt as much as worry now about who would take care of him if she had to go away.

Peter just couldn't let things go, could he? Manipulation had been his way just as it had been hers. You maneuver friends and foes alike into a box from which there was only one way out and for Peter, it had worked every time – now she was the one in the box.

"We should have burned the painting months ago like I told you," her father said.

Sarah smiled, on the verge of sleep herself. She touched Noah's nose with the tip of her finger. "I know you're right, it's what we should have done. But destroying the painting would have been like Peter dying a second time. I couldn't do it. I'm almost glad that it was taken from you. It's time I face up to what I did. It's time for you to face up to what you did – all of it."

Her father sighed, seemingly too tired to argue the point that they had gone over many times before. "We'll need to put together a statement – each of us. We should be able to make a deal with the DA that'll keep you out of jail and could give us some very useful publicity."

Sarah shrugged and nodded. Her father knew how to capitalize on every situation – even bad ones.

Five days later, with Noah in the care of a hired nanny, she sat beside her father, across from a portly detective who wore a thin black tie and black-rimmed glasses - a comic effect, she thought. At the head of the table was the assistant DA, a guy named Beamon. Everyone had a legal pad in front of them. Sarah teeter-tottered a pen between her fingers and, as Beamon began the process with some opening comments, she interrupted.

"We won't be answering any questions today, Mr. Beamon. You have the painting and we know where your investigation will ultimately lead, so we've decided to issue a statement that will save us all a lot of time and trouble. Does that make sense?"

Beamon nodded cautiously. "We can take your statement."

Sarah shook her head. "Not today and not here. It will be made in public at a venue of our choosing." She pulled out a typewritten sheet of paper. "These are our terms. If they are acceptable then we can proceed. If not, your office will be tied up unnecessarily for a very long time. You know how the evidence was obtained and you know how long it will take just to clear things for trial – if it even gets that far. Believe me, we can make things very difficult for you."

Beamon read the document then handed it to the detective who gave it a quick glance, grunted and handed it back.

Beamon stood up. "I'll need a few minutes."

"Take all the time you need," said Sarah. She glanced at her father as Beamon left the room. Being here was distasteful enough but at least the DA's office shouldn't give them any flak. She shook her head, remembering how she used to flash-analyze everything she did, tabulating pros and cons for doing one thing or another, anticipating probable outcomes. What would be the outcome today? That was easy: She would never be governor. She might go to prison for a short time – her father too. But then she'd be back with Noah and she would raise him as best she could. Not a bad outcome – not like Peter's. She felt a pang in her stomach at the thought of him. Was that guilt she was feeling? No, maybe just regret. Then she noticed the eyes of the portly detective. He was staring at her. "Something on your mind?" she asked.

"Yes, there is, and it's not about the Caruso case – not directly anyway."

Curious, she waited for his question.

"Did you know Patricia Harris?"

She must be slipping – she wasn't expecting *that* question. "The girl from Peter's high school who was murdered you mean? Now why would you think I knew her?"

"Maybe you don't know her, but do you know anything about her murder?"

Sarah pondered the harm in telling him what she knew and decided to go half-way. "No, not her, and nothing about her murder. But I do know she had been important to Peter."

"Do you know why?"

Sarah's mind drifted back to those dark times spent in Peter's gloomy apartment. "Patty Harris had been his first love – his only love, really – and even with her long dead, he seemed obsessed with her. He talked about her all the time, sometimes muttering things as he painted. I do know that she was his inspiration for *Woman in Winter*."

"Parks thinks Caruso killed her."

Sarah put her pen down and met the detective's eyes. "Peter

Caruso was a violent madman but he never could have killed his beloved Patty. She was everything to him."

The door opened and Beamon returned, papers in hand. He took his seat and spoke directly to Sarah. "Your terms are acceptable," he said. "We'll make the arrangements."

CHAPTER 25

Three mornings later, Cat pushed in the door at Bradshaw's. "Cat here," she yelled but there was no response. She tossed her cap and it caught the hook. Wow, it was going to be a good day.

Bradshaw, whom she hadn't seen in a standing position in months, came out of his office. "What're you doing here? Thought you were off working on your boyfriend's case – heard there was a big thing going on today."

"Yeah, I'm hoping it gets him off. I'll be at the courthouse this afternoon."

"Big case, lots of publicity." The old man scratched the bald spot on the back of his head. "The press might be wanting to talk to you, maybe you could mention us?"

Bradshaw was always working the angles. Well, good for him. He had his business to look out for and getting its name in the press was the least she could do considering all the time off she'd taken lately. And she had yet to tell him about Hiram's invoice. "If they ask me anything, sure I'll put in a good word."

"Good." Bradshaw nodded and shuffled back into his office.

Cat had plenty of work to catch up on but her mind was on Nate and on the clock. The DA's press briefing was at three and it had been hyped to be a public announcement related to the new evidence they'd received in the Caruso case. She thought they might even show the painting – it was about time.

The morning dragged by. She left at one-thirty and by the time she got there, she found the assembly room at the courthouse already filling up. The briefing was scheduled to begin at three.

She caught sight of Mooch.

"Saved you a seat near the front," he said, taking his coat off a third-row aisle chair. Then he leaned closer. "Sarah Crawford says she didn't know the Harris girl but she doesn't think he was the one who killed her."

"So she says."

"Right, she could be wrong. She could even be protecting Caruso's reputation, but I believed her Cat. She says Caruso was obsessed with her. Supposedly, she was in one of his paintings."

Cat wondered why Mooch was bugging her about this now. This was Nate's day for God's sake. She took her jacket off. "Oh yeah, which painting was that?"

"*Woman in Winter* – I checked it out on the internet."

"I remember that one—long, flowing white hair, white gown..." Cat was distracted by the sound-checks going on at the podium while, at the same time a guy came out from stage-left carrying an easel. Another man followed behind him with what could only be the painting. It was covered in a white sheet which was adjusted after it was placed on the easel. This set off a wave of conversation in the crowd.

"Look Mooch, can we discuss the Harris girl later? This thing's about to get started."

"Sure, sure, we'll talk later."

Cat was relieved when Mooch left – too many things happening at once. She took her seat and found herself staring at the enshrouded painting. Only ten days ago it had been in a storage garage at Phil's about to be burned. Too bad Meredith wasn't here, then Cat thought that maybe she was. She stood and looked around but didn't see her. She decided to call her.

"Thought you might be here at the courthouse today," said Cat when she answered.

"I'm watching on TV," said Meredith. "It's on all the networks. I saw you stand up a second ago."

"Oh yeah? Guess I should have worn a better outfit huh?" She turned and waved just as a man in a black suit stepped to the podium. "Oops, gotta go."

Cat ended the call as cameras clicked. The stage lights came on. She had the feeling she was at an off-Broadway production with the overture about to start. The man scanned the room with a threatening stare and things got quiet. Cat noticed slicked-down-Sam in the front row.

The podium was turned over to the DA who then thanked everyone for coming and gave some background on the Caruso case. Then he made his big announcement:

"A week ago we obtained new evidence which, because of its nature and because of the high degree of publicity already given this case, we've decided to make public. There will be no comments or official statements from my office until after the evidence has been disclosed and a prepared statement has been read."

He paused to heighten the drama – nice touch thought Cat.

"The new evidence is a painting created, ostensibly, by the deceased artist, Peter Lazar Caruso. Detailed photographs of it will be available to the media. We ask you please, no flash photography."

The DA gave a signal and another guy in a black suit walked behind the easel and pinched both corners of the white sheet. He stayed like that for a moment, exchanged a nod with the DA, then pulled off the sheet.

And there, for all to see, was Peter Caruso's last painting: *Death of the Artist*.

Everyone got to their feet. There were audible gasps from the front and the people in back tried to crowd in. From where she stood, Cat caught only a glimpse of the painting before she was shoved aside. She pushed back and inched her way forward, all while the DA was trying unsuccessfully to regain control of the room. Everyone had their cell-cameras raised hoping for a lucky shot. Cat slid into an opening just in front of the stage and then she saw it:

The painting showed a man, Peter, laying on his back diagonally across the frame. His face, tormented yet somehow relieved, looked out from it directly at her from the upper right corner. His eyes were a milky white with pupils of deep blue that seemed to float in a ghostly, other-world way, above the surface of the canvas. His mouth was open as if attempting one last breath. His checked shirt, wet with blood, clung to the contours of his chest. Pools of dark red lay in the hollows and spilled down onto the wooden floor. Beneath Peter, the seams between the dark floorboards were thin rivers of blood.

One arm lay stretched out from his body almost to the corner of the painting, the hand relaxed and curled slightly. The other arm crossed his body just above his beltline, its length almost out of proportion to the rest of the body. In that hand he held two green sheets of paper – no, they were tattered folders like one might find in an old file cabinet. They angled down toward the floor away from the observer and into shadow which made them difficult to see. There were spatters of blood on them and markings but Cat was too far from the painting to make any of it out. She noticed a tri-colored splotch in the corner of both folders: Blue, yellow, and red.

Were these folders the clue to the secret Peter had left behind? She strained her eyes and tried to get closer but couldn't. She'd have to pick up one of the photo-copies from the DA.

It took fifteen minutes for order to be restored. Cat and the rest of the people in the room finally took their seats and the room went quiet again. The DA, still at the podium, looked over the room, making sure that there'd be no more outbursts. He pulled out a sheet of paper and read from it: "Until recently, this painting had been in the possession of an individual who had purchased it legitimately. That individual has generously decided to come forward with the painting as it has a direct bearing on our investigation into the death of the artist Peter Caruso and on the pending trial of Mr. Nathan Parks. That individual will now come forward and read a prepared statement." He stepped off the stage and took a seat.

Cat had given a smirk at the 'generously decided to come forward' part of the DA's intro but knew the wording had probably been part of the deal struck by the Crawfords.

More waiting. Except for the podium and the painting, the stage was empty. There was a low, expectant buzz as everyone wondered what would happen next. Then, from the back of the room, there was a commotion and everyone turned.

Sarah had waited alone, sitting in a room on the second floor of the courthouse, watching the unveiling of Peter's painting and listening to the frantic, breaking-news commentary of the talking heads on CNN. Cold air wheezed from a vent over her head. She stood up – almost time. The room had a private bathroom which she used, splashing cold water over her face. She dabbed it dry then sat back down. She knew her father waited in a car outside. He'd wanted to be here with her but no, she needed to do this alone – or as alone as she could be with the dual personas she'd been exhibiting these days. She no longer had any idea which of them was in control at any given time – the ruthless, calculating lieutenant governor, or little Noah's meek and remorseful mother.

There was a soft knock and the door opened. "They're ready for us," said a black haired young man who looked like he was wearing his father's oversized business suit. She pegged him as third-year law and wondered when it was they'd taught him to use the inclusive pronoun that suggested he would somehow share in her fate.

They took an elevator down to a lobby area. A few people turned and stared as she crossed the room.

Third-year grabbed the handle on a wide double-door. "Ready?"

Sarah nodded and he pulled it open.

She felt like a bride making her grand entrance but there was no music, there were no bridesmaids, and there were no smiles. She kept her eyes straight and could feel the faces of everyone in the crowded room, following her as she walked. And she could hear the whispers. She climbed three steps onto the stage. Third-year was gone - so much for sharing her fate. She passed in front of the painting, taking no notice of it, then took her position behind the podium as she had so many times through the course of her political career. This time it felt distinctly foreign to her. She remembered her first time entering the confessional when she was a little girl in Catholic school - all alone, just she and the priest behind the screen. There was a glass of water on the podium. Her mouth was dry but she didn't take a drink.

All was quiet as Sarah looked down at the papers she'd prepared, left there for her by the DA. She began to read:

"My name is Sarah Crawford. I am the Lieutenant Governor of the State of New York and you may think you know me; but you don't. I am here today to tell the truth about the artist, Peter Caruso. I'm here to tell the truth about me. I'm here to tell the truth about something called genetic optimization."

The room reacted then quickly quieted.

"One October night in 1995, I was up in my room doing homework. I was twelve – a normal, healthy, happy schoolgirl. I'd never been a bright student and I was struggling with a composition assignment when, without warning and without apparent cause, I changed. Suddenly the assignment required no thought whatsoever. The words, good words, flowed from my pen as if my mind wasn't even involved. Over the next few months, I excelled at everything at school while expending very little effort.

"My father was very excited about this metamorphosis and had me put through blood tests, IQ tests, psychiatric tests and finally genetic tests. But I cared nothing about the results. My head was bubbling over with plans and ideas based on one overriding, undeniable premise: I was suddenly smarter than everyone else – smarter than my classmates and smarter than my teachers. I carried mathematical probabilities out to ten levels of what-ifs that I effortlessly factored into my daily life. And I had no anxiety in my thoughts, my actions or my decisions – I was right all the time and I knew it. I breezed through high school graduating at fourteen.

"Then, in my second year at Cornell, I discovered something I never suspected – there was someone else like me."

She took a drink of water.

"I met Peter Caruso at the Leyland Clinic while undergoing another series of my father's medical tests, which he had one day decided to resume. I didn't speak to Peter at our first meeting but did at the second. We became friendly in an uncomfortable kind of way. He was an artist and there was a dark, dangerousness about him that both attracted and repelled me. More than anything else, I was curious about him. He showed me some of his work. There wasn't much that impressed me in those days, but Peter's paintings did and I came to realize that my skills in law and politics were equaled by his in art. I began to wonder what might explain the unusual gifts we'd been given. I also wondered; if there were two of us like this, might there be others?"

Sarah paused, resisting the urge for another drink, wanting no display of her nervousness. She didn't look up. She continued reading:

"I began to look into my own past and learned that I'd been born in Romania to destitute parents who couldn't afford to keep me. There were thousands like us in Romania in those days, all victims of the government's decree that families – all families – must have no less than five children. Onerous taxation penalties enforced the decree. The more Romanians, the better for Romania, was the stupefying logic that led to people having more children than they could afford to feed. Desperate parents turned these excess babies over to the state.

"I'm told that, in our first few months of life, we were kept in buildings with dormitories that housed maybe fifty babies to a room. Conditions were appalling and in trying to take care of us all, the resources of the country were stretched to the limit. To most we were an unnecessary expense, an unwanted problem; but to one person in a research lab in Bucharest, we were an opportunity.

"The records were difficult to locate but I was able to find firm evidence that one hundred of these babies, ones that had been born with certain ailments like asthma and digestive irregularities, were separated from the others and were given a series of experimental injections designed to cure them and to somehow enhance their immunity to diseases. The babies were all between two weeks and three months old. All of them showed significant improvement, at first.

"Then, two months into the test, and without warning, one baby died. Then three others died. The experiment was aborted but that didn't stop the record-keeping. The fate of all these select babies was meticulously documented. Of the one hundred infants in the original experiment, four died, twenty-eight showed signs of their original conditions redeveloping at a more severe level, and sixty-seven exhibited signs of extreme hypertension. There were only five who showed no abnormalities. If anything, these five were in better condition after the injections than before. I was one of these five, Peter was another. Somewhere, the three others may still be alive – I don't know. Records for Peter and I were kept in folders – green folders like the ones you see Peter holding in his painting.

"He and I were adopted by Americans and taken to live here – me in up-state New York, he in a small town outside of Scranton.

"Five years after my first meeting with Peter, I confronted my father with what I'd found out about the experiments in Romania. It was then that he admitted that he was the man who had led the experiments. He profoundly regretted the harm he had done, especially to the children who had died or whose condition worsened and he swore to me that he'd been raising me as best he could as his way of atoning for his actions. Then he told me about his plan for Peter and I.

"As a way for him to achieve true redemption, and recognition, he wanted to carry his original experiment one step further. In doing so, he planned to give humanity a gift of immeasurable value – the gift he called genetic optimization. He wanted me to develop a relationship with Peter Caruso. He wanted me to have his baby."

There was an audible gasp in the room, then it turned dead silent. No one so much as moved.

"I brushed the idea off as absurd. Politics was my life back then. There was no room in it for a man. But this was my adoptive father asking, and he was only asking me to consider the idea. So I considered it and, in my usual cold, analytical way, I factored in all the what-ifs. Over time, the idea of vindicating my father while creating a place of historic importance for myself and for my offspring became so intriguing that I couldn't turn away from it.

"I began to visit Peter secretly at his apartment. On my first visit he recognized me from our time at Leyland but we didn't say a word the whole time. He only had time for his art, nothing else. I came back a few months later and then again and he started rambling on about the fulfillment of his destiny and about a high school love of his. We began to talk and it drew me closer to him and... we made love for the first time."

Sarah felt her stomach tremble and folded her hands to keep them from shaking.

"Peter was an animal. The act was a rape, violent and hideous and I was afraid for my life. When the bruises went away and the open cuts healed and I found that I was not pregnant, I knew I'd have to conquer my fears. I'd have to go back. To his credit, my father tried to talk me out of it. But I had to see this through. He bought me a gun – one with a silencer. I kept it in my purse and on the fourth time with Peter, the fourth time of being violated and beaten, I used it. He was relentless that night and he wanted me again and again and again. When he came at me the last time with his hands grabbing and his eyes red and wild; I shot him."

Someone shouted: "Self-defense." A few more yelled out their agreement.

Sarah took in a shaky breath.

"Peter didn't fall immediately. He kept coming. I fired twice more. His shirt was covered with blood. He bent forward, and as he did, his face changed from that of a wild man to that of a man who'd been suddenly freed, like a slave released from his chains. Rather than fall, he lowered himself to the floor where he stretched out very much like you see him here in his painting. He kept breathing for a while – short, rapid breaths. Blood pooled around him. I was horrified by what I'd done, but all I could do was watch. After a few minutes, his breathing stopped.

"At that moment, my survival instincts took over. I wiped the apartment clean. I cleaned everywhere I'd been. Then I walked ten blocks through the snow back to the busier side of town and caught a cab back to where I was staying. The next day I got rid of the gun in the east river and two months later I learned I was pregnant."

Sarah put her papers down and looked directly into the camera. "My father and I are cooperating fully with the authorities as they investigate the death of Peter Caruso." She scanned the people in the room, recognizing some. They were all still quiet, all waiting for her to say more but she had no more to give them – not today. She stepped off the stage and walked out of the room, her pace quickening as she passed through the doors and into the lobby area. There were some shouts but she ignored them all.

Outside, a black limo was parked at the curb a chauffeur beside it. He opened the rear door. Inside, her father waited.

Nate sat breathless, his heart pounding. With his feet chained loosely together, he had been allowed to watch the whole thing on TV. First had come the shock that Peter had been part of a genetic experiment. The disturbed boy he thought he knew back in Maysville and the brilliant artist he'd become had been designed and nurtured by a doctor who'd decided to play God with a hundred defenseless infants. How could Peter have harbored this secret all those years? But then Nate wondered if Peter even knew the truth back then. Maybe it had been Sarah Crawford who had told him.

When Sarah Crawford confessed to killing Peter, Nate had heard the crowd's reaction. Maybe she would get off with a self-defense plea, but that wasn't important to him right now. What *was* important was that he was about to be a free man again! He felt almost numb, unprepared to believe it.

As Sarah Crawford left the stage, Nate stood up and, hobbled by his chains, took a step closer to the screen. He looked behind him at One-Twenty-One.

"Wow, that was quite a story," said the guard.

Wow, that was quite a story, said the CNN guy at nearly the same time. Nate turned back to the TV as the commentator launched into some astute observations. Then the screen showed the DA stepping back up to the podium.

The DA wiped his forehead with the back of his hand. "My office would like to thank Ms. Crawford for her cooperation."

A woman in the third row, just on screen stood up. A mike was turned to catch her voice. Nate beamed when he saw who it was. He sat back down.

"I'm Cat Chaplin with the Bradshaw Detective Agency...in the Bronx," she said, more loudly than necessary. "Does this mean that all the charges against Mr. Parks will be dropped?"

The DA glanced to his left as if unprepared to go off-script but then relented. "Yes, Mr. Parks is now a free man. The State of New York regrets any inconvenience."

Nate shot up from his chair. "My God, it's over. I'm free!" he shouted, both hands extended as if he had just stuck a gymnastics landing at the Olympics.

"Good for you Mr. Parks," said One-Twenty-One, smiling. "Us guards were pulling for you."

"I need to make a call. Right now, I need to make a call." He tapped the pockets of his prison uniform half-expecting a phone to suddenly show up there.

"Here, use mine."

Nate dialed and listened to the ring: three times, four times. His foot began tapping. "Come on, pick up, pick up." Then she answered.

"Yeah? Who's this?"

"Come get me Cat. Come get me the hell out of here."

"Nate? Your caller ID said George Martinez. Oh, Nate, it's over. Finally, it's over – just like I said, right? We got you out. Okay, okay, I'll come get you. I'm on my way now."

"Cat?"

"Yeah?"

"Thanks."

Nate turned back to the TV and watched Cat take off down the aisle and off screen. His legs went a little rubbery as he handed the phone back to the guard. "You George?" he asked.

"Yeah, that's me."

"Pleased to meet you, George. Thanks for the use of your phone." They shook hands. "My girlfriend's on her way to pick me up and she'll be really pissed if I'm not ready. You don't want to see her when she's pissed."

George smiled. "I'll get you fixed right up Mr. Parks. Detective Moochakouski had a feeling that this'd be the way things would go down. He's got things all set up for you. There'll be a little paperwork, but it shouldn't take long. Step this way."

The process took three hours, which, Nate supposed, was pretty speedy by police standards. He was given back the clothes he'd been wearing when he was arrested. They'd been freshly laundered.

Mooch met him once he'd changed. "There're a few reporters out there who'll want to talk with you – second-stringers mostly. The big story's with the Crawfords now."

"Thanks for the warning but..." He made a move to push through the door but Mooch stood his ground.

"Cat's out there too. I drove her here myself. Treat her right – she's a good kid."

"You sound like a protective father."

Mooch smiled as he opened the door, "Yeah, something like that."

Nate stepped out into the lobby area. There were five reporters. He answered their questions quickly: Did you hear

Sarah Crawford's confession? – Yes. What's it like to be free? – Great. Had he known about the genetic experiments? – No. What does he think about the experiments? – Bad idea. It was that fast and, when they were done with him, they dispersed to file their stories.

Nate didn't see Cat until he'd taken a few steps further toward the outer doors. She stood beside a bench with a big smile on her face. He hurried over and grabbed her in a long embrace. Tears streamed down his cheeks, mingling with hers.

"I told you you'd be okay – right?"

"Yes, you did." They parted slightly.

"I called your mom and dad. They saw it all on TV. They want you to call them as soon as you can."

"Thanks, Cat, I will," said Nate who noticed Mooch standing close by.

"You two need a lift somewhere?" he asked.

Cat wiped both her cheeks. "His place."

Mooch ushered them outside then into the back seat of his waiting police cruiser.

"I told you your case was bull-shit," Cat told him as she got in. Nate called his parents on the way and Mom told him they'd be catching the next train up.

Mooch dropped Nate and Cat off in front of Nate's building and leaned over from the driver's seat. "Next time you need help from the Seventy-Third, let me know." Then he looked at Nate and extended a threatening finger. "And remember what I told you."

"What did he tell you?" asked Cat, after Mooch had driven off.

"He told me to treat you right."

She grabbed his hand. "Now there's a piece of good advice." They just stood there on the sidewalk for a moment. It was already dark.

"Your hands are shaking. Are you all right?" Cat asked.

He didn't answer. Was he all right? Well, maybe so, but he felt like a freshly graduated schoolboy who'd just been dropped off at his best girl's house. He gave Cat a kiss.

"Let's go up," she said.

He unlocked the door to his apartment and followed her inside, closing the door behind him. He tossed the keys on the table next to the door. The shades were pulled down and the room was dimly lit by a reading lamp he'd evidently left on. Cat's brown eyes looked up at him. He bent closer and kissed her, finding her lips soft and warm on his. He broke away gently and met her eyes again. He heard her breath quicken. She put a hand on the back of his neck. Her kiss lingered and her lips moved against his, softly at first then more intensely.

Nate's heart pounded with all the thrill and excitement of that schoolboy who stood there, all alone, with the girl of his dreams. He wrapped his arms around her and felt her feet leave the floor. They were both breathless when they parted.

"Cat, I love you. I don't know what else it could be. I think about you all the time. I mean, I know I was in prison, not much else to think about but..."

She touched a finger to his lips. "I was hoping that you'd be the first one to say it, Nate. I love you too. I've known for a while now but with you in jail there wasn't much point in telling you. You had other things to worry about."

He cupped her face with both hands, feeling the moistness of her cheeks. He brought his hands down, slipping them under her jacket and down her shoulders. Her jacket fell to the floor with a thud.

"I think you just broke my cell," she whispered.

But Nate's hands weren't finished. He felt the cloth of her dress rippling under his touch and the curve of her body beneath. From there, everything proceeded naturally, without a thought in his mind about what should happen next. He picked her up and took her through an open door into his bedroom. He laid her down gently.

"This all part of treating me right?" She said this softly, watching him as he took off his own jacket, then his shirt, then she held up her hand. "Stop, Nate."

It was Nate's heart that nearly stopped at her command. Stop now? How could he have mis-read her so badly?

Cat looked up at him from the bed and smiled as if taking delight in his confusion. Then she reached for him. "Come down here Nate, let me do the rest."

They made love with a passion that stripped away the long months of worry and stress. It felt warm and natural and right.

Then they slept.

"Hungry?" Nate asked in the morning, rolling over and whispering directly into Cat's ear from behind. The clock on the night-stand said nine and from the window, sunlight was peeking in around the shade.

She stretched out her legs, yawned, and rolled to face him. "Famished," she said.

Having been gone so long, Nate had no food in the fridge.

They showered, got dressed and headed a few blocks down to Tom's Restaurant on Vanderbilt. It was a place known for their eggs and crispy-fried bacon and Nate hardly ever went there, but he knew Cat would like it. Before going in, Nate was going to pick up a paper but they were sold out. He grabbed one from an empty table as they were being seated. The headline was exactly as he expected:

Lt. Gov. Confesses to Killing

He read the entire article aloud happy to see that he was only mentioned at the very end: *Local artist Nathan Parks is no longer being held.*

"So much for your fifteen minutes of fame," said Cat already downing her second cup of coffee and well into her plate of eggs, hash browns, bacon and toast. Having seen no GF pancakes on the menu, Nate had ordered the same – what the hell.

He went back to the paper. A black and white picture of Peter's last painting appeared on page two and, as he stared at it, an eerie feeling enveloped him. Maybe this had been Peter's plan all along. He'd just wanted to make things difficult so everyone might know how difficult and tormented his own life had been. He studied Peter's face, placing beside it in his mind the face of the boy he once thought he knew, sitting on a rock by the side of a stream. "Back in high school, I don't think Peter knew about Romania. I don't even think he knew he was adopted. It's something he would have told me about. Even though we fought a lot, we were pretty close back then."

"Up until the Harris girl was killed, you mean."

"Yeah, until then." Nate folded the paper over and tossed it back on the empty table next to them. He started into his eggs.

"Do you still think Peter killed her?" asked Cat.

"I think he did, but we'll probably never know for sure."

"Sarah Crawford says he didn't do it."

"Ha – now there's a reliable source of information. Did she say who did? Maybe she'll try to pin that murder on me too."

"No, I think you're in the clear on that one." Cat finished her plate and got a refresh on her coffee. "It could be that Peter knew who killed the girl. Maybe he told Crawford. They were lovers – lovers talk about a lot of things."

Nate let the waitress take his plate – half finished. "I think it's time for the Harris murder to go back into the cold-case file. It's better for her uncle that way. It's better for everybody."

"It's not better for Livingston. Who's going to want to see the Caruso paintings if everyone thinks he was a killer?"

"Always worried about the client, right?"

"Hey, they're the ones paying the bills."

As they were leaving their table, Nate glanced at the newspaper he'd discarded which was folded over showing a separate article he'd missed. It appeared under the headline:

Did Lt. Gov and Artist Create Super-Baby?

He just shook his head and followed Cat back outside. They walked back along the uneven sidewalks that ran along the brownstones. With the occasional breeze, leaves fluttered and fragrant white blooms shed their petals from the branches overhead. Nate had to pull Cat back into a stroll from her normal New-York hustle.

"Sorry," she said, "always in a hurry – bad habit of mine."

"Stay with me tonight."

Cat pondered the question for all of two seconds. "Oh, okay, what's one more mortal sin on my head? Once you have one, you might as well have a dozen."

"A dozen it is, then."

"But I'll have to go to work in the morning," she added quickly.

"Me too. It'll be good to get back to painting. I missed it."

"You know, Meredith told me she still has some checks made out to you from the gig she and Teddy threw. She's been holding them for you until you were cleared."

Nate stopped walking. "How much does she have?"

"Twelve-thousand."

Nate did a mental count of how many paintings he had ready and how many more he'd need, then factored in the time it'd take to teach the two classes he'd already lined up for the summer assuming Manhattan College still wanted him.

"You still up for an exhibit?" asked Cat.

"Maybe."

"I think you should. The whole thing with Peter and with Sarah Crawford is behind you. They're not your problem anymore. And people know your name now."

"Yeah, as the *Mozart Murderer*."

"We'll recast you as the *Vindicated Van Gogh* – how about that? Clever huh? I told you I was good at this publicity thing."

CHAPTER 26

The summer went quickly.

Nate kept to his painting while Cat handled the promotional work and planning. In June she got a stream of money coming in from a Kick-Starter site. In July, she and Eduardo organized a rally in the village that netted a few thousand.

In late July, Nate plunked down a deposit on a posh spot for the exhibit, just a block away from the Guggenheim. It took his breath away, writing a check for such a large amount but the commitment was made and the date for the big event was now set for September twenty-ninth.

Through the summer, the trial of Sarah Crawford and her father had been big news and, wanting to put that chapter of his life behind him, Nate had gone out of his way to not follow it. But he did know the outcome. In late August, Sarah Crawford had been found not guilty of murder based on self-defense. She was, however, found guilty of obstruction of justice in her attempt to hide the truth about Peter's death. The six-month suspended sentence she received felt like a slap in the face to Nate, who would never forget the tortuous days and nights he'd spent in jail awaiting trial. If Cat and Meredith hadn't found the painting, he might still be there. Nate wasn't sure what punishment for Sarah Crawford would have satisfied him but to see her go completely free, as if she'd done nothing wrong, was hard to accept.

It was early September when he was surprised to receive an email from her:

Mr. Parks,

I heard about your upcoming exhibit. Congratulations. I'd like to meet with you in advance of it at the New York Public Library. I'll be there on the fourteenth at 2PM and have reserved a private reading room. Stop at the front desk for the room number. If you decide not to come, I'll understand. I haven't been exactly pleasant to you in the past but I'd like to try to make up for that. I also have a favor to ask.

Nate called Cat and read the note to her.

"So are you going?" she asked.

"She says she wants to make up for what she did. You know, as if it's part of a deal she made with the judge – like doing community service. But I'm curious to hear what she has to say for herself. Yeah, I'm going. Want to come along?"

"Glad you asked. I was about to invite myself but you know me, I hate to be pushy. How's the painting going?"

"Don't ask." He had three paintings yet to finish, just to reach the minimum number for the exhibit. He'd never worked under such pressure and it was difficult for him to do his best work, but he wouldn't sacrifice his standards even if it meant falling short. "How's your end going?"

"The caterer I contracted with just backed out and the guy handling the lighting is re-figuring his quote – says he didn't know the place had such a high ceiling. We're going to need more lights. Except for that, everything's peachy. This meeting with Crawford better not take much time. We're going to be okay, but we've got a lot to do."

On the fourteenth of September Nate and Cat walked between the marble lions and up the steps of the New York Public Library. Inside, they were directed to a small room on the second floor. Nate knocked and opened the door.

For such a grand building, the small, windowless room was as plain as could be, and so was Sarah Crawford. She wore jeans and a Cornell sweatshirt and stood behind a six-chaired conference table on which sat a pitcher of water with a few glasses. A collapsed umbrella lay against the wall behind her. The rain had stopped well before noon so Nate figured she must have been there a while.

"Hello Mr. Parks. And you're Ms. Chaplin – Nate said you'd

be joining him. Thank you for coming. I wouldn't have blamed you for not showing."

Without shaking hands, they all sat and Crawford began: "I would have chosen to meet at a restaurant or some other more comfortable place but we might have attracted attention. I asked you here, Mr. Parks, for a number of reasons. The first is to apologize for my disgraceful behavior in the whole affair with Peter's death. As you may know, my condition then was such that my drive for the governor's chair clouded my sense of ethics and for that I'm very sorry."

Nate saw sincerity in her eyes but was in no mood to be sympathetic.

Neither was Cat who fired back on reflex. "Your cloudy ethics nearly got him convicted of murder. Were you really going to let him go to prison for something you did?"

Crawford kept her cool. "I don't think there's anything I can do that would make up for what I did. All I can say is that I'm a different person now."

"Different, how?" asked Nate, allowing more than a little self-righteousness to creep into his voice. He poured some water, handing one glass to Cat and taking one for himself. Sarah Crawford could pour her own.

"I can see the harm I've caused," said Crawford, "and I want to try to make amends. For one thing, I'm giving you Peter's last painting. I think he would have seen the poetic justice in you ending up with it."

Nate took a swallow from his water-glass and cleared his throat. "I appreciate that, but it should really go back to Mr. O'Neal. Peter wanted him to have it."

"O'Neal was going to destroy it. He may still want to. But what you do with it is up to you of course. It's worth about one point three million."

Nate sighed to himself, thinking about how quickly his money problems could be solved. "O'Neal could use the money. You only gave him a thousand for it. You stole it from him."

"Livingston probably still wants it," said Cat. "Their collection isn't complete without it."

"They're the ones who offered the one point three. I turned them down. But, as I said, what you do with it will be up to you. The police still have it and I've signed over my ownership of it to you. You can pick it up at the courthouse whenever you like."

Crawford then spoke quietly, her eyes glued to Nate's but not in the same intimidating way he remembered from their first meeting. "I also have some information for you that I think Peter would have wanted you to have. It's about the Harris girl."

Nate stiffened. "I don't need to hear how he killed her."

"Please, Mr. Parks, just listen."

Nate glared at her for a moment then relented. He slid his chair back a little and folded his arms. "All right, let's hear it then." Crawford kept her voice low. "The relationship I had with Peter was unusual. As fraught with violence as our sexual encounters were, you could hardly call us lovers, but in the times between those encounters we talked intimately. He mentioned his friendship with you and credited you with starting him on what he called his artistic path. And he talked about his first love – Patty Harris, his *Woman in Winter*."

Nate nodded as Sarah Crawford continued.

"It had been a day in early spring, trees still bare from the long winter. School let out early for one reason or another and Peter decided to take a roundabout way home by driving around a small lake a few miles out of town. He was nearly half-way around when, through the leafless branches, he happen to see a car parked well off the road near the water's edge. It looked like Patty's car. Curious, he pulled over and walked closer. He was nearly half-way there when he heard a heated exchange of words between Patty and whoever was with her – some man, he knew that much by the sound of his voice. He broke into a run thinking she was in trouble – and he was right.

"As he ran he got to a point where he could see them, standing out at the end of a short wooden dock. The man had her by the hair. He was bent over her shaking her violently trying to shut her up as she screamed. That's when Peter recognized him. He stopped running and stood there as if paralyzed. It was his father and he had a knife."

Nate's eyes snapped wide. *Peter's father?*

"Peter could see the glint of the knife that he clenched in his hand as he raised it over Patty's head. She screamed and struggled to get away. Then the knife came down with a swift, slicing motion. The screaming stopped and Patty collapsed there on the dock. Still a hundred feet away, Peter fell to his knees in the brush unable to believe what had just happened. He turned away, looking back to where he'd left his car. Suddenly he had to leave this place. He had to get away. As he got to his feet, he heard a splash but he didn't look back. He just ran, got in his car and drove off.

"He drove for hours until he'd convinced himself that he'd just imagined the whole thing. Maybe it wasn't really Patty. Maybe it hadn't been his father. Maybe nothing had happened at all. It was nearly dark and he was low on gas when he pulled up to his house. His father's car was there as it always was at that time of day and there was a light in the kitchen as there always was. He and his father had dinner and watched the usual TV shows then went to bed, but through it all Peter didn't say a word.

"Vivid dreams weren't unusual for Peter and he went to school the next day fully expecting to see Patty alive and well. But he didn't. Then the announcement came that Patty was dead."

Crawford paused and took some water.

"Why would Peter's father kill the girl?" asked Cat.

"Peter never speculated about that and I never asked him, but a middle-aged widower with an under-age girl – it's not hard to imagine what might have happened."

Nate breathed in deeply, his hands tightly folded. "When I met with O'Neal he told me that Frank Caruso had taken a shine to Patty. Those were his words – taken a shine. But I'm sure he didn't mean it in a sexual way. He never suspected anything."

"And Peter never confronted his father?" asked Cat.

Crawford shook her head. "If he did, he didn't tell me."

"I found the knife in Peter's hiding spot in his room. It had the inscription: *Only the Brave*. Do you know anything about how it got there or what the inscription meant?"

"Only the Brave - that was a phrase Peter often said to himself as he painted. I never asked him about it but I know that he thought of himself as a coward for not having run onto the dock that day to try to save Patty. He blamed himself as much as he did his father for her death. The season portrayed in *Woman in Winter* was different for reasons only Peter knows but the trees in the background were intended to resemble those around the lake. As for the knife, he never told me anything about that. He might have found it among his father's things and taken it. Maybe he planned one day to turn his father in."

Crawford stood up and put her hands on the back of her chair. "Peter told me this story under the condition that I never endanger his father. At this moment, Frank Caruso is a very rich man having sold all of his adopted son's paintings. But he's also a very sick man. He's in a hospital with liver disease and is not expected to live out the year. I figure there's not much point in making accusations against him now so it's probably best I think, if we all just keep quiet about it. Can we agree on that?"

The thought of Frank Caruso going free filled Nate with hate.

That despicable old man had cut Patty's life short and he'd ruined Peter's. He couldn't just let him get away with it. Then he thought about Mr. O'Neal and all he'd been through, and for a short time, he wondered what *he* would say right now if he were here. Then, he knew. "Agreed," said Nate quietly.

Cat opened her mouth to object but Nate shook his head.

The three of them sat in silence for a while until Cat asked: "Did Peter ever talk about his artistic transformation? Was it brought on by the trauma of Patty's death?"

"Yes, Peter said as much," said Crawford. "He described it as a sudden and powerful connection between hand and eye that he didn't know he had until the night of her death when, alone in his bedroom, he drew Patty's face in perfect detail. That was also the time when he said his dark moods began. His violent outbursts were his way of trying to escape from them. Depression can be a terrible thing."

Those words sent Nate back fifteen years. He could hear Peter, half-crazed, yelling down the stairs: *What if I killed Patty? What would you do?* What Peter had really wanted to say was – *My father killed Patty. What should I do?*

Nate ran both hands down over his face. "I'm sorry I didn't know him better. I was the one who wasn't a good friend."

Again, it was Cat who broke the silence that followed. "And what about you?" she said to Crawford. "You do seem to be a different person now – pretty normal despite the terrible things they did to you in Romania."

"My father thinks that's due to my pregnancy. I'm not sure if I'll ever be completely normal." Crawford stood and poured some water in her glass then sat back down. She took a drink and turned to Nate as if eager to change the subject. "By the way, did you notice the pattern in Peter's paintings?"

Nate looked up. "I thought there might be one, but I didn't see it."

"How many kids graduated with you in high school?"

"I don't know. It was a small school back then."

"Including Patty Harris, there were a total of forty students in your class and Peter devoted one of his paintings to something he knew about each one of you. For some he painted a representation of a greatest fear, for others it was their greatest hope, or it was the thing they valued most. Except for himself he painted them in the same order as you each appeared in your high school yearbook. You're in there somewhere, you know."

Nate remembered his first viewing of Peter's paintings and

suddenly the image of a particular painting came to him. He knew that Peter must have meant it for him.

Crawford continued, matter-of-factly. "The Caruso collection is much more than just a group of paintings. It's the collective portrait of a generation – Peter's generation, with all its hopes and dreams and fears. Interspersed within his violent nature was a startling understanding of people and that was what he painted."

Nate never would have guessed these things about his boyhood friend. Now it was Nate who wanted to change the subject. "In your e-mail to me you said you needed a favor."

"Yes I did," said Crawford, leaning forward just a little. She put her hands on the table. "I'd like to attend your exhibit and I'd like you to publicize the fact that I'll be there."

"You're welcome to come but why would we publicize that?" asked Nate.

"I want to speak to the people who attend. I want to draw as large a crowd as possible. The publicity should work for you as well as for me I think. Given the furor over my trial, the networks should all be there. Your TV exposure should be nationwide."

Nate brought himself back from the revelations about Peter. He imagined TV satellite trucks, an overflowing crowd, journalists, art critics. His exhibit could be the art-event of the season.

"What will you speak about?" asked Cat.

"I will honor your work of course," she said turning to Nate, "and I'll make a public apology to you. Then I will talk about genetic optimization and I'll talk about what my father's planning to do now."

They stayed in the small room at the library for another hour while Sarah Crawford did most of the talking.

CHAPTER 27

Early, on the evening of September twenty-eighth, Nate added the final touch to his last painting. It was a scene on a subway train, half-filled with travelers who sat or stood with expressions ranging from anxiousness to boredom. Some faced toward the observer and some faced away, their reflections vivid in the darkened windows opposite them. Of those facing away, one was a young woman holding a coffee and cell phone in one hand while poking at the cell with the other. Nate had been unable to resist painting Cat as he'd first seen her and his last brush-stroke had given her reflected brow a slight tilt that gave a hint to what she might be thinking at that moment. He blew lightly on drying paint then backed away.

"Okay, it's done," he told Mike, the moving guy who'd been waiting at the kitchen table. "You can take it now." Nate walked to the sink and washed out the brush.

"You cut things pretty close, Mr. Parks," said Mike, coming up to the painting with a wide, white sheet of heavy paper. He stood there for a moment staring at the painting without saying a word, then carefully covered it with the sheet. He taped the corners and carried it down to the truck.

Nate followed behind, his freshly dry-cleaned tux in a plastic bag draped over an arm. "Mind if I ride along?"

Mike jumped off the tail-gate pulling the paneled cargo door down with him. He latched it closed. "No problem," he said, "you'll have to squeeze in though."

Nate hopped in next to Mike's high school kid helper who'd

been sleeping in the truck. "Hey, what's up?" muttered the kid making room.

"We're on the move Robbie," Mike told the kid, starting the truck and pulling out.

Nate texted Cat that he was on his way then winced at every bump, listening for sliding or bumping sounds from the back.

"A little like sending your kids off on the bus on their first day of school, isn't it?" observed Mike, avoiding an upcoming pothole with a deft swerve that caused Robbie's head to loll over to his other shoulder – he was half asleep.

"I don't have kids," said Nate, "but yeah, I imagine it's exactly like that."

"We had a tough job last night," explained Mike pointing a thumb at the boy, "then he had school all day and now this. He's a good kid – works hard when he has to."

Forty minutes later they pulled up at the store-front gallery. Mike double-parked. Nate hopped out and met Mike at the back. Robbie got there a moment later, rubbing his eyes. Mike unlatched the cargo door and pushed it up, revealing the wrapped paintings still lined up neatly on their racks. "See, they had a good ride," he said.

Robbie hopped onto the tailgate.

As they started unloading, Nate walked up to the gallery where bright lights blazed through the front windows. He could see that the walls were white and clean but the dark gray cement floor was pock-marked and littered with cardboard boxes, strips of shipping tape and scrap panels of dry-wall. A yellow tri-pod sat in the middle of the floor. He rapped on the door and, a moment later, saw Cat hurrying up from the back, her face flushed.

"Nate, thank God," she said. "I've been trying to reach you. I was worried we wouldn't get the paintings in time. The guys who're supposed to hang them left an hour ago. Why didn't you call me?"

Nate propped the door open. "I texted you. There were some last minute things I had to do." He gave her a quick kiss then noticed the strong odor of fresh paint in the room. He hoped it would dissipate by tomorrow. He gave directions to Mike and Robbie. The paintings had been numbered and would be arranged in order around the room. It took them less than half an hour to get them all inside and placed on the floor by their numbered spots. Cat wrote out a check that Nate knew, for once, wouldn't bounce. At the moment he had a million-three in his account from the sale of *Death of the Artist* to Livingston. In a few days he'd be sending a cashier's check for that amount to David O'Neal. It would be from an anonymous donor. Still, it was nice to be rich for a little while. He made sure Cat gave Mike a nice tip.

"Good luck with things tomorrow," said Mike on his way out.

"Hold on a sec," said Nate. He stuck his hand in his pants pocket. "Here're a couple of VIP tickets. They'll get you in the door. Hope you can make it." He handed them to Mike.

Mike smiled and accepted them. "Yeah, I'd like to come. Mind if I take the misses instead of the kid? – I don't know if you picked up on it, but this really isn't his thing."

"Yeah, I got that. I'll see you and your wife tomorrow then – we'll open at five."

Cat locked the door after them then leaned her back against it. "We've got a lot to do, Nate. Carpet arrives tomorrow at eight, tables right after that. You and I have to hang all your paintings tonight, then clean everything up." She gave a light kick to a box on the floor. "We've got all the hooks and anchors we'll need, we've got tape measurers and a couple of hammers. What do you say, Mr. Artist? You up for it?"

They were startled by a knock on the door. It was Robbie.

"Here, you might need this." He handed Cat the tux Nate had forgotten in the truck then left.

"Wow, that was a close call," said Cat. "Can't have you looking like a bum tomorrow. There've been a lot of close calls in this project and things are down to the wire now. We'd better get a move on."

Nate smiled and gave her a hug. "We'll get it done. What good is an artist who can't hang his own paintings?" Then he noticed the yellow tripod again. "What's that thing?"

"The guys explained it to me before they left," said Cat. "It's a laser leveler. It'll make sure we hang your paintings straight and at the same distance off the floor." She turned it on and a motor whirred into life. "See that?"

A red line of light swept around the walls of the room.

"It's at eye-level. All we do is put all the hooks on that line and we'll be in good shape."

Nate swallowed.

"What? What's the matter?"

"That's not the way it's done, Cat," said Nate. "The paintings are all different sizes and the center of each one has to be at eye level: sixty inches off the floor."

"Oh." Cat put her hands on her hips.

Nate walked closer to her. "And galleries always have wood or wood-laminate floors, not carpet."

Cat was crestfallen. "Not a real big deal though, is it? It'll all be okay, right?"

Nate smiled. "No, not a big deal – let's get to work."

Three hours later they were finished with the hooks. Then they started clearing debris off the floor and sweeping up, around the paintings that were still wrapped, and still laying on the floor. They were careful not to raise too much dust.

One by one, they unwrapped then hung each painting. Some of them Cat had seen before, others not.

"Nate, these are incredible," she said as they worked their way around the room. Then they came to the last one – the subway painting. She knelt over it as it lay on the floor. He let her unwrap it by herself. She paused mid-way, apparently seeing what it was. The corner of her mouth quivered slightly as she pulled the rest of the paper off. She put a hand to her mouth and stood up, tears flowing down her cheeks.

"Cat, what's wrong?" He put his hands on her shoulders. Maybe she didn't like it?

"Oh, Nate, it's beautiful. I remember that moment too – like it just happened."

"I call it the coffee-spiller," said Nate. "What do you think?"

She landed a fist on his chest. "You did not."

With the last painting in position, they walked together to the center of the room. Seeing all of them on display, Nate had to take a deep breath. He realized he was tearing up too. Here was his life's work. Every brush-stroke in every one of these paintings had been laid down by his hand. This was The Parks Collection he was looking at, all gathered in one place, all on display for the first time.

"What did you really call it?" asked Cat.

Nate turned to face the subway painting again, his eyes focusing on his last brush-stroke. "The Girl with the Brown Eyes," he said.

They slept in the gallery that night on two folding cots.

The carpet installers woke them up at eight, pounding on the door. In his bare feet, Nate hurried over and unlocked it. The foreman of the work crew walked in, assessing the room, hands on hips, without a glance at the paintings on the wall. "Man, you got some serious sweeping to do. We don't do that, you know."

Despite the cleaning they'd done the night before, Nate saw that there was still a thick residue of drywall dust on the floor and isolated scraps here and there. "No problem, we'll get right on it," said Nate, Cat yawning beside him.

The foreman walked to the back and pulled open a janitor's closet. "There's some sweeping compound in here," he told Nate, pointing to a gray five-gallon bucket. "Be sure and use it. It'll keep the dust down. And start here at the back, we'll follow behind you and work our way up to the front. Best we can do is to give you a ten minute head start so you better get cracking." He turned back to the men with him and clapped his hands three times. "All right, let's unload. Let's go let's go, let's go!"

Two hours later the carpet installers were gone and the floor was covered with a plush goldish-red weave that looked a little garish to Nate. White plastic runners crisscrossed it temporarily.

"What do you think?" asked Cat.

"Looks great, feels good on my feet."

"We're supposed to walk on the plastic while we're setting up," she admonished.

He went out and got a couple of coffees with breakfast sandwiches which they gobbled down fast. Cat checked the time. "Tables will be here anytime. They'll bring a portable bar and a small stage."

"A stage?"

"Sure, you'll need to say a few words, you know – thanks for coming, how's the cheese? And Sarah Crawford will need it for her thing."

Nate had been so immersed in finishing his paintings that he'd forgotten their deal with her.

"It'll be good, Nate. We're getting a ton of publicity out of her being here. All the local stations have picked up on it."

"You don't think she's too controversial?"

"Nate, it's hard to get publicity without controversy. We talked about this."

He rubbed his jaw. "Guess I'm just a little nervous."

"I am too Nate. This is a big deal. But just look around the room. This is your big show. And how could the critics not like what they see?" She kissed him. "It's beautiful, Nate."

The table people came an hour later and took an hour and a half to set up. The signage and programs were all laid out. The brass plaques engraved with the title of each painting were in position. Things were coming together nicely, thought Nate. They were almost running out of things that had to be done. He looked at the stage. "Do you have a microphone coming?" he asked Cat.

"A mike, my God Nate, I forgot about a mike."

"It's okay. We've still got a few of hours."

"We'll need speakers too."

Nate made a call and by mid-afternoon Eduardo showed up at the door with a few women friends. They peered in as Nate unlocked the door. "Did you bring the audio stuff?"

"In the trunk," said Eduardo pointing to the cab.

They had it set up quickly and Cat seemed to breathe a little easier.

Eduardo stepped onto the stage and gave it a test run. "This is fabulous, Nate – oh, I should call you Nathan today – just fabulous." His voice boomed from the portable speakers that had been positioned in each corner of the room. Eduardo rambled on with a few more comments and a few tasteless jokes, which generated an enthusiastic response from his small audience. Finally, he stepped down and walked over to Nate. "Who's your MC for this big event?"

"MC?" He looked at Cat. "Do we have an MC?"

"I didn't think we needed one. This is an art exhibit for God's sake."

Eduardo held up his hand. "Never fear, I'm available. And don't worry, I have totally different jokes for more formal occasions such as this."

A short time later, Nate and Cat ducked out to the room they'd reserved in the hotel next door. They got cleaned up and changed and were back by three – Nate in his tux, and Cat in her blue Bradshaw gown.

A TV truck was already setting up a few doors down. Cat tapped her hand nervously against her thigh. "Booze and food should be here – half hour tops." A few people were already starting to gather outside. The caterers arrived with their provisions and started setting up.

Then it was five. The sidewalk was jammed and a line of spiffy-dressed people wound up the street and around the corner. Nate walked to the front door that was still locked and, as if going through a pre-launch checklist at NASA, he glanced around the room. The doorman nodded. The bartender nodded. The waiters with their platters of Champagne-filled flutes nodded. From the stage, Eduardo in his tux nodded. The three-person chamber music group gave him three thumbs-up. Then he looked at Cat standing next to him.

"It's show-time, Mr. Parks."

Nate took a deep breath. He unlocked and pulled opened the doors while from behind him Eduardo loudly announced the official opening of the Nathan Lido Parks Exhibit.

The VIP-ers came in first, Nate's parents among them. He hugged them both, noticing the tears in their eyes. Then there were Teddy and Meredith – he hadn't seen them in months. He shook their hands and Meredith gave him a light kiss on the cheek.

Cat stood beside him. "I hear you've got a fitness studio going," she said to Meredith.

Meredith smiled. She looked good, thought Nate. Maybe a little of the mystery in her eyes had been replaced by a little more self-confidence. "Yes," she said, "we just opened two months ago and we're doing great."

"She's too modest," said Teddy. "She's a born fitness guru and an excellent business manager." Then he glanced around the room. "I see you've been busy Nathan. I think we'll have a look around."

"The room is yours," Nate told him. "Thanks for believing in me. You made this happen – both of you did."

"It's kind of you to say, but we know talent when we see it. Don't we, my dear?"

Meredith smiled at Teddy then turned back to Nate. "It's all so beautiful. I'm excited for you, Nate. And for you too, Cat. Let's be sure to get together sometime."

Other familiar faces checkered the crowd, some of whom Nate had met at Teddy's gathering, some of whom he hadn't seen since his college days. Mike the moving guy and his wife were there and Nate greeted them heartily.

"Must have been a long night for you last night," said Mike looking around. "It looks good." He had Nate sign his program.

The next two hours for Nate passed in a blur then he saw heads turn toward the door. Sarah Crawford had arrived.

Nate had been watching for her limo but overheard someone say that she'd been dropped off by a taxi. The crowd parted for her but, for a while, all Nate could see was the top of her blond head. Camera's snapped all around and finally she made it up to where he stood.

Nate took a step closer and shook her hand. "Good to see you, Sarah." More cameras flashed. Any reporters in the crowd were probably disappointed that they hadn't broken into a fist fight, thought Nate.

Her eyes looked bright and determined. "Thanks for letting me come. You have a nice crowd."

"A lot of them are here to see you," said Nate.

She shook her head. "Maybe that's why some of them came, but they'll all leave remembering your art and, as you know, that plays into my message here tonight."

"I'm up at nine," said Nate, "and you'll be right after me."

"Perfect," said Sarah.

When Sarah left to view the paintings, Nate put a hand over his breast pocket, reminding himself of the other event he'd been planning for this evening.

At nine, Eduardo took the stage and again welcomed everyone to the exhibit. He told a few more jokes than necessary then gave Nate a rousing introduction. Enthusiastic cheers and applause greeted him as he stepped up to the microphone.

Nate looked out over the crowd for Cat and saw her standing with Meredith in the back near the musicians. With the rest of the room, they were both applauding. Then he caught sight of old Mr. Whitaker who'd somehow managed to slip in unnoticed. A couple of high school age kids stood next to him. He thought he recognized one as the boy who'd asked about the money side of the art business.

When the room became quiet, it took Nate a while to get his nerves under control. He had no podium to stand behind and he was suddenly afraid that his nervous foot thing might take over. Then, from the back of his head, he heard a voice. Calm and steady, sounding somehow kinder now than he'd ever been in life, it was Peter: *Go ahead Nate, only the brave have moments like this*. Nate smiled, then began.

"There are so many people to thank for making this night possible. My parents are here, my art teacher from high school is here, my many donors are here, and..." he pointed to Cat, "my partner and my confidant, Cat Chaplin is here. It was her encouragement that really got the ball rolling on this whole thing." He shook his head. "Just a few hours ago, she and I were sweeping the floor for the carpet guys. Now you're all here taking time out of your busy schedules to see my paintings. Thanks to you all for that. I hope you like what you see." This raised a round of applause.

"I paint people. I paint them doing ordinary things: A farmer looking up to see if it's going to rain, a baker kneading dough for his ovens, travelers in a subway going off to work. These scenes are the experiences of life that we can all identify with and feel a part of and that's why I love painting them. I've never warmed up to the abstract symbolism of some who feel obliged to take up the artist's burden of teaching society some great new artistic insight or some high moral truth. We artists learn about life in the same ways everyone does – through our own ordinary experiences.

"So when you look at my paintings, don't look too hard for meaning or abstraction. Look for yourselves. You know what that baker's thinking. You know what those subway riders are thinking. You are who I paint and if you can identify with my art, if it gives you some real and personal attachment, then I am satisfied with the job I've done."

The room was totally quiet. Everyone, even the people at the door who'd been on their way in or out were standing perfectly still and they were all looking at him. They expected him to say something else but his mind was suddenly a blank. He glanced to one side of the stage and saw Sarah Crawford. Then, he knew what to do.

"As most of you know, I've had a trying summer as has had a guest of mine. Both of us were mixed up in a series of twisted events that were not of our making. I hold no malice toward Sarah Crawford and, after a few lengthy conversations with her, have agreed to let her speak to you today on a matter of utmost importance to both her and to me." Nate extended a hand. "Ladies and gentlemen, Ms. Sarah Crawford."

The room exploded with applause. Nate shook Sarah's hand as she stepped onto the stage. He gave a last wave to the crowd, then took a spot in the back of the room beside Cat. She gave him a hug. "How was I? Was I okay?"

"Nate, you were wonderful," she sniffed and dried her cheeks with a Kleenex.

He took a deep breath. "Glad that part's over," he whispered as Sarah started to speak.

If her pregnancy had caused her to lose her emotionless, calculating, political skills, it had no effect on the poise she displayed on stage. She owned the crowd from the start, first giving Nate an eloquent and heartfelt apology then praising him as a true artistic genius - that was the word she used: genius. And the room agreed, breaking into applause and cheers, heads turning in Nate's direction. She waited for the room to go quiet again, then launched into what she really came to talk about:

"When the story came out about my involvement with Peter Caruso and about my adoptive father's role thirty years ago in the genetic experiments that led to it, I expected the story to be received with the same sense of outrage that I felt. How could innocent, newly born babies be injected again and again with experimental drugs designed to alter their genetic makeup – to transform them into some kind of enhanced human species? What kind of people would carry out such experiments? What kind of people would allow it? That was the kind of public outrage I expected from Peter Caruso's story and from mine. Instead, the reaction was nothing like that.

"Instead, people from all over the world have been bombarding my father and his new Genetic Optimization Developments Corporation with applications to have the treatments administered to their, as yet, unconceived children. As we speak, treatment centers are being set up in several backwater countries where government regulation won't interfere. Everyone's anxious to make their son or daughter a stand-out in one field or another; to make them part of a new breed of humans that may one day supplant everyday humans just as we Homo sapiens once bested the Neanderthals. There's even an underlying fear among perspective parents, that if they don't opt into genetic optimization, their children are going to get left behind, relegated to the lower rungs of this new social ladder that's being built.

"I'm here today to oppose my father and to oppose genetic optimization."

There were murmurs around the room and Sarah paused for a moment to survey the faces glued to hers. "We are here today to honor the works of Nathan Lido Parks. He's worked hard at his craft and, over time, he's become an extraordinary artist. He's what most would call gifted. But what he has accomplished came from skills built up over years of dedication and perseverance. Nathan Lido Parks has climbed his Everest through hard work and an unbounded love for the creative process. It's in our nature that we humans strive for things that are just out of reach for most of us, and those few who are able to achieve those high goals, well, they become our heroes. They are the ones who shine a light for the rest of us and, with them in the lead, we all make this world a better place for each succeeding generation.

"Some, like my father, argue that making the world a better place is the essential justification of genetic optimization. I speak from personal experience: this is a falsehood. Genetic Optimization is an experiment with, at best, uncertain consequences. It saps emotion and replaces it with a skill-set that is precise and cold and calculating. While I am alive I will do all that I can to defeat it."

There was a smattering of applause around the room as if only a few were convinced. But Sarah persevered.

"My son Noah was intended to be the continuation of my

father's original experiment. He was conceived in violence and delivered into this world with the cold, analytical projection that he would one day be a kind of prototype super-human who would show amazing capabilities. Will he trade human empathy for those capabilities as Peter did? Will he plot and connive to achieve his ends no matter the cost, as I did? In truth, no one knows.

"But as Noah's mother, and as a person who has, in a sense, become more human since his birth, I do know that there is one thing I can add to the experiment. It's the one component that no doctor or scientist could ever formulate and inject into his body. I will give to Noah his mother's love."

She paused and took a few steps closer to the front edge of the stage. "Genetic optimization might one day be a wonderful thing. But, take my word for it, it's not there yet and, at the peril of turning the next generation into a giant and very inhuman experiment, we must proceed slowly and with great care. This course of prudence is my cause and I know it's a cause that Nathan Parks is one-hundred percent behind."

"If you agree with us, you will sign the petition I've brought with me tonight. Its aim is to keep genetic optimization in the lab where it belongs so we can learn more about it. There may be a time, my friends, when we can call it safe and maybe even beneficial, but that time most definitely, is not now."

Sarah wrapped up her talk and, from the stage, handed out the green and red pamphlets she'd brought. Some took them and some signed her petition, others did not.

When she finally stepped down, Eduardo took to the stage to encourage more wine and cheese tasting. The chamber music started back up.

After leaving the stage, Sarah made her way to the back of the room. "I'm not sure if I did more harm than good tonight," she confided to Nate and Cat.

"You did what you could, but everyone must decide the issue for themselves," said Nate. "All I know is that Peter Caruso could paint beautifully yet he was a very troubled boy and man. I don't think he was ever truly happy. That's not a life I would want for our sons or daughters."

Sarah nodded. "Thanks to both of you for letting me speak. If there's anything I can do for you in the future, let me know." They shook hands and, with an uncertain smile, Sarah Crawford left.

"You said 'our'" Cat said to Nate, keeping her eyes straight ahead.

"What?"

"Our sons or daughters – you said 'our'." She gave him a sideways glance.

"Slip of the tongue."

"That's not what Freud would say."

Nate fidgeted for a while. *Now, it should be now.* His heart was thumping when he grabbed Cat's elbow. "Come with me," he said, guiding her toward the back wall, then behind some hanging drapery. She moved easily, letting the drapes swing closed behind her. There was just enough light for Nate to see that they were now standing in front of the janitor's closet. There was a whiff of sweeping compound in the air – a fine, romantic choice of venue he thought with a grimace. Still, he could hear the strains from the cello and violin so maybe it wasn't so bad.

She looked up at him and spoke in a whisper. "Are you going to say something Freud-like now?"

He gave her a long, lingering kiss then parted from her gently. He reached into his shirt pocket, took her hand and slid the ring onto her finger. He spoke softly. "Marry me. Spend your life with me, Cat. Have sons and daughters with me."

Cat's lips wavered. "You're a famous artist now Nate. Are you sure you want to link up with me - Cat Chaplin from the Bronx?" Her eyes brimmed, a tear escaping down her cheek.

Nate dried it with his hand, feeling his own eyes filling. "Cat Chaplin, famous private detective, finder of missing paintings and purveyor of fine wine and cheese? Yes, I do want to link up with her; if she'll have me." He waited, his heart pounding. "Say yes, Cat."

She kissed him. "Yes Nate, yes, I will marry you."

Nate held her close. "I love you," he whispered.

"I love you too, Nate." She ran the back of her hand over her eyes. "Man, you've got me doing a lot of crying tonight."

Nate held her hand when they parted the curtains and walked back into the gallery. It took a moment for his eyes to dry and then to adjust to the light. Up at the front, the after-dinner crowd was filtering in and the wine continued to flow. Everything looked the same as it had a few minutes earlier, but Nate knew things were completely different now. He grabbed two glasses from a waiter and handed one to Cat. He was just about to clink his glass to hers when Mr. Whitaker came up.

"I'm just about to leave, Nate. I'm sorry I haven't had a chance to talk with you."

Nate was embarrassed that he hadn't sought him out after spotting him from the stage. There was just too much going on tonight. He put his wine down and shook his teacher's hand with both of his. "I'm so glad you took the time to come." He reached for Cat's hand. "This is my fiancé, Cat Chaplin."

"Well now, pleased to meet you. Congratulations to you both."

"Mr. Whitaker was my art teacher all through high school," Nate told Cat. "Without him, I would never have become an artist. He still teaches."

"It's a hard profession to give up," said Mr. Whitaker. "I have one of my current and most promising students here." He introduced Frank Madison, the boy standing next to him. Frank smiled shyly and shook hands.

"Still want to be an artist?" Nate asked him.

"More than ever, Mr. Parks. Who wouldn't want all this?"

"You aren't worried about a genetically altered artist coming along some day to show you up?"

Young Frank didn't know what to say but Mr. Whitaker smiled. "Baseball's dealt with its performance enhancing steroids Nate, I expect we'll find a way to deal with genetic optimization. If anything, we'll need artists more than ever to remind us of who we are and what we aspire to be."

Nate nodded at the old man's insight. "And we'll always need good teachers like you, Mr. Whitaker."

It was three in the morning when the last guest left. Cat locked the front door then joined Nate in the center of the room where they sat for a while on two folding chairs. They looked around. Wine-stained glasses, napkins and party-toothpicks littered the floor but from the walls, Nate's art looked down at the scene, unaffected. The room seemed unnaturally quiet. Nate took a breath. The air carried the scent of wine and cheese and perfume and cologne.

"It'll be good to sleep in a real bed tonight," said Cat. "You ready to go?"

"In a minute." Nate stood up and put his hands in his pockets. He found himself staring at his paintings, one at a time, shifting his gaze from one to the other and then onto the next. His thoughts were interrupted by a wood against wood sound behind him. Cat was setting up the cots.

She caught his eye and walked closer to him and whispered: "It's okay Nate, we can stay."

A short time later, as they lay in the darkness, Cat asked: "So which of Peter's paintings was yours?"

Nate smiled to himself and rolled to face her. He could make out her form and could see the glint of her eyes. "Mine's the one of the old man sitting on a park bench, alone and oblivious to the falling rain."

"I remember that one. So Peter thought of you as being afraid of old age, afraid of being left out in the rain like a forgotten dog?"

"I guess he did."

"Well, that's depressing. I don't think he knew you too well. He just liked painting dark clouds and dark things. When you paint the rain you have a little girl in the middle of it, having fun, splashing in the puddles." She reached out and found his hand. "Promise me you won't ever forget about that little girl, Nate."

"I promise," he whispered.

"Good, then she won't ever forget about you."

∞∞∞∞∞

The Nathan Lido Parks Exhibit had been held on New York's Upper East Side on a chilly night in late September. It had been well attended and, in addition to the detailed write-up in the still to come Sunday issue of the Times, it also warranted a mention near the bottom of page six of the morning edition the next day.

The third-stringer who wrote it knew that few readers would see it there and fewer still would remember it for long. But those who did, might just be able to put aside their worries about murder, high rent and bad pizza, long enough to realize that there were still good things happening in the world every day and that there could still be happy endings—even in New York City.

AUTHOR'S NOTES

Thank you for reading *The Caruso Collection*, I hope you enjoyed it. Just to clarify:

Though used in the narrative to further the plot, there is absolutely no evidence that I am aware of to indicate that the tragic plight of Romanian orphans has ever been misused for medical experimentation. At its worst in the 1980's, the dingy, underfunded orphanages of Romania were home to at least 100,000 infants and children. In those years it was the misguided ideology of the Ceausescu regime that an increase in population would drive a stronger national economy. More than that, it was believed that the state could raise a child better than his or her own family. Taxation laws, quotas related to family size, and birth control policies were used to further this ideology. A severely broken economy left an impoverished family little choice but to give up their "excess" children to the state.

As of this writing, there are roughly 60,000 orphans still passing through the Romanian system. So, thanks to the tireless work of many reform-minded Romanians and the warm hearts of foster parents around the world, things have gotten better and slow progress is being made. As for genetic optimization, steroids for the brain, and other intelligence-altering efforts, the ethics jury remains in recess.

But I sense that change is coming. Who knows, in the future the most important credential on your doctor's wall may be his or her genetics documentation providing evidence of their suitability to practice within their medical specialty. I'm sure this would raise an uproar among many but, with tongue in cheek, I can say with certainty that I'm okay with it—so long as they don't adopt similar requirements for novelists.

PRAISE FOR TOM ULICNY'S FIRST NOVEL

THE LOST REVOLUTION

A top, 5-Star rating was received from *Readers' Favorite*: "Brilliant descriptions, a complex mystery, and a fantastic naval adventure make *The Lost Revolution,* by Tom Ulicny, an exciting story well worth reading. Strong characters and exciting action make this book very difficult to put down." *The Lost Revolution,* a work of historical fiction, is available on Amazon and on other on-line outlets as a paperback and as an E-book for the Kindle and other E-readers. Check it out at: The Lost Revolution

If you have comments about Tom's books or would just like to say hi, please visit him at www.tomulicny.com he'd love to hear from you.

Made in the USA
Middletown, DE
18 February 2016